Criminal Kabbalah

▼ ▼ ▼ ▼ ▼ ▼ ▼ ▼ ▼ ▼

An Intriguing Anthology of Jewish Mystery & Detective Fiction

Edited by Lawrence W. Raphael

Foreword by Laurie R. King, author of *O Jerusalem*

For People of All Faiths, All Backgrou...

JEWISH LIGHTS Publish...

Woodstock, Vermont

D1040399

Criminal Kabbalah:
An Intriguing Anthology of Jewish Mystery and Detective Fiction

Library of Congress Cataloging-in-Publication Data
Criminal Kabbalah : an intriguing anthology of Jewish mystery & detective fiction / edited by Lawrence W. Raphael ; foreword by Laurie R. King.
     p.   cm.
ISBN 1-58023-109-8 (Paperback)
1. Detective and mystery stories, American. 2. American fiction—Jewish authors. 3. Judaism—Fiction. 4. Jews—Fiction. I. Raphael, Lawrence W.
PS648.D4 C75 2001
813'.0872088924—dc21

2001000542

10 9 8 7 6 5 4 3 2 1

Manufactured in the United States of America

Cover design: Bronwen Battaglia
Text design: Chelsea Cloeter
Typesetting: Sans Serif Inc.

For People of All Faiths, All Backgrounds
Published by Jewish Lights Publishing
A Division of LongHill Partners, Inc.
Sunset Farm Offices, Route 4, P.O. Box 237
Woodstock, VT 05091
Tel: (802) 457-4000   Fax: (802) 457-4004
www.jewishlights.com

This book is dedicated to the memory of my mother, Florence Raphael, who loved books. She gave me her passion for reading and learning. It is a gift that I hope my own children, Matthew, Andrew, and Rachel, will treasure too.

Contents

▼ ▼ ▼ ▼ ▼ ▼

Foreword   *Laurie R. King*   7

Acknowledgments   9

Introduction   *Lawrence W. Raphael*   11

The Banality of Evil   *Terence Ball*   17

Silver Is Better Than Gold   *Sandra Levy Ceren*   39

Death Has Beckoned   *Martin S. Cohen*   57

The Golem of Bronx Park East   *Richard Fliegel*   81

Truth in a Plain Brown Wrapper   *Michael A. Kahn*   103

The Tenth Man   *Stuart M. Kaminsky*   127

Bitter Waters   *Rochelle Krich*   141

Thy Brother's Bloods   *Ronald Levitsky*   159

Your Papers, Please   *Lev Raphael*   183

Reconciling Howard   *Shelley Singer*   193

Hospitality in a Dry Country   *Janice Steinberg*   213

Without a Trace   *Batya Swift Yasgur*   229

Foreword

▼   ▼   ▼   ▼   ▼   ▼

Crime and Kabbalah

LAURIE R. KING, AUTHOR OF *O JERUSALEM*

Criminal Kabbalah, the Kabbalah of crime—what does an esoteric form of mysticism have to do with common lawbreakers? Nothing, we declare with indignation. And yet . . .

The word Kabbalah grows from the Hebrew root *kbl,* which has to do with things received. Specifically, Kabbalah is a system (or, this being Judaism, a number of systems) by which a person might attain union with God, not despite everyday reality, but through it. There are divine sparks in each of us, says the Kabbalist, placed there in Creation. Tradition—the things received, the powerful symbols of everyday reality—lead us back to that spark that we might restore the perfect state in which we began.

The word Crime comes from the Latin *crimen,* which has to do with faults and flaws. In the context of traditional (that is, received) crime fiction, an offense is committed, establishing a flaw in the perfection of the writer's created world. The story then follows the efforts of the investigator to restore order, to set things back; not as they were, but in balance with how they used to be. The writer employs everyday reality—fingerprints and witness statements, the time of day and the human motivations of greed and fear and loyalty—to seek after the spark of truth that, once liberated, will restore order to this fictional universe.

Crime fiction, then, has essentially the same goal as Kabbalistic mysticism—on a considerably less exalted level, true, but sharing the core psychological and emotional experience of restoring harmony. A satisfying mystery imparts the feeling that the reader has been united, however briefly and frivolously, with Truth. For a short time, the reader becomes the fictional detective seeking to restore order; at the story's end, the investigator's revelation is the reader's own.

And who better to lead the way to Truth than a Jewish investigator? Judaism, more than any other tradition, recognizes the rules inherent in existence: If I do this, then such and such will happen; if I eat that, I will not remain ritually clean; if Adam and Eve choose to defy the given boundaries, they must leave the Garden—not punishment, simply consequence. A crime story reasserts the inevitability of consequence: The wrongdoer is caught, and suffers as a result. A pious Jew is described not as "devout" so much as "observant," sensitive to the consequences when God's laws are broken. And what, after all, is the chief characteristic of an investigator but that he or she be observant?

You are receiving *(kbl)* here: the efforts of twelve writers seeking to restore a little order to our flawed *(crimen)* universe. They will bring you sparks of pleasure, and possibly even of Truth.

Acknowledgments

▼   ▼   ▼   ▼   ▼   ▼   ▼   ▼   ▼

THE PROCESS THAT LED TO THE PUBLICATION of this book began in 1995 at a now-defunct New York City bookstore. There one evening my wife, Terrie, and I were browsing, and we found Paula Woods's important study *Spooks, Spies, and Private Eyes: Black Mystery, Crime, and Suspense Fiction* (Doubleday, 1995). Inspired by that book, Terrie suggested that I should consider putting together something about the Jewish contribution to crime and detective fiction.

Not long after that evening I participated on several mystery writers' panels with two wonderful mystery writers, S. J. Rozan and Marissa Piesman. Those experiences, and the many conversations that the three of us have had, were instrumental in my approaching established mystery writers and asking them to contribute Jewish mystery stories to an anthology. Stuart Kaminsky encouraged my efforts very early on. To these three superb writers I owe many thanks.

In the spring of 1998 I met with Stuart Matlins, publisher of Jewish Lights Publishing, and his enthusiastic response to my idea to collect and publish such an anthology led to *Mystery Midrash: An Anthology of Jewish Mystery & Detective Fiction*. Working with Stuart and his staff helped me create that first volume of stories. This volume owes much to the excellent editorial efforts of Bryna Fischer. Her expertise in Judaica and editing has improved this book immeasurably.

Throughout this experience of soliciting, reading, evaluating, and editing

9

these mystery stories Terrie was and continues to be all that I could ask for in a life companion. She is supportive, constructive, imaginative, and willing to take the time necessary to give me her valued opinion about contributions to this genre. My efforts would not have been possible without her.

My continued interest in Jewish mystery fiction has led me to create a web site where an annotated bibliography of contemporary American Jewish mysteries is listed. Readers who are interested in this field, and anyone who has suggestions for stories that might be included in future volumes of Jewish stories, should visit www.jewishmysteries.com.

Introduction

▼   ▼   ▼   ▼   ▼   ▼   ▼

LAWRENCE W. RAPHAEL

YOU ARE HOLDING IN YOUR HANDS a mystery trip into Jewish culture and philosophy through well-crafted stories. If you love a good tale, if you want to know more about Jewish tradition, if you would like to create order out of chaos and the complexities of daily life—turn to any story in this collection. Crime stories that illuminate the mysteries of life are as old as Jewish tradition and as new as today's temptations.

In the fall of 1999 the first collection of Jewish mystery stories, *Mystery Midrash,* was published. Since that time I have traveled all over the country lecturing about Jewish identity and mystery fiction. My audience has included synagogue groups, book fair attendees at Jewish community centers, rabbinic associations, and the dedicated fans of mystery who have gathered in bookstores from Phoenix to New York City. In each location I have been delighted by the response and the interest from readers who enjoy good stories, find pleasure in reading quality whodunits, and want to expand their knowledge of Judaism through the medium of interesting fiction.

That first collection of Jewish mystery stories was groundbreaking. Other collections have featured mystery stories written by women, mysteries centered on cats, mysteries focused on food, or mysteries that pinpoint a particular place. *Mystery Midrash* was the first anthology that included only

Jewish mystery stories. And now, *Criminal Kabbalah* offers all of us who are intrigued by this fascinating genre a collection of more Jewish mysteries and more ways to explore the uncertainties that are a part of contemporary Jewish identity.

Why *Criminal Kabbalah?* Most people think of Kabbalah as Jewish mysticism, especially the forms it assumed in the Middle Ages from the twelfth century onward, which address the problems of evil and sinful behavior in the world. According to a major kabbalistic source, the *Zohar,* the realms of good and evil are to an extent commingled, and it is our human mission to separate them. The general kabbalistic position is that evil is a necessary component of our unredeemed world. It is not until the time of the Redemption and the day of final judgment that the power of evil will be destroyed and will thus disappear. The principal instrument for repairing the broken world, according to Judaism, is the activity of good deeds. Solving crimes, righting wrongs, establishing order from chaos, then, parallels the Jewish mystical tradition of Kabbalah. These acts of righting wrongs are exactly what happens in the stories in *Criminal Kabbalah.*

The Hebrew term *kabbalah* has a literal second meaning: "received," as in "received tradition." Kabbalah is used in *shalshelet ha-kabbalah,* the "chain of tradition" that includes important customs, teachings, or wisdom, frequently in the form of stories that are passed from one generation to the next. For example, in early rabbinic literature, the chain of tradition traces the passing of Jewish leadership from Moses to Joshua, then to the prophets, and on and on until it reaches the rabbis of the first century.

Why do so many of us have such a passion for solving riddles? Such a fascination is one reason why mysteries are part of traditional and popular culture. The passion and fascination of this type of problem solving addresses a human interest that long preceded any classic crime story. The classic mystery story is about good triumphing over evil. In separate interviews that appear in *The Fatal Art of Entertainment,*[1] the writer Sue Grafton, creator of the private investigator Kinsey Millhone, notes, "I always think of mystery writers as the great moralists of fiction" (p. 48). Popular British mystery writer P. D. James concurs: "I think there can be little argument that the crime novel can be literature. After all, man has always concerned himself with problems of moral choice, with the nature of good and evil, and with

---

1. Rosemary Herbert, *The Fatal Art of Entertainment: Interviews with Mystery Writers* (New York: G. K. Hall, 1994).

that unique crime for which there can be no reparation to the victim, murder. Our earliest myths are concerned with violent death, and with the bringing of order out of disorder" (p. 77).

These stories that concern violence and mayhem are found in the very beginning of Jewish sacred literature. Cain and Abel are part of the primal struggle that ends in violence and death. The biblical tale of the rape of Dinah includes the story of her brothers' revenge. Indeed, for thousands of years, Jewish tradition has discussed the dilemma between existence and justice in the world. In a midrash (rabbinic inquiry into the meaning of Bible stories), the rabbis comment on the verse from Genesis 18:25, in which Abraham is arguing with God over the fate of Sodom and Gomorrah, and teach, "If You, God, would have absolute justice, there can be no world; if You would have a world, there can be no absolute justice. You would hold a rope by both its ends: You would have a world, and You would have true justice. But if You will not be a little indulgent, Your world will not be able to endure" (*Leviticus Rabbah* 10:1). Our understanding of the human condition is that this imperfection exists.

The sleuth in crime and detective stories addresses this imperfection in our world. In the introduction to *Fatal Entertainment,* its author, Rosemary Herbert, cites several writers when discussing the purposes of mystery fiction:

> Mortimer[2] testifies that the sleuth ought to be "the man who can understand everything in a wicked world and who also imposes order upon chaos. . . . " And Aird agrees that the appeal of the mystery novel is to "those in search of an orderliness"; she notes that "although personally you may inhabit a world that is not reliable—within the hard covers of a book you know perfectly well that justice will be done."
>
> But a desire for orderliness is not the whole story. . . . As Grafton puts it, "Each book is always a brand new adventure. The exciting thing is how you keep learning about yourself. That's what mystery writing is about, teaching us about ourselves" (p. xviii).

The collection of stories in *Criminal Kabbalah* are Jewish mystery stories. They are Jewish stories because they fit into one or more of the categories suggested by Dov Noy, the founder of the Israel Folktale Archive

....
2. John Mortimer is the creator of British barrister Horace Rumpole; Catherine Aird's novels feature Inspector Christopher Sloan.

in Haifa. According to Noy, there are four major qualities of Jewish stories. The first is Jewish time, the second is Jewish place, the third is Jewish characters, and the last is a Jewish message or moral. The phenomenon of learning about other cultures through mystery literature is illustrated by the popularity of Tony Hillerman, who has written best-selling mysteries that take place in the Navajo reservation of Arizona, Utah, and New Mexico; of Walter Mosley, who writes about African Americans in Los Angeles; of William X. Kienzle and Andrew Greeley, who both write about American Catholics; of Georges Simenon, who writes about the French; and of Batya Gur, who writes about Israelis. Some Jewish mystery writers use Judaism to provide information about and insights into a way of life that is fascinating to many. The material concerning Jewish culture is not merely used as background. It also provides insight into character, which in turn demonstrates motive. A bonus for the reader is the ease with which such material as Jewish ritual, observance, learning, and tradition contextualizes or amplifies the story or plot and is used as the occasion for the occurrence of a crime.

The stories in *Criminal Kabbalah* will entertain you and, along the way, may teach you something unexpected. They are stories that have conflict, crimes, memorable scenes, and characters a bit like people you already know or might one day meet. Like all crime fiction, the stories make us want to know what happened next and why, and explain something about the mysteries and imperfections of life.

Each of the contributors to *Criminal Kabbalah* offers us a glimpse into Judaism and the finding of riddles and their solutions.

- In "The Banality of Evil," Terence Ball tells the story of the retired Minneapolis policeman–turned–private investigator Abe Feldman, who puts together the pieces of a puzzle that includes neo-Nazis, the defacing of a synagogue, and murder.

- Sandra Levy Ceren brings us Cory Cohen, a psychotherapist in San Diego who normally sees patients in cases related to sexual abuse. In "Silver Is Better Than Gold," a new client requires that her work take on a very different dimension.

- Martin S. Cohen introduces a long-lost journal that transports us back almost two hundred years to the Austria of composer Franz Schubert and Cantor Salomon Sulzer. "Death Has Beckoned" tells a remarkable mystery story that is pieced together from the "notebooks" discovered by the grandson of a student of Sulzer's son.

- Richard Fliegel is known for his novels about former New York City police detective Shelley Lowenkopf. In "The Golem of Bronx Park East," Shelley is working as a private eye; as a result of his saying Kaddish on the occasion of his father's *yahrzeit*, he gets involved in a case in the Bronx.

- Michael A. Kahn provides another chapter in the story of St. Louis lawyer Rachel Gold in "Truth in a Plain Brown Wrapper." Here she defends a Holocaust survivor who has become an aristocrat within the local fashion world and is now enmeshed in a libel case.

- Stuart M. Kaminsky's Abe Lieberman is a Chicago police lieutenant. "The Tenth Man" transports us back to a time when Abe had just been promoted to police detective and still attended *shul* with his father and brother.

- Rochelle Krich tells a story of sibling rivalry and jealousy. The experiences of the twin brothers in "Bitter Waters" are as ancient as the beginnings of Jewish stories.

- Ronald Levitsky reintroduces us to First Amendment lawyer Nate Rosen. In "Thy Brother's Bloods," we are immersed in the criminal mind of a convicted killer on death row as the doomed prisoner presents Rosen with a most unsettling challenge.

- Lev Raphael has written an atypical mystery story. It is not a mystery with a puzzle. Rather, "Your Papers, Please" is the story of someone primed to crack: it strives to illuminate the complexities of human nature. In fact, this is not a story about a crime and its detection or aftermath; it is deliberately a tale about the creation of a criminal.

- Shelley Singer presents her private eye Jake Samson, who takes on the case of a childhood acquaintance now conducting reconciliation groups for people who hate one another. In "Reconciling Howard," Jake seeks to find out who is threatening the life of Howard, who is from Jake's old neighborhood.

- Janice Steinberg has written a story that is a mixture of midrash and crime story. In "Hospitality in a Dry Country," we meet the ancient Israelite judge Deborah, the Canaanite general Sisera, his mother, and Jael.

Steinberg's ancient yet modern story illuminates the biblical text and gives us an insight into the motive behind the crime.

- Batya Swift Yasgur has a police detective take us inside the Orthodox Jewish community and provides insight into a little-known aspect of Jewish marriage law. "Without a Trace" combines Jewish religious tradition with the investigation of a Jew-by-choice policeman.

Criminal Kabbalah will entertain you and illuminate the Jewish tradition. It too is part of a chain of tradition of Jewish stories. It provides an answer to the question asked in a traditional Jewish saying: "Why were human beings created? Because God loves to hear stories."

TERENCE BALL teaches political theory at Arizona State University; he has also taught at the University of Minnesota, the University of California, and Oxford University. His first mystery novel, *Rousseau's Ghost,* was published in 1998. "The Banality of Evil" is the first in a series of projected Abe Feldman mysteries.

The Banality of Evil

▼ ▼ ▼ ▼ ▼ ▼ ▼ ▼ ▼

TERENCE BALL

THE PHONE KEPT RINGING, but Abe Feldman refused to pick it up. He had looked at the caller ID display and knew who was calling. After eight rings the answering machine came on.

"Abe, if you're there, pick up. Hello? Abe, are you there? It's your brother, Joel."

That would be Rabbi Joel Feldman, Abe's younger and only brother. Joel only called when he wanted something. More precisely, when he wanted Abe to do something for him or his family for free.

"Abe, I know you're there. Look, I need to talk with you right away. It's urgent. Something's happened at the temple."

Abe picked up the phone.

"What's happened?"

"Swastikas. They've painted swastikas and shit on the walls and on the cornerstone."

"Who's *they?*"

"Who do you think? Devout Jews?"

"No, I'd put my money on anti-Semites. Neo-Nazis, maybe."

"Maybe my *tukhis.* Of course it's neo-Nazis. Who else would it be?"

"Kids. Could be kids. Punk kids playing a prank."

"Some prank. No, I tell you, Abe, it's gotta be Nazis. I know it. I can feel it in my gut."

17

"So what do you and your gut want me to do about it?"

"Do your job. Investigate."

That was Abe Feldman's job. After taking early retirement from the Minneapolis Police Department two years ago, he had gone into the detective business for himself. He was one of three Jewish private investigators in the Twin Cities and the only PI in Saint Louis Park, the affluent ghetto of a western suburb that the goyim called Saint Jewish Park. He worked mostly for insurance companies and sometimes for a local law firm in which his ex-brother-in-law was senior partner. But he had never before been retained by a synagogue.

Working for his brother and Temple Beth Israel would be something entirely new. And not a very welcome novelty, either. Abe Feldman had not gone to temple even once in the last twenty of his forty-six years. Abe's irreligiosity was a sore point between him and his brother and had been an even sorer one between Abe and his now ex-wife Leah, who midway through their fourteen-year marriage had rediscovered her religious roots and had tried unsuccessfully to bring her indifferent husband along.

Abe leaned his lanky frame back in his chair and put his feet atop the gray metal desk. His scuffed brown wingtips needed a shine in the worst way.

"Why me? I don't do Nazis. I do insurance fraud and fun stuff like that. I suggest you call the cops."

"We did call the cops, early this morning, just after Rachel got here and discovered this shit."

"Who's Rachel?"

"Rachel Bronstein, the assistant rabbi. You know her."

"I do?"

"Of course you do. You met her a couple of years ago. She certainly knows who you are. Always asks me how you're doing and why you never come to temple. And you don't remember this woman who remembers you?"

"Oh yeah, now I remember. Nice looking. Great hair. Really thick and curly."

"Forget the hair already. Rachel is upset. Very upset. She can't stop shaking. When she called me she could hardly talk for crying. I called the cops and then came to the temple right away and without even shaving."

"You don't shave twice a day you look like Yasir Arafat."

"Very funny, Abe. Jerry Seinfeld you're not. But this is no laughing matter. I've had tsuris enough, but this is the worst since I came here seven years ago. I—we—need your help. The temple needs you. Your people need you."

"People, *schmeeple*. You know better than to try to take that line with me. I've never taken any guilt trips and I'm not about to start now. So, enough already. Let the cops handle this, Joel. They've got a hate crimes unit that specializes in cross burnings and swastika paintings and suchlike."

"Fat lot of good they are. They're treating this like it was some ordinary act of vandalism. They're here for less than half an hour. They asked some half-assed questions and took some pictures and dusted for fingerprints and then they left."

"Left to talk to the neighbors, probably. To ask if anyone saw anything. It's standard procedure. Don't drop your tefillin just yet. Keep calm and let the cops do their job. And speaking of jobs, I've got work to do here. So if you don't mind . . . "

"Abe, I do mind. I mind a lot. Come over here and check things out. Maybe you'll see something that the cops missed."

"Most likely I won't. But if you insist and if the temple wants to retain me, I get $500 up front and $200 a day plus expenses. I find something that results in a conviction, I get a bonus, $2000 minimum."

"That's not funny, Abe."

"What am I, a comedian? I work for a living. I charge the going rate."

"Well, we'll see about that, after you've had a look around. Maybe you'll change your mind after you've actually seen the swastikas and the slogans. They're ugly, Abe. Really ugly."

Abe sighed audibly. He knew there was no way he was going to win this one.

"Okay, okay. I'll have a look-see. Give me half an hour, forty-five minutes tops."

Last week's early spring snowstorm, followed by bright sunshine and steadily rising temperatures, had turned the streets and sidewalks to a brownish gray slush. Abe Feldman kept turning on the windshield wipers of his rapidly rusting '91 Pontiac, which smeared the slush into an ever-harder amber glaze. He remembered that he had forgotten, once again, to refill the windshield washer fluid. Twice he had to pull over, pick up handfuls of snow from the curbside, and smear them over the windshield. Then, as they melted on the muddy windshield, he turned on the wipers. Clear vision again, if only temporarily. Abe turned left off Lake Street onto Lyndale Avenue, heading north to Twenty-eighth. Temple Beth Israel stood on the northwest corner of the intersection, low and austere, as though not to offend the neighbors. He pulled into the parking lot in back.

The lot behind Beth Israel was abuzz with activity. Two TV trucks with satellite dishes were surrounded by technicians stringing cables and setting up lights and cameras. A blonde TV news reporter was checking sound levels and her hair and makeup. Behind her was a jagged black spray-painted swastika, about five feet in both directions. To the right were three words, one atop the other:

> K ill
> K ike
> K weers

The KKK was in red spray paint, the rest in black. Abe felt a wave of revulsion that started in his stomach and stopped in his throat. He tried saying "Bastards!" but nothing came out.

Abe felt a hand on his shoulder. He turned around and saw a grim but familiar face. Eric Brown, a reporter from the Minneapolis *Star Tribune,* stood there, notebook at the ready.

"So we meet again, Abe. Haven't seen you since you retired. How's life?"

"Life's been better. Until today. Can you believe this shit?"

"Unfortunately, yes. And this won't be the last time we'll see this. But we've both seen worse, Abe. At least this time there's no dead body."

Thank God for that, Abe thought. Seeing one more dead person would surely unhinge him and send him over the edge, maybe into madness. That was the real reason he'd retired.

"So why'd you quit the force? The guys downtown always said you were the best in the business. And then suddenly one day you up and quit. Why was that?"

"Time to do something different, to be my own boss—you know, the usual," Abe lied.

The reporter looked down at his notebook and up at Abe. "I believe the rabbi's name is Feldman. Any relation?"

"Yeah, he's my brother."

"And you've come to lend some moral support?"

"Not really. Joel—that's my brother—he wants me to have a look around. So I said I would. Not that I expect to find anything the cops haven't already found. So yeah, I guess I am here to lend moral support." Abe paused, surprised by his own words. "Well, catch you later, Eric. Good to see you again."

"Likewise. I wish the circumstances were different."

"C'mon, Eric. The only times we ever saw each other were at crime scenes. So nothing's changed all that much. But, as you said, at least this time nobody's dead."

With a wave of his hand, Abe ducked behind a TV camera and between two sets of lights and entered the back door, the shortcut to the rabbi's office. At the top of the stairs he stopped to cough and catch his breath.

"Abe, is that you?" a familiar voice called from inside.

"Yeah," Abe rasped, stepping inside the open doorway. "It's me." He saw his short, slightly overweight and unshaven brother, who with his black curly hair and gray whiskers was the spitting image of their late father, Samuel.

"Thanks for coming, big brother. I appreciate it."

"We appreciate it," chimed in a female voice from behind.

Abe turned around and saw Rachel, the assistant rabbi, just before she caught him off guard with a hug that seemed to warm him all the way through. Startled, he pulled away and then immediately regretted it.

"Abe, you remember Rachel . . . "

"Of course I remember. I never forget a pretty face," Abe said, not entirely truthfully. Rachel Bronstein's dark brown eyes were puffy with crying. Tears had made her eye shadow and mascara run down her cheeks. She looked more like Alice Cooper than the comely, slightly zaftig rabbi he remembered from before.

"A fine-looking pair, the both of you," Abe said, trying to chuckle but not quite making it.

"We're upset," Joel said. "Terribly upset. It's been hard for both of us."

"And it's going to be even harder on the congregation," Rachel added. "Especially the older ones—the ones who remember . . . " She meant to say those who remember Kristallnacht and the other warning signs of the event that no Jew could ever forget. But her words trailed off into silence.

"Rachel and I have been debating something. Maybe you can help us out—give us a fresh opinion."

"About what?"

"About whether to call the sandblasting crew in today, to remove all traces of this abomination and to spare the feelings of our older members. Or whether to leave it there for a few days, to let the young ones see with their own eyes what their parents and grandparents used to see when they were young. It could be a kind of bond. And besides, maybe the neighbors should see it too, to give them a little taste of what it's like to be Jewish. Might make them a little more sympathetic. So what would you do, Abe?"

"I'd remove it as soon as possible. But not before I've had a chance to look around and to ask you both some questions."

"Okay, shoot," said the rabbi. "We're all yours."

"First thing I need to know is whether you've had any threats. Any personal encounters, notes, phone calls, whatever?"

"Just the usual," Joel answered.

"What do you mean, the usual? What usual?"

"You know," Rachel interjected. "Phone calls. Nutcases calling and asking to speak to Judas—"

"Or to Rabbi Christkiller," Joel interrupted. "That's my favorite. I've even thought of answering the phone that way. 'Hello, Rabbi Christkiller speaking.'"

"With your luck, Joel, old Mrs. Friedman would be on the other end of the line, and she'd have the Big One right then and there. And then how would you feel?" Rachel asked, almost smiling.

"Like maybe I had one less yenta kvetching at me ten, twelve times a week?"

"Look, about these phone calls," Abe said. "Are there threats? Threats of physical or bodily harm?"

"Oh, sure, sometimes," Joel answered. "We just hang up."

"Or let the answering machine take it," Rachel added. "That's what I do when I'm here alone. I use the machine to screen most calls."

"You don't have caller ID?" Abe asked. "So you can see who's calling and from what number?"

"No. Our budget is tight. We cut corners where we can. The extras and service charges add up."

"Well, this is one extra I'd spring for, if I were you. So when you get these calls, you call the cops?"

"No."

"Why not?"

"Because we'd be calling them at least once a week, and they'd get irritated," Joel said. "And because nothing has ever come of these threats. Until now, that is."

"So there were threats leading up to this . . . this incident?"

"Not specific threats, no," Rachel answered. "But someone's been calling and saying nothing and then hanging up."

"Sounds like someone wants to know when you're here and when you're not," Abe said, frowning. "You should record these calls. Do you have tapes? Answering machine tapes, I mean."

"I don't think so. Do we, Rachel?"

"No, I rewound the tape yesterday just before I went home. Which reminds me: In all the confusion this morning I forgot to check for messages. I'll do that when we've finished here."

"Do it now," Abe said, sounding sterner that he meant to. "Please," he added.

"All right," Rachel said. "Come into my office."

The brothers followed her into the next room. It was small and cozy, the walls lined floor to ceiling with shelves groaning under the weight of books. Rachel pressed the blue button on the answering machine.

"Rachel, hello, it's your mother. If you're there, pick up, it's your mother speaking. . . . So . . . I guess you're not there. Maybe you've got a date, then? A date would be nice. So I won't call you at home. Far be it from me to interrupt anything. Call me tomorrow, tell me how your date went." A click, then a beep.

"I should be so lucky," Rachel said.

"Rabbi, it's Baruch Mandelbaum. My Rose had another stroke last night. She's in Methodist Hospital, the intensive care unit. I think maybe she's not coming home this time. We're married now sixty-one years. . . . Well, that's all I have to say." *Click, beep.*

"Yeah, hi, Rabbi. This is Walt from B & D Heating Contractors. I vacuumed out your furnace and the ducts, but I gotta tell you, that old thing is on her last legs. The burners are shot and the core's corroded real bad. She's prob'ly not gonna make it through another winter. To be honest with you, we're lookin' at big bucks here. We're talkin' asbestos removal, which don't come cheap, and cuttin' the old girl into pieces so's we can get 'er out of the basement. Same deal with th' oil tank. Anyways, I'm sendin' a estimate so's you can look at it. Gimme a call 'n' let me know. You have a good day now."

Click, beep. Then another message. Or rather, no message at all. Just the sound of someone breathing, saying nothing. In the background were mechanical clanking, clanging sounds, like large metal pipes being banged together. A foundry, maybe? Abe thought to himself. A machine shop?

Click, beep. "Hello, Rabbi Feldman or Rabbi Bronstein? This is Ruth Lipke. I know you're not there—it's five o'clock in the morning—but I didn't know who else to call. My Danny's gone. I don't think he even slept in his bed last night. If you see him, please tell him to come home. Or call me, at least. I'm very worried about him. He seemed really upset yesterday. He hardly touched his dinner. That's not like my Danny. Please tell him to call his mother. Thank you." *Click, beep-beep-beep.* No more messages.

"Who's Danny?" Abe asked.

"Danny Lipke, Mrs. Lipke's son," Joel answered.

"That much I've already figured out. I mean, who is he and why is his mother calling the rabbi? And at five A.M. no less?"

"Danny's retarded. He has Down syndrome. He's maybe thirty-five, thirty-six, lives at home with his mother. He hangs around the temple sometimes, does the occasional odd job, but mostly he moons over Rachel." Joel turned to Rachel. "Now there's a date to make your mother proud."

"Really, Joel. You shouldn't tease. Danny's sweet, he's gentle. And he's more of a mensch than most men I know."

"From what his mother said, I gather that he doesn't do this—run away from home, or whatever you want to call it—very often. Is that right?" Abe asked.

"Right," Joel replied. "Never, in fact, that I know of."

"His mother said he was upset about something. Do either of you have any idea what that might be?"

"I think I do," Rachel replied. "When Danny was here yesterday he overheard me saying to Joel that I didn't even want to answer the phone any more because the silent guy scares me. I guess I got a little emotional and probably more upset than I should have. Anyway, Danny rushed in from the hallway and said he'd always protect me and I shouldn't worry. His face was flushed, red as a ripe tomato about to burst. Said he had friends in the JDL . . . "

"The Jewish Defense League?" Abe asked.

"Yes," Joel said. "But that's just a figment of Danny's overwrought imagination. Danny doesn't actually have any friends. He's a loner. And besides, there is no JDL in the Twin Cities. I think he was just trying to impress and reassure Rachel."

"And did he succeed?" Abe asked.

"Not really," Rachel replied. "He impressed me with how sweet and sincere he is. But no, I didn't feel reassured. If anything, I was frightened by his

. . . I don't know, his anger on my behalf. I'd never seen him like that before and didn't know how to react, how to comfort him, calm him down. He's a big boy, I mean man—well over six feet, maybe 250 pounds—and when he gets upset like that, it's scary."

"You were scared of him?" Abe asked.

"No, I was scared *for* him. I didn't know what he might do—to himself or maybe to someone else. Joel and I did our best to try to calm him down. Told him that everything was okay, gave him a hug, offered him a nosh. Which, unusually for him, he didn't take. He went and sat in the corner and put his head down."

"It's the 'time-out' position," Joel interjected. "His mother makes him take a time-out when he gets upset. Mrs. Lipke told me it's become second nature to him and he now imposes it on himself without her having to do or say anything."

"And the time-out worked?" Abe asked.

"I'm not sure," said Rachel. "Temporarily, maybe. But after ten or fifteen minutes he got up and walked out without saying anything. I called Mrs. Lipke and told her that Danny was upset and that she should call if he didn't come home or if she wanted to talk."

"So did she call you back?" asked Abe.

"No," Rachel said. "Not until five this morning."

"She's a brave woman, is Mrs. Lipke," Joel said, "living under the same roof with her meshugga son."

"That's not fair," Rachel said. "Danny's no meshuggener. Because he's mentally retarded he's often confused."

Abe was feeling too warm, too confined in this hothouse of familial troubles and intrigues. He needed air. Fresh air. "Let's go outside," he said, "and have a look around." He stood up. Joel stood up. Abe looked at Rachel. "Coming?"

"No," she said. "You go ahead. I've seen enough. Too much already. Way too much."

The air outside was sunny and crisp. Abe followed Joel down the steps at the front of the temple and turned left.

"You saw the swastika and stuff at the back," Joel said, "but you probably didn't see the other one."

"Where's that?"

"On the cornerstone, northeast corner, just around here." Joel led the way across crunchy, half-frozen slush. "Here, you can see. . . . " Abe saw the familiar spray-painted scrawl, a large swastika with a vertical slogan to the right, though this time with a difference:

K ill

K ik

K

"So what do you make of that?" Abe asked. "Better yet, what did the cops say about it?"

"That the vandals ran out of spray paint—used so much on the other side that they didn't have enough here to complete the job."

"Or maybe . . . " Abe thought aloud.

"Or maybe what?" Joel asked.

"Maybe they were surprised—so surprised that they didn't or couldn't finish the job."

"Surprised by what?"

"I don't know," Abe replied. "Something. Or maybe nothing. It's only a guess on my part. I'm just following my gut here."

Even Joel knew that his brother had the best gut in the business. Part instinct, part intellect, part past experience and part intuition, Abe's gut was like no one else's. It was a finely tuned instrument that he could play like Itzhak Perlman plays his fiddle. But like any virtuoso, Abe Feldman was temperamental. Sometimes he felt like playing, sometimes not. He hadn't felt like it when Joel first called him this morning. But now he was getting in the mood, warming to the task. Joel felt better. He watched as Abe took a small yellow-and-silver Stanley measuring tape out of his coat pocket and measured the distance from the ground to the top of the swastika.

"Just over eight feet," Abe announced. "Eight-three, to be exact. Which means that our perp is maybe six-four, six-five."

"How can you tell?" Joel asked.

"See the bar at the top of the swastika? It's the same width as the other lines. Which means that it was sprayed face-on, just like the others."

"So?"

"So the perp wasn't spraying above his reach, but within it. If he'd been stretching, pointing the spray nozzle up, the top bar would have been wider and messier, less well defined than the others. But as you can see, it's the same. So, yeah, this guy's tall. Either that, or we're talking about a midget with a ladder. I'd put my money on the tall-guy theory."

Joel paused and frowned, touching his forehead. "*Oy vey,* are you thinking what I'm thinking?"

"I don't know. What are you thinking?"

"That maybe Danny did this? To . . . I'm not sure. Maybe to impress Rachel in some weird way. Like he'll be able to protect her or something. He was acting really strange yesterday. The timing—it's maybe too much to be a coincidence?"

"The thought had crossed my mind," Abe said. "But then I remembered something you said upstairs. So, no, I don't think he did this."

"What did I say that lets Danny off the hook?"

"That Danny is a loner."

"So?"

"The perp had a partner. His partner is probably shorter."

"Partner? He had a *partner*?"

"Yeah. There were two of them. They had a division of labor. Tall guy painted the swastika and the *KKK*. Shorter guy painted the rest."

"And this you *know* for a fact?"

"Look, Joel, this isn't exactly rocket science. See the lines on the swastika? Compare the width and texture of those with the lines in *KKK*."

"I don't know. Except for the color they look the same to me."

"That's because they *are* the same. Now look at the lines in *ILL* and *IK*. Same or different?"

"Different, I think."

"You think right, little brother. They're noticeably different. Narrower, for one thing. And darker. Which means that the shorter guy was spraying closer up. Probably because he's less confident, less handy with a spray can than tall guy."

"Next thing you'll be telling me is how many cans they used."

"That's easy," Abe said. "Three—two black, one red."

"Oh, come on, Abe. Now you're just pulling my leg."

"No, really, three. Think about it. Say you're gonna deface a temple or some other building of your choice. You want to be mobile, you want to be quick, you want to travel light. To be in and out as fast as you can. Which means you schlep only as much equipment as you need. In this case the equipment is simple—cans of spray paint. You want to bring only as many cans as needed to do the job. And you're artistic, in a twisted kind of way.

You don't want your work of art to be dull and monochromatic, so you use two colors of paint—and preferably the black and red that the original Nazis favored. You're working with a partner, so you divvy up the job. The more skilled, more experienced guy can work faster, so he does the lion's share. His partner does less. Tall guy has two cans—one black, one red. Short guy has one can of black paint. Tall guy probably begins the job by painting KKK in red. Then, while short guy finishes writing the words, tall guy paints the swastika. It's a kind of artistic collaboration."

"You're sick, Abe. You have a twisted mind."

"In this business, believe me, it helps. You go after sickos, it helps to be a little sick yourself. You have to know how they think." Abe paused, frowning. "So, we've done the easy part. Now comes the hard part."

"Which is?"

"Figuring out why they didn't—or couldn't—finish the job. Here's how I see it. Tall guy painted KKK in red, went to work on the swastika, finished that, waited for short guy to finish his part. Then something happened."

"What happened?"

"That, I don't know. Something—or someone—stopped them, interrupted them midjob. Maybe they saw a cop car cruising down Lyndale, shining its spotlight on the nearby businesses. Maybe they heard something that scared them off. Until we know what that was, we've got *bupkas*."

"So we're stymied?"

"Not quite. Put on your thinking yarmulke, Rabbi. Put yourself in the place of an anti-Semitic vandal interrupted in the middle of doing your dirty deed. What do you do?"

"Run?"

"If you can, yeah, you probably run. Or . . . "

"Or what?"

"You fight. If you're cornered and can't get away that's what you'd do. So let's say our two perps are surprised by someone. Let's say they make a run for it. Where do they go?"

"Maybe up Lyndale? Or down Twenty-eighth?"

"Think again. They're not gonna run along well-lighted streets. They're gonna duck along the north side of the building where it's dark and make a run for the alley. So let's follow out that path. The snow on the north side—the shady side—won't be melted. So don't walk on the sidewalk—stay off to the side. Just in case we disturb anything."

As soon as they turned the corner Abe spotted something that stopped him cold.

"Look at this," Abe said.

"Look at what? I don't see anything."

"The snow next to the temple is disturbed. It's kind of bowl shaped, about six, seven feet in diameter. The few footprints that are still visible show a waffle pattern. Size twelve, thirteen Doc Martens, I'd guess. Then over here are parallel tracks, about a foot apart, almost like ski tracks," Abe said, his voice reduced to an intense whisper, "but they weren't made by skis."

"How do you know?"

"Because the tracks are cupped, which suggests—"

"What? Suggests what?"

"Somebody's heels. Someone grabbed somebody from behind, probably by the shoulders, and dragged him along the sidewalk up to . . . here," Abe said, pointing to a large metal plate with a handle on the top. "What's this? Looks like an old coal chute."

"It *is* an old coal chute. We don't use it anymore."

"There's no lock on the hasp. Looks like somebody's used it, and fairly recently."

"That would be the heating contractor. He wanted to run his large vacuum hose down the chute so he could clean the furnace. He asked me for the key. Well, the key has long since disappeared. Then he asked if he could cut the lock off, and I said yes. I was going to buy another lock today, but . . . other things got in the way. I forgot all about it until now . . . Abe, are you okay? You're not looking so good."

Abe felt himself barely able to stand up straight. He was dizzy to the point of nausea. He spoke in a hoarse whisper.

"The tracks end here, at the coal chute. I've got to get down to the basement. How . . . ?"

"Around this corner to the back entrance, then down the steps to your right."

Abe had no sooner turned the corner than he stepped between a TV camera and the blonde reporter.

". . . is being investigated by the Minneapolis Police, who . . . *Hey!* You just ruined my shot! *Hey!* I'm talking to *you*, asshole!"

Abe ducked in the back door and down the stairs. He turned left at the bottom and walked slowly and none too steadily toward the coal chute. The chute emptied into a large steel bin about chest high. Abe peered over the top. A pair of large, bulging eyes stared back at him. He recoiled, reeling backward, bumping into his brother, who steadied him and then looked down into the coal bin, empty except for a body.

"Oh, my God. My God, poor Danny. Poor Mrs. Lipke. It'll break her heart. And Rachel . . . " The silence was broken only by the thumping of the heating pipes overhead. Finally Joel said, "How . . . I mean, how did Danny—"

"It's murder," Abe rasped. "Danny was strangled. With a chain. A chain with small links—like on a dog collar. You know, a choke chain." Abe paused, pondering the grim double entendre. Then he took the cell phone out of its holster and punched in several numbers. He waited. "Yes, I'd like to talk to Captain Anderson, please. Tell him it's Abe Feldman . . . No, Feldman, F-E-L-D-M-A-N . . . Yes, that's right. And tell him it's an emergency." Again Abe waited. Joel prayed over the crumpled lifeless body of Danny Lipke.

"Hello, Bill. Yeah, it's me . . . No, I'm not doing okay. Not today. Look, you know that synagogue that was vandalized with swastikas? . . . Yeah, down on Lyndale and Twenty-eighth. Well, it's not about vandalism anymore. There's been a murder. Retarded kid name of Danny Lipke. I'm pretty sure he surprised the two perps . . . Yeah, two . . . I'll tell you later. Anyway, he catches these two guys in the act. There's a fight. They strangle him with a chain and stuff his body down a coal chute . . . In the basement of the temple . . . Yeah, I'm there now. We just found the body . . . My brother and I. He's the rabbi . . . Yes, I'll tell him . . . Okay, thanks, Bill."

"Tell me what?" Joel asked.

"That he's sorry."

The TV trucks and crews were about to leave when the black and white, siren screaming and lights flashing, pulled in and slid to a stop. A grim-faced, heavy-set plainclothes detective got out and walked quickly, but not quickly enough, toward the back door. The blonde reporter from Channel 6 stepped in front of him.

"Has there been some new development, Captain—some break in the case?"

"For Chrissake, Wanda, give it a rest. Can't you see I'm busy?"

"Busy with what?"

"No comment," he growled as he brushed past her and stepped inside. In the basement he found Abe Feldman sitting on a wooden crate. The two rabbis, visibly upset, were discussing who should tell Mrs. Lipke and how, and making plans for the washing and "watching" of the body before burial, and for saying Kaddish afterward.

"Abe, you look terrible," Anderson said, as quietly as he could.

"Then the outside matches the inside," Abe said, rising and pointing toward the coal bin. Anderson walked over, had a look, shook his large head.

"God in heaven," he wheezed, bending toward the body of Danny Lipke. "As usual, you're right," he said to Abe. "It's strangulation. And apparently with a small-link chain of some kind—like the ones dog trainers use. A . . . a . . . "

"Choke chain," Abe said. "And yes, I appreciate the irony." As he filled Anderson in on the details, the basement was becoming crowded with a medical examiner, a photographer, and several uniformed officers whose main job was to keep the media at bay. "One last thing, Bill. My guess is that those spray paint cans were discarded around here somewhere, maybe along the alley in a garbage can, maybe in someone's backyard. If we're lucky we can pull some prints off of them. If not, maybe we can find where they were bought and by whom. So if you can spare a couple of guys to do the legwork, it might pay off."

"Okay, will do. We'll take it from here, Abe," Anderson said at last. "Go home. Have a brewski for yourself—and one for me."

"I never drink in the middle of the day. But I am going to visit a bar."

"Bar? What bar?"

"The Iron Works, down on Minnehaha."

"The hell you say," Anderson exclaimed. "That's a biker bar. But more than that, it's a goddamned neo-Nazi hangout. Bad idea, Abe. *Very* bad idea."

"Yeah, well, it's the only idea I've got. So I'm going with it. But I'm sure I'll be safe."

"How's that?" Anderson asked.

"Because I've got your number on my speed dial," he said, half-smiling and patting his holstered cell phone as he headed toward the stairs.

Outside, the TV crews had once again unloaded and set up their equipment. The blonde reporter was applying fresh lipstick and adjusting her carefully coiffed hair when she spotted Abe coming out the door. She frowned and then, suddenly, she smiled and followed him to his car.

"You must be important," she said. "Could you identify yourself and give us a statement for the evening news?"

"Say 'Please,'" Abe said as he unlocked the car door.

She frowned again and then tried, not quite successfully, to smile. "Please," she said, thrusting her microphone into Abe's face.

"No."

Abe drove east on Lake, turning right on Minnehaha Avenue down into what had once been south Minneapolis's thriving industrial hub. Empty grain silos towered over long-abandoned factories and warehouses with broken windows. All looked down on rusted rail lines that ran north and south to nowhere.

The Iron Works was easy to spot. Above the entrance was a large German-style Iron Cross flanked by Confederate flags. As Abe pulled into the muddy parking lot, he noticed that most of the motorcycles and pickup trucks had bumper stickers announcing their owners' political views. Hitler was Right, said one. Six Million: A Good Start, said another. Think White! shrilled a third. Like we think in colors? Abe asked himself as he slopped through the parking lot toward the front door. He took a deep breath, opened it, and stepped inside.

The dank cavernous room smelled of stale beer, body odor, sweat, and cigarette smoke. He heard a familiar sound, coming from above. Looking up, he saw large steel pipes of various lengths and diameters, suspended from the ceiling just close enough to one another that the slightest breeze set them off, like a gigantic industrial wind chime. It was the sound he'd heard on the answering machine tape. He looked down and into a pair of distinctly unfriendly eyes.

"Yeah—you got business here?" the burly shaved-headed bartender asked. It sounded more like a threat than a question.

"Matter of fact, I do," said Abe. "I want to talk with the guy who calls himself The Commander."

"He don't call himself that. Other people call him that. Commander X. That's what he's called. But that's not his real name," he added conspiratorially. "His real name's a secret."

Secret *schmecret*, Abe thought. He knew that The Commander's real name was Paul Doolittle and wasn't surprised that the neo-Nazi preferred the mock-heroic Commander X to the teasing 'Paulie, who can Do Little,' as he was called back at West High School, where he and Abe had been students. The years since then had shown that the little that Paulie could do—and do very well—was to impress people who were too easily impressed by empty hate-filled slogans backed only by swagger and bravado. Even so, Abe knew that Paulie's being ridiculous didn't make him any less dangerous. If anything, his never-far-from-the-surface absurdity made him all the more mercurial and unpredictable, and therefore more dangerous. Especially to Abe Feldman and his kinsmen, not to mention blacks, Hispanics, immigrants, gays, Catholics, and race traitors—this last a term of art referring to people who have friends or who date or marry outside the white race, whatever that is. Abe could understand the White Rabbit, most of the *White Album,* and even "White Christmas"—maybe because its composer was Irving Berlin—but the White Race remained for him a mystery. If I "Think White!" Abe thought, what am I thinking? Maybe—who said this? Hannah Arendt?—I'm not *thinking* at all. Abe's reveries were interrupted by the sudden appearance of a very tall young man with light brown hair and matching starched brown shirt.

"You're here to see The Commander?" he asked in a tone so officious that Abe almost smiled.

"Yes, please take me to your leader," Abe mocked, without eliciting even a smile. "And you are . . . ?" he said, extending his hand.

The young man instinctively started to offer, and then quickly withdrew, his right hand. But not before Abe noticed traces of red paint on his nails and fingertips. Now we're getting somewhere, he thought grimly as he followed the brown shirt to a table around the far end of the bar.

"Wait here," he was told. Abe sat down. He looked around. Men with very short hair, some with shaved heads, eyed him warily from across the room as they played billiards and drank beer from bottles. The uniform of the day seemed to be black leather, motorcycle boots or Doc Martens, tattoos from knuckles to shoulders and God only knows where else. Wrapped around their necks and waists were chains that looked like longer versions of canine choke chains. Abe was just close enough to see that most of them were smoking Camels—unfiltered, of course. Isn't that just too perfect, Abe chuckled to himself. These guys show the world how tough they are by double-daring lung cancer and emphysema. Yeah, works for me. I'm convinced.

Abe was eyeing the Nazi memorabilia on the walls when he became aware of an eerie presence. He looked around and saw a familiar pockmarked face.

"What're you doin' here?"

"I came to see you, Pau . . . Commander X. Interesting name. Any relation to Malcolm?"

X glowered at Abe. Brown shirt stood nearby, arms folded, eyes fixed on Abe. The billiards players had stopped to watch, leaning on their long hardwood sticks. The industrial chimes overhead bonged ominously.

"I heard you retired," X hissed. "That right?"

"Yes. Two years ago."

"Then you can't be here on police business. So get your Yid ass the hell outta here."

"If I do I'll be back, next time with company. You wouldn't like the company I keep. They'd be doing wants and warrants on you and everybody in here and every vehicle outside, calling in the Health Department to do a very thorough sanitation inspection, the Fire Department to check for code violations—you name it. I may be retired, but my friends aren't. They're still very, very active."

"You're a nervy bastard, I'll give you that. Could it be that you're wearin' a wire?"

"Would I tell you if I were?" Abe wasn't sure he could pull this off.

"Okay, you got three minutes, startin' now," X said, looking at his wristwatch. Abe noticed it had a swastika where the Mickey Mouse should have been.

"I don't enjoy your company any more than you enjoy mine, so I'll be brief. First off, who's been making the threatening phone calls to the synagogue on Lyndale and Twenty-eighth?"

"Ain't nobody been makin' no phone calls I know of."

"Stop screwing around with me or so help me God I'll call my friends. I know for a fact that somebody's been calling from here because it sounds like the goddamned *Gong Show*."

X leaned back in his chair. "So, yeah, okay, some of the boys get a little liquored up, make a few phone calls . . . to their friends . . . " The black-leather-clad boys laughed at this clever riposte.

"It's a felony misdemeanor in Minnesota to make threatening phone calls," Abe said loudly enough to be heard by all.

"Don't you think I know that? That we all know that? So tell me, what threats were made? What threats?"

Suddenly Abe knew why the anonymous caller said nothing. No words equals no threat, technically speaking. He had to let this one slide.

"The point is that these calls constituted an implied threat," Abe finessed, "and the threat preceded an act of vandalism and"—he paused for dramatic effect and looked straight at X—"a murder."

X recoiled. "Hey," he roared, "don't try to pin no murder on me. I don't know nothin' about no murder."

"So you and the boys here just make threatening phone calls and deface synagogues with painted swastikas and shit, but you draw the line at murder?"

"Okay, the phone calls, yeah. But nobody's been paintin' anything." X paused, looking around the room and then at Abe. "I'd know about if it any-body did. Me and the boys don't keep no secrets. Everybody's got braggin' rights, if you know what I mean."

Abe knew exactly what X meant. And strangely, he found himself thinking that X might actually be telling the truth. But something still bothered him.

"Any of these 'boys' have day jobs?" Abe asked.

"It's none of your business."

"Humor me," Abe said, "or I call my friends."

"Yeah, sure, some of 'em work, some don't."

"What about Martin Bormann here?" Abe asked, pointing at brown shirt.

"Go ahead, Eddie, tell him where you work," X ordered.

"Down at Wilson's Auto Body Shop. On Forty-sixth."

That would explain the red paint residue on brown shirt's nails and fin-gertips. Back to square one, Abe thought.

"Okay, no more questions. I'm outta here," Abe said, standing up and surveying the room. "One more thing. Not that you'd want to know what I think, but I'll tell you anyway. I think that you and your boys here are zits on the backside of humanity. And that's when I'm having a good day and feeling charitable. Well, I gotta go." Suddenly, and certainly luckily, Abe's cell phone began to ring. "That would be my friends. They're expecting me right about now, wondering what's happened to me. You remember my friends?" No one made the move that all wanted to make, and Abe sauntered safely out the door.

Once outside Abe pulled out his cell phone and answered, "Hello, and thank you *very* much . . . Oh, Bill, hi. Boy, talk about being saved by the bell! . . . No, I'll tell you later . . . Tell me what? . . . In a garbage can? All three? Good work. Any prints? . . . Too bad . . . Excellent! Almost as good as prints. . . . Okay, I'll meet you over there in ten minutes."

So, Abe thought as he drove west along Lake Street, his hunch had paid off. Sort of. When combing the alley that runs north-south behind the temple, a patrolman had found three almost-empty spray paint cans—two black, one red—nearly three blocks away. All had been wiped clean, and none had any clearly discernable fingerprints. But one still had the price tag on it, and on the tag was the name of the store.

Abe parked the old Pontiac behind the black and white in front of Jay's Hardware on Twenty-ninth and Hennepin. As he walked inside, the door buzzer announced his arrival.

"This is Jay Nelson, the owner," Anderson said to Abe. Abe nodded. "Tell Detective Feldman what you just told me."

"Well, yesterday afternoon late, just around closing time, these two kids came in. Teenagers, maybe fifteen, sixteen years old. One was real tall, like he was a basketball player or something. He was trying real hard to be cool. The other one—a little dude—he seemed real nervous. They were both wearing black leather everything—head to toe—and, to tell you the truth, they looked a little scary, especially with the big boots and the chains. I mean, I know that's the fashion now and lots of kids dress like that. I thought for a minute that they might be here to rob me—that would be the second time this year—so I felt relieved when they pulled out money to pay for the three cans of Rust-Oleum, two black, one red. But then I think, wait a minute, I bet these kids are up to something. Maybe, I'm thinking, they're going to paint graffiti—boy, that's been a problem like you wouldn't believe, just ask any of the store owners around here. And so I have an idea—."

"Here's the best part," Anderson interrupted. "You're not gonna believe this."

"Well," Nelson continued, "I say to the boys, 'Hey, have you boys heard about our drawing? We're giving away a mountain bike'—I point to the blue-and-red one over there—'in a drawing tomorrow. Just write your name and phone number on here,' I say, giving a pad and pencil to the short kid. Well, he's so anxious to get out of here that he writes his name and phone number down. The tall one tries to snatch it away but I'm faster. I tear off the top sheet and give the pad to him. 'Here, son,' I say, 'you can take a chance too.' 'No,' he said, and they both left. They had a big argument outside, and all the way down the block you could hear them shouting. As you've probably guessed, there is no drawing—that was my little white lie—but here's the short kid's name and phone number." He showed Abe a small piece of paper with the hardware store's name and logo at the top. "So any-way, what did these kids do? It's graffiti, isn't it? Am I right?"

"It's a lot more serious than that," Abe said. "We can't give you any more information right now. Read tomorrow's paper. And Mr. Nelson?"

"Yes?"

"Good work. I wish we could clone guys like you."

Anderson rang the front doorbell. A short, baby-faced kid opened the door. "My dad's not home," he said.

"We're not looking for your dad, Glen, we're looking for you," Anderson said sternly but not unkindly as he showed his badge. "We're the police. You know why we're here."

The boy began to shake and sob. "I didn't wanna do it. Honest, I didn't. But Freddie he kept saying, like, 'Let's stir things up in this boring 'hood, get a buzz goin',' you know, like it was fun or somethin'. And I go, 'no I don't want to' and he goes 'chicken' and I go 'okay.' So we buy some spray paint and wait 'till it gets dark. Around midnight we get there—"

"Where's there?" Abe asked.

"You know, that church place over on Lyndale."

"The Jewish synagogue?" The boy nodded yes. "What do you have against Jews?"

"Nothin'. I mean I don't know anything about 'em, except . . . "

"Except what?"

"Like they're really smart and stuff."

"How do you know that?" Abe asked.

"Freddie told me. He's pretty smart too. He, like, planned everything— the whole deal."

"So you get to the synagogue. Then what do you do?"

"Freddie paints, like, *KKK* and then does the . . . that whatchamacallit."

"Swastika."

"Yeah, that thing. And me, I'm like, tryin', you know, to remember what I'm supposed to write, and Freddie's gettin' mad and tellin' me to hurry up. Then we go around to the other side and we're gettin' started and then this crazy dude comes runnin' out of the bushes and starts shoutin' some-thin' about how we're not gonna hurt his girlfriend and stuff and he's just, like, completely crazy. We tried gettin' out of there—we didn't want no fight—but he kept grabbin' us and like, man, that dude was strong. He's like some big retard and just wouldn't let go. I was real scared. I hit him in the nuts and when he turns on me, like, Freddie, he puts his belt chain around the crazy dude's neck and, like, just keeps holdin' on while the big dude's tryin' to turn around. We knew if he, like, ever got loose he'd kill us for sure. Finally he stops movin' but Freddie, he like, keeps holdin' on . . . "

Abe Feldman felt sick. He stepped outside onto the darkened porch. What stupid, senseless, thoughtless waste, he thought. Then he remembered a phrase from long ago. The banality of evil. Who said that? Rachel would know. He walked down the stairs and along the slippery sidewalk toward the old Pontiac.

SANDRA LEVY CEREN, a native New York, presently lives in California, where she practices clinical psychology. She is the author of mystery suspense novels featuring Dr. Cory Cohen, psychologist and amateur sleuth. In this story, as in the novels, Cory grapples with her patient's intriguing problems.

Silver Is Better Than Gold

▼   ▼   ▼   ▼   ▼   ▼   ▼   ▼   ▼   ▼   ▼

SANDRA LEVY CEREN

CORY STEPPED INTO THE RECEPTION ROOM to greet her new patient. "Hello. Joshua Silver? I'm Cory Cohen."

The tall, well-dressed red-haired man with shadows under his eyes stared at her, a puzzled expression on his face. "Oh. *You're* Dr. Cohen. I'm sorry. I expected a Jewish woman."

"I am Jewish. My Asian features fool people." When brought to her attention, the incongruity between her appearance and her identity gave her discomfort. The daughter of a Japanese mother and a Jewish father, she had been reared by her Jewish grandparents.

After Cory ushered him into her office, Joshua Silver rushed to the window and carefully, from the corner, peered out at the blue Pacific. "Can anyone see into this room?"

"No." Was Mr. Silver paranoid?

He paced the floor, stumbled on a potted plant, and landed on the couch.

"I'm a klutz." His face reddened as if he were used to a lifetime of awkward accidents.

"I don't know about that. Since the cleaning crew moved Yankel the Yucca, a few people have tripped over the plant today. I'm sorry."

"Funny name for a plant."

"And my name is funny for me, too." She hoped Joshua Silver would lighten up.

"Look, I'll get straight to the point. I'm afraid that I'm going to be murdered."

The hair on the back of her neck rose. "Have you reported this to the police?"

"I can't. I'm being watched."

"By whom?"

"Neil Gold's henchmen. Have your heard of him? The financial guru."

Cory nodded. A recipient of frequent invitations to Gold's financial seminars, she had declined them all. "How can I help you?"

"I need to feel safe. Like in a locked ward in a mental hospital."

Hmm, this was the oddest request she had gotten in a long time. "You'll need a proper diagnosis for admission."

"I'm sure you will find something substantive when you hear my story."

With rapt attention to his words, she crossed her slim legs, notepad on her lap and pen in hand.

"The story is about Neil Gold and my father. Neil and I go way back. We studied for bar mitzvah together. Now, my dad is a very outspoken shul board member and was well respected in the Jewish community until Neil offered $500,000 to Congregation Beth Shalom to build an annex. Since Dad doesn't trust Neil, he advised the board to conduct an investigation into his business practices before accepting what may be tainted money."

"Why does he distrust Neil?"

"Back in Brooklyn, where Neil and I were raised, he was always cooking up some cockamamy scheme to line his pockets at the expense of others, as far back as when we took bar mitzvah classes together. He was more interested in studying the racing form and bragging about his winnings than studying the Torah. He conned me into placing my savings on a sure-thing horse. The horse lost, and my father hasn't forgiven him or me for it since. He believes Neil pocketed my money and didn't place any bet. My dad knew all of the neighborhood bookies and they said Neil was a *no-goodnik* and that he wasn't a customer. From that day on, my dad forgot my name. Calls me *schmegegge* and schlemiel. He doesn't respect my judgment."

"Some parents don't realize how their words affect their children," Cory pointed out.

"I know he loves me, but he doesn't know how to show it. He said I was a schmuck for marrying Cheryl—that she was only out for my money."

"What do you think?"

"She *is* materialistic, but she does care for me. Watches my diet, has me working out with her personal trainer. Another guru, Ed Finnegan."

A small world. A patient had ended an affair with her personal trainer, Ed Finnegan, after discovering him in a compromising position with another woman.

"But your experience with Neil was—how many years ago?"

"Well over twenty years. My father has the memory of an elephant. He's angry at me for befriending Neil when Neil and his wife moved here two years ago and joined our shul. I wanted to let bygones be bygones and invited him to the house. Our wives got along well. They're both young and aren't ready to start a family yet. Think too much about their figures."

Cory wanted to follow this thread, but she couldn't see that it was relevant to his present circumstance. "Let's go back to the board meeting"

"Lisa Marks, another board member—tight with Neil—denounced my father as a man who committed a sin."

"The sin of *lashon hara*. Maligning a person's character," Cory observed.

Joshua's eyebrows raised. "So you do understand."

"Yes."

"Lisa accused my father of condemning an innocent, charitable man and is trying to force Dad's resignation."

"How does this connect with Neil going after you?"

Silver pulled a tissue from the box on the table and mopped his sweaty brow. He began to tremble and his face paled.

"Are you okay?" Cory poured a glass of water from a pitcher on her desk, leaned forward, and handed it to him.

He took a few sips. "Better now. Last night I woke up with heart palpitations. Cheryl called 911. I wound up in the emergency room. After a bunch of tests, doctors assured me it was only anxiety. Hah! *Only* anxiety! I've brought you a copy of the results of my exams." He handed her a sheet of paper.

"Thank you. Your thoroughness is admirable." She skimmed the test results and read the diagnosis. "It's natural to feel anxious when threatened. Please go on with your story."

"Neil invited me to his office to discuss a professional arrangement. I'm a CPA with more than enough clients and I needed his work like a hole in the head, but I was curious and Cheryl coerced me. She's gullible and very impressed by his fame and fortune, and she thought it would be good for me to find out what he had in mind." Joshua sighed. "Anyway, yesterday

I examined his *farpatchket* books. It didn't surprise me when I found substantial proof that Neil Gold is indeed a genuine gonif."

"How so?"

Silver cleared his throat, shifted his position and sat erect in his chair, his fingers forming a pyramid. He appeared ready to address a boardroom.

"Neil has convinced his clients that in order to take swift advantage of changes in stock values arising from market volatility, they would need to sign over to him power of attorney. In reality, he invested their money in his name and paid them only a portion of any gains. At the inception of the business, there were substantial losses, but he paid some investors money that he apparently had taken from other investors. He keeps a double set of books. Imagine my disgust when I actually saw how he defrauded people." A little vein in Joshua's forehead swelled and pulsated. Cory watched with interest and some concern.

"When I confronted him about it, he said his clients were grateful for the money he made for them and were relieved he didn't *shtup* paperwork on them. He wasn't the least bit embarrassed at my catching him. That *mamzer* had me pegged for the schlemiel he took advantage of twenty years ago. He had the chutzpah to offer me a generous share of the business in exchange for my handling his books—and I presume for my silence. When I told him I wouldn't participate in his illegal scheme, he got upset and said if I squealed on him, I'd regret it."

"That's scary, but maybe the threat was an empty one." She was beginning to think that maybe Silver did have a reason to be afraid.

"Oh, no. The way he looked at me, I'm sure he wants to have me killed."

"That is a serious allegation. What do you want to do about this?" She was torn between maintaining clinical objectivity and a rising concern for the man's safety.

"I know what I should do, but I'm afraid. I don't trust the police and I wouldn't put it past Neil to hire a hit man. I'm sure he knows my every move. I've hired a bodyguard. Told him I was threatened by a crazy client. He's waiting outside your office."

Cory studied Joshua's grave face—the face of a man who feels doomed. "Have you decided to blow the whistle on Neil Gold?"

"My father's humiliation is painful both to my parents and to me. With my proof of Neil's fraud, I can restore Dad's dignity and finally earn his respect." Silver paused to catch his breath. "Only if I do so, I risk losing my life."

"Your conflict adds to your anxiety. You are an honorable man. I saw the anger in your face when you spoke about how Neil cheated his clients. You want no part of that."

"You're right. I couldn't live with myself if I cheated anyone. My parents raised me to have principles, to live according to the Ten Commandments and follow God's injunctions."

Religious Jews believed God commanded them to be fruitful and multiply. How did that sit with Joshua, whose wife, Cheryl, chose to remain childless? Cory avoided the subject. Josh had enough tsuris. She watched him run his fingers through his thinning hair. "I understand. You didn't need Neil as a client, but you checked out his books because you were curious. Sure. Your father fueled your suspicion about Neil. Perhaps you wanted to find something amiss—something that would put your father in a better light with the congregation. You didn't create the opportunity, but you took advantage of it."

"I don't think that was wrong."

"Fine. Now, if your assumption about Neil's threat is correct, he may not have yet devised a damage control plan." Cory wanted to protect Joshua Silver, but she pondered the wisdom of giving him advice. She must lead him to draw his own conclusion. "Have you considered your options?"

"Cheryl begged me to stall Neil—tell him I've reconsidered, pretend to be friends. But I'd be lying."

"Would you lie to save your life?"

For the first time since he had entered Cory's office, Silver smiled. "Of course, but if Neil believed me, he'd be a poor judge of character."

"He proved that when he asked for your professional help."

"Oh, thanks for the compliment." Joshua stroked his chin. "I bet last week Lisa Marks told Neil about the board meeting. You see, when I came out of Neil's office yesterday, there she was, seated in the waiting room, all dolled up, sexy looking, wearing a short skirt and low-cut blouse. When she saw me, she seemed embarrassed—like I'd caught her with her pants down." Silver blushed. "Neil was trying to use me to get my father to leave him alone."

"You may be right."

"This situation is making me meshugga. I'll call him tonight. Tell him the big lie. The delay would give me time to notify the Securities and Exchange Commission. Then I'd stay in the hospital for awhile, go abroad until it works out. Money isn't a problem. I make a good living."

"A change of environment could help reduce your anxiety. Why not go on a vacation immediately?"

"No. My nerves are really shot. I need help."

"I agree, and the emergency room notes substantiate the diagnosis of anxiety. I'll get you into a hospital by tomorrow. When do you plan to notify the authorities?"

"I'll call the SEC early in the morning. My CPA credentials should make them take notice. They act fast."

"Good. Go home. Pack necessities. I'll make the arrangements." Cory handed him her card. "Call me at seven in the morning. Tell your family where you'll be, but please instruct them to keep it to themselves."

"Then you do believe me?" Silver seemed relieved.

"I believe you have a reason to *feel* threatened, but I don't know if the threat is genuine."

Silver slid a thick envelope from his pocket. "I've prepared a signed, notarized statement authorizing you to contact the police and my father and reveal the content of this session in the event any harm comes to me. For my father, I've included proof of Neil's guilt. I might not reach him for a few days. He's traveling abroad, and I want him to have these documents."

"I don't feel comfortable as guardian of these papers. Why not give them to your attorney?"

"He hasn't returned my calls and his office is closed now. There's no time to lose. Please, I'd feel better if you had the documents. Cheryl is—well a bit flighty, and I don't want to worry my frail mother. Please," he begged. Reluctantly, Cory filed the sealed envelope in the case folder marked with Joshua's name. Caught up in this unusual case, she blurted out, "If you believe Neil is having you watched, it might be wise to make your calls to me and the SEC from a secure line."

After Joshua's session, Cory made several phone calls and finalized arrangements for his admission to a hospital.

For a while after seven the next morning, Cory sat in the den sipping coffee, waiting for Joshua Silver to call. She turned on the TV for the local news. Southbound traffic was backed up for ten miles along Interstate 5 due to an accident at the merge. Cory figured Joshua might be traveling that route and could be delayed in making the calls, but he could have reached her from his cell phone, at least to say he was stuck in traffic.

When 7:45 rolled around without a call from Joshua, Cory became alarmed. Could he have had an accident? Was he Neil's victim, after all?

She phoned Joshua's home and reached an answering machine, so she left her name and number. Next, she called the local hospitals, but no information about Joshua Silver was forthcoming.

It was time to rely on her good friend George Lewis, a San Diego police detective. She phoned and reached him immediately. "Sorry to bother you, George, but I need to know if a Joshua Silver, a tall red-haired man, age about thirty-six, has met with an accident."

George grunted. "Since you've been right about these things before, I'll check for you. Call you right back."

Cory rinsed her breakfast dishes, put them in the dishwasher, and then paced the den. Finally the phone rang.

"Bad news, Doc." The voice was George's. "A Joshua Silver was killed this morning when his car exploded in front of his house."

Cory's stomach clenched and she was speechless.

"Hey, Doc, are you okay?"

She felt guilty. Why had she waited to hospitalize Joshua Silver? It was very upsetting. "Yesterday, he came to see me, afraid he'd be murdered."

"I need details, Doc. I'll be there in a few minutes."

"Thank you."

"No. Thank *you*."

Although Cory had only known Joshua Silver for one hour, she found herself weeping for this religious man, dedicated to doing the right thing and trying to be deserving of his father's respect. She paced the floor until the doorbell rang and she let in George Lewis.

"Whatcha got, Doc?"

"I have Joshua Silver's permission to tell you that Neil Gold threatened him two days ago." She gave him as much of the story as she could, while maintaining some confidentiality.

"Thanks, Doc. I'll get on this right away, and keep in touch." Cory saw George to the door and he hurried off.

Cory called the hospital and canceled the admitting order before leaving for her office, grateful for other patients to distract her.

At the end of the day, and the workweek, as she was about to leave her office, a well-tailored, husky man entered the reception room. "I'm looking for Dr. Cohen. I'm Lieutenant Tom Bains, detective, San Diego Police Department."

Cory knew lieutenants usually didn't conduct investigations. Moreover, familiar with most of the detectives on the force, she didn't recognize Bains.

She took note of his elegant suit and his highly polished Italian leather shoes. She stiffened—afraid the probably bogus detective was there to collect Joshua Silver's documents or force her to reveal information about him. What else could it be?

"May I see your credentials, please?"

As the dark haired man reached into his pocket, her fear rose. What if he had a gun? Cory edged closer to the reception desk, where the security panic button was hidden. If she pressed it, would the alarm scare him off? She froze as he pulled a badge from his pocket. It looked authentic, but she figured, like him, it must be counterfeit.

"What is this about?"

"Joshua Silver."

"Who?"

"Don't pretend you don't know him. I tailed him to your office yesterday."

"Many people come here to offer goods or services. My receptionist just stepped out. I'll ask her when she returns. Please leave your card, and she'll contact you. Has he done something wrong?"

"I can't answer that."

Afraid of what might come next, her fingers inched toward the panic button. Just as she reached it, the door opened and in sauntered the three-man cleaning crew. The large men, with heavily tattooed, rippling biceps showing from short-sleeved, gray-colored uniforms, pushed in mops and metal buckets.

The fake detective turned on his heel. "I'll be back," he warned.

Cory resisted the urge to hug her new heroes, the cleaning crew. Shaken, she called the San Diego police department, identified herself, and asked for Tom Bains.

"Sorry, no one here by that name."

"A man impersonating a police officer has just left my office."

The dispatcher took the report, promised an investigation, and accepted Cory's urgent message for George.

Trembling, Cory phoned building security for an escort to her car. As the guard accompanied her downstairs, she glanced around. No sign of the phony cop.

Driving home, she checked the rearview mirror. Someone driving an old Porsche followed too closely behind. Unnerved, Cory suspected the person was tailing her. She turned up a dead end street; the Porsche stayed on her track. She made a U-turn, the Porsche followed. At a traffic signal, she made another U. Again, the Porsche was directly behind her. Heart pounding, Cory headed straight into the parking lot of the popular Beach House restaurant and the safety of valet parking. Tires screeching, the Porsche sped away.

She had ditched the pursuer—for the time being. She tipped the valet and drove home, worried that the pursuer—maybe the bogus cop—would return. She would be vigilant.

Sunday morning, George called and asked to meet Cory at the new café near her office. When she arrived, she spotted George, clad in a pair of blue sweats and seated in a quiet corner, a mug of steaming coffee on the table. He rose to greet her. With his sandy buzz haircut and his fit physique, George looked the part of the retired Marines officer he was.

"Must be your day off," she remarked.

"My first free morning. I've pulled two overnights this week. Plenty to tell you, Doc."

The bright-eyed young server interrupted, and Cory ordered two egg whites scrambled, a bagel, and coffee.

"Same here," George said, lifting his coffee mug. The server filled his cup and scurried away.

Cory stared at George. "I left you a message Friday afternoon. Someone impersonating a police officer and calling himself Tom Bains came to my office to question me about Joshua Silver. I shudder to think what would have happened had the janitorial crew not arrived. And that's not all. I was followed by someone in a Porsche, but I ditched whoever it was."

"Get a license number?"

"It was too dark." Cory was surprised that he hadn't called. She had expected George to show more concern.

"Sorry I didn't get your message. We've had some clerical problems. You know, Doc, there's little we can do about what happened to you."

"That's a comfort."

"Ask building security to make frequent checks of your office. We'll send an extra patrol to your office and house. Be vigilant."

She rolled her eyes.

"Listen, Doc. Neil Gold couldn't have been responsible for the murder of Joshua Silver."

Cory dropped her jaw. "Why not?"

"Gold's receptionist reported that soon after Joshua Silver left Gold's office on Wednesday, Gold had a stroke. She called 911. That was the only call made from his phone after five in the afternoon. Gold's completely paralyzed, in critical condition. Sorry, Doc, but he's got a perfect alibi."

Now she was puzzled. "Could the explosion have been an accident?"

"No. Our demolition experts found remnants of a bomb, set off when Silver started the engine. A neighbor said the Silvers were having some major landscaping done to the garden and when Joshua arrived home, several feet of soil blocked his driveway and he had to park his car on the street overnight."

"Any suspects?" Cory didn't know enough about Joshua Silver to think of any. She was afraid of what her involvement in this case might lead to. Should she have refused to accept the documents?

"We usually concentrate on the victim's spouse," George explained. "Apart from the neighbor, she was the only one who knew his car was parked overnight on the street. She's sedated, and we haven't been able to talk with her. Listen, your pal was a very rich man. His financial documents show large endowments for various charities and plenty left over for his wife, Cheryl. She's the sole beneficiary of his substantial life insurance policy."

"Is she your only suspect?"

"Right now, yes."

"I don't know her, but I doubt she had anything to do with it." Cheryl knew Neil had threatened her husband. She could have jumped at the chance to have her husband killed and Neil would be the prime suspect, but this wasn't enough to convince Cory. She'd seen Cheryl's loyalty through Joshua's eyes.

"I've asked to be assigned to this case. The funeral is at El Camino Memorial Park at two o'clock today, and I plan to interview Cheryl Silver afterward. She probably knows nothing about planting a car bomb. She'd need an accomplice."

"Who else would gain?" Cory wondered. Then she flashed on Lisa. Supposing Lisa and Neil were lovers. Would Lisa have had Josh silenced to protect Neil?

George raised his eyebrows. "Whatcha thinking, Doc?"

"Check out Lisa Marks, a member of Congregation Beth Shalom. See if she spoke with Neil before he went to the hospital," Cory suggested. "I can't say more."

Cory reflected on Joshua's session and the envelope he'd left with her for safekeeping. "I'd like to go to the funeral with you."

"Sure, Doc. I'll pick you up at one-fifteen."

Wearing a long-sleeve black dress and a black hat, Cory waited for George on her doorstep. This day would be hard for Joshua's family. Her heart ached for parents who lost a child. Children should outlive parents, not the other way around. She steeled herself for the upcoming weeping and wailing. Would she know any of the mourners? In a small Jewish community, most Jews knew one another. More than likely, their grief would mask any curiosity about George and Cory and her relationship to Joshua. She rehearsed what she would say to Mr. Silver.

George arrived on time, wearing standard funeral attire—a dark blue suit. She doubted he had many occasions to dress up. Too bad this was one of them. "You look spiffy, George. Handsome. I'm glad for your company today. Find out anything about Lisa Marks?"

"Conveniently unavailable for questioning. Took off on a two-week cruise yesterday. She's made a big bundle with Neil. His secretary said Lisa and Neil were together about fifteen minutes before he fell ill."

"Enough time to plan a murder?"

"Doc, you're a cynic."

"I caught it from you, George." She frowned. "Maybe I could have prevented Joshua's murder by getting him into a hospital right away."

"You're always too harsh on yourself, Doc."

She handed him a blue velvet yarmulke, borrowed from her son's stack. The little skullcap perched precariously on George's crew cut. "Now, I'll fit right in. Intruding on a grim, private event makes me uncomfortable, but in a murder investigation, we've got to check out the guests."

They made the trip to the cemetery in silence and linked up with a long procession of cars to Joshua Silver's final resting-place. After George parked behind a Rolls Royce, Cory clung to his arm as they climbed the hill to join the service. Three mourners, dressed in dark clothes, sat on canvas folding chairs. Cory figured they were Joshua's parents and Cheryl—a slim, petite, curly-haired brunette beauty in her twenties. Cheryl held hands with the frail-looking woman seated beside her—no doubt Joshua's mother. The two women clutched handkerchiefs and dabbed their faces. Joshua's mother rocked back and forth as though *davening*. Joshua's father, stone-faced and red-eyed, sat stiffly with his arm around the older woman's shoulder.

Joshua had closely resembled his father. The same fair complexion and red hair. The elder Silver had a fuller physique and gray hair at the temples. Cory imagined that had Joshua lived, he would have matured into the image of his father. Her eyes welled with tears. Who could have killed him? And most of all, why?

The crowd circled at the newly dug grave. Cory clung tightly to George's arm for emotional support and nodded to a few people she knew.

After the funeral, guests were handed directions to Josh's parents' home. Cory stooped to wash her hands at a small faucet on the cemetery grounds and beckoned George to do likewise. "Still think Cheryl wanted her husband dead?"

He shrugged. "She could be performing the bereaved widow role."

Cory didn't think it was an act. A woman wouldn't call 911 fearing her husband was having a coronary if she wanted him dead, nor try to protect him with her sage advice.

"Take a gander at Neil's wife—the one in the outrageous outfit—the tasty dish—two plump strawberries on a tiny glob of whipped cream," George suggested.

Cory scanned the crowd. Her eyes rested on a tall, slender blonde in a red tube top and white satin mini skirt that barely covered her butt. "You *are* a good detective. I didn't notice her. How do you know who she is?"

"I interviewed her at the hospital. She's not the brightest bulb in the chandelier. Seems like a kid, young enough to be Gold's daughter."

Cory smiled. "Rich men are very attractive to women of all ages. She probably went to the funeral to support her friend Cheryl."

"Then how come she didn't go near her?"

"Very interesting. Let's find out."

They headed to Rancho Santa Fe, a wealthy San Diego suburb where giant eucalyptus trees lined the road and orange groves hid the estates from view. Soon they reached a large wrought-iron gate left open for cars. George turned onto the driveway and parked his jalopy behind a late model Ferrari at the end of the long path leading to the Silvers' home. She hoped George, like many other goyim, didn't assume most Jews were wealthy. Quickly, she chastised herself for her own prejudice.

As George was about to ring the bell, Cory placed her hand on his arm. "Don't. When visiting Jewish mourners, the custom is to enter unannounced so as not to disturb them."

"Thanks for explaining. I'll learn some cultural lessons today. Then maybe I'll find me a nice Jewish *maidel*."

"Why not a nice shiksa?" She jabbed him playfully in the ribs.

George pushed open the ornate front door, and they entered a wide foyer facing an enormous room furnished with antiques. Persian carpets graced the parquet floor, and huge European paintings hung from velvet cords on the wall. Cory felt as if she had stepped into an eighteenth-century painting. The family stood in front of a marble fireplace and received condolences, hugs, and handshakes. A server carried a large tray piled high with corned beef sandwiches on rye. Another server passed a tray filled with knishes.

A white linen sheet hung over the fireplace mantle, covering a mirror. "A Jewish mourning custom," she explained.

Someone had wanted Joshua Silver dead. Had it been Lisa? Did Lisa know something—anything at all? "I'll snoop around while you get us some drinks," Cory said.

Cory strolled around the buffet table. She collected a bagel and a napkin and moseyed to a quiet, secluded corner where Neil's wife sat with a husky man. They appeared unaware of her presence. Cory munched on the soul food and focused her attention on the couple. The man was dark-haired, tall, and built like a bouncer, but his back was toward her and she couldn't hear what he was saying.

Neil's wife resembled a California-type model. Her sun-streaked, smooth blonde hair caressed her tanned, naked shoulders. This strawberry sundae looked to be in her early twenties and was a knockout—in a cheap sort of way. If the large diamond on her finger were on a dowager's, it would have looked authentic, but on Ms. G. it looked fake.

Pouting, the young woman raised her voice. "Damn it, Ed, you promised you'd stop seeing Cheryl."

"You know I'm nuts about you, babe, but I can't drop Cheryl at a time like this. She'd be devastated," the man said.

Their voices dropped and Cory couldn't make out the rest of the conversation. Was the man Ed Finnegan, the personal trainer? Was he having an affair with Cheryl Silver? She was shocked. This opened up a whole new line of possibilities. Could he have murdered Joshua to get closer to Cheryl and her money? How dreadful.

Cory sauntered over to the bar where George waited in the middle of the line for the drinks. "This may be important." She whispered the snippet between Ed and Ms. Gold. George nodded that he had heard and understood.

As a pretty, petite Asian server passed, George stopped her. "Pardon. Please find out if the gentleman seated in the far corner is Ed Finnegan."

"The one with Ms. Gold? Yes, that's him."

"Thanks." Then turning to Cory, he told her, "I need privacy. I'll be busy awhile."

She walked George to his car. Grateful for comfortable shoes, she strolled around the lush rose garden and moved to the orange grove. The citrus scent mingled with honeysuckle. Lovely.

She checked her Timex. After fifteen minutes she returned to the house and cornered the cute Asian server. Tall Cory felt awkward, towering over the petite woman. "Hi. Since you know Ed Finnegan, perhaps you know someone who can recommend him as a personal trainer?"

"Oh, sure. He have many clients. I too work for them. The Golds, the rabbi's family, the Silvers, Lisa Marks. I afford, I go. He too expensive for me."

"Maybe for me, too. Thanks." Cory wanted to offer her condolences to the Silver family, but a crowd surrounded them and she resumed her post in the shadows near Ms. Gold and Ed.

Cheryl approached the couple. Ed rose, hugged her, and stroked her hair. Red-faced, Ms. G. stormed out of the house.

To an unsuspecting onlooker, Finnegan was comforting his client, a grieving widow. Ed faced Cory, but she was certain he didn't notice her—his eyes devoured Cheryl.

Now Cory had a good view of him. She gasped. He was the man who had impersonated a police officer!

Cory slipped out of the house, ran to George's car and tapped on the window.

George was using his laptop. "Best tool for fast data retrieval. Here's what I just got on Finnegan: A Marines demolition expert. Suspected of stealing explosives. Dishonorable discharge. You know, from the bomb fragments we've recovered at the explosion site, within a few weeks forensics can determine if the explosive was the type used by the military. Something else. His credit report shows he's in serious debt."

"An impressive résumé," Cory said. "Add one more. Impersonating a police officer."

"What? I'll have a police car out here to arrest him. You'll make the I.D.

The rest is circumstantial evidence, but something or other is bound to stick."

"He's in debt, yet the server said Finnegan has a big clientele."

"This came in a few minutes ago. Silver's neighbor, an insomniac, reported that at three in the morning the day of the explosion, he'd heard a car and looked out the window. It was a clear night with a full moon and Silver's Mercedes was parked under a street lamp. An old Porsche with a battered door on the driver's side pulled in front of Silver's car. A man jumped out, carrying a tool kit, and approached the Mercedes. The neighbor was about to phone the police, but he had a nature call. When he returned to his window, the Porsche and the man were gone, but he had gotten a good look at him. The man he saw fits Finnegan's description, and Finnegan owns an old Porsche with a battered door. It'd been in a motor accident a month before the explosion. I checked out the license number of the Porsche parked over there." George pointed to a row of cars behind them. "It's Finnegan's."

Cory gasped. "Someone in a Porsche nearly scared the wits out of me!"

"That'd be a big job." He winked. "Your hunch about Lisa Marks, Doc? She couldn't have known Silver's car would be parked overnight on the street."

"Maybe Ed acted on his own. You said he was in debt. Maybe Neil or Lisa, or both of them, paid him to silence Joshua."

Cory thought it ironic that Joshua's father had accused Cheryl of marrying for money and then along came Finnegan, aiming to capture her heart and Joshua's cash. Had Finnegan come to Cory's office to collect information—or to dispose of her?

George checked his watch. "For now, we'll charge Finnegan with impersonating a police officer. We don't need to know why he killed Silver yet. Motive may be revealed at plea bargain time. You know—exchange the name of a conspirator for a reduced sentence. I'll wait here for the arresting officers."

Cory went back into the mansion. She ate a poppy-seed pastry, washing it down with a cup of aromatic coffee, and felt vaguely guilty about enjoying the respite. Soon guests drifted out.

She opened the front door and was confronted by a commotion in the driveway. Cheryl was shouting obscenities at Finnegan as an officer cuffed him and placed him in the rear seat of a police car. Hysterical, the widow collapsed into the nearest pair of arms—Cory's.

"Ed told me he killed my Josh," she shrieked. "He said he did it for us. Us? He's crazy. We weren't lovers. I thought we were friends. He was in debt and I felt sorry for him. I sent him clients, gave him money, tried to help him. Josh even hired him as a bodyguard, and this is what I got for it? That rotten bastard took away my best friend in the whole world." She sobbed.

Cory put her arm around Cheryl's waist and helped her into the house. The angry, grief-stricken young woman curled up on a sofa and wept. Cory tried to comfort her. "Ed mistook your kindness for love. He doesn't understand friendship."

When Mr. Silver approached the two women, Cory rose to meet him. "I'm Cory Cohen. I'm deeply sorry for your loss. May I talk to you in private?"

"Do I know you, Ms. Cohen, is it?"

"It's actually Doctor Cohen. I'm a psychologist."

"You knew Josh?" He asked in a raspy voice.

"Yes." She followed him down a long hallway into an office and sat beside him on a leather couch. "Josh asked me to give you this." Cory handed him an envelope from her purse. "He suspected his life was in danger and he wanted you to have this should he meet with foul play before he could reach you."

The elder Silver's posture stiffened. He cleaned his eyeglasses and hooked the stems around his ears and carefully opened the envelope. He read slowly, his eyes moist, then let the letter fall to his lap, a surprised look on his face. "My boy found proof that Neil Gold is a crook!"

"Your son had planned to call the SEC the morning he was killed. Neil had threatened that if Josh squealed on him, Josh would regret it. Your son was willing to risk his life in order to halt a crime, redeem your reputation, and earn your respect."

Josh's father's eyes filled with tears and his shoulders shook as he sobbed. Finally, he stopped, pulled out a wad of tissues from a box on the table, and then blew his nose and blotted his face.

"Thank you, Doctor. You don't know how much this means to me."

"I can only imagine." Cory held back her tears.

"Please send your bill to me."

Even at this moment, money was on Mr. Silver's mind. "Your son has paid up."

"In more ways than you know," he muttered. "Neil Gold is a crook, but I doubt he'd have had my boy murdered. Now Neil is paralyzed. He's in critical condition from a stroke. When the time comes, his clients will ask for an accounting from his estate. Then, the board will believe me, but it doesn't matter now. Who'd want my Joshua dead? He was very well liked.

A do-gooder. He led daily minyan services. Was going to become a big brother. He wanted his own children, but . . . " His voice trailed.

"Were there marital problems?" Cory felt uncomfortable questioning a grieving parent.

"Cheryl wasn't ready for motherhood, but we expected she'd come around. They had a few counseling sessions with the rabbi. Joshua could have divorced her over it, but he is—uh—was a patient man."

"So you don't know if there was talk of divorce."

"If it had, my generous son would have given her a pretty penny. I don't suspect my daughter-in-law of having anything to do with the car explosion. The bomb could have been planted in the wrong car. Meant for someone else. A mistake." He wiped his eyes. "I trust the police to find the culprit. I have to help my fragile wife cope with the loss of our dear son, our only child. And take care of my dear daughter-in-law. We are her only family."

Cory swallowed her tears. The conversation with Mr. Silver validated her opinion that Cheryl wasn't involved in Joshua's murder.

Mr. Silver continued. "Joshua lit up my life. I loved him more than I ever thought possible. He was good as gold and smart as a whip." He started to weep again. "I never said it out loud. I wish I had. I should have praised him more, but that wasn't my style. I never made time to read parenting books. Too busy chasing the dollar. I raised my boy the way my father raised me. I made mistakes. I must suffer."

Cory didn't wish to cause him any more grief. Soon he'd learn that a so-called friend of his daughter-in-law was in police custody, perhaps because he had mistaken her generosity for a budding affair.

"All parents make mistakes, Mr. Silver, and whatever yours were, they didn't stop your son from loving you." She knew Joshua's parents would mourn their loss for the rest of their lives. "In the short time I knew Joshua, I felt connected to his life and his family. He loved you very much." She rose to leave.

He escorted her to the front door. "You've done a great mitzvah here, Doctor Cohen. I presume you know what that means."

"I may not look Jewish, Mr. Silver, but I am."

"I never doubted it for a moment," he said.

In the fifteen years since he left academics to become a full-time congregational rabbi, **MARTIN S. COHEN** has published four books of essays about different aspects of Jewish spirituality and four novels, each one concerned with the ordinary mysticism of everyday Jewish life. In addition to his work as rabbi and author, Cohen serves as editor of the international quarterly *Conservative Judaism*. He is an avid amateur pianist and is especially partial to the music of Franz Schubert.

Death Has Beckoned

▼   ▼   ▼   ▼   ▼   ▼   ▼   ▼   ▼   ▼

MARTIN S. COHEN

FRANZ SCHUBERT MAY HAVE DIED IN 1827 at the tragic age of thirty-one, but his life itself was anything but tragic. Indeed, he was blessed his entire life with a huge circle of friends, among whom was one single Jew, the same Salomon Sulzer who served during the last decade of Schubert's life as the cantor of the Seitenstettengasse Tempel in Vienna.

What I know of Schubert—I mean what *I* know of Schubert, as opposed to what *everybody* knows of him from his biographers' efforts—comes to me through this Sulzer fellow: my grandfather was a cello student of his fourth son, Josef, and once bought several hundred of Sulzer *père's* books (including some two dozen volumes of handwritten reminiscences) from his teacher's son when the latter was down on his luck years later and in need of funds. What follows, then, is an excerpt from the first of those volumes, written by Sulzer in the fall of 1874 and devoted solely to the events of the summer of 1820, the year Salomon was sixteen and Schubert, twenty-three. It was, as you shall see presently, a very interesting season for both of them.

* * *

(The first page of the first notebook is missing.)

. . . but 1820 was a very good year for Franzl. He was hard at work on

Lazarus. His songs were becoming better known. And he had two major openings in Vienna: the first performances of *The Twin Brothers* at the Kärntnertor Theater in June, and the premiere of *The Magic Harp* at the Theater an der Wien in the middle of August.

In between the Brothers and the Harp, Schubert fled to Atzenbrugg Castle, a country property near Tulln owned by the monks of the Klosterneuburg Monastery but administered by an uncle of Schubert's friend—and, in the eyes of many, his ruination—Franz Schober. Now, as it happened, my family spent the summer of 1820 not far from there. But as none of *my* uncles ran castles, we had no choice but to be content with the tiny thatched cottage Father rented for us in Pfrimmbach. It was small, but it did have a lovely garden and an excellent piano. . . . *(The last few lines on the page are illegible.)*

. . . sixteen years old. I had grown some hair on my chest, and was consequently looking for as many opportunities to walk around without my shirt that summer as possible. I took up sunbathing, but after a few days I was so red I looked more like an Edomite than an Israelite.[1] I took to "forgetting" to wear my *tallis koton* and leaving the top few buttons of my shirt undone.[2] That seemed to do the trick. My father, as usual, was too self-absorbed to notice, and my mother didn't seem to care. I was happy. Karlsruhe was long behind me[3] and the Hohenhems pulpit was not due to be occupied by myself until the holidays in the fall.[4] I was, in short, free—free of school, free of obligations, and free of the burdens of life—but without quite being free of the roof my parents still felt obliged to provide over my head and the food they still felt honor-bound to put before me three times a day. Really, the ideal situation.

It was a Sunday in mid-July when Herr Freudenthal, the president of the local synagogue, came to our door just before lunchtime to ask if I would be available to sing at the funeral of a Jewish man who had died in Pfrimmbach that morning. I had no plans—and just about no interest in taking on a job like this.

----

1. The name of the ancient nation of Edom is related to the Hebrew word for "red."

2. A *tallis koton* is a kind of fringed undershirt worn by the pious to fulfill the commandment to wear fringes on one's garments at all times.

3. SS studied composition and conducting in Karlsruhe from 1817 to 1819.

4. SS was appointed cantor in Hohenhems in 1817, but only began to work there in the fall of 1820.

My father, however, not even *thinking* to consult with me, agreed on the spot. My salary, of course, was to be . . . nothing at all. It was, he explained, my pleasure *and* my honor to participate. And my mother appeared to feel the same way: she was so delighted with the invitation that she invited Herr Freudenthal to return for tea in three days' time.

The next day, Monday, was one of the most beautiful days I can recall. The sky was bright blue, the sun a golden yellow. The air was cool and warm at the same time, and as I walked through the forest from our cottage into Pfrimmbach, I could see that the trees were filled not merely with the usual pigeons and crows, but with cardinals and larks and blackbirds as well. I was happy that day, Fanni . . . happy and young and carefree.[5] Was I smart enough to understand how lucky I was to have such a day to remember forever? I can't quite recall . . . but I doubt it.

The funeral was set for ten in the morning, and I arrived at the shul shortly after nine. Other than the deceased and three old men muttering psalms by the bier, there was no one present at all. Still, my early arrival was not entirely without its advantages. I had taken up coffee as my morning beverage of choice in Karlsruhe, you see, and now felt quite out of sorts if I was unable to find a cup to start my day. My parents hadn't approved of my new habit and they had tried quite assiduously to wean me off the stuff, but now that I was early—and alone—I decided to try to find a *Kaffeehaus* where I could have a hot drink before singing over Sigmund Levy's casket. It was, as they say, a serendipitous decision.

The synagogue was on the Bergstrasse, a street that seemed to have no commercial life at all other than a bootblack's shop directly across from the synagogue's side gate. After I walked only one block further toward the center of town, however, I came to the corner of the Döppstrasse and there I found a *Kaffeehaus* called *Zur Grünen Nachtigall*. The thought that the trees in the back garden might be filled with nothing but green nightingales intrigued me, but I must admit that what drew me to the front door of the *Kaffeehaus* far more strongly was the promise of a pot of black coffee and a basket of hard rolls and some fresh butter *and* a quiet twenty minutes to eat them in before having to sing my heart out over the casket of someone whose death I could mourn only theoretically.

I went in and sat down, wondering what my father would say if he could see me behaving like a grown man and, at least in my own eyes, looking

----

5. SS addresses most of the entries in most of the diaries to his wife.

like one as well. I don't believe I had ever walked into a café before all by my-self, but the waiter came right up to me nonetheless and took my order. Sud-denly, I felt very well indeed. I ordered precisely what I wanted for breakfast. I had the money to pay for it in my pocket. I was off to work—if it is possible for someone to go off to work without actually having a job—in a few minutes. In the few seconds it took me to sit down and order my break-fast, I could practically feel myself warming to my new role in the world. In as offhand a manner as I could muster, I asked for the Vienna newspapers, then looked on with almost total amazement as the waiter brought them over without any comment at all. I almost asked for a mirror to see if I looked as grown-up as . . . *(The bottom right hand corner of page 4 of the jour-nal has been ripped off.)*

. . . early morning patron of the Nightingale was seated in the far corner of the room by the fireplace. He was a short, stout fellow with curly hair and a receding hairline, yet for all his incipient baldness, he did not look to be more than twenty-one or two.[6]

Surrounded by piles of paper and empty coffee cups, he was scribbling fu-riously in a notebook that lay open in front of him on the only unoccupied piece of tabletop within arm's length and tapping his foot up and down. I wondered if he too was a musician and then, when he lifted the manuscript leaves off the table to fold them back on themselves, I could see that the man was indeed writing out music of some sort. I was intrigued. Emboldened by my success with the waiter—and I assure you that I considered having sat down in a coffee house and placed an order to be a success of the great-est magnitude—I found myself walking over with my coffee to the stranger's table.

"I see that you can write music," I said, somewhat uncertain how to begin a conversation with a total stranger.

The man said nothing.

To retreat was impossible; to repeat my idiotic observation, unthinkable. For a long moment, I just stood there, coffee cup and saucer in hand. And eventually the curly head did look up. *"Du bist?"* the man asked, using a suc-cinctness of language I found no less engaging than terrifying.

"Sulzer."

He extended his pudgy hand. "Schubert."

I shook the proffered hand. "A pleasure."

---

6. Schubert was twenty-three in 1820.

Without waiting to be asked, I sat down. Awkwardly. He smiled at me as he shoved some papers aside to make room for my saucer. The waiter brought me my rolls. Schubert ordered another *Schwartzer.* And then he asked the question that changed my life. *"Jawohl, yes,"* I answered, "as it happens, I can read music."

After Sigmund Levy's interment, we returned to the Nightingale. (Schubert, who told me he hadn't ever attended a Jewish funeral—or any Jewish ceremony of any sort—had insisted on coming along.) He had, he said, enjoyed the experience, but what made the greatest impression on him was my singing. Did I ever sing outside the synagogue? Would I agree to sing a song he had written, one no one had never sung before—the song, in fact, he had been working on when I first noticed him that same morning in that same *Kaffeehaus?* Did I know Mozart's song, *Abendempfindung?* Schubert—whom I was now to call Franz or Franzl—thought my voice would suit that song very well. I did know it? Then could I sing it right there for him? Indeed, I could.

The late Sigmund Levy had spent most of his adult life as the local *melamed.*[7] The irony that a man who had no children of his own should have ended up as a teacher of other people's offspring was lost on no one, but, at least according to the several eulogies I was obliged to sit through during his funeral, the man had been an excellent teacher and somewhat of a country scholar; the Jewish community of Pfrimmbach considered itself lucky to have had him in their midst for as long as it did.

His eulogies made the details of his life sound ordinary to the point of being banal, but a bit of a mystery had apparently presented itself in the context of his demise nonetheless. People, it turned out, remembered clearly that many years earlier there had been a Frau Levy—a stout, prickly woman named Hannelore. But when the men of the burial society had checked their records, the location of her grave could not be ascertained. Indeed, when a hasty search had been carried out in the graveyard itself, no headstone could be found that bore her name and neither could anyone be located who precisely remembered her funeral.

Schubert and I ended up discussing the situation over more coffee.

"Surely it isn't so odd that a man's wife should be buried somewhere

7. SS uses the traditional Jewish term for a teacher of young children.

other than in the town in which she lived. There could be a thousand reasons."

"But," I countered, "there's surely something odd in that no one can remember her actually dying. They all say—this goes back twenty-five years, so you can excuse them for being a bit vague—but they all say that she was just here living a normal life and then one day she was gone."

"Surely they must have asked where she had gone off to."

"Well, that's just the thing. No one really remembered what he said. She was just . . . gone. He was all prickly about it though—they all remember that clearly enough."

"And she never came back to Pfrimmbach?"

"She never came back at all. She just remained gone and then, one day, Sigmund announced in synagogue that she had died. He said Kaddish—the Jewish mourner's prayer—for a month, then returned to the classroom."

"So what's so mysterious in that? She died, he said the prayer, he went back to work." Schubert's forehead wrinkled slightly, almost as though he could sense a certain lack of logic in his own words, but without being able precisely to put his finger on the flaw in his reasoning.

"Well," I said, suddenly unsure how involved I wanted to be in any of this, "it wouldn't be too mysterious at all. Except that Levy's will, which his lawyer made public early this morning, specifies that it was his wish to be buried next to his wife. That's why they were searching for her grave in the files and in the cemetery, but to no avail. Wherever she's buried, it's not there."

It was dusk now and I knew my parents were expecting me home for dinner. A blue haze of pipe smoke filled the room and the pleasant smells of an old country inn were wafting through the establishment and making me hungry. There was roast duck on the menu that evening—and, although I would never have dreamt of eating any meat that wasn't kosher, the smells were delicious. Schubert was waiting for his friend Franz Schober—known, he said, in his circles as the *other* Franz—to join him for dinner. I would have liked to meet him, but I knew I couldn't stay. As I tore myself away from the table, I felt more happy than I had ever felt before. I had sung well. And I had a new friend—and a *goy* at that! What Papa would think, I couldn't imagine. Or rather, I could.

The next morning, Tuesday, I announced I was going to prayers at the synagogue, then headed for the Nightingale as soon as the service was over.

Franzl was in his accustomed place. I sat down at the same table and signaled to the waiter to bring my breakfast.

I brought Schubert up to date. "It turns out they are going to pay me after all."

"You weren't going to be paid?"

"Of course not. But now I am—and you'll want to know how."

"If you say so. How?"

"Well, the will lists no relations at all, and no heirs. All his property was willed to the community. But it turns out there is a fair amount of music among Levy's effects—he was, of all things, a cello player as well as a teacher. The president of the community told me that I was a good lad for singing at his funeral and that since there's no cantor here, I can have as much of the music as I want. Even all of it."

"Do you know what's there?"

"Not the slightest idea."

Schubert leaned in a bit closer over the table. "When are you going to take a look?"

I smiled, reeling in my catch. "Tonight," I said gamely. "Want to come along?"

Schubert sat back and thought for a moment. "Why not?" he asked eventually. "Everybody at Atzenbrugg is going to a swimming party at a lake about two hours from here, but I have no interest in going. Schober said he'd stay behind with me, but I'll send him along and we can go investigate Herr Levy's secret music library."

"Well, its contents are—temporarily—a secret from us, but I doubt it's much of one in any other sense."

Schubert nodded as though this were some wise, gnomic remark. "We'll see," he said.

Shortly after eight o'clock that evening, Franzl and I met in front of the house at Mailandstrasse 18. It was a bit late—and I had had to cook up *some* cock-and-bull story to explain to my parents where I was going—but Schubert's Atzenbrugg crowd was only . . .

(There is a hole in the manuscript at this point, apparently a cigarette burn.)

. . . half past seven and it took at least half an hour to walk from there into Pfrimmbach. In the meantime, I had attended evening services at the synagogue and retrieved the key to the house from the lawyer in charge of the estate. Meister Krugg didn't look at all pleased to part with the key to Herr Levy's home, but the house *and* its property was the Jewish community's now, not his, and he had no real choice but to comply. He gave me the key, told me tartly that it would be an act of larceny to take anything other than music from the house, and left me standing in the street in front of the shul. That was about half past seven. As the Mailandstrasse was only a ten-minute walk from the Bergstrasse, I had time to kill. I spent it walking lazily around town, reveling in my newfound freedom. I caged a cigarette off a fellow my age who left the synagogue about when I did, but made a point of walking off in the opposite direction. Eventually, I came to Mailandstrasse 18 and stood in front smoking the cigarette as slowly as I could until Franz showed up almost precisely on time.

The house was typical of the time and place. A large, airy foyer. A curved staircase up to the second story. A library with a magnificent cherrywood piano to the right and a large sitting room to the left. There were gas lamps everywhere and, as we had been instructed, we lit just three or four. The stairs down to the basement—where Joachim Krugg had told me the music cabinet was to be found—were at the far end of the library. Schubert ran his hand lightly along the edge of the piano's reddish wood, but neither of us wished to linger in the library. We opened the door to the staircase and headed downstairs. I remember feeling a certain fear for the first moment, then an equally unexpected surge of lightheadedness.

"Odd that Herr Levy didn't keep his music up near the piano, isn't it?"

"I guess so."

Downstairs, we saw a single gas lamp on the wall and I think we both felt a bit calmer once it was lit. The room was just a storage cellar filled, as far as I could see, with junk. But at the extreme far end of the room was a huge wooden armoire with a weird design of musical notes painted on its doors.

Inside the cabinet, we found a real treasure trove of music. You've seen the music, Fanni—several dozen printed volumes of music by various composers, but also some manuscripts, including one of some sketches by Beethoven—it was signed only with the letter *B*, but Schubert recognized the master's hand immediately—and another that appeared to be some childish *écossaises* by the young Mozart.[8] Schubert was enthralled by the

....
8. Subsequently published as "First Steps in Mozart" by the Pflumverlag (Berlin and Leipzig, 1950).

manuscripts, so much so that it was I who noticed one final volume that appeared to have fallen under the cabinet so that only its upper right-hand corner was peeking out. I could see it clearly enough, but when I tried to pull it loose, it wouldn't budge.

"Lean it backward."

"Too close to the wall."

"Then pull it forward." I had the smaller hands, so it was I who reached for the manuscript while Schubert pulled the cabinet onto its near legs.

"I almost have it—"

But when I pulled at the manuscript, it somehow up-ended the armoire, and Schubert lost his grip. The cabinet fell to the floor, leaving the space it had covered completely exposed.

The manuscript I had been reaching for was face down.

"What is it?"

Schubert looked at it carefully. "It's a cello sonata in the style of Haydn, but not by him."

"How do you know? Maybe it *is* by Haydn."

Schubert smiled. "Not in this key."[9]

He tossed the music on the pile. But as we squatted down to lift the armoire back up to its standing position, Schubert saw that something was buried just beneath the floor.

"There's something there."

"What?"

"How should I know? But I can see its outline in the dirt."

I looked more carefully, but could see almost nothing. "What do you think it might be?"

Schubert laughed. "Only Salieri knows everything. I only know that I can see something buried under the floor in a most inconvenient place."

We set the armoire back down and began to dig, using our finger tips to displace the loosely packed soil . . .

An hour later, we were sitting in the pitch black of Herr Levy's backyard on a wrought-iron bench. Someone in the adjacent building lit a lamp, then extinguished it almost immediately.

....

9. See M. Donner, "An Unknown 'Cello Sonata by J. Haydn?" *Canadian Journal for Musical Research* 43 (1969), pp. 145–208.

"There's no real question. She has to have died somewhere."

I could sense, rather than actually see, Schubert pushing his spectacles back up his nose. "If she's dead, then she must have died somewhere. But that doesn't mean—"

"It does mean. What *else* could it mean—a box of bones in the basement of a dead man whose wife's grave just recently could not be located? She lived here—I told you all this, didn't I?—she lived here, she disappeared, and then he finally mentioned it around town that she had died. Yet *he never left town to attend her funeral.* That's what they were saying in shul—that she *had no funeral.* That she just vanished and after a while he said she had died." As I said these words, something drew my eyes up to the window in which the lamp had been lit for just the briefest of moments. I saw the curtain move slightly.

"And you are putting this all together into a cogent narrative?" Schubert asked.

"I am indeed. The poor woman didn't go anywhere. She lived here and here she died—but her husband was so unable to accept her death *or to take his leave from her* that he just told everyone she was traveling while he kept her body in the house. Eventually, when there was just a skeleton left, he gathered up her bones and buried them in his basement. So she died, all right, but was never buried anywhere other than at Mailandstrasse 18. That's it. *Sof pasuk.*"

"What?"

"The end of the story."

"And no one knew?"

"Look, he was an old man and she was an old woman. No one knew because no one cared to know. Because no one suspected foul play. Because, in the end, no one really gives much of a damn about anyone's death that doesn't touch them personally."

The moon had risen over the Pfrimm while we were inside Herr Levy's house, and it now shone brightly over the town. We ourselves were shielded by some sort of overhang from its silvery rays, but the *Hintergarten* was shimmering in the evanescent light of the midsummer moon. Impulsively, I took Schubert's hand.

"You know what we must do. . . . " A kind of unfinished statement rather than an outright question.

"Not actually."

"We must help avoid scandal. The memory of Herr Levy, may he rest in peace. . . .

(The top of p. 12 of the manuscript has been ripped off.)

. . . must bury the bones of Frau Levy before anyone finds them."

"And where precisely did you have in mind?"

"There's only one safe place—and they belong there anyway."

"And where would that be?"

"In his grave. Where else? He did say in his will that he wished to be buried next to his wife, after all." The curtain in the window fluttered again ever so gently, but I refused to be intimidated. We had every right to be in the house that evening. And if we wished to sit for a moment in Herr Levy's *Hintergarten* and chat for a few minutes, then why would anyone find that peculiar or irresponsible?

As to my plan for disposing of the bones, where else could they have gone? I suppose we could have brought them to the police—or at least to the rabbi—but, at the moment, burying the bones in Herr Levy's grave felt like a rational next step. It seemed . . . natural. *Logisch.* Reasonable. Even, dare I say it . . . proper! *Anständig!*[10]

There were two shovels in the gardening shed, and Franzl carried them. I, out of some sense that Frau Levy should be borne to her final resting place by Jewish hands, carried the box of bones. (It wasn't a very big box—just about the right size to hold a cocker spaniel.) The cemetery was on—I forget the name of the street, but it was just behind the Bergstrasse where the synagogue was located, was it the Pfrimmgasse? Maybe, but I knew just where it was—I had been there only the day before—and we found the cemetery and the grave without any difficulty.

Our plan was simple enough, Fanni. Dig down to Herr Levy's coffin, place the box of bones on the casket, put the dirt back into the hole, leave the shovels where it would look as though the cemetery workers themselves had forgotten them, and go home. Schubert sang one of his Goethe songs as we walked the few blocks—the one about how silvery moonlight has the ability to unlock the power of the human heart. It was—is—a beautiful song—Schubert later set the song again, but I'm talking here about the first setting, the simpler one—the one, in my humble opinion, of the more

....

10. Decent.

exquisite beauty.[11] I had never heard it previously, but I was to end up singing it at my first recital in Vienna years later.

At any rate, that was the plan. We found the cemetery locked but were able to squeeze through between the loosely chained gates nonetheless. We found the grave. We were alone and unobserved. We dug quietly. Schubert sang quietly. I worried quietly. The moon passed overhead most quietly of all. We got to Herr Levy around four feet down.

The deed was done in less than forty minutes. We stopped to rest from all that digging, then pitched the shovels against the wall and left, we hoped, totally unobserved.

When we went back to the house on the Mailandstrasse to retrieve the music, Franz took the manuscripts and I took most of the printed books. I locked the front door, then left the key in the terra cotta urn by the side of the house as instructed by Meister Krugg. I went home and was delighted to find my parents fast asleep in their beds. My brothers were up making music—my parents had learned years earlier to sleep through *that*—and I was, they said, welcome to join them. I showed them the new music I had acquired, sang a song or two by Zumsteeg that we all liked, then went off to bed.

It was late the next afternoon that Herr Freudenthal came to tea. The conversation passed from one thing to another uneventfully, however, until the late Levy's name came up.

"Well, I have something to report on that front too," Herr Freudenthal said, obviously delighted to have something interesting to tell. "We located the wife's grave."

"Where?" I could feel the color draining from my face.

"In Berlin. It turns out that Frau Levy was there visiting some elderly auntie when she had a heart attack and died. Her parents were buried there, and it would have taken weeks to summon Herr Levy to Berlin, so they just buried her there next to her parents. I think he was embarrassed to have missed the funeral, so he just said nothing. Eventually, when people began to wonder what had become of her, he simply said she had died out of town, said his Kaddish, and left it at that. I suppose in the will he must have meant that he wished to be buried by her side in Berlin, but it's too late now!" Herr Freudenthal attempted to chuckle, but it came out somewhere between a cackle and a cough. "Much too late!"

---

11. The two settings are numbered 259 and 296 in the Deutsch catalogue of Schubert's works.

It was indeed much too late. No one seemed too interested in discussing Frau Levy's final resting place in any more detail than that and the conversation moved on to other things. But I myself could not concentrate on any other topic because I found myself entirely absorbed with the question Herr Freudenthal's comment had inadvertently provoked: if Frau Levy was buried in Berlin, then whose bones were in the box Schubert and I had buried in his grave?

I saw Schubert a few hours later at the *Nachtigall*. His friends were returning to Atzenbrugg later that evening, he said, and he was happy to have my company until they got back to the estate. . . .

"Nothing can happen to us," he said after I finished reporting to him what I had learned from Herr Freudenthal. We spoke about it at length, but without coming to any firm conclusions. There was, in any event, nothing to be done about it. We were hardly going to dig the box of bones up again and put it back where we found it!

With that, we passed to other topics. Schubert and his friends were having a musical evening at Atzenbrugg the following evening to celebrate their return and I was invited. To listen and, if I wished, perhaps to sing for them as well. I wasn't to be shy.

I countered that I had nothing prepared, that I hadn't ever sung anywhere except in synagogue, that I had nowhere near the kind of musical training it would take to sing in public, but Franzl was uninterested in my protestations. I was to sing Mozart's *Abendempfindung,* something by Haydn (FS suggested the English one about the sunbeams dancing on the mirror-smooth sea—I forget its name for the moment[12]) and one of his own songs, perhaps even *An den Mond,* the song he had been singing on the way to the cemetery. If I wished, I could even sing something from the synagogue liturgy—the people, he insisted, would be fascinated.

I, of course, was appalled. I was sixteen. I hadn't ever been *anywhere* unsupervised. What would I wear? Would I keep my head covered? What would I eat? Or drink? And what if they teased me—or worse—about my Jewishness? I was overwhelmed with the whole concept; plus, of course, my father would never allow it. There would be women! And liquor! And perhaps even Jesus music! That settled it. There wasn't even a choice. Not even something to discuss. It was completely out of the question, not even worth the debate at home the proposal would have undoubtedly occasioned.

....

12. *The Mermaid's Song,* words by Anne Hunter.

I accepted gratefully and with the most enthusiasm I could muster without sounding pathetic or peculiar.

I spent the whole of Thursday concocting the story I would tell my parents to explain where I was going that evening, but, to my amazement, they seemed quite uninterested in my plans. That I made some friends in town who had invited me over seemed to strike them as genial and reasonable. That I was going to sing for them, appropriate and nice. I spent the day practicing Mozart and Haydn, and learning Schubert's *An den Mond*.

When I arrived at the estate, Schubert was standing on the path waiting for me in a state of visible agitation. He paid off the driver, then waited for him to drive off before dragging me into a greenhouse, lighting a lamp, and thrusting a single piece of paper into my hand.

"What is this?"

"It came an hour ago. Addressed to me. Nothing else on the envelope, only my name and the words *Schloß Atzenbrugg*."[13]

"What does it say?"

"You tell me."

I unfolded the piece of paper and stepped closer to the lamp. On it were written two Hebrew words.

"Can you read them?"

"Of course."

"What do they say?"

"*Loi sirtzach.*"

"Which means?"

"Thou shalt not kill."

Someone knew, Fanni. But who? And what did he know? Or *she*? It had to have something to do with the bones—but whose bones were they? And who had seen us? And why had they chosen to write to Schubert instead of confronting him in person? And why in Hebrew? Did the sender think us guilty of murder? Or was the Hebrew merely to make it clear to Franzl that he had stumbled into somebody else's business—or maybe to make it obvious that whoever had sent the letter knew who I was, too? Perhaps it was to force Schubert to involve me?

....

13. Atzenbrugg Castle.

The evening at Atzenbrugg passed uneventfully. If I do say so myself, I sang well. The crowd loved my rendition of *An Den Mond,* which remains to this day one of my favorites among Schubert's Goethe-*lieder*.[14] There was a great deal of food served, but everybody was so drunk that no one seemed to notice or care that I only nibbled on a few crusts of bread and had a couple of apples. Or that I drank water instead of wine from the crystal goblet a servant handed to me as soon as I entered the main reception area.

Later, when everybody was walking around the grounds and smoking, Schubert and I had a few private moments together.

"So what do we do now?" An unexpected tremor in my voice. I suppose I was nervous.

"Nothing."

"Nothing at all?"

"*Genau*. Precisely. Nothing at all."

"But the note said—"

"The note said what? Not to kill? Killing is when you make a living person dead, not when you bury a dead person in the ground. All we did was bury the remains of a person in the grave we thought they belonged best in."

"Perhaps we were wrong."

"Indeed."

There were going to be charades later on, but I begged off. Schubert didn't seem miserably unhappy that I was anxious to go. He had Schober order the castle's trap for me and, not forty minutes later, I was back at my parents' rented cottage.

Friday was a very warm day, and I was feeling more determined to get to the bottom of things than worried about the consequences of doing so. Would a murder never be discovered, and its perpetrator consequently never brought to justice, because of me? If *Levy* was the murderer, of course, he was beyond the punishment of the earthly tribunal. But if the bones weren't his wife's, then what connected Levy to them other than the fact that they were buried beneath the floor of his basement? Surely someone else could have put them there. I honestly didn't know what I was going to do. And then, Fanni, my hand was forced.

It was late that Friday afternoon. The Sabbath table was already set. My mother had finished her cooking and was sitting in the garden mending some linen napkins. My father was napping. My brothers were in the front

---

14. The song was sung at Sulzer's funeral by the celebrated baritone, Mendel Schwarzfuchs.

room playing chess when someone came to the door, rapped on it with enough force to make the pane of glass in its window shake, and ran away. I was in the backyard reading by my mother's side when my older brother brought me the envelope. I recognized it immediately, but dared not show any particular response at all in front of my family. On the outside of the envelope was only my name: Salomon. No last name. No address or return address. I recognized both the hand and the envelope. My mother looked curiously at me as I played nervously with it. I was smart enough not to open it in her presence, but I did open it as soon as I was able to flee to my bedroom. Inside, as I knew there would be, was a single piece of paper with two Hebrew words on it: *veloi signoiv.* Thou shalt not steal.

That Saturday was the least pleasant *Shabbos* of my young life. I hardly slept, couldn't really rest, felt distracted in synagogue *and* at home. I had a fight over something ridiculous with my younger brother. I was cranky toward my parents, who seemed almost amazingly uninterested in knowing who sent me the note or what it said. I just couldn't settle down knowing that *someone* out there felt that Schubert and I had disturbed somebody's bones and put them where they didn't belong. Was that theft? Was it the equivalent of murder? I thought us innocent on both counts—but someone obviously did not.

Franz was off on a three-day hike in the country as of Sunday morning and, to tell the truth, that suited me just fine. I needed some time to think and to try to figure this all out.

After services Sunday morning, I took myself to the Mailandstrasse and sneaked around to the back of Herr Levy's house. The key was gone from the urn, presumably retrieved by Meister Krug. Not at all disappointed to be unable to gain entrance to a place I had no real desire to enter, I sat on the same wrought-iron bench Franz and I had sat on just a few days earlier and tried to organize my thoughts. But I found that my mind seemed to have— is this silly to say?—a mind of its own. I tried to focus on what I thought were the most important aspects of the situation, but I kept returning, almost involuntarily, to the question of the Hebrew notes. Finally, I gave in and began to consider them seriously.

The same person, I thought, had definitely sent both of them—the German handwriting on the envelopes was the same, the Hebrew handwriting of the notes was the same, and the envelopes themselves were identical, as were the pieces of paper on which the notes were written. I pondered those hands. The German was the handwriting of an educated person, someone who had been trained in penmanship. And the Hebrew hand was equally elegant. So the author of the notes was an educated man, undoubtedly a Jew. But surely that wasn't going to narrow the field anywhere near enough.

Suddenly I had an idea. Or rather the glimmer of an idea. Something . . . something had triggered a thought . . . a fleeting idea that needed fleshing out. I wasn't even certain what, but something needed investigation. I leaped up from my bench and, hurrying toward I didn't even know what, I took myself to the synagogue.

The Bergstrasse shul was unlocked, but no one was inside. I went in and headed straight for the bookcase at the rear of the synagogue, then sat down at one of the long tables at the side of the sanctuary. In the *Chumash*, I quickly found what I was looking for—the text of the Ten Commandments in the twentieth chapter of Exodus.[15] It read just as I remembered it. *Loi sirtzach.* Thou shalt not kill. *Loi signoiv.* Thou shalt not steal. I looked at the words, silently praying for some sudden burst of inspiration. And then I had it.

I took the letter I had received the previous Friday afternoon from my pocket. Something had seemed odd about it when it came, but I hadn't focused on it too carefully. Now, however, the oddity presented itself for my full inspection. The text was wrong. It didn't say "Thou shalt not steal," but "*and* thou shalt not steal," a single extra letter indicating the extra *and*. That *and* had sat in the back of my mind for two days incubating, and now it came to the forward and insisted on my attention. I turned the matter over this way and that in my mind. Then, as though Providence were guiding me, I began to turn the pages of my book. Slowly, as though I were acting out a role in some preordained drama, I came to the fifth chapter of Deuteronomy. There I found, as I knew I would, Scripture's second version of the Ten Commandments. The text was the same as in Exodus, but not entirely, precisely, *absolutely* the same—just mostly the same. And one of the differences mattered to me a lot. I read carefully: *veloi signoiv. And* thou shalt not kill.

At that moment, I knew quite a few things. No one, surely not any shul-Jew, would ever cite the Ten Commandments from Deuteronomy. Over the ark of the Bergstrasse shul, for instance, were twin tablets of the Law, and the text given was that from Exodus. I had heard my own father quote those lines over and over to us while I was growing up. I could hear him

---

15. A printed edition of the text of the Torah is called a *Chumash* in Hebrew.

thundering at me when I had once taken a few coins from a kitchen drawer to buy something at school—*loi signoiv. Loi signoiv. Loi signoiv.* Thou shalt not steal. But I also knew something else: that the previous week, we had read precisely the second section of Deuteronomy in shul—the one that presents the second version of the Ten Commandments. So my correspondent was someone who had been lately reviewing the text of Scripture, someone who had (I hoped) *inadvertently* cited the Bible text he had been going over and over and over so as to read correctly during the service, rather than the text a Jew would normally have cited.

My mind turned to the synagogue service I had attended the previous *Shabbos*. It had been the twenty-second of July last Saturday, the day we read the Ten Commandments from Deuteronomy. I thought back to that day, Fanni, and I found I could remember it almost perfectly. It had been very warm in the sanctuary and I had felt myself dozing off a few times during the service, but I had stood up with everybody else when the Ten Commandments were being read. I could just hear the . . . the what? Who had been reading? Suddenly, this struck me as the solution, even before I could say with any certainty what the question I had answered actually was. The reader—now I could see him in my mind's eye. A fat little man. Rosy cheeks. A bald head, as pink as it was utterly hairless, under a black *yarmulke.* In my mind's eye, I could see the beads of sweat with which the July heat had adorned the man's smooth forehead glistening in the yellow light that poured through the window over the Holy Ark. The man's voice hadn't been unpleasant, only excessively nasal, as though he had a cold of some sort. But his reading, I recalled, had been flawless. Every letter, every vowel, every cantillation mark—all perfect. I had been impressed.

Now, *there* was a man with Deuteronomy on his mind. I replaced my book in the bookcase and went next door to the rabbi's manse. I knocked on the door, then was surprised when Rabbi Wolff himself opened the door in his shirt sleeves. He had, he said, been studying his daily Talmud, but he was just about done. Would I like to come in? I said I would like very much to come in.

Something about Rabbi Wolff made me feel confident. I told him I had a few questions I'd like to ask him, and I promised him he would understand their importance before I left if he would just let me ask them before explaining fully.

"Why not?" The rabbi seemed utterly calm, utterly unflustered by my arrival.

"I don't wish to pry into business that isn't my own," I began, "but I'd like to ask you a few question about the fellow who read Torah in shul on *Shabbos*."

"About Moritz Fuchs? Why?"

"Well, I'll tell you in just a moment. But first let me ask you this—has Herr Fuchs's life changed in the last while? Or the last few years even?"

The rabbi's demeanor suddenly darkened. His face seemed to grow narrower as I looked on. His eyes focused directly on mine. "What is this all about?"

I could see I had touched a nerve. "I'm just asking if this Herr Fuchs's life has taken a turn lately. For the better."

The rabbi seemed deeply interested in what I was asking. "An uncle of his in Holland died and left him a lot of money almost five years ago. Why do you ask?"

"Did he spend it all at once? On a house, for example? Or a country estate?"

"I don't think it was *that* much money. But he did sell his house and move to a much larger home just behind it in the Schützgasse. In fact, he sold it to the man we just buried, Sigmund Levy."

A light went on in my head when he said Levy's name. "The new house was directly behind the house on the Mailandstrasse?" I had noticed the Schützgasse while walking around town—it always pleases me when streets are named for composers—and it was one single street past the Mailandstrasse. And now I was certain I knew which house the rabbi meant: the one in which a lamp had been lit, then almost immediately extinguished, while Schubert and I were talking in Levy's back yard the night we buried the bones. *The house with the curtain that had fluttered almost imperceptibly back and forth while Franzl and I chatted in Herr Levy's garden.*

"Yes, precisely. How did you know where Sigmund lived?"

"Meister Krugg sent me to retrieve some music there the other night."

"I see."

"And Frau Fuchs, did she move into the new house with Moritz?"

The rabbi's face darkened noticeably. "Why do you ask about her?"

"I don't know. I suppose I'm just curious. Did she?"

"Did she what?"

"Did she move into the new house with her husband?"

"No, she did not."

"May I ask why not?"

The rabbi's eyes widened perceptibly as a single bead of translucent sweat appeared just over his left eyebrow. "She . . . she ran off."

I sensed the interview was over. The rabbi said nothing. I said nothing. After a while, I took my leave. Rabbi Wolff failed even to rise to see me to the door. I let myself out, then walked slowly home.

The morning after Franz returned from his walking trip, I was waiting for him at the *Nachtigall*. We ordered coffee, then retired to a table by the fire to talk. Forty minutes later, we were on our way to visit Moritz Fuchs. Were we expected? I felt certain Herr Fuchs had sent us those notes to warn us off, but if he truly thought they would have the desired effect—that, obviously, I could not say.

The house was easy to find. It was just past ten in the morning. The air was already warm. The sky was clear, the sun warm. We were both excited as Franz knocked on the door. It opened almost immediately. Herr Fuchs looked pale, almost as though we were the very last people on earth he expected to come calling. But if he *was* shocked, he recovered quickly enough and, when Herr Fuchs spoke, his voice was calm.

"Please come in."

We stepped inside. The concept that apparently guided Moritz Fuchs's life was heaviness. He himself was quite heavy, but so were the appurtenances of his home. The furniture was heavy. The frames that hung on the walls were all immense. Even Herr Fuchs's cat was fat. I expected him to say something when we had come inside, but he said nothing at all, merely turning and waddling into the sitting room that adjoined the front vestibule. We followed.

In the sitting room, there was a lovely rosewood piano almost identical to the one in Sigmund Levy's home, a couch, two armchairs, and not too much else. We sat down on the couch, but Herr Fuchs remained standing.

For a long moment, we sat in silence. But then, just when I thought we were going to sit there forever without speaking, our host spoke.

"You have something of mine."

"Not any longer."

"Where is it then?"

"We thought it . . . that it belonged to Herr Levy, so we . . . we returned it to him. But if it belongs to you, we'll gladly retrieve it and give it to you."

A long silence ensued, almost as though issues that had lain dormant for long years were now returning one by one to Herr Fuchs's consciousness and laying claim to some specific part of his brain. He looked weary and deeply unhappy, yet there was still an air of vitality and purpose to him.

In the end, it was Franzl who broke the silence. "You . . . those were your—" He cleared his throat and began again. "Was it your wife whom we found?" A simple question, almost elegantly put.

Herr Fuchs looked at us both, then appeared to come to an internal decision and spoke in a clear voice. "Lives aren't lines," he said. "They're circles—and not *just* circles, but interconnected, swirling ones that can never quite be successfully separated—*not even for a moment*—from the others with which they intersect. My wife, Lilianna, was an unhappy woman in every way, but she was mostly unhappy with me. I offered her a divorce, but she preferred an alternate solution to her unhappiness, and one day I came home to find her in our bed with Sigmund Levy—and I don't really remember much after that. Levy pulled his pants back on and ran home, and I faced her in a state of rage so great that I felt transported from this world into some other realm, some place where anger is the air men breathe. I became a monster that day, and I punished my Lilianna in the only appropriate way. Doesn't Scripture decree death both for the adulteress and her lover? Well, the lover I wasn't interested in, but I didn't even know what was happening—and before I did, Lilianna was lying on the floor dead at my feet. I didn't feel remorse, didn't feel sorrow or grief, just a sense of inner peace more total and more totally satisfying than I had ever felt before or have ever felt since.

"I came to my senses soon enough. I buried her under the floor of our basement, then lugged a huge *Kleiderschrank* over the makeshift grave. I told everyone she had run off, but I told Sigmund—my *friend* Sigmund whom I had rescued from bankruptcy not once, but twice—I told *my friend* Sisigmundus—does it amuse you to know we felt so close so as to have chosen pet names, intimate names, for each other?—I told my *friend* Sisigmundus the truth. He was shocked and not shocked, I think—that's the best way to put it—he was both shocked *and* not at all surprised. But for all he was a scoundrel and a knave and an adulterer, Sigmund Levy was no fool. When I ordered him to buy my house years later—I had come into a bit of money and I wished for a larger home with a library and a proper music room—when I ordered him to buy my house *and never to sell it,* he didn't hesitate. I mean, I wasn't about to dig Lilianna up, and whom else could I trust never to say a word?"

Schubert cleared his throat before speaking. "You could have sold the house to anyone. No one would have thought to dig up your cellar."

"That may be true, but I wanted Sisigmundus to have his due. He liked having her under him. I trust you will pardon my vulgarity, but there it is: he liked having her under him, and now he would have her under him for the rest of his life. *That's* what appealed to me, not *only* the thought of never being found out. But he knew something more potentially ruinous about me than I knew about him, and, in the end, he outsmarted me. I have to give that to him. He outsmarted me and I am, therefore, undone. I see his plan all too clearly now: just by storing his treasures—honestly, you'd think he owned the manuscripts of Don Giovanni *and* Magic Flute, not a few bagatelles and some boyhood sketches by Herr Beethoven, may God grant him a long life—at any rate, by storing them in the basement instead of by the piano in the parlor and then by leaving his estate to the Jewish community, he could be sure someone would go down there to poke around. And he found a way to point you in the right direction. . . . "

"There was a book stuck under the cabinet."

"I assumed something like that."

"When you heard the music was mine to take?"

"Yours or someone's. I knew someone would come."

I looked directly at Moritz Fuchs. "And you watched to see—"

"If you took more than music—"

"And we did."

"And you did."

Now Franzl sounded intrigued. "And the notes?"

"Just an old man's attempt to scare you out of making public your find."

"And now?"

Moritz looked at us both as though he hadn't expected to be asked where we were all to go from here. Or perhaps he considered it self-evident that *we* weren't going anywhere at all together. "Well, it must seem to you that my fate is in your hands. You know now whose bones you found beneath the basement floor, and you know how they got there. You must feel that you have complete, or almost complete, power over me. All you have to do is say the word, and the police will arrest me and a judge will indict me and a jury will convict me and a hangman will dispatch me to which ever ring of hell they reserve for men who take their marriage vows as seriously as I took mine. Isn't that how it seems to you?"

Later, Franz told me that he took this as a serious question and was about to answer. I took it that way too—but before either of us could say anything, Herr Fuchs withdrew a pistol from his jacket pocket, put the barrel in his mouth, and pulled the trigger. We were both stunned, but there was nothing to do. We left him where he was, exited the house, and walked briskly into town to tell Meister Krugg what had happened and to ask him what we were to do.

I was silent as we walked, but Franz was already at work, the melodies in his head coming just barely audibly to his lips as we walked. I heard the end of a song I had heard the other evening at Atzenbrugg. The words had struck me then, but now I first understood what Mayrhofer had meant when he wrote that to die, one must first be beckoned by Death itself. He sang:

> The old man takes up his harp and steps towards the wood,
>   singing softly . . .
> Soon I shall sleep the long sleep which frees from all affliction.
> The green trees rustle.
> The trembling blades of grass whisper.
> The birds sweetly sing, "Oh let him rest . . . "
> The old man listens and keeps silent.
> Death has beckoned. [16]

---

16. From Johann Mayrhofer's poem, *Nachtstück,* set by Schubert in October of 1819 and catalogued by Deutsch as no. 672 among Schubert's works.

RICHARD FLIEGEL has published seven Shelly
Lowenkopf novels and written for television. He
serves as an administrator and teacher at the University of Southern California in Los Angeles. His latest
novel, which is not a mystery, is *Inspiration Point;* his
latest screenplay, *The Goddess of Pelham Parkway.*
This is his first short story featuring detectives Shelly
Lowenkopf and Homer Greeley, both former homicide officers in the Bronx.

The Golem of Bronx Park East

▼　　▼　　▼　　▼　　▼　　▼　　▼　　▼　　▼　　▼　　▼　　▼

RichARD FliEGEL

SHELLY LOWENKOPF WAS NOT A RELIGIOUS MAN, but as the days of his fifth
decade on earth collected like odd socks in his drawer, his thoughts turned
more and more often to memories of his father. His own aging was responsible for it. When he shaved in the morning, his left eye would scrunch up
in the mirror, making a face that looked less and less like his own. In moments of frustration, when he missed a bus or turned a key the wrong way
in a lock, the little "Ah" from the back of his throat had somehow converted
to an "Eh." At the newsstand, he found himself laying down two quarters on
the counter beside the cash register, with the same crisp clink his father had
always used in laying down one. It caught the ear of the newsman, who
had given Shelly's father the same quick nod he now gave to the next generation of Lowenkopfs.

Once a year, on the anniversary of his death, Isabelle would light a candle
in memory of their father. The date was calculated by the Jewish calendar, so
Shelly was usually surprised to find it burning in his sister's empty sink, a
yellow flame flickering through the facets of a drinking glass. "It is that
time again?" he would ask, and Isabelle would reply: "Do you want me to remind you?"

"Of what?"

"Of the date, next year."

No, he never wanted to light a *yahrzeit* candle, and this year was no different. But on the Friday night following Isabelle's candle lighting, Shelly drove up to a synagogue on Bronx Park East to say Kaddish for his father. Not to say it, exactly, since he didn't know the words of the Aramaic prayer and could not read Hebrew fast enough to keep up with the men who recited it under their breath several times in the course of the service. But listening to it might also do some good for his father's spirit, as the rabbis said. Shelly was not a practicing Jew and did not belong to a congregation, but he had done some service for a tiny synagogue on Bronx Park East, where his son Thom had studied for his bar mitzvah. Shelly had not set foot inside the place since but knew that no one would turn him away from a service, especially because they were often short the ten Jewish men they needed for a minyan.

When he arrived at the synagogue, the service was already in progress, and Shelly was surprised by the number of eyes that rose to meet his own. A sheer white curtain fluttered in the central aisle that ran from the rear of the sanctuary to a raised *bimah* at the front. At least a dozen men sat in chairs on the right side of the curtain as Shelly entered, but what surprised him more were the seven women who sat in chairs on the left. The traditional place of these women on Friday nights was at home, preparing the Sabbath meal. On holidays or special occasions they came to the shul, but what had brought them out on a Friday night in October, after the High Holy Days? Then Shelly noticed something even stranger: some of those faces belonged to young people, and three of these to women, who sat together in the first row. What on earth could have drawn those young people here?

Shelly found his answers at the front of the room.

A new, young rabbi stood beside the ark, watching as the old *hazzan* interrupted the mumbling congregants occasionally to sing out a section of the service. The rabbi couldn't have been older than his early thirties, Shelly guessed, although he wore a curly beard that he twirled in the fingers of his left hand, while his right rested on the lectern. He was dressed in a frock coat that hung nearly to his knees, with a snug waist and fine black stitching around its edges. The cut and embroidery made it stylish in a way Shelly had not realized rabbis could be stylish. And when the rabbi reached up to smooth a curl at the edge of his beard, there was an undeniable charm in the gesture. Shelly found a seat along the third row, between the Minsky brothers and an old-timer who seemed to float between waking and sleeping, his eyes closed and lips trembling. He never consulted the prayer book open on his knees, but never ran out of prayers, either. After a brief struggle with his own siddur, Shelly gave up trying to follow along. He closed his eyes and listened to the jumble of voices, standing up when Joel and Jonathan Minsky scraped their chairs, sitting again when they did. Shelly hoped it was doing some good for his father's spirit in heaven, because it wasn't doing much for his own on earth.

It did remind him of his son Thom's bar mitzvah, when Shelly was called to the *bimah* to recite a blessing before the reading of the Torah. Shelly remembered that Thom's left cheek had been sucked in as if he were biting it, as they stood side by side before the *davening* congregation like blasphemers on judgment day. Shelly's ex-wife, Ruth, had sat in the second row, boiling over the discovery that she would not be called to the *bimah,* as she would in a Reform synagogue. Yet, despite the daggers shooting from Ruth's eyes, Shelly had felt a surge of warmth as he hovered beside his son at the parchment scroll neither of them could read. Shelly had stumbled over the Hebrew words of his blessing, and Thom had chanted his portion by memory, and the two of them had never felt closer.

That was why he had come back to say Kaddish for his father.

After the service, when the men and women gathered for wine and honey cake, some familiar faces came up to greet Shelly. Dave Horowitz was no longer president of the congregation, a distinction that had fallen to the former chair of the ritual committee, Jacob Zweizig. Sol Schneider was talking to his mother, Helen, and his niece Julia, while Stanley Blumberg had come with his wife, Rachel. Shelly didn't see the old-timer with the trembling lips who had sat in the third row, but he didn't have time to wonder about it before Rae Blumberg had him by the sleeve.

"Nu?" she asked Shelly, "What do you think of our new rabbi?"

"Nice," said Lowenkopf. "He's very young, isn't he?"

"And handsome, don't you think? Half a dozen mothers in the congregation have him matched already with their daughters."

"A catch, huh?"

"You shouldn't know from it. Come on, I'll introduce you."

The rabbi stood at the center of a knot of congregants, disentangling himself from one set of talmudic questions only to face another. Either the parashah was of particular interest to the women tonight, or something less spiritual had prompted their desire for a deeper understanding of the text. However, as soon as Rachel managed to squeeze in "Excuse me, Rabbi, but I thought you should meet Shelly Lowenkopf," the young rabbi's eyes swung around to greet him. They were large and watery brown, like the eyes of a deer caught by surprise in the woods. "Shelly, meet Rabbi Nathan Glickman."

"Detective Sergeant Lowenkopf?" Glickman asked.

"Not any more, Rabbi."

"Ah. I didn't know. But you're the one who helped Stan Blumberg with his business, aren't you? And Sholem Pirsky, *oliv-hashalom* through his terrible time of trial?" The young people around the rabbi didn't recognize the names, but their ears perked up at the sound of a terrible time of trial.

"I did what I could."

"Good! Then perhaps you can help me, too."

Shelly didn't like the sound of that, but fifteen minutes later, he found himself in Sholem Pirsky's former study, across from Rabbi Glickman. What a transformation the younger man had wrought! The bookcases were still crammed with volumes, but many of them were in English, and Shelly could make out titles on counseling the bereaved or on Jewish divorce and alcoholism, as well as texts in Hebrew and Yiddish. The old desk had been replaced by a slimmer model in teak, with half the number of drawers, and the overflowing ashtray that had dominated the desktop was nowhere in sight. Instead, a sign hung on the bulletin board above the rabbi's desk: "The Evil One smokes. Should you?" It was in English but printed in letters that looked like Hebrew script. These days, Shelly allowed himself one cigar a week and, remembering the haze that had permeated Pirsky's personal space, had already taken a Corona out of his jacket. But a pained glance from Glickman reminded Lowenkopf that the Sabbath evening was not a good time to light up. He sniffed the cigar briefly and tucked it back into his pocket.

"We were burglarized last week," said the rabbi, settling back in his chair as if such incidents were routinely discussed in rabbinic schools. "We called the police, who said from what they saw it was most likely some neighborhood kids who broke in and took what they could find before their nerve ran out. The sanctuary below us is deserted at night, but I often come down from my apartment to work a few hours in this office, and they might have heard my footsteps overhead."

Shelly nodded. "If that's what the police said, it's probably right. I can't do any better than they can."

"I believe it," said Glickman, "and count us lucky. No one was hurt breaking in, thank God, and nothing irreplaceable was lost."

"What did they get?"

"Not much—a silver *yad*. Do you know what that is?"

Shelly felt the heat of the stuffy room. His hair, which was always curly, curled a little bit more, and the back of his neck grew itchy. He took off his wire-rim glasses and wiped a spot of perspiration off the inside of the lenses, near the little brace for his nose. "A pointer for reading the Torah, isn't it?"

"Yes, that's right, a pointer. We can replace it for a couple of hundred dollars. We were much more concerned about what they passed up. Have you any idea what a Holy Scroll is worth in dollars and cents?"

Shelly shook his head briefly. Was there really a market for something like that? He knew the answer well enough: there was a market for anything.

"Thousands," said Glickman. "Not to mention what it would cost us in anguish, if our Torah were stolen from us."

"But they left it, didn't they? You think they'll come back?"

"I'm worried that they'll learn what a Torah is worth from whoever buys the *yad*. Some of us have already seen something . . . "

"What?"

"I should say someone lurking around the shul overnight. Somebody big. He never comes to the door and never makes a sound, but returns from time to time to stare at the windows of the sanctuary."

Glickman parted the curtains over his own window to check on the street below. Shelly looked out but saw only a gnarled oak tree in the front yard, lit from above by a streetlight on the corner. Its leaves, orange and yellow with an occasional flush of pink, stirred restlessly in the late October breeze. Farther back along the fence, closer to the sidewalk, stood a few twisted stalks of ailanthus whose bare trunks had already lost their heavy, compounded leaves.

"Have you reported him to the police?"

"What complaint could we make to the authorities? That a man stood under a tree on our corner of the block? What would they say to us?"

"They could send around a patrol car."

"They did. And the officer stopped in to chat. He explained to me that a burglary takes a psychological toll on its victims, who may feel less safe than they did beforehand. Those fears can stir the imagination into seeing new threats everywhere. He said the best thing to do was sleep on it and let time do its work. He invited us to call him again when another crime has been committed."

Shelly grunted. That was what he might have said himself, sent on a call like this. But he was no longer on the force and now spent hours placating the fears of his clients. From what he knew of the synagogue's resources, this would be pro bono work, which fell between private snooping and public service. He patted his jacket until he found a pen in his pocket, then asked the rabbi for a piece of paper.

Glickman hesitated, reluctant to give him scrap paper from the pile in plain view on the desk-top. "If you don't mind, on *Shabbos* . . . "

"Of course," agreed Shelly, remembering the restriction among Orthodox Jews that prohibited writing on the Sabbath. He didn't exactly know how he could take notes if he couldn't write them down, but he stuck his pen back in his jacket and tried to pay closer attention. "Have you actually seen this man yourself?"

"I'm not certain," said Glickman. "I saw something out of the corner of my eye, under the tree, one night. But it could have been a shadow."

"Has anybody seen him?"

"Apparently, yes. You should talk to Julia Bronstein, who has a harrowing story to tell, and the shammes, Pinchas Perets. You know what a shammes is?"

With every one of these questions Shelly saw himself reflected in the rabbi's eyes as a Jew who hardly knew his own language. True, he had asked for a piece of paper, and Glickman might even have noticed that he hadn't kept up with the liturgy during the service, but that didn't mean that Shelly knew nothing at all. "It's a synagogue's sexton. A beadle."

"A beadle? I like that word! I'll have to call Pinchas a beadle sometime and see what he says about it."

"Do you have a number for each of them?"

The rabbi offered his Rolodex. "Please, help yourself."

Shelly memorized the two names and telephone numbers and figured he had cut his losses. How long could it take to interview Julia Bronstein and Pinchas Perets and ease their apprehensions? His partner, Homer Greeley, never cared whether a client could pay, so long as the case offered some detail of professional interest—although Shelly doubted if this case held anything that might hone the edge of Homer's methodical mind. It sounded more like an exercise in sympathy, which was Shelly's own area of expertise. He would write a report, reassuring the rabbi, who could in turn calm the fears of his congregation. Shelly closed the Rolodex with a flick of his wrist and asked, as always, "Is there anything else I should know?"

Glickman hesitated and finally shook his head.

"What?" pressed Lowenkopf.

"It's nothing. Only—do you know Shakespeare? When Hamlet warns Horatio, 'There are more things in heaven and earth than are dreamt of in your philosophy'?"

"He's talking about the ghost, right?"

"A ghost, yes. But there are other things, too, in God's Creation. And when you talk to some of these people, it might be a good idea to keep an open mind."

When Shelly went downstairs again, the congregation had gone, but there was a noise in the tiny kitchen just off the social hall. Julia Bronstein was cleaning up after the wine and honey cake. Her attention to the cleanup prevented her from hearing Shelly when he came in behind her, so he had a moment to size her up in silence before making his presence known. She looked to be in her middle thirties, ten years younger than Shelly himself, with light brown hair swept up in back, showing a slender neck. She wore a beige plaid dress that zipped up close around the base of her throat. Gathered at the waist, it flared slightly below so that the skirt stood away from her hips and thighs, revealing nothing. Below, she wore brown stockings and browner shoes with low, square heels. She startled and turned around, discovering Shelly a moment before he would have spoken up.

"Oh! Mr. Lowenkopf! I didn't know anyone was still here."

"I was talking to the rabbi."

"Quite a find, isn't he? Not long for the Bronx."

"Is he going somewhere?"

She nodded profoundly. "He's got a big future ahead of him."

"He asked me to talk to you."

"Did he?" She cleaned her hands on a dish towel.

"About someone you saw around the synagogue the other night? He said you had a harrowing tale to tell."

"It harrowed him? It certainly frightened me."

"It?"

"Him. Whatever it was."

"Can you tell me about it? Or was it so harrowing? . . ."

"No, I can talk, if Rabbi Glickman wants me to. It was on a Tuesday night, after the adult study group. Our group is on Kabbalah, on Jewish mysticism—which is a hot topic among younger Jews today." She laughed self-consciously. "Believe it or not, I'm considered a young person in this synagogue."

"I believe it."

"Very nice of you to say so. Anyway, after the group, I was cleaning up, as you see tonight. Some of the other women helped, but I told them to go while I finished up."

"You were alone?"

"My car was parked out front. Unfortunately, I lost the blue plastic ring around the door key, so I tried the trunk key in the door lock first. And while I was fumbling, trying to get in, I noticed—across the street—someone moving under the trees."

"Outside the park? Or in it?"

"He had been sleeping on one of the benches that line the black iron fence. I must have awoken him, jangling my keys. He sat up, looked my way, and started down the block in my direction. Well! As you can imagine, the sight of him moving toward me had the worst possible effect on the keys in my hand. Suddenly none of them would fit the door lock. There are only two keys on the ring that look alike—I tried one that didn't fit, and then the other didn't either. He stopped for a minute, on the far side, watching me struggle. One hand went into his pocket. And then he started to cross the street, coming directly at me." She shivered, and her eyes widened as she told this part, but she went bravely ahead.

"I stopped trying to get into my car, and put the keys between my fingers, the way they tell you to do. I thought of running back into the synagogue, but the sanctuary was empty downstairs, and Nathan had taken Chaim up to the attic, where we had packed away Rabbi Pirsky's books. So I knew no one would hear me if I screamed. I was preparing to scream anyway and thinking about the best time to do it, when something stopped the man right in the middle of the street.

"He stood for a minute where he was, on the broken white line divider. I could see him better there. He wore a red flannel shirt with black checks over a dirty undershirt. Filthy khakis without a belt hung from his hips. He wasn't looking at me any more, but at something else, on the corner, under the street lamp. I couldn't see what it was, because the tree on the front lawn of the shul blocked my view. But I could feel it there, if you know what I mean—a great, hulking shadow, round as a stove. He must have been eight feet tall. His head was in the leaves.

"The man in the flannel shirt turned back up Bronx Park East, running down the center of the road. He didn't want to go back into the shadows, either. And he wouldn't turn his head, to see where he was going—his eyes stayed right on whatever it was under the lamp on the corner. When he got about two blocks away, he finally turned and continued running, until he disappeared into the park. I wouldn't go into the park after dark, myself. I don't know how it is for the homeless people—you hear all sorts of stories. But you could tell by the way his red flannel shirt flew out like a flag behind him that whatever he had seen under the street lamp on this corner scared him more than anything lying in wait for him in the tall grass of the park."

"What do you think he saw?"

"I have no idea." She tucked the last plate into its place in a cabinet over the sink and smiled in embarrassment, as if her whole tale were a joke that had fallen flat. "But I wouldn't refuse if you offered to walk me to my car."

Shelly walked Julia to a red Toyota Corolla parked in front of the synagogue and waited for her to drive off. After she left, he stood for a moment, watching the lamplight drip through the leaves that still clung to the oak in the corner of the yard. Nothing stood under it now, but he could imagine a shape lurking in its shadows, and the picture sent a chill up his spine. What it must have felt like to a woman alone on the street at night was beyond his conjuring power. Who could it have been? All of the congregants knew one another, and a man large enough to conceal his face among the leaves would have stuck out among the others like a football player at a chess tournament. It couldn't have been a congregant—but if it wasn't, what was the fellow doing on that corner in the middle of the night?

"It was a golem," Pinchas Perets told Shelly Lowenkopf fifteen minutes later, when the two of them were alone in the synagogue. The duties of the shammes included maintaining the *ner tamid*, the eternal light burning over the ark. The bulb was flickering, presenting a problem for the beadle: should he turn on a light on *Shabbos*, or allow the *ner tamid* to dim? Finally, it failed, and Perets made his decision, climbing up on a rickety chair and unscrewing the bulb from its socket.

"At the end of the sixteenth century, when the Jewish community of Prague was accused of terrible crimes, the Great Rabbi Loew shaped a man of clay to protect them. On its forehead he wrote EMET—Truth—a sacred name of God. And the giant came to life: a silent creature with enormous arms and legs, who moved through the alleys of the city like the shadow of death itself."

Perets must have been seventy years old, but the muscles bunched in his chest and forearm like electrical cables as he screwed in the replacement light bulb. Shelly asked, "Are you in trouble here?"

The shammes stepped down from his chair and headed for the door, shaking out his ring of keys. They all looked identical, but he knew immediately which one fit the synagogue's main entrance. "We never used to lock this door," he said. "If the Almighty wanted to invite some poor soul into His house, who were we to interfere? But all you have to do is look to see why we don't do that any more. Now in our hour of need, when vandals break into the sanctuary, steal our *yad*, and dream of coming back for the Torah— is it any wonder the golem came back to protect it?" Perets turned up his wrists, a gesture that implied one didn't have to be a scholar to reason thus far.

Shelly needed more than talmudic logic. "Did you ever see him yourself?"

"Of course I saw him! I'm the shammes here." He closed the door between them and locked it, as if he had said all that anyone needed to hear. Shelly tapped on the wood, which hardly made a sound; he picked up the iron knocker and clanged it against its black ring. The door cracked ajar and a lone eye waited on the other side.

"All right," said Shelly, "let's call it a golem—it can't be easy to bring one to life. Who would know enough to create one?"

Pinchas Perets blinked a couple of times, thinking it over. "Only a rabbi," he said and shut the door between them for the night.

Chaim Rabinovitz had nearly a mile to walk home after services, making his way along the facades of buildings nearly as old as himself. As he passed, shadows retreated into the courtyards, and bricks squatted down upon bricks—but the old man paid them no attention. He was thinking about the trees across the street, in the deeper darkness of the park, whose branches rustled behind the iron bars like the immaterial world behind the prison of the senses. If he listened, he could hear the voices of the leaves, whispering to one another the secret names of God. What did it matter that the streets were strewn with garbage, that violence and ignorance coupled naked in the stairwells? In the lowest was the highest; in the filthiest pit of the sewer lay the sparks of Creation, covered with trash, waiting to be released and returned to their Creator. Holiness waited here, around every corner, a new opportunity to redeem the world. Every scholar who studies late into the night and every boy who learns his *alef bet* contribute to the redemption of Creation. Even Martin Ceda, who practiced his vowels on the floor behind a sofa while his brother watched wrestling on the TV, late at night—

Whang! Chaim looked up. His reverie was interrupted by an aluminum can, bent in half and projected from behind him so that it struck a fireplug and bounced off, rolling past his feet. "Hey, look'a who's back!" Soft soles struck pavement behind him; somebody jumped off a mailbox. "Didn't I warn you last time, Pops? Not to come by here again?"

Yes, indeed, Chaim had been warned, but what else could he do? The shul was at the south end of Bronx Park East, and his apartment building halfway to the north end. After *Shabbos* services he couldn't ride in a taxi, so what other choice did he have but to walk past their courtyard? He turned to explain it, but at the sight of his inquisitor, the words caught in his throat. Thick arms, broad shoulders, but a face no longer in his teens. A twenty-year-old man threatening strangers? What did he think would be waiting for him in the afterlife?

"Tonight," said Chaim, "it's my turn to warn you. Leave me alone."

The face showed yellow teeth when he smiled. "You're warning me?" The short sleeves of his T-shirt were already rolled to his shoulders, so he couldn't roll them up—but if he could, he would have. He made a fist as big as a pot roast and stuck it under the old man's nose. The tangy smell of his hairy knuckles was strong enough to overcome the sickly sweet pomade that made his cropped hair glisten, even in the darkness. Chaim closed his eyes. His lips began to move.

"You best say your prayers," the punk hissed, while his two *compañeros* made gurgling noises. They sat on a low wall that marked the outer limit of their building's real estate. Around them, at the base of the concrete, empty beer cans littered the sidewalk, like the can that had flown after Chaim. The smaller one sat with his back to the wall and balanced a stick across his knees. His partner hid something along the flank of one leg, long and silver with a pointed tip—the stolen *yad*. The gall rose in Chaim's throat. Who would miss these creatures? Not the neighbors, chased away from their own courtyard. Chaim squeezed his eyelids together and left their fate to the Lord.

He did not feel a blow, and heard only the littler one, who still sat on the wall: "Holy shit! What's that?" Nobody answered, but the smelly fist disappeared from under Chaim's nose. He turned his back and did not listen to the awful noises behind him: the shouts and the thuds, the screams and the crunch of bones.

When Shelly returned to the synagogue on Sunday, his partner Homer Greeley came with him. Homer had listened to Shelly's story of the night before at the shul, and when he had finished, Homer had buttoned the cuff of his neat white oxford shirt and asked, "So that's what you're looking for, Shell? A sixteenth-century Frankenstein?" That didn't sound good to Shelly either. He'd tried to explain how he had felt when Julia told him her story, but Homer had interrupted. "Why don't we stop by there together and see what else we can find?" The second *we* in his sentence stood in for *I*.

But Homer did not join Shelly in the rabbi's study when Lowenkopf went back to see Glickman. Instead, Shelly watched Homer through the office window as his blond partner squatted down beneath the oak tree on the corner, climbed the fence into the yard, and crawled on his hands and knees through the synagogue's sparse grass. It distracted him, and when he forced his attention back to Glickman, he found the rabbi in the middle of a discourse on the great Rabbi Loew.

"Rabbi Yehudah ben Bezalel was a scholar of discernment, a man of great piety and spiritual insight. In 1592, he was called to a personal audience with Rudolf II to answer mystical questions on the Hapsburg emperor's mind. Rudolf gathered at his imperial court the painter Jan Breughel, the Danish astronomer Tycho Brahe, and Brahe's brilliant assistant, Johann Kepler."

This lecture was at least partially for the benefit of Julia Bronstein, who had been sitting beside the rabbi counting out piles of supermarket scrip when Shelly entered his study. Now, as Glickman talked, she watched every flicker of his mouth, as if the secrets of the Kabbalah were about to drip down his chin. The rabbi continued:

"The Jews of that time were often victims of blood libels—do you know what those were? Accusations that Jews had murdered Christian children to mix their blood in the flour when they made matzah at Pesach. A terrible affront to holiness, but people will believe what they choose to believe. The bodies of children were dumped on Jewish property and terrible accusations leveled against the owners. To refute these charges, the legend tells us, Rabbi Yehudah ben Bezalel—who was called the Gaon Rabbi Loew or the Maharal of Prague—used the Kabbalah to create a man out of clay, a giant to do his bidding.

"When you ask me for my thoughts about a golem, what are you asking, exactly? If I know the legends about the Gaon Rabbi Loew? Whether I believe in those stories? Or are you driving at something else?"

Shelly hesitated. "You don't know how to make one, do you?"

Glickman smiled, and stroked the beard on both sides of his mouth with one hand. It was a practiced move, Shelly noticed, that allowed the rabbi to look thoughtful while he stalled for time. "The instructions are readily available," he said at last, "missing only an incantation or two. So in a sense you might say that I do know how to do it, as any careful reader of the Maharal's son-in-law would. But if you mean, have I ever tried to bring a golem to life? The answer is no—definitely not. I wouldn't presume to claim the spiritual authority to wade into those mystical waters."

Julia was pleased with the rabbi's answer, Shelly plainly saw. Knowledge of the Kabbalah might confer upon its reader the power to instill life into matter, but it also conferred the humility to refrain from encroaching upon the prerogatives of the Divine. The rabbi could create a Frankenstein, if he wanted to—but the same wisdom that taught him how also taught him why he shouldn't. Shelly couldn't help wondering if those two lessons always went hand in hand.

"Is there anyone else," he asked, "who might know how to do it, but might not be so clear on the self-restraint?"

The rabbi took a minute to resettle in his chair. "Is there anyone?" he asked rhetorically, and stroked his beard again. Then he seemed to remember something: he turned to Julia and said, "Did you show Sergeant Lowenkopf the *yad*?"

"Did I show him?" asked Julia.

"Just a moment," Glickman said, and stepped out of the room. At first, Julia wouldn't say a word in his absence. It was odd, Shelly thought, that she had felt so free to talk the night before, but the next day in the rabbi's office, she sat like a stranger waiting for a bus—or was that doubt on her face? She seemed to be growing agitated, twisting her ankle back and forth, until, just as they heard a step outside the office door, she leaned forward and whispered, "Rabinovitz."

"Pardon me?"

"Chaim Rabinovitz. He joins our group sometimes—"

But whatever he did in the Kabbalah group Shelly was not to learn, because a moment later Glickman entered, carrying something wrapped in a white handkerchief. He laid the object down in the center of his desk and unfolded the cloth, flecked inside with spots of reddish brown. Inside was a silver rod, ten inches long, carved around with ornate Hebrew letters and tapering to a point.

"When he unlocked the front door of the shul this morning, Pinchas Perets found this hanging from the black iron knocker. It's our *yad*."

"The one that was stolen?"

"The same."

"How do you account for that?"

Glickman shook his head and lifted his shoulders. "Guilt, perhaps? Whoever took it might have learned what it was used for and repented his crime. He didn't want to reveal himself—out of shame, maybe?—so he left it where he knew that we would find it for ourselves. It's difficult to unravel any human purpose. One way or another, we can say with certainty that God willed its return and address our thanks to the Almighty, who can soften the heart of the most hardened criminals."

The rabbi was writing his sermon already. Shelly understood but didn't believe a word of it. He inspected the *yad,* which looked undamaged, except for a semicircle of reddish brown below the pointed tip that had partially rubbed off on the handkerchief. If it was blood, then the thing hadn't been returned in repentance. Guilt was a definite possibility. Glickman picked up the tool by its shaft and offered it to Shelly, who asked, "How many people have touched it this morning?"

"Nobody," the rabbi insisted, then noticed it in his hand. "Only me. And Pinchas, when he found it. Julia, when she wrapped it in the handkerchief. And whoever hung it on the door."

Whose fingerprints were now lost among Glickman's and Perets's and Bronstein's. Shelly's own fingers closed around the *yad.* It had a nice weight, heavier in the back of the shaft, with a tip sharp enough to do some damage. Anyone on the street would have recognized what a handy weapon it made. It even had a chain at its blunt end. "Do you mind if I borrow this?"

The rabbi and Julia exchanged a quick glance. "We thought it was gone forever," said Glickman easily. "We can do without it for another couple of days."

When Shelly joined Homer on the corner, under the oak tree, the blond detective was still crouching near the ground.

"Find anything?" said Shelly, checking out the panels of smooth concrete with an occasional leaf of grass growing between them.

Homer tugged on the cuff of his gray flannel trousers until it rested crisply on top of his shoe. He wore oxblood loafers of some fine, soft leather, with carefully tied tassels that dangled to the left. If either one dangled to the right by accident, Homer would bend over to shift it to the left. "Somebody waited out here for at least half an hour," he said. "With very human likes and dislikes."

"For shoes?"

"For Life Savers." Homer opened his palm, revealing two circles of candy.

"He likes green ones?"

"He dislikes green ones. That's why he left them, Shelly. He ate the yellow and the red, the white and the orange. But when he got to the green ones . . ." Homer mimed pitching it over the fence. "He ate at least one, tossed the first greenie, ate some more, and tossed another. Let's say it takes five minutes to dissolve one of these things in your mouth. That's twenty minutes between greenies, plus another five minutes for the one he ate before the first greenie. Twenty-five minutes, minimum. If our suspect waits a few minutes between candies, or if he eats even one greenie before he decides that he doesn't really like them, we're talking even longer."

Shelly examined the candy life preserver. "What if he chews them?"

Homer shook his head. "Did you ever chew a Life Saver? They crack. If he takes the trouble to stand under a tree so that no one can see him in the lamplight, he's hardly going to risk making himself conspicuous by cracking one of these in his teeth."

"Does it give you his name any place?"

Homer made a face. "Did you get a name, inside?"

"As a matter of fact," said Shelly, suddenly remembering Julia leaning toward him as the rabbi's foot fell on the carpet outside. What did she say? "Rabinovitz." And to his partner's doubtful face, he repeated with some satisfaction, like a blessing he was learning to recite: "Chaim Rabinovitz."

When Chaim Rabinovitz first rode the subway north from Brooklyn Heights to the dense green canopy of the Bronx, the train cars had seat cushions woven of cane, and he could see farms in the distance through the sliding windows. East of the park, across from a high fence of wrought-iron spears and stone pillars, stood the grandest buildings, with courtyards of multicolored brick and sculptured concrete planters for ferns and flowers and sometimes murmuring water. If the Jews who lived in those splendid palaces were inclined to argue over politics rather than points of halakhah, others, who lived on the side streets a little farther from Bronx Park, found their present pleasure and hopes for the future in the white, two-story synagogue toward the southern end of the boulevard. Chaim had been called there in his early thirties, when Rabbi Horowitz of blessed memory keeled over while opening a window in his study to a breeze that smelled of grass. Chaim filled in for the rabbi during his recovery and afterward became his student, performing services when the rabbi was busy and teaching the boys to chant their Torah portions. Chaim never had to wait for a minyan in those days, and the soft light on the tops of the trees always told him when it was time to leave off his studies in esoteric texts and prepare for the service welcoming *Shabbos,* bride of Israel.

It had come as a terrible disappointment when Reb Horowitz asked Sholem Pirsky to take his place as rabbi of the tiny congregation. His illness had prevented him from explaining his thinking to Chaim, who had grown so accustomed to his supporting role in the life of the shul, he hardly raised a peep. Sholom Pirsky told him he would always have a place to continue his studies, to teach, and to pray. But he did not make good on his pledge when parents began to complain about Reb Rabinovitz's influence on their sons. It was true, Chaim admitted, that most bar mitzvah tutors did not set their instruction within the context of the larger spiritual universe—but he never shared with his boys any subtlety of religious thought that might disrupt their normal development. Chaim was disappointed once again when Sholem Pirsky decided that it might be best if he himself took over responsibility for bar mitzvah training, leaving Chaim more time to devote to his own learning. Depriving him of his students and the contact they provided drove him deeper into the mysteries of the great sages, where he had uncovered secrets that should perhaps have remained hidden. He had taken on students, privately, no one else would have taken. He wondered about the state of his own soul as a result. But had he wondered too late?

His reverie was interrupted by a soft knock at his door. He looked at the clock. Was it eight already? Where had the evening gone? He had eaten his dinner of a boiled egg and a dry piece of matzo, and had washed it down with black coffee, steaming hot and fully caffeinated. He didn't mind if it kept him up, later on. He wasn't planning to sleep that night anyway. His books were waiting, and if a night of study began with trope for a boy who hardly knew his name, what of it? What more fitting place was there to search for the Divine light lurking behind the commonplace? The knock at his door grew a trifle more insistent, and Rabinovitz stood, clearing his kitchen table.

He was coming, yes, he was coming. He wiped the last clay from his hands and stuck the trowel deep into his pocket.

"Are you sure that's his?" asked Shelly, peering through the windshield of the Reliant, over the dark playground to the windows at the back of an old brick building—the second from the left on the third floor up, where a yellow window shade filled the dingy panes. Shelly's own car was a Lexus these days, but he kept the old Plymouth for surveillance work because the car was invisible on the streets. Nobody admired it or thought about stealing it. There might have been a bit of nostalgia, too, for their old days on a stakeout. Homer never seemed to think about cars and took a cab when he needed one. But he lived in lower Manhattan, a different galaxy from Bronx Park East, or even from Shelly's apartment in Washington Heights.

"It's his, all right," declared Homer, hardly looking up. The fingernail on his left thumb was not entirely rounded and required most of his concentration. Homer's posture implied an innate sensitivity to the slightest change in the window overhead. How else could he rest so easily against the seat cushion, with one calf crossed over the other knee, and his gaze fixed on his cuticle? He still had his clean-shaven good looks, and his suits were better than ever, though Homer's middle had been thickening lately from too much scrupulous dining. Shelly's eyes were glued to the ancient window shade, watching for a difference in the yellow hue while he wondered if Julia hadn't been pulling his leg when she whispered, "Chaim Rabinovitz."

"What do you expect to see here, Shell?" Homer yawned. It was a fair question. The playground was closed for the night, but shapes still moved under the maple trees, crossing from the handball courts to the basketball courts and lingering behind the square, brick playground house in the middle of the block. They weren't spirits, Shelly knew, but adolescents who had climbed the fence to find one another under cover of the night. Yet, as the branches shifted overhead and their shadows leaped from the glow of one streetlight to the next, their soft voices on the night air might have been the whispers of ghost children who had fallen off the monkey bars and tumbled off the swings in the years since the playground was built.

Shelly sighed. "You believe in science, don't you, Homer?"

Homer's face showed what he thought of these conversations—he called them stakeout philosophy. The silence and waiting were as effective as alcohol at convincing men the time was right to expound on their personal visions. But Homer was trapped, with nothing better to do, and he knew it.

"You don't have to believe in it, Shell. That's the thing about science. It works, whether you believe in it or not."

"So you believe in it?"

"I believe in what science has discovered."

"Uh huh. What about what it hasn't discovered yet?"

"Like what?"

"Like—nuclear physics. Or even radio waves. There was a time before science discovered them, right? Did they exist?"

"Radio waves? Of course they existed. We can prove it."

"But what about before they were discovered? Did they exist then?"

"Things don't wait until they're discovered to exist, Shelly. They exist all along. We just learn about them when we're ready."

"What if some people sensed them before they were discovered?"

"Good for them. But until science noticed them, the rest of us didn't believe it."

"Even though they existed?"

"That's right."

"Then how do you know that there isn't a golem, Homer?"

Now it was Homer's turn to sigh. "You can't know there isn't anything," he said. "You can't prove that anything is impossible. But until science has proven that there is such a thing as a golem, I'd just as soon hold onto my skepticism."

"But you would have been wrong about radio waves, wouldn't you?" said Shelly. "And nuclear physics. In fact, with that same skeptical attitude, you would have been wrong about every single discovery in the history of science."

"So what are you saying? You believe that a golem broke into the synagogue, stole the silver pointer, and put it back when he was done with it?"

"I'm just trying to keep an open mind."

Homer didn't let it go so easily. "I understand the temptation, Shell, the desire to believe. It would be nice if somewhere in the universe lived a creature whose job it was to look out for decent people and punish the creepy crawlers. But—how many years did we spend on the force?"

"Between the two of us? Maybe thirty."

"In all that time, did you ever see anything that made you think that the righteous were protected and the guilty held accountable? Except by us?"

Shelly turned to the windshield, lifted his eyes—and gripped the padded shoulder of Homer's twill jacket.

The blond detective brushed him off the fabric. "What?"

"Look," whispered Shelly, very distinctly.

On the window shade of Chaim Rabinovitz's third-floor apartment, the shadow of something large stretched from one side to the other: six and a half, maybe seven feet tall, with massive shoulders and a small head. It hunched over a smaller figure, who only occasionally emerged from the looming shadow.

"Rabinovitz," said Homer.

Shelly found his voice. "Him I recognize. But who's his big brother?"

Homer sat forward, one hand on the dashboard, peering at the monster through narrowing eyelids. Despite the awful silence that filled their car, Shelly felt a certain satisfaction, watching his partner's logical mind wrestle with something it could not get around. Finally, Homer was interested.

They took the back stairs to the second floor, and knocked on Rabinovitz's door. He opened it just a crack and stood squarely behind it, blocking their line of sight into the apartment. To open the door further, they would have to shove the old man out of their way—which Homer seemed to be considering, as Shelly said:

"Good evening, Reb Rabinovitz."

"Do I know you?"

"My name is Shelly Lowenkopf. This is Homer Greeley. Rabbi Glickman told us we would find you here."

"Glickman, you say?" As if he couldn't quite place the name. From behind him came the scraping of a chair.

"It's rather urgent. Would you mind if we came in?"

"Do you have a warrant?"

"We're not with the police. At the moment."

Rabinovitz tried to work out the ambiguity: did Lowenkopf mean they had once been with the police, or that they could come back later with a policeman at their side? He decided not to risk misunderstanding, and let the door swing open as he disappeared inside. "Close it behind you," his voice lingered.

The small living room behind the door was empty except for an old sofa that sagged in the middle, an overstuffed chair in a flowered print, and a coffee table, stained, with a dried-up tea bag still sitting on the wood. Between sofa and chair, an end table supported an old lamp. Across from this arrangement was the window shade Shelly and Homer had been watching. Under the window stood a wooden cabinet in blond wood, paler than the coffee table. There were holes in the front panel, which told Shelly that the top of the cabinet could be lifted to reveal a turntable. Beside it was a stack of records with Hebrew labels: recordings of Torah portions. The third wall had a closet door and another into the kitchen, where a brighter light still burned.

"Sit," said Rabinovitz, indicating the couch. Before they could obey, he inquired, "So what did Rabbi Glickman say I could do for you?"

Shelly had worked out a story on the way up: they were investigating the theft of the synagogue's *yad*, and talking to all the members of the Kabbalah study group, in case any of them noticed anyone unusual on their way home. Anyone on the corner, perhaps? But Shelly never got a chance to try out this line because before he climbed out of the sofa's limp springs and perched himself on the wooden board that ran along the front of its threadbare cushions, somebody was standing in the doorway to the kitchen. "Rabbi? You coming back?" a small voice said.

He was black, no more than eight years old, in a red-and-black T-shirt and baggy white jeans. He had red Converse on his feet, no belt around his waist, and the tiniest *yarmulke* Shelly ever saw. Under the boy's elbow was a paper workbook with Hebrew letters on its cardboard cover, and in his hand was a pencil.

"I think it's enough for tonight, Martin," Rabinovitz said. "Practice your *alef bet* and we'll pick up the reading on Thursday."

Martin went back into the kitchen to pack up his books.

"You're teaching him Hebrew?" Shelly asked.

Rabinovitz shrugged. "They won't let me tutor the bar mitzvah boys at the shul anymore," he said. "One day Martin Ceda knocked at my door and asked to be taught. My first reaction was just like yours. He said, 'They told me if your mother is Jewish, that makes you Jewish, too. Doesn't that apply to people like me?' So I agreed to give him one lesson, to see how serious he was. And, don't you know, he was more serious about it than half the boys at the shul."

Martin came out of the kitchen with his workbook and another text under his arm. "G'night, Rebbe," he said, but hesitated before crossing to the door. His big, brown eyes crept over to the two men on the couch.

"Maybe we should walk him home," Shelly suggested. It was almost nine o'clock and the sky in the window was starless.

Rabinovitz shook his head. "It isn't necessary. His brother Jose is waiting for him in the candy store, reading comic books off the rack. Besides, you're here on a mission for Glickman, aren't you?"

Martin took it as his cue to head for the door, which seemed to loosen up Homer. Sitting further forward, so that only his tailbone rested on the couch, he said, "Unless I'm mistaken, Rabbi, I smell clay. Are you a potter, by any chance?"

Rabinovitz studied him carefully. "Clay?"

"I have a pretty good nose for plastics. It says, clay."

"As a matter of fact," the old man said uneasily, "I am a fair potter. I don't have a wheel myself, but I took a course at the home." The Beth Abraham Home, on Allerton Avenue and Bronx Park East.

"Could you show us some of your handiwork?"

"In the closet." Rabinovitz nodded toward the door beside the entrance to the kitchen. But he didn't get up from his chair, so Homer leaned over and opened it. From where he sat, Shelly caught a glimpse of a glazed yellow ashtray, a blue bud vase, and something else that disappeared into his partner's hand.

"Tell us about this," the blond detective said, setting the third object on the coffee table in front of them. It was a humanlike form, three inches tall. The head was merely a sphere of clay with a mouth and pair of eyes poked into it by an ice cream stick. It had not been glazed, so that the dried clay gave off a pungent smell. When Shelly touched it, the surface felt powdery, and the head nearly rolled off its shoulders.

"What is there to tell?" said Rabinovitz. "It's a small clay figure of a man."

"Did you make it yourself?"

"Yes."

"Do you mind telling us why?"

"I told you, already. For a class."

"And did making it give you any other ideas?"

Rabinovitz's eyes focused on Homer, and Shelly saw for the first time how dark they were and full of anger. The man carried himself wearily, as if the effort of moving from the kitchen to his armchair were almost more than he could manage. And yet, when his guard fell, there was still a passionate vehemence inside him—enough to fill another soul with energy and perhaps even an animating desire for revenge.

"What do you mean, ideas?"

Homer smiled pleasantly. "We saw something on the your shade tonight, and I was wondering if this"—the clay figure—"might not explain it. Do you mind?"

Rabinovitz shrugged. "Why should I mind? The adult education class is over. Do whatever you want with it."

"Thank you," Homer said. He carried the clay figure carefully to the end table, where he stood it up, so that the head and shoulders rose to the edge of the old lamp's shade. By raising and lowering the figure, he adjusted the shadow on the window shade, until something appeared that resembled a golem—a smaller version of what they had seen from their stakeout car below.

"Now, Shelly, if you could just tilt the window shade towards us, I think you'll find that it changes the apparent size of the object in shadow."

Shelly walked over to the window and lifted the stiff shade. As he did, his eye fell on a streetlight at the far end of the block, just as two figures were passing below it. One of them was Martin Ceda. He was holding the hand of the other, who must have been his brother Jose—a comic book was rolled in his back pocket. Except Jose looked too old to be reading comic books. He stood six foot five, carried two hundred pounds, and bobbed his head as he walked. He wore plaid shorts that drooped below his kneecaps and a baseball shirt with the name of New York's other team scrawled across his back: the Mets. His right hand was bandaged, and Shelly was willing to bet that under the strip of gauze was a puncture wound in the shape of the pointy end of a *yad*. Somewhere in his pocket his paw probably held the ragged end of a roll of Life Savers. Or had he bought a new one in the candy store?

The bottom of the window frame was crooked on its track. It rested uneasily on the sill, and a draft of air whistled through. For a moment Shelly felt his father's presence beside him, warming the cool air—when he heard Homer's calm voice:

"You see what I mean, Shell?"

The clay figure's shadow filled the tilted shade from one end to the other. Shelly let it drop back over the window, as Martin and his brother crossed the side street and disappeared into the Bronx. "Yeah. I see what you mean."

MICHAEL A. KAHN is a trial attorney and the author
of six mystery novels featuring St. Louis attorney
Rachel Gold. His latest novel is *Bearing Witness*
(Forge, 2000). His short story "Bread of Affliction,"
featured in *Mystery Midrash*, won a 1999 readers'
award from *Ellery Queen Mystery Magazine*. He lives
in St. Louis with his wife, five children, and assorted
pets.

Truth in a Plain Brown Wrapper

▼   ▼   ▼   ▼   ▼   ▼   ▼   ▼   ▼   ▼   ▼   ▼

MICHAEL A. KAHN

I WALKED JACOB CONTINI TO THE HALLWAY outside the courtroom and
waited for the door to swing shut behind us. "They have a final settlement
proposal," I told him.

My white-haired client straightened warily. "Now what?"

I peered through the window of the courtroom door. Cissy Robb and
Milton Brenner were huddled in conversation near the empty jury box. I
turned to Jacob. "You're not going to like it."

He crossed his arms over his chest, his face grim. "Tell me."

"Cissy will drop the lawsuit if you give her five designer dresses and a
formal letter of apology."

He stiffened, eyes ablaze. "Never. That woman is nothing but a common thief—a *gonif*." He raised his right hand, pointing his index finger toward heaven. "Jacob Contini apologize to that woman?" He shook his head
firmly. "As God is my witness, never."

Several heads turned to stare at the diminutive, elegantly attired gentleman. I doubted whether any recognized him, but many sensed that they
should have, that they were in the presence of a personage, perhaps an Italian duke. Although Jacob Contini had indeed been born in Milan, his father had not been a duke but a tailor—and a poor one at that, eking out a
living in the Jewish section. In the late 1930s, terrified by the rise of fascism

and anti-Semitism, Yitzhak Contini brought his young family to America, eventually settling in St. Louis.

Despite these humble origins, the son of Yitzhak Contini had risen to aristocracy within the fashion world of St. Louis. He was, after all, the Jacob of Jacob's On Maryland, the snootiest boutique in the Central West End. Through nearly four decades and countless weddings, debutante formals, and charitable balls, he had clothed the grandmothers, wives, and daughters of the ruling class of St. Louis.

"I understand your feelings," I told him, lowering my voice, "but compare the cost of five dresses to the cost of this trial. You can end the case now, eliminate your risk, and actually save money."

"Money? This is more important than money. That woman has violated my honor, and she has violated the honor of my religion. She, not I, is guilty of slander. In the Talmud, Rachel, it is said that he who speaks slander has no portion in the world to come."

"Let's first worry about this world. If you lose, there could be a big verdict. She's asking for a million in actuals and a million in punitives."

"And I ask merely for justice."

He shook his patrician head gravely. "I have been an American citizen for fifty-four years, Rachel. I understand my constitutional rights. I choose to exercise them here. I demand my day in court."

I studied him a moment and sighed. I gave his arm an affectionate squeeze. "Okay, boss."

Cissy Robb and Milton Brenner looked over as we entered the courtroom.

"Wait there," I told Contini, pointing him toward the rows of benches in the gallery.

Brenner approached with a big smile. He was a stocky man in his early sixties, with a ruddy complexion, a shock of gray hair, crinkly blue eyes, and a crooked smile that displayed tobacco-stained teeth. Ironically, Brenner had made a name for himself defending media defendants in libel cases. Today, though, it wouldn't have mattered if he'd been on retainer as special libel counsel to the *New York Times*. That was because Cissy Robb happened to be the wife of Richie Robb, who happened to be the founder and CEO of Pacific Rim Industries, which happened to account for 32 percent of the annual billings of the law firm of Harding Brandt LLC. Although Harding Brandt LLC might trace its origins and carefully burnished image back to the genteel professionalism of the 1800s, when the wife of your biggest client is unhappy, your job is to make her happy, and if that means dressing up Milton Brenner as a plaintiff's libel shark, so be it. The business of modern law is business.

"Well, counselor," Brenner said with hearty good cheer, "do we have a deal?"

I shook my head. "Nope."

He frowned. "Jesus, Rachel, does your client understand his exposure here?"

"Last time I checked the cases, Milt, truth is a complete defense."

He tugged at the loose skin on his neck, his lips pursed. Finally, he gave me a grudging chuckle. "You drive a hard bargain, counselor. What's your counteroffer? I probably can whittle her down to two dresses."

"No counter, Milt. Let's go see the judge."

The Honorable LaDonna Williams leaned back in her chair and looked down at her desk with a scowl. Judge Williams had been on the bench for just two years, having previously served for sixteen years in the city prosecutor's office, where she'd been a respected, hard-working attorney. During those years, she'd been a guiding force of the Mound City Bar Association, the association of black attorneys. Now in her midforties, Judge Williams was a plump woman with a gentle smile and soft features that masked an incisive legal mind.

"Now let me see if I have this straight, Rachel," she said. "Mrs. Robb bought a dress from your client, and when she attempted to return it your client refused to take it back. Correct?"

"Yes, Your Honor."

"The reason being?"

"Mr. Contini examined the dress," I explained, "and concluded that it had been worn."

Judge Williams turned to my opponent. "And how exactly does this incident metamorphose into a libel claim, Mr. Brenner?"

"Very simple, Judge. When the defendant refused to take back the dress, there were heated words." Brenner attempted to look indignant. "He accused my client of fraud. He accused her of dishonesty. He accused her . . . of theft. These scandalous charges were overheard by three other women in the store, all of whom knew my client on a social basis." He paused to shake his head sadly. "Mr. Contini's false, defamatory, and malicious accusations have tarnished my client's reputation, and her reputation is her most precious asset, her most treasured—"

"Counsel," Judge Williams interrupted, "save the violins for the jury." She turned to me. "Those are harsh words from your client."

"He was furious at the time, Your Honor. When he refused to take back the dress, Mrs. Robb called him, and I quote, 'a dirty Jew bastard.'" I paused. "Those were the worst possible words she could have chosen. My client is fervently opposed to any form of anti-Semitism. He's obsessed by it, and with good reason, Your Honor. He lost many relatives in the Holocaust, which he blames on lies about the Jewish people spread by Hitler and others."

The judge turned to Brenner with a puzzled look. "Not that it's relevant, Mr. Brenner, but isn't your client Jewish?"

"She is, Your Honor," Brenner said with a forced smile. "However, I would point out to the Court that her alleged words are not an issue in the case. We will be filing a motion to exclude any testimony on the subject. The defendant has filed no counterclaim for libel."

I said, "That's because Mr. Contini refuses to stoop to her level."

The judge sighed. "Settlement prospects?"

I shook my head. "We have two stubborn litigants who believe that what's at stake here is their honor."

"Honor." The judge rolled her eyes wearily. "That's what makes lawyers rich. Well, let's pick a trial date, folks." She opened her calendar. "Is this on the jury docket?"

"Judge," Brenner said, "our first priority is to get this case to trial. My client needs to clear her name as soon as possible. If that means waiving a jury, so be it."

Judge Williams turned to me. "Rachel?"

I tried to mask my delight. Libel plaintiffs tend to love juries, and juries tend to love libel plaintiffs. Judge Williams was far more likely than a jury to resist Milton Brenner's closing argument histrionics. Nevertheless, I could see why his client might choose speed over greed. Cissy Robb was an indefatigable social climber. With a net worth north of fifty million dollars, she needed the money far less than she needed to remove this blemish from her reputation.

I said, "We're prepared to waive a jury, Your Honor."

"How long will this case take to try?" she asked.

Brenner rubbed his chin. "Oh, two days?"

Judge Williams turned to me. "Rachel?"

"Sounds about right."

"Two days," the judge repeated as she studied her calendar. "You're in luck. I have an opening a week from next Thursday. How's that?"

"Well," Brenner stammered, "I suppose that's fine with me, Judge, but I'm sure Miss Gold could use a little more time to get her case ready."

He was right. I could use a lot more time. But I couldn't ignore the hitch in Brenner's voice, which seemed more important than additional time.

"A week from next Thursday is perfect," I said. "We'll be ready."

"Nine A.M.," Judge Williams said, entering the date on her calendar. She looked up with a smile. "I'll see you then."

Out in the hall a somewhat edgy Milton Brenner asked, "Are you going to want to take Cissy's deposition before trial?"

I smiled and shook my head. "What for, Milt? We're already loaded for bear."

We weren't, of course, but bluffing is part of the battle.

I gazed at the purse on the edge of the desk and shook my head in disbelief. "Five hundred and twelve dollars for that?"

Jacki shrugged. "It's a Salvatore Ferragamo. All leather."

"Forget the damn purse," Benny said. "What about the high heels? Who in their right mind would pay eight hundred and seventy dollars for a pair of shoes?"

"Oh, but you have to admit," Jacki cooed, touching one of them lovingly, "these are exquisite."

"Hey, girl," Benny said, "if I'm going to shell out that kind of money for a pair of pumps, they better come on the feet of a babe wearing nothing else but a G-string."

It was the end of the day. Benny had dropped by my office after his antitrust seminar with a pair of tickets to a blues concert that night. Jacki had just returned from Plaza Frontenac with the purse and shoes we'd been examining. Benny and Jacki were, to say the least, an unusual pair. Benny Goldberg was unique by any standard: vulgar, fat, gluttonous, and obnoxious. But he was also ferociously loyal, wonderfully funny, and—most important—my very best friend in the whole world. We met as junior associates in the Chicago offices of Abbott & Windsor. A few years later, we both escaped that LaSalle Street sweatshop—Benny to teach law at De Paul, me to go solo as Rachel Gold, Attorney at Law. Different reasons brought us to St. Louis. For Benny, it was an offer he couldn't refuse from Washington University. For me, it was a yearning to live closer to my mother after my father died.

As for Jacki Brand, she was a former Granite City steelworker who was putting herself through night law school while working days as my secretary, paralegal, law clerk, and all-around aide. Standing six feet three inches and weighing close to 240 pounds, with plenty of steelworker muscles rippling beneath her dress, she was surely the most intimidating legal secretary in town. I'd call her my Girl Friday, except that anatomically she was still a he— and would so remain until her operation next summer. Jacki (née Jack) was now in her fifth month as a woman and her fifth month as the greatest assistant I'd ever had.

I'd sent her to Plaza Frontenac to pick up the materials turned over in response to subpoenas we'd served on Neiman Marcus and La Femme Elegànte. As part of my pretrial preparation for Cissy Robb's libel lawsuit against Jacob Contini, I'd obtained a copy of her Visa statement for the crucial month of August. It showed the $4,558.56 charge for the Adrienne Vittadini dress that she'd purchased from Jacob's On Maryland on August 11 and unsuccessfully attempted to return the following week. August 11 was a Tuesday. The next day (August 12), according to her Visa statement, she'd made a $512.35 purchase at Neiman Marcus and a $870.67 purchase at La Femme Elegànte. What made those two purchases noteworthy were two subsequent entries on August 18: a $512.35 credit at Neiman Marcus and a $870.67 credit at La Femme Elegànte. The subpoenas I'd served asked each store to produce the paperwork surrounding the transaction plus the actual items purchased on the twelfth and returned on the eighteenth.

I lifted one of the shoes from La Femme Elegànte. It was a sleek black pump by Yves Saint Laurent. I turned it over and studied the sole. There were a few faint scratches around the ball of the foot that suggested, at least to my inexpert eye, that the shoe may have been worn.

"When's this crazy trial start?" Benny asked.

"Next Thursday," Jacki said. She lifted the Salvatore Ferragamo purse by the straps and stood up, turning to looking at her reflection in the window. Although it was a standard-size black leather bag, against Jacki's bulk it seemed to shrink to a child's play purse.

"It looks smart," I told her.

She gave me a doubtful look.

"You think it'll settle?" Benny asked.

I shook my head. "Neither one is in it for the money." Still holding the pump, I leaned over and placed it alongside one of my shoes. They seemed the same size.

"It's principal versus pride," I said to Benny. "Jacob is convinced that she bought that dress with the intent of wearing it somewhere and then returning it. He claims she's done it before. When she called him a 'dirty Jew,' he went ballistic. Anti-Semitism is his hot button." I glanced at Jacki. "Right?"

"You can say that again." She sighed. "Rachel was stuck in court last week when he showed up for an appointment. During those thirty minutes I learned all about the Dreyfus affair in France and the *Protocols of the Elders of Zion* and the Russian pogroms and the blood libel and his personal hero, Joseph Bloch."

"Who?" Benny asked.

"I'd never heard of him, either," I said. "He was an amazing guy."

Jacki said, "Bloch started off as rabbi in Austria in late 1800s, which was not a good time or place to be Jewish. In 1882, fifteen Jews were accused of murdering a girl named Esther Solymosi to use her blood to make unleavened bread for the Passover ceremonies."

"What?" Benny said, incredulous.

"The infamous blood libel," I said. "And that was hardly the first time."

"According to Mr. Contini," Jacki explained, "blood libel claims against Jews date back to the twelfth century."

"So what happened to the Jews accused of murdering the girl?" Benny asked.

"This powerful priest—" Jacki turned to me. "What was his name?"

"Father August Rohling. He was a professor at the University of Prague."

"Rohling claimed that he could prove the existence of the blood ritual," Jacki said. "Bloch fought back, almost single-handedly. He gave speeches and wrote articles. He accused the priest of ignorance and dishonesty. Rohling sued him for libel, but Bloch's arguments were so powerful that he was forced to drop the suit. After the fifteen Jews were freed, Bloch started publishing a newspaper that fought anti-Semitism. Later, he became a member of the Austrian parliament, and eventually he got three powerful Christian men thrown in jail for accusing a group of rabbis of the blood ritual."

Benny raised his eyebrows, impressed. "Cool."

"Jacob sees his fight here as a personal tribute to his hero," I explained.

"It's all about principle. For Cissy, it's all about social standing. Don't forget that just ten years ago she and Richie were shopping at Kmart, driving an old Chevy wagon, and celebrating their daughter's bat mitzvah with *mostaccioli* and green Jell-O in the temple basement. Now the guy's worth big bucks. Cissy's come a long way. She's not backing down."

"So what does she want?" Benny asked.

"Total vindication," I said as I slipped off one of my shoes. "She wants either a public apology from Jacob Contini or his public humiliation at trial."

"Can your guy prove she wore the dress?" he asked.

I glanced over at Jacki, who raised her eyebrows and sighed. I looked back at Benny. "Not yet."

"Excellent," Benny said sarcastically. "Does the Great Contini understand that he'd better get ready to bend over and kiss his principled *tokhes* good-bye?"

I slipped my foot into the pump. "Hey, it fits."

I stood up, wobbling on one heel.

"Here you go, Cinderella," Jacki said, handing me the other one.

I kicked off my other shoe and slipped on the second pump. I did feel like Cinderella. I'd never owned anything by Yves Saint Laurent. "Do you realize," I said, "that this pair of shoes costs more than all of my shoes combined?"

"Nice," Jacki said, admiring the shoes. "They're you, Rachel."

I tilted my head back and fluffed my hair in an exaggerated Hollywood pose. "Thank you, dahling."

I took a few sashaying steps and looked back toward Jacki. We both started giggling like school girls. It was a nice respite from the grind of this case.

Benny looked heavenward and shook his head. "What the hell is this," he said, "a costume party?"

"Hush, Grumpy," I told him. I returned to my chair and slipped off the heels.

"Rachel," he said in exasperation, "the trial is a week away and this is all you've got? A couple of returns? She's just gonna say she bought this crap, brought it home, decided she didn't like it, and took it back. Then what are you going to do?"

I put the shoes on my desk. "Here's what we're going to do." I turned to Jacki. "Brenner has no clue what we're up to. After class tonight, stop at the library and get the *Post-Dispatch* for the Sunday of that week. August sixteenth. There's a section in there called Style Plus. They run a column on society events, especially charity fund-raisers."

"What am I looking for?" Jacki asked.

"Best case scenario," I said, "Cissy's name. Otherwise, you're looking for every event mentioned and every person identified as attending."

Jacki was jotting down my instructions. When she finished, she looked up with a puzzled expression. "Why?"

"A hunch," I said, gesturing toward the purse and the heels. "In a two-day period, Cissy Robb spent close to six thousand dollars on a dress, a pair of shoes, and a purse. The following week, she returns, or tries to return, everything. Maybe Benny's right—maybe she just had second thoughts. But Jacob is convinced she wore the dress. If he's right, we have an alternative scenario, namely, that she bought the outfit specifically for an upcoming social event. Given the Visa statement, that would mean that the event had to take place sometime between August twelfth, when she bought the shoes and purse, and August eighteenth, when she returned them and tried to return the dress."

Jacki was smiling and nodding her head. "I like it."

"Check with Jacob, too," I told her. "If there was some big event that weekend, some of his other customers may have mentioned it." I looked at Benny, who raised his eyebrows skeptically. "Well, Professor, you have any better ideas?"

He grunted. "Yeah. Get your client a good bankruptcy lawyer."

I dropped by the office after the concert that night. Jacki had left a nice surprise in the center of my desk: a photocopy of the society column from the Style Plus section of the Sunday, August 16, edition of the *Post-Dispatch*. She'd circled the middle paragraphs, which described the highlights of the Carousel Auction Gala at the Ritz-Carlton put on by the Friends of the St. Louis Children's Hospital:

> Guests gathered last Friday night under the carousel in the smaller of the two ballrooms at the Ritz, where a bar had been set up in the center with bartenders serving on all four sides. High above the bar was a carousel horse, and at each of its four corners was a smaller gilded carousel horse dressed in burgundy and teal blue. Waiters passed silver trays of delicious hot hors d'oeuvres to guests as they signed up for the silent auction items displayed around the room.
>
> Chairwoman Cynthia Barnstable said the event netted more than $450,000, including $145,000 from the auction itself. 350 guests paid

$150 and up for their tickets to the event. The money will be used for the new neuro-rehabilitation unit at Children's Hospital.

The article included a photograph of two women standing in front of a carousel horse. The caption identified them as Cynthia Barnstable, chairwoman of the event, and Prudence McReynolds, president of the women's auxiliary of Children's Hospital. The photo credit named Charles Morley. I circled his name and drew an arrow to the margin, where I jotted a note to Jacki: *We need to subpoena this guy. Let's talk in the morning.*

Jacob Contini crossed his arms over his chest and shook his head firmly. "Never, Rachel. I would view it as a betrayal."

Ozzie groaned. We both looked over, but he was sound asleep on the rug.

It was Sunday morning. Jacob and I were in my office going over a few matters in preparation for the libel trial that was just four days off. I'd gone for a jog through Forest Park earlier in the morning with Ozzie, my golden retriever. We'd dropped by a Jewish bakery afterward for a snack—an onion bagel with cream cheese and a large coffee for me, a pumpernickel bagel and a small bowl of water for him. Then we drove over to my office, where Ozzie promptly fell asleep, his paws over his ears.

Jacob and I made quite a Sunday contrast—me in my St. Louis Browns baseball cap (to keep my curly hair out of my face as I jogged), an oversized gray Jane Austen Rules! sweatshirt, black jogging tights, and Nikes; Jacob in an elegant navy, pinstriped, double-breasted suit, white shirt, gold-and-gray striped tie, and black Italian shoes buffed to a brilliant shine.

"Jacob, I can tell your customers that I got their names from a guest list for the event. They'll never know my real source."

"But I would know, Rachel. A secret betrayal is no less a *shanda* than a public one."

"It's hardly a sin," I said, trying to hide my frustration. "Three of your customers bought dresses for the Children's Hospital benefit. You said yourself that all three are loyal patrons. If one of those women remembers what Cissy Robb was wearing that night, and if it turns out that it was your dress, I'm sure she'd be happy to help you by testifying at trial."

Another adamant shake of the head. "Out of the question. That woman slandered me and my people. I would never ask one of my ladies to sully her hands in this coarse dispute. This is my problem and my responsibility. I must force this slanderer to drop her case."

He reached into the breast pocket of his suit, removed the white handkerchief, patted it against his forehead, and replaced it, making sure to position it perfectly in the pocket. I leaned back in my chair and sighed. Ten thousand retailers in St. Louis, and I end up representing the Rabbi Bloch of designer dresses.

"Jacob," I said patiently, "Cissy Robb has sued you for millions of dollars. She will swear that she never wore that dress."

"But she's a liar."

"We still have to prove it's a lie. Otherwise, she's entitled to a judgment in her favor."

He gave me a serene smile. "Ah, but that will not happen."

"Oh? And why not?"

He made a sweeping gesture with his hands. "Because, my dear Rachel, you will not allow it to happen."

I smiled in resignation. "Jacob, my name is Rachel Gold, not Perry Mason. I'm limited to admissible evidence, and, frankly, we could use some more."

"But, Rachel, I thought that you found some. What about that fellow from the newspaper—the gentleman who took the photographs?"

I shrugged. "Jacki went through the one roll he developed the day after the event. Cissy isn't in any of the pictures."

He grimaced. "A pity."

"He thinks there may be a few more pictures from the event on another roll he hasn't developed yet. He promised to do it over the weekend. We'll find out tomorrow."

Jacob nodded with satisfaction. "There. You see?"

"Don't get your hopes up." I leaned back and sighed. "I'm not optimistic."

"Oh, but you should be. You are such a lovely young lady, Rachel, and so intelligent. God smiles down upon you, my dear. I am certain you will find us our evidence. And if not, well—" he paused and gave me a shrug "—such is the way of the world. But," he said, placing his hand over his heart, "you must not chide me for refusing to allow my darling ladies to get dragged into this case."

I rested my chin on my fist and smiled at my courtly white-haired client. "I would never chide you, Jacob."

He leaned over and patted my hand. "I promise to be a good witness. It will be her word against mine. That may be the best we can do. We will pray that justice prevails."

I said nothing. My client was in a sentimental mood, and I saw no reason to shake him out of it. This was Sunday. I had four days to come up with something more than a prayer.

"Well?" Jacki said.

I stepped back, crossing my arms as I studied the poster. It was a blow-up of a color photograph of two cars parked side-by-side on a wide circular driveway. The car on the left was a silver Corvette. The car on the right was a silver Mercedes-Benz coupe with gold trim. An ornate Spanish tile mailbox was visible in the left foreground with the address stenciled in gold: #6 Sienna. Looming above the cars in the background was the 21,000-square-foot Mission-style home of Richie and Cissy Robb. The vanity plate on the silver Corvette read I'M RICH. The vanity plate on the Mercedes read ME, TOO.

I looked over at Jacki and nodded. "I like it. I like it a lot."

"Mark it?" she asked, reaching for her trial exhibit stickers.

"Yep. Exhibit H, right?"

"Right."

It was eight-thirty the night before trial. We were at my office doing the usual last-minute preparations—marking trial exhibits, making copies of key documents, outlining direct examinations, making notes for cross-examination. Benny had dropped by to help. He was in a chair in the corner reading through a pile of recent libel decisions in an effort to breathe some life into Jacob Contini's affirmative defenses.

I watched as Jacki peeled off the back of the exhibit sticker and carefully affixed it to the upper right corner of the poster. The sticker read Defendant's Trial Exhibit H.

"Okay," I said. "We'll need to wrap it and mark it." I pointed to the other poster. "Let's make this Exhibit I."

I turned to the third poster, which was already wrapped in plain brown paper and sealed with tape. I picked up the black marker, took off the cap, and walked over to it.

"Which makes this one," I said as I bent down next to it, "Exhibit J." Using the marker, I printed Defendant's Trial Exhibit J across the brown paper. I straightened up, replaced the cap on the marker, and stepped back to admire my handiwork.

Benny looked up from his cases and shook his head. "Let's hope you never have to unwrap that present, Hanukkah Joe."

I turned toward him and crossed my fingers. "As my father used to say, from your lips to God's ears."

"Does your client know about Exhibit J?" Benny asked.

I shook my head. "He's nervous enough as it is."

Benny slowly shook his head. "Good grief." He looked over at Jacki. "What's your take on Exhibit J?"

She shuddered. "I don't want to think about it."

At 9:05 A.M. the next morning, I rose at counsel's table. Jacob Contini was seated next to me, ramrod straight, his hands steepled beneath his chin.

"Defendant is ready," I announced.

Judge LaDonna Williams nodded gravely. "We'll start in a moment." She leaned over and said something to her docket clerk, who got to her feet and came around behind the bench to confer with the judge. As they talked in hushed tones, I turned toward the gallery, which was usually empty save for one or two elderly court watchers. Today, though, a crowd of two dozen was scattered on the benches. I recognized the society correspondent and the gossip columnist for the *Post-Dispatch,* seated side by side in the third row. Behind them was a reporter from Channel Five with a steno pad open on her lap. One row over was Charles Morley, the photographer from the *Post-Dispatch*—here today not as a spectator but as a witness. Jacki had served him with a trial subpoena. I caught his eye and smiled. He acknowledged me with a nod. I spotted two other witnesses we'd subpoenaed. With any luck this morning, they'd never have to take the stand.

Seated in the first row directly behind us were Jacob Contini's stout wife, Dorothy, and their stouter son, Isaac. Isaac had Down syndrome. He was in his thirties and had an absolutely angelic disposition. I winked at Dorothy Contini, who nodded nervously. Isaac smiled and gave me a thumbs-up.

On the other side of the courtroom, in the first row behind plaintiff's table, was Richie Robb, CEO of Pacific Rim Industries and husband of the plaintiff. Richie was flanked by two members of his entourage. In contrast to his grim lieutenants, Richie seemed almost languid this morning. With his heavylidded eyes, shiny black suit, and dark, slicked-back hair, he reminded me of a drowsy, well-fed panther.

"Counsel," Judge Williams said, peering down at us over her reading glasses, "I've read your trial briefs and I'm familiar with your legal theories. We'll dispense with opening statements." She turned to my opponent. "Mr. Brenner, call your first witness."

"Thank you so much, Your Honor," Milt Brenner said in his fawning manner. He turned to his client, who was seated next to him. With a sweeping gesture, he announced, "Your Honor, we call the plaintiff herself, Mrs. Cecelia Robb."

She rose with steely poise and strode across the courtroom to the witness box, where the clerk was waiting. At forty-eight, Cissy Robb was a striking figure, with an aura that seemed regal. And with good reason. Whatever nature omitted had been supplied by the finest collection of plastic surgeons, orthodontists, personal fitness trainers, hair stylists, fashion consultants, makeup artists, personal tutors, and diction coaches that Richie's money could buy. Today she wore a subdued but elegant red wool suit and matching neck scarf that brought out the highlights in her shoulder-length, auburn hair.

"Please raise your right hand," the clerk told her.

And thus the trial began.

Many who knew her claimed that Cissy Robb had ice in her veins. Just last year, for example, she'd refused to pay her $10,000 pledge to the St. Louis Special Olympics when, instead of being seated for the luncheon at the A table (with guest of honor Barbara Walters and the wives of several St. Louis CEOs), she found herself at a table that included two of the gold medal winners at the day's competition. As she angrily informed the chairwoman of the event, "I didn't pledge ten grand to eat lunch with a couple of retards."

Perhaps to soften her image, Milt Brenner started his examination slow and gentle—marital status, children, pets, hobbies. I glanced over at Richie, who had momentarily perked up when his wife took the stand. He soon lost interest, though, and turned to one of his assistants to whisper something. The assistant nodded intently, jumped to his feet, and scurried out of the courtroom. Richie turned with a bored expression to watch him leave.

Richie hadn't always been surrounded by an entourage. Twenty years ago, he was a smalltime jobber named Richie Rubenstein who'd cornered the U.S. market in cheapo, made-in-Singapore work boots at a time when no one cared about cheapo work boots. Which was fine by Richie. His margins on the schlock he peddled to the inner city discount houses were just enough to cover the mortgage, the Blues season tickets, and the twice-a-year junkets to Vegas.

But then a miracle occurred: the fickle finger of fashion pointed to work boots. Richie was so far ahead of the curve that it took years for the rest to catch up. With his Asian factories working triple shifts, Richie went from penny ante to pennies from heaven. When he took Pacific Rim public on a Thursday morning in March eight years ago, his net worth shot from $23,124 to $36.3 million in the space of six hours. Richie went berserk that weekend: he chartered a plane and flew his twenty-two best buds, including the entire bowling team, to Vegas for three days of booze, blackjack, and broads. Cissy went uptown that weekend: she took the wife of Richie's securities lawyer to Hilton Head Island and spent three days pumping her for information on St. Louis society. Richie returned with a cosmic hangover and a genital rash of indeterminate origins. Cissy returned with climbing ropes and pitons.

While Cissy's social aspirations might never quite surmount her husband's crudeness, I conceded that the woman had resolve. Looking at her seated in the witness box, elegantly groomed and perfectly coifed, it was obvious that the former Cissy Gutterman was breathing thinner air these days.

We were now nearly an hour into Brenner's warm and cuddly preliminaries about her background and family. Finally, he reached the day that Cissy called, in a halting voice, Black Tuesday.

"Tell us about it," he said compassionately.

What followed was a performance that deserved a Tony nomination. We heard about her initial confusion when Jacob Contini responded with a silent scowl to her request to return the dress. Then the embarrassment of having him place the dress under a high intensity lamp and inspect it with a magnifying glass. Then the dismay of struggling to maintain her composure while he fired questions at her, his voice "literally dripping with hostility." And finally, the mortification of public disgrace.

"There were other women in there," she said, her lips quivering, "women I know, women I admire, women I respect." She paused to dab her eye with a handkerchief. "He raised his voice to me. He was practically shouting at me. He called me a liar and a cheat. Those women heard every one of his vile accusations." She paused and took a deep breath, her face contorted in anguish.

Brenner, in an empathetic tone, asked, "Was it painful, Cissy?"

She sighed, her hands fluttering helplessly onto her lap. "Oh, you have no idea."

"Tell the court, Cissy."

As if on cue, she covered her face with her hands and began sobbing. Brenner allowed it to continue until Judge Williams quietly announced that the court would be in short recess. Brenner helped her off the stand and walked her out of the courtroom. Richie, barely acknowledging his wife's condition, huddled with his two aides.

I used the break to get my exhibits arranged. Brenner had to know that he couldn't top that last scene. His expression confirmed as much when he strolled back into the courtroom alone. He could not have looked more pleased with himself.

"Rachel," he said, "I'm afraid our last settlement offer is off the table."

Five minutes later, with his restored and composed client back on the witness stand, Milt Brenner stood to announce, "No further questions, Your Honor." He turned to me with a sympathetic smile. "Your witness, counsel."

I checked my watch as I stood up. Eleven-fifteen. We'd break for lunch around noon, which gave me forty-five minutes to set it up. So far, things were going according to the plan—the one I had worked out in the wee hours last night. If the plan worked, the case would end over the lunch hour. If it didn't, we'd be stuck in a high-stakes mud-wrestling match for at least another day and a half.

I came around counsel's table to face her. "Good morning, Mrs. Robb," I said courteously. "My name is Rachel Gold and I represent the defendant."

She nodded, her eyes chilly.

"I have a few questions for you, but before I ask them I'd like to make sure I understand your claim." I moved back over to Jacob Contini and put my hand on his shoulder. "You've sued my client for libel. You claim he said some defamatory things about you, right?"

She looked from me to Contini and then back to me. "That's right," she said, sounding almost annoyed by the question.

"In fact, you allege that Mr. Contini said you were lying about whether you wore the dress. You allege that he accused you of trying to cheat him by asking for a full refund on something that you had already used."

Her nostrils flared. "That's exactly what he said."

I nodded. "And you allege here that his accusations were false, correct?"

She nodded imperiously. "They were lies."

"In fact, Mrs. Robb, you allege that you didn't wear that dress at all, correct?"

"It's not an allegation," she snapped. "It's the truth."

"Thank you." I nodded politely. "I think I understand your position."

I walked over to the wall hook where the dress hung, tagged with an exhibit sticker. "Now, I'd like us to go back to Tuesday, August eleventh. That was the day you bought this pretty Adrienne Vittadini dress from Mr. Contini, right?"

"Yes."

"You bought two more expensive clothing items the next day, right?"

She shrugged indifferently. "I'm sure I don't remember something that far back."

I smiled politely. "I understand, Mrs. Robb. I can't even remember what I had for breakfast today. Let's see if I can jog your memory."

I spent the next fifteen minutes refreshing her recollection with charge receipts, credit slips, and her credit card bill for August. When I finished, Cissy found herself cautiously eyeing Defendant's Trial Exhibits E and F, which were resting on the ledge of the witness box directly in front of her. Exhibit E was the pair of Yves Saint Laurent black pumps that she had purchased for $870.67 on August 12. Exhibit F was the Salvatore Ferragamo handbag that she had purchased for $512.35 on the same day.

"Let's make sure our dates are correct," I said, turning to the blackboard. "On Tuesday you bought that pretty dress. On Wednesday you bought the matching pumps and purse. Then, on the following Tuesday, after the weekend, you returned the purse to Neiman Marcus and the shoes to La Femme Elegànte." I turned and gave her my perky kindergarten teacher smile. "Right?"

She frowned at the blackboard and then looked down at the receipts already admitted into evidence as trial exhibits. "I suppose."

"Is that a yes?"

She looked at me, her eyes narrowing. "Yes," she hissed.

Another perky smile. "I thought so."

I walked back toward counsel's table. I sat against the table edge, facing the witness. "Tell us about the night of August fourteenth. It was the Friday of the week you bought the dress and the shoes and the purse."

She laughed. "Get serious. That was months ago. I have no idea what I did that night."

I nodded. Leaning across the table, I lifted the next exhibit off the pile. "Let's see if we can refresh that memory of yours again."

I walked over to the witness box. "I'm handing you what I've marked Defendant's Trial Exhibit G."

I gave an extra copy to the Judge and one to Brenner. Turning back to the witness, I said, "Identify it, Mrs. Robb." No warmth in my voice now.

She stared at the document for a moment and then looked over at Milt Brenner with a frown.

"Identify Exhibit G," I repeated, turning toward Brenner. He dropped his eyes.

"It's a program," Cissy said carefully.

"A program for what?"

"For, uh, a fund-raiser."

"Specifically, the Carousel Auction Gala sponsored by the Friends of the Children's Hospital, correct?" Fortunately, the Ritz-Carlton had kept several copies of the program.

She shrugged, trying to sound offhand. "That's what it says."

"What's the date of the event?"

She looked at the program. "According to this thing, August fourteenth."

"According to that thing?" I repeated, incredulous. "You can surely do better than that, can't you. You were there, correct?"

She sat back with a frown, as if trying to remember. "I might have been. I can't recall for sure."

"Let me help you, then. Let's see if we can jog that foggy memory of yours."

Brenner leaped to his feet. "I object, Your Honor."

Judge Williams peered down at me over her reading glasses. "Sustained. Easy on the adjectives, Miss Gold."

"Your Honor," Brenner continued with an obsequious smile, "perhaps this would be a good time for a break."

I glanced at the clock. Ten minutes to twelve. "Judge," I said, "could I at least conclude this line of questioning? It won't take long, and then we can start on a new line after lunch."

Judge Williams nodded. "Proceed, Counsel."

I turned to Cissy, who was eyeing me warily. "Open that program to page five, Mrs. Robb." As she flipped to the page, I noted with satisfaction that Judge Williams had also turned to the same page of her copy. "Do you see the list of committee members for the event? Look in the second column, sixth name down. That's your name, right?"

"Yes," she said with a trace of disdain, "but that doesn't prove anything. I serve on committees for many worthwhile causes. That doesn't mean I have time to attend every single one of their events."

"Turn to page three."

She did. The Judge did. Milt Brenner did.

"You see that list of featured auction items? Do you see the fourth item? What is it?"

She looked up slowly, sensing for the first time that maybe, just maybe, she'd wandered into dangerous territory. "A Corvette."

I turned to my client. "Mr. Contini, could you set Exhibit H up on the easel."

All eyes in the courtroom watched him walk over to the side wall, where three poster-size objects wrapped in brown paper were leaning against the wall. The first one was marked in bold black marker Exhibit H. He brought it over and set it up on the easel facing the witness box and Judge Williams. Brenner got up and came around to watch.

"Mrs. Robb," I said, turning to her, "take a look at what I've marked Defendant's Trial Exhibit H."

I glanced over at Jacob Contini and nodded. He reached up and tore the brown wrapping off the poster board, revealing the enlarged side-by-side shot of the two cars in the Robbs' driveway. I leaned back on the edge of the table, crossed my arms over my chest, and waited.

Cissy stared intently at the photo, her brows knitted in concentration. You could almost hear those neurons firing. Eventually, she shifted her gaze to me.

"I remember now," she said with a frosty smile. "My husband and I attended that function."

"As a matter of fact, you bought the Corvette there, didn't you?"

She gave me a haughty look. "We didn't simply *buy* that car, Miss Gold. We acquired it in exchange for a very generous donation to a very worthy cause."

I couldn't help but smile. Might as well take a freebie. "A very worthy cause," I repeated as I came over to the witness box and took away the program. As I returned to counsel's table, I said, "And what exactly was that worthy cause?"

There was silence. I kept my back to her, waiting.

"Objection," Brenner finally said, scrambling to his feet. "Irrelevant."

I turned around. I'd already scored the point, as was clear from Judge Williams' efforts to keep a straight face.

"I'll withdraw the question, Your Honor." I turned to my client. "Mr. Contini, could you bring over Exhibit I?"

He walked back to the side wall and fetched the second wrapped poster. This one had Exhibit I printed in bold black letters on the brown paper.

I turned to the witness. "Do you recall the article on the charity event in that Sunday's *Post-Dispatch?*"

Cissy glanced uncertainly at her attorney and then back at me.

I sighed patiently. "Okay, let's see if we can refresh that memory again."

I nodded at Jacob Contini. He tore off the wrapping paper, revealing the blow-up of the society column from the Style Plus section of the Sunday, August 16th edition of the *Post-Dispatch*. This was one that Jacki had found for me. The blowup included the photograph of the two women standing in front of a carousel horse.

I pointed to the caption beneath the photograph. "Do you see this photo credit down here?"

Cissy leaned forward. "Yes," she said cautiously.

"Charles Morley," I read. Turning to her, I said, "Do you remember Mr. Morley?"

Uneasy, she shook her head. "I don't think so."

I turned toward the gallery. "He's out there. Charles," I called, "hold up your hand."

Self-consciously, Morley raised his hand.

I turned back to Cissy. "Remember him? He was there that night. For over an hour. Walking around among the guests, taking photographs." I paused. "*Lots* of photographs."

Her eyes darted between the photographer and me. "I—I don't remember."

"Really?" I gave her a look of mild disbelief. "You don't remember him taking *lots* of photographs?"

She looked at Brenner. I turned to look at him, too. He had a rigid smile that looked more like gas pains.

"Well?" I repeated.

"I—I don't—I'm not sure."

I turned to Jacob Contini. "I guess that means it's time for Exhibit J."

Jacob walked over to the wall and brought back the final wrapped poster. As he set it on the easel, I said to him, "Just a moment."

Rubbing my chin thoughtfully, I turned toward the dress hanging from the hook. Then I looked over at the shoes and the purse resting on the ledge in front of Cissy Robb. Her eyes were wide as her gaze kept shifting from me to the wrapped poster on the easel to her lawyer and back to me again.

"Let me move these to a better position," I said. I walked over to the dress and removed it from the hook. I carried it back to the easel and handed it to my client. "Jacob, could you stand with the dress on this side of the easel?"

"Certainly."

I walked over to Cissy, who leaned back as I approached. I picked up the fancy shoes and the handbag and carried them over to counsel's table, where I lined them up on the edge of the table near where Jacob was standing. Then I stepped back, like a set designer, to study the arrangement. As I did, I glanced at the clock on the back wall. 12:11. Perfect.

I turned back to the Judge with an apologetic smile. "Your Honor, I wonder if we could take a break. Before I move to the next line of inquiry, I would like to ask Mrs. Robb to put on the dress and the shoes."

Cissy's eyes widened.

Milt Brenner was up like a jack-in-the-box. "Actually, Your Honor, if we're taking a break perhaps we could make it for lunch as well."

Judge Williams looked up at the clock and then back down at me with a knowing smile. "Very well, Mr. Brenner. Court will be in recess until two o'clock. That should give the plaintiff ample time to eat her lunch and put on the dress and the shoes before she returns to the witness stand."

With a bang of her gavel, Judge Williams stood and left the bench. As soon as the door closed behind her, Jacob Contini came over and hugged me.

"Oh, Rachel, *mazel tov.* You were magnificent."

"Wait," I cautioned, "it's not over yet." I glanced nervously at the easel. "Excuse me a moment." I walked over to take down the wrapped poster board marked Exhibit J. I carried it over to the bailiff. "I need this locked up," I told him.

He was an elderly black man with a big paunch and a pleasant moon face. "Oh, that's okay, Miss Gold, we lock the courtroom doors during the lunch recess."

I leaned in close. "I can't leave it in here. I have to put it somewhere else."

He shrugged good-naturedly. "We can put it in the vault. Follow me."

The vault was three floors down, inside the office of the circuit clerk. Once I got Exhibit J safely stowed, I stopped at a pay phone outside the clerk's office to call Jacki.

"Oh, my God," she squealed, "tell me what's happening."

I filled her in on the morning's events.

"Oh, my God," she said, "what if it doesn't work?"

"I'll improvise."

"Improvise?" She sounded apoplectic.

"I don't know. I'll have her stand there in the outfit—make sure my witnesses get a good look at her. Maybe it'll jog their memories about what she wore that night. Don't worry, Jacki. I'll think of something."

I checked my watch when I got off the elevator. It was almost one o'clock. Although I didn't have an appetite, I could hear my mother's voice telling me I had to keep up my strength for the afternoon. *Also,* she would no doubt add, *you have guests, Doll Baby—your client, your client's wife, their son.*

Yes, Mother.

I headed back to the courtroom to gather the Contini clan for a lunch somewhere near the courthouse. As I pushed through the door, Jacob jumped to his feet. "Ah, Rachel, hurry. They're waiting for you in the judge's chambers."

I frowned. "Who's waiting?"

"Her lawyer and the judge. The clerk told me to send you back there immediately."

Thirty minutes later I emerged from Judge Williams's chambers and found Jacob pacing in the hallway while his wife and son watched from a bench.

He came dashing over. "Well?"

I smiled. "I have a new settlement proposal from them."

He straightened. "What now?"

"Twenty-five thousand dollars."

He snorted. "I wouldn't pay that woman a dime."

"And you won't. Their opening offer was to drop the lawsuit in exchange for your agreement to keep the settlement terms confidential. I told them you were willing to keep the terms confidential but that you expected to be reimbursed for your time and your legal fees. They offered a thousand. I demanded fifty. The judge convinced them to split the difference. I told them to wait while I sought your approval."

He gaped at me in astonishment. "*She* will pay *me* twenty-five thousand dollars?"

I nodded.

"And drop the lawsuit?"

I nodded again.

"Oh, my God," he mumbled. Then he stiffened, uncertain. "What are these confidential settlement terms?"

"One, we have to destroy all photographs of her, and, two, we can't let anyone know she paid you to get rid of the lawsuit."

There were tears in his eyes. "Rachel, I told you last Sunday that God smiles down upon you." He placed his hands on my shoulders and kissed my lightly on each cheek. "Thank you, my dear."

We drew up the settlement papers right there in the courtroom, and Jacob signed them before we left for a victory lunch at a nearby Italian restaurant. I called Jacki to have her join us for lunch. Milt Brenner promised to deliver a fully executed copy of the settlement agreement to the restaurant along with a certified check for $25,000. Both arrived during dessert. By then we were on our third bottle of Chianti.

"Ah," Jacob said with a wistful smile, "I have only one regret." He gazed at me across the table. "I wish I could have seen that woman's expression when you unveiled Exhibit J."

I glanced over at Jacki, who stifled a giggle. I turned to Jacob. "Then you have no regrets, Jacob. No one ever would have seen that exhibit."

Jacob frowned. "But it was the next one. It was on the easel. I put it there myself."

"If trial had resumed after lunch, the easel would have been empty."

Now he was baffled. "I don't understand."

"Can you keep a secret?" I asked.

"Certainly."

I looked around the table and leaned forward. "The photographer checked the other roll of film. He didn't have a single picture of her that night. Not one. Exhibit J was a blank piece of poster board."

Jacob looked at his wife and then back at me. "I don't understand."

"Have you ever played poker?"

He stared at me for a moment and then smiled. "Ah."

I pressed my index finger against my lips. *"Shhhh."*

STUART M. KAMINSKY is author of more than forty
mystery novels and an equal number of short stories
in addition to biographies and textbooks. He has
been nominated six times for the Mystery Writers of
America's prestigious Edgar Allen Poe Award, which
he won for best novel in 1989. His screen credits in-
clude *Once upon a Time in America, Enemy Territory,
A Woman in the Wind,* and *Hidden Fears.* He is the
director of the Sarasota Festival of Jewish Films.
"The Tenth Man" is a new story in the Abe Lieberman series.

The Tenth Man

▼　▼　▼　▼　▼　▼　▼　▼

STUART M. KAMINSKY

THE LITTLE OLD MAN WAS NODDING HIS HEAD and mumbling to himself as
he walked down the gray corridor of the synagogue. It was not an unusual
sight, but this particular old man was unfamiliar to Morrie Greenblatt, who
approached him.

Morrie towered over the old man, who wore a black yarmulke atop his
freckled, nearly bald head and a white-fringed tallis over his shoulders.
Under his arm the old man was carrying a black prayer book.

From the main sanctuary, the sound of voices, a man's and a woman's,
went back and forth nervously.

"Excuse me," said Morrie.

The old man stopped and looked up at the tall, slope-shouldered man
who had stopped him.

"We need you," Morrie said, glancing at his watch.

"Me?" asked the old man in a voice that sounded raspy from too many
hours of prayer.

"We need one more for the morning minyan," Morrie said. "A tenth man."

"But I . . . " the old man began, looking toward the main sanctuary.

"It won't take long. I promise. Prayers, and then if you have time we have

127

bagels and coffee. We need you. Sid Applebaum was supposed to be here but he has a stomach something and with the rain—"

"You need me?" the old man said.

"Yes."

The old man shrugged and said, "Then I'll come."

Ten Jewish men over the age of thirteen were required to meet the minimum number set forth in the Holy Bible for morning prayers. Morrie, who owned a bath and tile store on Lawrence Avenue, was the congregation's unofficial shammes, the one who saw to it that things got done.

No one, not even Morrie, was sure whether Morrie had volunteered for this job or if it had simply evolved. Morrie, now almost fifty, accepted the responsibility, the principle task of which was to see to it that there was a minyan for each morning's prayers.

The regulars, if they were healthy, were no problem. He could always count on Rabbi Wass and his son, Cal Schwartz, Marvin Stein, Hyman Lieberman, Joshua Kornpelt, Sid Applebaum, and himself. He would check the night before with phone calls and if it looked as if they would be short, Morrie would ask Marv Stein to bring his brother or Hy Lieberman to bring his sons. Some days they had as many as sixteen or more. Some days they had walk-ins who were from out of town or regular congregation members there to observe a *yahrzeit*, the anniversary of a loved one's death.

When he had counted this morning, Morrie had been sweating. Both of Lieberman's sons had come, looking none-too-happy to be there. Maish Lieberman explained that their father wasn't feeling well. Maish was thirty-four, and by this time in the early morning was usually at the T&L, the new deli he had opened with a loan from his father and Sid Applebaum. Abe, at thirty, was the puzzle of the lot. Short and lean like his father, with the same dark curly hair, Abe was a policeman who came to services only when his father pressured him into doing so. Just last week Abe had been promoted to detective and an unimposing detective he was, a shrimp beanstalk with a sad face too old for his years. A few minutes ago, Maish, his yarmulke perched precariously atop his head, had nodded and talked about the price of eggs and the courage of astronauts. Abe, in a sport jacket and tie, and looking like a shoe salesman, had politely asked Morrie, "You want me to call Alex?"

"I'll find someone," Morrie had answered. It was a matter of pride, but time was against him.

"Alex can be here in ten minutes," said Abe.

"I'll find," Morrie had repeated.

"Morrie, this is my third day on the job. I've got to be downtown in an hour and a half."

"You'll be there," Morrie assured him. "The bad guys'll wait."

"Bad guys don't wait," Abe said. "Let me call Alex."

"I'll find," Morrie repeated. "With God's help, I'll find."

Abe Lieberman had shrugged and moved over to talk to Rabbi Wass's son, who at the age of thirteen was almost as tall as the policeman. The boy wore thin glasses that kept creeping down his nose. A sudden jab and they were back up, ready to start slipping again.

Now, less than five minutes after he had left, Morrie entered the small chapel across from the central sanctuary and announced, "We have a minyan."

As Morrie ushered his treasured old man in, Marv Stein let out a loud sigh of relief. Marv was reliable, but he was also retired and had a tee-off time in a little more than an hour. God willing, the rain would stop.

"This is Mr . . . ," Morrie began.

"Green," the old man said taking Marvin's outstretched hand.

"Nice to meet you, Green," Marv said, and then added, "Let's get started."

The rabbi moved to the front of the small room, lectern before him, son at his side. The eight men and the rabbi's son sat in the chairs facing Rabbi Wass, a somber, clean-shaven man with well-trimmed white hair. To Abe, Wass looked like Lee J. Cobb with a stomachache.

Morrie smiled in relief, ready to lose himself in the comfort of daily prayer, looking forward to eating a poppy-seed bagel with cream cheese and arguing with Josh Kornpelt on some point about the U.S. role in Viet Nam or God's role in John Kennedy's murder or why none of the astronauts were Jewish. Astronauts were on everyone's mind. The first man, an American, was scheduled to land on the moon, walk on the moon in two days.

Green, the old man from the corridor, stood next to Morrie, who smiled at him. The Lieberman boys stood on the other side of the old man. Green gave a tentative smile back and the services began.

They didn't last long. Maybe five minutes. Maybe ten.

They were stopped by a loud, high-pitched raspy voice behind them. Not a shout, but a high-pitched insistent demand.

"Hold it," the man said.

Rabbi Wass stopped and looked up through the narrow aisle that separated the cluster of ten men.

All heads turned toward the man who had entered. They saw a tall man in dark pants and a black T-shirt. He was about forty, with long, uncombed dark hair and bad teeth. He was carrying a gun.

He didn't look like an Arab. Morrie concluded that he was a drugged-out wanderer who was there to rob them. Just so he wasn't an Arab terrorist.

"We are at prayer," said Rabbi Wass, guiding his son, who had run to his side, behind him.

"You think I'm fucking blind?" said the man, pointing his gun at the rabbi. "I can see what you're doing. I know where I'm at. I didn't think I was at the damned Dominick's Supermarket or some shit."

The gunman shook his head and looked around at the men who had turned to face him. There was no doubt that the intruder was drunk, on drugs, or insane, possibly all three.

"You can have our money," Rabbi Wass said calmly.

"I know I can have your money," the tall man said, closing the door behind him. "I can have your money, your shirts, your shoes. I can have your goddamn lives."

He looked into each face before him, growing more agitated.

"I don't want your goddamn money," he said, willing himself, without success, to be calm. "Maybe I just want to come in here and let you know Jesus is coming and your asses are not getting into heaven. Don't matter how much you pray. You're going to hell."

"We shall take your opinion for what it is worth," said the rabbi, who had now completely shielded his son with his body.

"You're boning me," said the man with the gun.

"Boning you?" asked the rabbi.

"Making fun of me."

"I'm not in a position to make fun of you," said the rabbi.

"You're goddamn straight not in a position," the man said. "You are not in a position. Which one of you is Lee-burr-man?"

"Why?" asked the rabbi.

"I don't have to tell you why," the man said, stepping down the aisle. "I've got the gun. Just which one of you is Lieberman?"

"What do you want with Mr. Lieberman?" asked the rabbi.

The man with the gun shook his head.

"What do I want with him? I want to blow his damn head off. That's what

I want with him. Now let's get it down and done with and I'll get out of here."

"Why?" asked Rabbi Wass.

Someone was praying softly. Cal Schwartz. Cal was over eighty. His eyes were closed and he was gently swaying.

"What's he saying?" the gunman demanded.

"It's Hebrew," said Morrie. "He is saying that God is Almighty. That there is but one God and that His will *will* be done."

"Jesus, you people," said the gunman. "Lieberman, which one are you?"

"Why do you want to kill Mr. Lieberman?" asked Rabbi Wass again.

"Okay," said the man. "I got out of prison last week. I went home. I found out my little brother was dead. Over a year dead. A cop named Lieberman had shot him when Lance was just minding his own business. They kept it from me, told me Lance was away or some shit. Then I find out. I ask my mom where's Lance and she says, 'Connie, he was killed by some Jew in a uniform, killed for doing nothing, for being in the wrong place minding his own business.'"

"What makes you think Lieberman is here?" asked the Rabbi.

"Because I'm no fucking dummy," said the man, tapping the barrel of his gun against the side of his head. "He's right in the phone book. I went to his apartment, brushed my hair back, smiled, and said to the pregnant girl who opened the door that I was an old friend of Lieberman. She told me he was here. Short walk. Big gun."

"I'm Lieberman," Abe said.

"I'm Lieberman," Maish said.

And, not to be outdone and having seen *Spartacus* twice, Morrie said, "I'm Lieberman."

Then, one by one, even Mr. Green who had been brought in as a stray from the hall, identified himself as Lieberman. The only ones who didn't were the rabbi and his son.

"All right, then," the man with the gun said, "I can shoot all of you."

"You ever shoot anyone, Connie?" asked Abe.

The man looked at him, cocked his head to one side, and leveled the gun toward the thin young man who had asked the question.

"If there's got to be a first time," the man said. "It should be for good reason. I've got good reason."

"To kill eight, ten people?" asked Maish.

"If need be," said the gunman. "If need be."

"And if we rush you?" asked Kornpelt. "We get you. You shoot one, maybe two of us, and you probably don't get Lieberman. The electric chair or life in jail is what you'll get."

"You're Lieberman," the gunman said to Marvin Kornpelt.

"I already told you I was," said Marvin.

The gunman was looking decidedly nervous now, his fingers clasping and unclasping the weapon in his head.

"I'll start with you," he said to Maish. "I shoot you. Odds are I've got the right guy. If not, Lieberman can let me know now who he is. How about them apples, Lieberman? I'm going to shoot big mouth now unless you step up like a man."

Maish tried to move past his brother to the gunman. Abe barred his way with his hand and stepped past Mr. Green and Morrie into the narrow aisle between the chairs.

"If you shoot any one of us," Abe said. "We'll all tell you that you shot Abe Lieberman. And we may be telling you the truth. Odds are eight to one you're wrong. Or maybe you're right. You kill another one of us and you still won't know. You said we're all going to hell. What about you? You kill innocent people and Jesus'll take you to heaven on a big white bird?"

"I'll repent," the gunman said.

"You'll be lying," said Lieberman. "You think Jesus won't know you're lying?"

"Shut up," shouted the gunman, pushing the gun inches from Abe's nose. "I'm starting with you. Right now."

"I'm Lieberman," Abe said.

"You're a smart-ass Jew, probably a lawyer."

"I'm Lieberman," Abe repeated.

"You armed?" the man answered.

"We don't wear guns in the synagogue," said the rabbi.

"You have a last name, Connie?" asked Lieberman. "If you're going to shoot me, I think I've got the right to know your name."

"You have the right? And what right did Lance have? You're Lieberman? Prove it."

The solution to this confused man's problem was evident to Morrie. Just tell everyone to pull out his wallet and show his driver's license. But Connie the gunman, Connie the intruder, was clearly not operating within the realm of reason.

The gun was now aimed at Lieberman's right eye. Lieberman blinked wearily.

"Your brother Lance had just beaten a pharmacist nearly to death. Your brother Lance had a Kmart bag full of money and drugs in one hand and a gun bigger than yours in the other. The pharmacist hit the alarm before he passed out. My partner and I got there as your brother was coming out of the store. He shot at us. We shot back."

"Bullshit and a half," the gunman sputtered, his face turning crimson. "Bullshit and a half. Lance was a good kid."

"The pharmacist nearly died. He still can't talk so you can understand him," said Lieberman.

"I will have my revenge. A life for a life."

"I prefer live and let live," said Lieberman. "Or 'Vengeance is Mine,' saith the Lord."

"I know the Good Book from cover to cover and back again," the gunman said. "I had seven years behind the walls. I read it. Now, I've made a promise to myself, to Jesus, to my dead brother. I made a vow. Moses said, 'If a man vow a vow unto the Lord, or swear an oath to bind his soul with a bond, he shall not break his word, he shall do all that proceedeth out of his mouth.'" The gunman looked around the men proudly. He could outdo these Jews with his eyes closed, outdo them with their own Bible.

"I took an oath," he said. "And I mean to keep it."

"'But if any man hate his neighbor, and lie in wait for him and rise up against him, and smite him mortally that he die, and fleeth into one of these cities," said Rabbi Wass, "then the elders of his city shall send and fetch him thence, and deliver him into the hand of the avenger of blood, that he may die.'"

"Amen," said Morrie.

"Connie, let's go outside," Lieberman said to the gunman.

"Here suits me just fine," the man said. "I'm going to blow your head off right here. Mess up your walls and all of your memories, the way I'm messed up about Lance."

Lieberman was in the aisle facing the man. Something touched Lieberman's back. He reached back slowly, keeping his sad eyes on those of the man with the gun whose bad breath wasn't overridden by the smell of alcohol.

"Mortal sin going down here," said Lieberman, taking from Maish's hand whatever it was he had poked Lieberman with.

"Maybe. Maybe not. That's the future," the man spat. "This is now. I'll be here tomorrow. You won't. I saw on the TV we're putting a man on the moon in a couple of days. Going to be right there live on television. Let me ask you. Are they sending NB fucking C TV up there to the moon? What the hell will you care? You'll be dead like my brother."

"One of the other astronauts, Collins, Murphy, something," said Morrie. "He'll have a camera."

The gunman's face was inches from Abe's now. He whispered, "Won't that be something to miss?"

The gunman saw a movement over Lieberman's shoulder. He stepped to the side just in time to see the rabbi's son duck through a door behind his father and slam it shut.

"Shit. *Shit,*" said the gunman, shaking his head. "Now I gotta hurry. I didn't want to hurry. I wanted to stretch this, make you sweat, beg."

"We don't beg," said Maish.

"Give me the gun, Connie," said Abe wearily. "We've got a service to finish. We all have to get to work or home to our families."

The gunman stepped back, shaking his head and smiling. Then he started to laugh. "You got balls for a Jew. I give you that. But you'll be making 'em laugh in hell in a minute."

Lieberman pulled his hand from behind his back, holding the gun that Maish had pressed into it. The gun was small. Abe hoped it was loaded.

"Give me the gun," Abe repeated.

The gunman's mouth dropped open. He looked from the gun to the sad face of the thin policeman.

"Like hell," he said leveling his own weapon at Abe Lieberman. "Looks like we're in for stormy weather."

"I'm not waiting for it," said Lieberman. "Give me the gun."

"Can you beat that?" Connie the gunman asked, looking around at the frightened faces of the men about him. "Can you beat that? Hell, I might as well shoot. Maybe we'll both die. No way I'm going back inside the walls, back inside and no evening up for my brother."

"Suit yourself," said Abe, unsure of the weapon in his hand, concerned that a wild bullet might kill someone else in the small sanctuary.

"A suggestion," said Rabbi Wass behind Abe.

"It better be a goddamn good one," said the gunman, looking into Lieberman's eyes. "We got ourselves one hell of a situation here and running out of time."

"You put down your gun," Rabbi Wass said. "And Detective Lieberman lets you walk out. We all pretend you were never here. We thank God for having saved us and we pray to him to have mercy on you."

"And he'll have mercy on me, your God?"

Rabbi Wass shrugged.

"Our God will do whatever He wants to do. We ask. He does what He wants to do."

"Very damn reassuring," the gunman said. "Makes me feel all safe and comfortable. The hell with it."

He raised his weapon at Abe, who did the same to him.

"Let's get it on," the gunman said.

"You're *shikkered*," said Marv. "Drunk."

"If I wasn't, I couldn't be doing this," the man shouted.

"I'm going to shoot you in the eye," said Lieberman. "The right eye. That should be very painful, but it should work. You're shaking. You can't shoot straight, and I'd say you haven't spent any time on the range. I've got a good chance of living and you've got a sure chance of dying. Think about it."

The gun wavered in the man's hand. He chewed on his lower lip and considered his fate.

"Hell," he said with a sigh. "I can't see Lance coming in here and doing this for me. He was always a selfish little prick, but don't tell my mom I said it."

He backed toward the door.

"Stop," said Lieberman. "Drop the gun."

The man turned his weapon quickly away from Abe, aiming it at Rabbi Wass.

"I'm going," he said. "Or I'm going to kill a priest."

"I'm a rabbi," said Rabbi Wass. "We haven't had priests for almost two thousand years."

Odds were, Lieberman calculated, that at this distance and shaking drunk the man with the gun might not hit Rabbi Wass. But then again, he might.

Abe watched as the man stepped back to the door through which he had come, fumbled at the handle, and opened it.

"Forget I was here," he said. "I'll find a better time." He was looking at Abe now. "I'll come back sober. I'll come to your apartment. Your wife's got a baby growing in her. I'll come and pay your family a visit. Think about that

. . . . Lance wasn't much but he was my brother and I got to live with myself."

"Who says?" said Morrie.

The man with the gun went through the door and slammed it behind him.

Abe ran to the door, hearing the voices behind him, hearing his brother shout, "Abe, wait."

Abe didn't wait. He went through the door. The gunman was running awkwardly down the synagogue's hallway toward the front door. Across the hall, the door to the main sanctuary was open. A group of men and women were talking in front of the small platform, the *bimah,* setting up flowers. One of the women turned and looked at Lieberman and the gun in his hand.

Abe, tallis flying like a cape, yarmulke held down by his free hand, charged after the fleeing man, who was now out the door and into the morning. The man looked back before running to his left and falling momentarily out of sight. Abe followed into a light morning drizzle.

The man was running more slowly now, drunk, out of shape. He looked back at Abe, who leveled his weapon. There was no one on the street. People inside the houses adjoining the synagogue were just waking up. Abe was aware of a few cars moving down the street.

"Stop," Abe called, not exactly a shout, more like a resigned call.

The man stumbled forward, turned, and fired a shot that went in the general direction of the dark clouds. Abe fired back. The bullet from the small gun hit the concrete sidewalk a few feet behind the now gasping man.

The man turned, breathing heavily, and lifted his gun. It was hard to read the look on his face—confusion, hate, maybe a little self-pity. Abe fired again and the man tripped backward and fell, his gun leaping from his hand and skittering down the sidewalk away from him.

Abe stepped forward and stood over the fallen man.

"My leg," he said. "Damn, I picked the wrong day to do this."

"Want your gun back?" Abe said, evenly aiming his weapon at the man's face.

"My gun? I want an ambulance, a doctor. You shot me in the goddamn leg. I'm bleeding to death."

"I'll give you your gun back and shoot you in the face if that will make you feel better," said Abe, hearing voices behind him coming out of the synagogue. "No more pain."

"A doctor," the man said.

Abe knelt next to the man and said, "I'm not a religious man, but that—" he said, glancing back at the synagogue, "—is where my father and brother pray, where my friends and their families feel safe. You made it dirty. You went to where I live and you came here and threatened my wife and unborn baby. I take umbrage at that. Can you blame me?"

The man, looking up at him, shook his head.

Footsteps were moving quickly toward the detective and the gunman now.

"I'm calling an ambulance and I'm having you booked and if I ever see you again when you get out the next time," said Abe, "I will kill you on sight. You understand? No questions. No discussions. I'll kill you."

The man nodded, looking over Lieberman's shoulder at the men hurrying toward them, tallises flying, a flock of Jew birds swooping down on their prey.

"I understand," the man said, closing his eyes. "It hurts. It goddamn hurts."

"It's supposed to. It'll hurt for a few years," said Lieberman standing. "Then it'll go away. One more thing, Connie. I didn't shoot your brother. I was there but another cop did it."

"Why didn't you just say that in there?" the man groaned.

"Would you have believed me?"

"No," said the man, gritting his teeth, blood streaming from his leg.

"You believe me now?"

"No. Yes. I don't know. My leg."

"Abe," Maish called behind him. "Are you all right?"

"Fine," said Abe, moving to pick up the gunman's fallen weapon by the barrel. "Someone call an ambulance and the police."

"My son already called the police," said Rabbi Wass.

"I'll call an ambulance," said Morrie, scurrying back to the synagogue.

Abe looked at the men who had come to help him, Josh Kornpelt, Marv Stein, and behind them old Cal Schwartz and the tenth man Morrie had pulled from the corridor, Mr. Green. They were shuffling forward, clutching their prayer books. Rabbi Wass moved to the fallen, moaning intruder.

"A gun in the synagogue?" Abe said to his brother reproachfully.

"When did I ever have a gun?" Maish said, pointing to himself, his droopy face looking hurt.

"It's mine," said Green.

"He handed it to me," said Maish. "I passed it to you."

Abe looked at the old man.

"You have a permit for this?"

"I was a cop," said Green. "Long time ago, but I was a cop. I got a permit."

Abe was about to ask another question when he saw a tall, thin woman in her late thirties come running out of the synagogue, holding a black hat on her head with the palm of her hand. The woman was heading for the men and screaming, "Pop."

They all turned to watch her join them. Her hair was red, her eyes green and frightened. She looked at Abe, who held two guns, at the fallen man, and at Mr. Green.

"I'm a police officer," Abe said.

"He is," said Rabbi Wass.

"Pop," the woman said to Green. "What's going on? What happened to you? You go to the bathroom and get lost and then I find you out on the street with guns."

"They needed me," said Green.

"For what?" she asked. "We're here for Dolly's son's confirmation."

"Bar mitzvah," said Marvin. "It's called a bar mitzvah."

"That's why we're here," she said, ignoring Marvin.

"I know," said Green. "But they needed me."

"For what?" the woman demanded.

"Prayers," Green said proudly. "They need ten men for prayers."

"They need ten Jews for prayers, Pop. Ten *Jews*. You're Catholic."

"They needed me."

"My father's name is Patrick Ryan Green," the woman said in exasperation to the men around her as the drizzle stopped. "He doesn't count."

"I think he does," said Maish.

"Let's get to Dolly's boy's confir . . . bar mitzvah," she said, taking her father's arm and leading him back toward the synagogue.

The man stopped abruptly and faced Abe.

"Is it always like this?" Patrick Green asked.

"Not always," said Abe.

"When are you doing it again?"

"Tomorrow," said Maish.

"Can I come back?" asked Green.

"Anyone's welcome," said Marvin.

"Amen," said Cal Schwartz.

"Pop," the woman said, rolling her eyes and leading her father away.

"I'll get the gun back to you," called Abe. "Thanks."

Green looked over his shoulder, smiled, and said, "I'll pick it up tomorrow."

ROCHELLE KRICH (www.rochellekrich.com) won the Anthony Award for *Where's Mommy Now?*, filmed as *Perfect Alibi*. She is the author of five stand-alone thrillers, including *Speak No Evil* and *Fertile Ground,* and a mystery series featuring LAPD homicide detective Jessica Drake, who is exploring her newly discovered Judaism while solving crimes. Her novel *Dead Air* features Jessie Drake, as does the most recent book in this series, *Shadows of Sin*.

Bitter Waters

▼   ▼   ▼   ▼   ▼   ▼   ▼

ROCHELLE KRICH

REUBEN STOOD ON THE FLAGSTONE PATIO, nursing a glass of wine, and watched his wife float among the guests near the pool. There was something extraordinarily graceful and at the same time sensuous about the way she lifted her hand, about her posture, about the tilt of her golden head. He willed her to look at him and was pleased when she suddenly met his eyes. She flashed a shy smile before she turned—reluctantly, it seemed to him—to the woman with whom she was talking, and he could see the pink tinting her skin, luminous under the light, reflected from the moon and the lanterns spaced around the garden.

"Great party," said his twin brother, Jonathan, saluting Reuben with a wine glass as he walked toward him. "And Isabelle has done wonders with the house. I'm ready to hire her to do mine, if that's okay with you."

"Of course." Reuben felt expansive, and his chest puffed with pride. "I have to warn you, though—she has a long waiting list of clients."

"Isabelle is worth waiting for." Jonathan gazed at her. "She looks particularly beautiful tonight."

"Yes, she does."

The ankle-length burgundy silk dress was a striking contrast to her delicate ivory complexion, and to the blond hair she'd worn in a chignon to

141

please him. He liked the fact that her upswept hair exposed her bare shoulders and the long, slender column of her neck, shoulders and neck that only he could kiss.

"There's a real glow about her," Jonathan said. "I guess it's true what they say about pregnancy. Congratulations, Reuben." He punched him lightly on his arm.

Reuben swiveled toward his brother, sloshing the wine in the crystal goblet. "Isabelle told you?" he asked with forced casualness.

"Don't be upset." Jonathan smiled, amused by his brother's discomfiture. "I saw her at the Ivy the other day. She was coming out of the restroom and looked pale and shaky. I was worried and insisted on driving her home, so she *had* to tell me. Mom and Dad will be thrilled. When are you planning to let them know?"

"Not for a while. Isabelle hasn't even seen a doctor yet." The results of the home pregnancy test had been positive, though. "But I guess she told you all that."

"Actually, she didn't say much. I think she was nervous about how I'd react. But seeing you together in your new home—it feels right, Reuben." Jonathan squeezed Reuben's shoulder. "And Isabelle's obviously crazy about you, though I can't figure out why." He laughed. "I'm happy for you, bro. For you and Isabelle."

"That means a great deal to me." Reuben heard his own clipped tone and wished he didn't sound so stiff. Jonathan had obviously taken pleasure in revealing Isabelle's breach, a pleasure enhanced by Reuben's reaction.

Jonathan lifted his glass. "To your happiness with Isabelle, and to the baby." He clinked the crystal against Reuben's goblet and took a sip. Reuben did the same. "I'm going to spread the Bruckner charm." Jonathan flicked the front of Reuben's shirt and smiled. "I suggest you change. It's not seemly for the host to go around with a wine-stained shirt."

Reuben frowned at the shirtfront. He was annoyed with the smile, which was really more of a smirk, and with the condescension he detected in his brother's voice. "Tell Isabelle I'll be right back, would you?"

"Don't worry, I'll take care of her until you return."

Was Jonathan mocking him? Walking through the open French doors into the family room, Reuben stopped to greet several guests, glancing behind him toward the pool as he did so. Jonathan had placed his hand on Isabelle's shoulder. She turned and looked at Reuben. Anxiously, he thought.

Upstairs in the master bedroom suite, he ripped off the offending custom-made shirt, sending two buttons flying, then balled it up and hurled it into the corner. Jonathan had definitely been smirking—just as he had at the wedding. The rabbi officiating under the *chuppah* had spilled red wine on Isabelle's gown. Club soda had removed most of the evidence, but Reuben, who was a perfectionist, had been upset, more so than Isabelle or her mother. Jonathan, handsome and dignified and aloof in his tuxedo, had shaken Reuben's hand and planted a chaste kiss on Isabelle's cheek. And he had smirked, no doubt pleased with the mishap. Sour grapes, because he'd had every expectation of being Isabelle's groom. Well, the better man had won.

Reuben supposed he should feel guilty—if he hadn't stolen Isabelle, Jonathan would probably be producing the first Bruckner heir. But Jonathan didn't seem to be carrying a grudge, and his toast had sounded sincere.

That was disappointing, Reuben admitted to himself as he buttoned a fresh, crisply starched shirt. In his heart Reuben knew Isabelle's initial allure had been the fact that Jonathan had chosen her. "You always want what Jonathan has," his mother had told him several times, and there was truth to that.

The brothers had been fiercely competitive, though Jonathan pretended otherwise, and Reuben had been driven to succeed because he wanted to best his brother, who was older by five minutes. He had done so only once—*he* had been valedictorian, not Jonathan, at the private college they'd both attended. He had earned his MBA from Wharton, while Jonathan had earned the same degree from Kellogg—a tie, in Reuben's opinion. In three years Reuben had built up a technology company whose shares were worth a hundred eighty dollars on the market. Last week the shares of Jonathan's rival company had topped two fifty. And while Reuben had outbid his brother for this two-story Beverly Hills mansion, Jonathan had found a larger, more beautiful home, just a few blocks away but with a more impressive address, because it was north of Sunset Boulevard.

And then there was Isabelle. Capturing her away from Jonathan had given Reuben a heady rush of sweet success, and though he had come to truly love her, he would have preferred a heart-broken Jonathan, pining for his lost love, to a forgiving brother whose benevolence and magnanimousness grated.

He couldn't help wondering whom Jonathan would marry. She would be beautiful and accomplished, of course. She would have to outshine

Isabelle in looks and class—that would be Jonathan's revenge. Reuben had been steeling himself for that moment, though he told himself he didn't really care. Jonathan could choose the most exquisite woman in the world, and that wouldn't diminish Reuben's feelings for Isabelle. True, he'd felt the bitter taste of soured pleasure with the business and the house after Jonathan had outshone him; with so many other events, large and small, that had pricked at him throughout his life. But this was his wife, not a company or a car or an art collection. He truly loved her.

It surprised him that his brother had waited this long to marry. Reuben and Isabelle's wedding had taken place a year and a half ago, but Jonathan didn't seem to be in a rush to find the perfect woman, or to race to sire the first Bruckner grandchild.

Reuben had been brooding about that. Why not? he wondered again. *Why not?*

He slipped the onyx-and-diamond links, a gift from Isabelle, into his cuffs and pondered the smirk again. And then he had an appalling thought. *Maybe Jonathan wasn't looking because he didn't have to.* The notion made his heart pound and brought beads of sweat to the skin above his thin lips.

"Isabelle is worth waiting for," Jonathan had said. "I'll take care of Isabelle until you return," he'd promised. And he'd placed his hand familiarly on her shoulder, touched her bare skin as if he had the right, as if he did so all the time.

Maybe he did.

Reuben told himself he was being ridiculous. Isabelle loved him. She was carrying their child. Not fifteen minutes ago she had looked at him adoringly, basking in his admiration.

Or maybe she'd been looking at Jonathan. That would explain the shyness, the guilty blush, the anxious look he'd caught just before coming upstairs. She had told Jonathan about the baby and hadn't revealed the admission to Reuben.

Why not, unless she felt guilty? Unless the baby, the first Bruckner grandchild, was Jonathan's, not his? They were probably laughing at him right now.

Reuben finishing dressing and went downstairs.

"I'm tormented," Reuben told the lean-faced rabbi who had spilled the wine on Isabelle's gown. "I don't sleep well. I'm not able to function at work."

Everyone had noticed. During the past few weeks he'd been snapping at the staff. Morale was down; productivity, too. Some days he felt like walking away and never coming back.

The rabbi stroked his graying goatee. "If you'll pardon my frankness, Reuben, why have you come to me? I've known Isabelle since she was a child, but I've met you only twice—under the wedding canopy, and once before that."

"I'm not a man of faith," Reuben admitted without apology. "But I'm troubled and I need help. Isabelle told me she's been talking to you." A lie. The private detective he'd hired had told him. "I thought you could help me, too. We're having problems."

"I can't discuss what Isabelle has confided in me."

"She's having an affair with my brother." Reuben paused to let the words take effect, but saw no reaction in the rabbi's liquid brown eyes. "I'm sure of it, but I don't have proof. I need to know."

The detective had reported Isabelle's frequent visits to Jonathan's home—twice at night—when Reuben had gone out of town for several days, to test her. Isabelle had mentioned the evening meetings to Reuben. Business dinners, she'd told him, so clever in her seeming candor, and how could he complain? He'd urged her to take Jonathan on as a client, expecting her to refuse. That had been the first test, and she'd failed it. Reuben hadn't confronted her about the affair—he wouldn't give her or Jonathan the satisfaction—but he was no longer taken in by her duplicity. He wondered how he'd ever been fooled, how he had missed the truth. Love is blind, he comforted his wounded pride.

The rabbi looked pained. "My conversations with Isabelle are confidential, but I think you're jumping to false conclusions. Why don't both of you come in together, and perhaps I can help you begin to communicate."

The rabbi knew—he was equivocating. Reuben shook his head. "Isabelle won't admit the truth. But it's clear she no longer loves me. She used to be so affectionate. Now she's awkward around me and avoids me." And there was guilt in her eyes. How was it that he hadn't seen it till now? And hadn't she betrayed before, leaving Jonathan for another?

The rabbi looked at him with pity. "Love can't thrive under a cloud of suspicion, Reuben."

"I could divorce her, but what if I'm wrong?" Reuben said, as if the rabbi hadn't spoken. "What if the baby *is* really mine?" That would be just like

Jonathan, he thought with a surge of anger, to poison his mind against Isabelle so that Reuben would divorce her. To ruin Reuben's life.

The rabbi sighed. "I have no answers that will satisfy you. You need counseling, Reuben, if you want to save your marriage."

"I need to *know*." Reuben clenched his teeth so hard that they hurt. "I can't live like this. You're a rabbi. There must be a way for a husband to *know*."

"In biblical times, yes." The rabbi nodded. "The Torah talks about a *sotah*—a woman whose husband suspects her of infidelity. He has no proof. If he had proof, he would have to divorce her. But he suspects."

Reuben was intrigued. Desperate hope filled his heart. "What does he do?"

The rabbi shook his head. "Get counseling, Reuben. Talk to Isabelle."

Sotah, Reuben said as he walked down the street to his car.

Locking himself in his office later that day, he thumbed through an English translation of the Pentateuch that he'd picked up in the Fairfax Avenue Judaica store where he'd gone with his mother and Jonathan to buy prayer shawls for their joint bar mitzvahs sixteen years ago. The shop clerk, a clean-shaven, erudite young man in his twenties, had found and marked with a red ribbon the section Reuben wanted: a portion titled *Naso* in the Book of Numbers.

"Any man whose wife shall go astray and commit treachery against him," Reuben read aloud, his heart breaking at the simple truth of the words, "and a man could have lain with her carnally, but it was hidden from the eyes of her husband, and she became secluded and could have been defiled—but there was no witness against her, and she had not been forced. And a spirit of jealousy had passed over him and he had warned his wife. . . . "

Yes, a spirit of jealousy! Reuben's eyes filled with tears of relief. Someone understood! Someone else was familiar with the invisible vapor Reuben inhaled with every waking breath, a vapor that assumed a leering, gleeful shape as it snaked its way into his head and around his heart and soul, a phantom that kept him up nights whispering, whispering, planting images in his eyes of Isabelle and Jonathan that made him want to weep and squeeze the life out of her lovely neck until she would confess. All those afternoons and evenings that she'd spent alone with Jonathan—*and she became secluded and could have been defiled!* There were probably other times the detective didn't know about.

"The man shall bring his wife to the *Kohen*," Reuben continued, recognizing from his childhood the Hebrew word for "priest," "and he shall bring her offering for her, a tenth-ephah of barley flour; he shall not pour oil over it and shall not put frankincense upon it, for it is a meal-offering of jealousies, a meal-offering of remembrance, a reminder of iniquity."

Coarse barley flour, Reuben learned from the commentaries, because she had behaved coarsely; barley, usually used to feed animals, because she had been an animal in her behavior, shameless in her nakedness, rutting like a pig on the designer sheets covering Jonathan's bed. There would be no frankincense to beautify the offering, no perfume like the one Reuben, stealing upstairs last week into his brother's bedroom, had detected when he'd pressed his face against the silk pillows his wife had chosen and sniffed her scent.

The *Kohen*, Reuben read, would take sacred water in an earthenware vessel and mix into it earth from the floor of the Tabernacle. Uncovering the woman's hair, he would place the meal-offering of remembrance on her hands while he held the vessel with the "bitter waters that cause a curse." Not bitter of themselves, the commentaries added, but bitter for the wife if she is guilty.

The *Kohen* would administer an oath to the woman, whose consequences she accepted: if she had not committed adultery, the bitter waters would have no effect. But if she was guilty, Reuben read with growing fascination and dread, the waters would cause her "stomach to distend and her thigh to collapse. And the woman would respond 'Amen, amen.'"

Reuben blanched, picturing Isabelle's beautiful body distorted. And what about Jonathan? he wondered angrily. Jonathan was the seducer! Reuben took comfort in learning from the commentary that the same fate would befall the guilty woman's partner in adultery.

After administering the oath, the *Kohen* would write the words of the oath onto parchment and erase the oath, including God's sacred name, into the bitter waters. The *Kohen* then placed the meal-offering on the altar and gave the woman the bitter waters. And she was proven either innocent or guilty.

Like Isabelle. Reuben smelled the musk of deception when he held her, tasted betrayal on her beautifully shaped lips. But what if he were wrong? He needed concrete proof, stronger than what any detective could provide.

He needed God.

He bought a bag of barley flour at a pet food store. He didn't know the equivalent of the tenth of an ephah, and neither did the young man in the Judaica store. Reuben didn't want to ask Isabelle's rabbi, so he chose a synagogue from the Yellow Pages and spoke to the rabbi, who told him the equivalent was approximately five pounds. A heavy amount, and Reuben remembered reading that the *Kohen* placed the meal-offering in the suspect wife's hands to encumber her and make her confused to the point that if guilty, she would confess. He was quite certain Isabelle wouldn't confess. He'd given her several openings, all of which she'd ignored.

He would have to make substitutions, of course. There was no Temple, no sacred water or laver, no *Kohen* to present the meal-offering at the holy altar or to write and administer the oath. And he couldn't ask Isabelle to participate with full knowledge in this trial-by-water. He had caught her staring at him more than once, a curious look on her face, and only yesterday she had urged him to see a doctor.

"You don't look well, Reuben," she had told him, pretending to care. "You're not yourself. Please tell me what's wrong."

She would laugh at him at first, then call him crazy. Maybe that was the plan, Reuben thought—to drive him insane with jealousy and have him committed. Jonathan's idea, not hers. He couldn't believe Isabelle could be that cruel—but then, what did he really know about her?

So he would have to improvise and conceal, as well as substitute. But God knew his intention was worthy. God would understand.

In the evening, wearing a navy jacquard silk robe (his most priestly garment—it would have to do), he lit the logs in the living room's marble-faced fireplace and went into his office. With painstaking care, calling on skills he'd abandoned after his bar mitzvah along with the fringed prayer shawl, he picked up a fountain pen and began copying the *Kohen*'s oath onto a sheet of parchment he'd bought at an art store. He had practiced earlier on plain paper at his downtown office, but his hand shook now as he formed the letters.

The first attempt was embarrassing. Jonathan would have done better, he knew. Red-faced, though no one was around to witness his clumsy effort, Reuben tossed the crumpled parchment into the trash can at the side of his desk and pulled over a fresh sheet. His hand was surer this time, and he was pleased as he inked the Hebrew words. Now he had to scribe God's sacred name. The rabbi who had explained about the ephah had told Reuben that God had several sacred names, and why was he asking?

Reuben had told him he was curious.

"One isn't allowed to use God's sacred name in vain," the rabbi had cautioned, his voice almost melodramatic.

Reuben had returned to the Judaica bookstore and searched through several texts on mysticism until he found what he wanted. Now, his hand poised over the parchment, he reflected and chose.

When he was done, he waved the parchment to help dry the ink. For a fleeting moment he wondered whether the words would fly off the paper. That would be a sign that he shouldn't continue, he decided. But of course, the words were there, thick and bold against the parchment.

After testing the leg of the first letter, he took an ink eraser and abraded the letters, one by one, into a glass of red wine into which he'd stirred some earth from the garden. Wine was fair, he'd decided. Wine was sacramental, and God couldn't expect him to find sacred water or to convince Isabelle to imbibe something in which she saw particles. And though Isabelle didn't know about the erased oath, God knew. That was what counted.

Isabelle had been resting, but she joined him in the living room when he asked. The morning sickness was taking its toll, and she looked pale, but to Reuben her pallor and the hollowness in her cheeks only accentuated her fragile, delicate beauty. Jonathan probably thought so, too.

"You've started a fire," she noted with pleased surprise. "That's so romantic, Reuben." Drawing close, she linked her arms around his neck and kissed him.

"The altar of our love," Reuben said, his lips an inch away from her treacherous ones. He took a step backward out of the seductive prison of her arms. "Close your eyes, Isabelle, and give me your hands."

"A gift?" she asked with the ingenuous delight that had always charmed him. "But it's not my birthday or anything."

"Close your eyes and you'll see."

She did as he asked. When he placed a barley-filled plastic bag in each upturned palm, she opened her eyes and looked at him, disappointed and puzzled. "Is this a game?"

"A ritual." *Whore,* he thought as he smiled. "I read about it in a book. We pledge our love and drink to it."

Isabelle crinkled her lovely brow. "What's in the bags? They're heavy, Reuben."

"Barley flour. For all the blessings of the earth, for an easy pregnancy and delivery. That's why you hold the bags. We pledge our love and fidelity, and put the barley flour on the fire. If our love is true, our offering is accepted. And if not . . . "

"It seems so pagan." Isabelle tilted her head. "What book did you find this in?"

"What's the difference? I'll go first." He cleared his throat. "I love you, Isabelle. I will always love you."

"I feel silly."

"Come on," he coaxed. "What can it hurt?"

"Okay." Her uneasy laugh tinkled. "I love you, Reuben. I will always love you. These bags are so *heavy*." She made a motion to sit on the white brocade sofa.

He held her elbow. Liar, he thought. "We have to stand," he said, filtering impatience from his voice. "I love only you, Isabelle. I swear I have been faithful to you in that love. Since we were joined, I have never been with another. Your turn."

She frowned. "I don't like this."

"It's no big deal, Isabelle. Why should saying you've been faithful bother you? It's true, isn't it?"

"Of *course* it's true." Her voice quivered with hurt. "We shouldn't have to say it, though. It seems wrong."

"But it's part of the ritual." He flashed his most convincing smile, the one he'd used to persuade her to go out with him that first night, behind Jonathan's back. "I want to do it right."

"All right." She sighed her resignation. "I've been faithful to you, Reuben," she said without emotion. "Since our wedding, I haven't been with anyone else. Can I sit down now? My shoulder hurts."

"You have to swear it, Isabelle."

"Reuben." She shook her head.

"You have to swear it, or it won't count."

"This is ridiculous, Reuben!"

Her cheeks, so pale of late, were flushed with color, and he could hear the fear in her voice. *Because she knows that I know.* The thought gave him a queer pleasure.

"Just say the words, Isabelle. Humor me."

"Fine." She sighed again. "I swear there's no one else, Reuben. Are we done now?" Her voice was cool with annoyance. "I'm tired, and I haven't been feeling well all day. I think I'll go upstairs."

Liar, he thought. Liar, liar, liar. He removed the bags from her hands. "In a minute."

He emptied the barley flour into the fireplace, which sizzled its acceptance of the offering. A cloud of smoke seeped into the room, like a ghost seeking its shape, and he felt a thrill of fear coursing through him. He could stop now. He could stop, and try to live with the doubt.

But he had to know.

Steeling his heart, he handed her the prepared glass of wine and took another for himself. "To our eternal love," he said.

She frowned at the glass, and for a moment he feared she suspected. "I'm not supposed to drink alcohol, Reuben."

He released the breath he'd been holding. "I read that a little wine is good for you. It won't harm the baby." Jonathan's baby? A weight pressed against Reuben's chest. "To our love," he said again and drank the wine.

Raising the goblet hesitantly to her lips, she took a few sips and crinkled her finely shaped nose. "There's sediment, and a bitter aftertaste. How old is this?"

"Really?" Reuben frowned. "It's an expensive wine. I'm sorry you don't like it." *Not bitter of themselves, the commentaries had said, but bitter for the wife if she is guilty.* Even a sip should be potent enough. His hands were suddenly clammy. Taking her glass, he set it on the coffee table.

"Let's sit and enjoy the fire," Reuben said.

She scowled at him, dubious. "No more ritual? I hate it when you get so intense."

"No more ritual," he promised.

Moments later she curled up next to him on the sofa. His chest and face felt on fire, pricked by thousands of tiny, hot needles. Inhaling the floral perfume of her shampoo for what he knew would be the last time, he listened, only half hearing, his heartbeat drumming in his ears, while she told him about her day. She'd had lunch with his mother, had met with a prospective client. . . .

He hated her for betraying him but felt like weeping. She was so beautiful, and he had loved her so much. He dreaded witnessing the awful proof of her guilt—her stomach distended, her thigh collapsed (he wasn't quite sure what this meant, and the commentaries hadn't explained). He wondered where Jonathan was now, wondered whether his body would be distorted at the very same time, or sometime later. . . .

"Reuben?"

He stared at her, startled. "What?"

"I asked if you'll be coming to the doctor with me next week. They're going to do another ultrasound. We'll be able to see the baby."

"Of course, I'll go with you. I wouldn't miss it for the world." He checked his watch and was shocked to see that minutes had passed. Nothing had happened. He had been so sure.

"Are you all right?" She touched his cheek. "You look flushed. Do you have a fever?"

He removed her hand. "I'm fine." Maybe it would happen later. Sometime during the night, with only God as witness.

Upstairs in their king-size bed, he tried staying awake, but at some point he fell asleep. He awoke with a start to the gray morning and darted a furtive glance toward Isabelle, lying motionless on her back.

His breath quickening, he touched her skin—warm, alive. He lifted the comforter. Her stomach under the white silk nightgown was flat, with no outward sign yet of the two-month-old fetus, still so tiny. He traced the outline of her perfect thigh.

She stirred and opened her eyes, smiled lazily at him. Moving closer, she pressed against him. "I love you, Reuben," she whispered.

Maybe she did. Maybe the spirit of jealousy was just that—air, without form or substance, a demon of his own creation, sent to plague him.

"I don't want to do this again." Isabelle moved her clenched hands behind her back.

"I wasn't honest with you last time," Reuben said. "We have to do it over."

For three days Reuben had struggled to believe in Isabelle's innocence, but his belief had been shattered by the detective's report. She had been with Jonathan. And—more damning!—she had kept the visit secret.

"I don't understand," Isabelle said, scowling.

"It's because of Jonathan." Reuben had decided on the truth—God demanded no less. That was why the first attempt had failed. "He's been saying things that make me think you're having an affair with him."

"That's crazy." She stared at him.

"You're constantly alone with him at his house. You saw him two days ago and didn't tell me."

"Because you're upset when I mention his name." Isabelle hesitated. "I'm worried about you, Reuben. You seem so upset lately. Jonathan's worried, too."

Clever, he thought. So very clever. "Jonathan wants to ruin our marriage, because I stole you from him."

"No." Isabelle shook her head. "Jonathan is happy for us. Even if he isn't, that has nothing to do with you and me. I love you, Reuben. Why can't you believe me?"

"I *want* to believe you," he said. "That's why I need you to swear. If you love me, you'll do this for me."

She gazed at him thoughtfully. "The book you told me about doesn't exist, does it?"

"It's the Bible." He told her what he had learned, aware that she was watching him in the sad, careful way people observe the mentally unbalanced. He didn't care.

"You're ruining everything with your suspicion, Reuben." Isabelle's eyes filled with tears. "I love *you,* not Jonathan. I married *you,* not him. How can I prove that?"

He grabbed her hands. "Swear that you're not having an affair with Jonathan, Isabelle. Swear that if you're lying you'll accept the punishment."

"And if I swear?" Gently, she removed her hands. "You're not a priest, Reuben. This fireplace isn't an altar, and we don't have sacred water. We're not living in biblical times."

"Then why won't you do it? If you're innocent, what are you afraid of?" He had her now, he thought with grim satisfaction.

Isabelle didn't answer immediately. "If I do this now, will that be the end of it?" she asked, her voice as soft and light as down.

His heart skipped a beat. "Yes."

"Because if you don't trust me after this, Reuben, then our marriage is over. You understand?"

A feathery shiver ran up his spine. "Yes."

"Give me the barley, and the water." She stretched out her hands, palms up.

He had never loved her as much as he did now. She was innocent, and she was willing to go through this hell to prove it to him.

He placed the barley bags on her palms and recited the oath. He shivered when she said "Amen" with grave simplicity, her love for him bright in her eyes.

His script was surer now as he wrote the oath, swifter. He erased the letters into a water-filled goblet into which he had sprinkled earth from the garden. He scattered the barley into the fireplace and turned to Isabelle.

She had been watching him without speaking.

"You think I'm crazy," he said. "You're going to leave me, aren't you?" He could see it in her eyes. Why had he done this? *Why?* She was obviously innocent, and he had abused her trust.

"I want you to have peace of mind, Reuben. If this helps . . . " She reached for the goblet.

He loved her so much. Lying in their bed, watching the gentle rise and fall of the breasts that would suckle their child, he marveled at her selflessness, at her courage, at her devotion. How many wives would do what she had done for him tonight? Most would have stormed out of the room, revolted, frightened, and left forever.

Not Isabelle. Isabelle was true. Isabelle was pure. He couldn't imagine why he had ever doubted her.

"Reuben," Isabelle whispered.

"You're up?" He had doubted her because of Jonathan, a small voice reminded him. Because Jonathan *wanted* him to suspect Isabelle. And Reuben had played right into his game.

"I don't feel well."

He looked at her beautiful face, at her golden hair splayed on the pillow. She was a goddess, and she was his. He would give his life for her. "What's wrong, sweetheart?"

"I'm having pains." She winced.

He stroked her hair. "Where?"

"In my stomach. It started on the right side, but now it's all over. The pains are sharp."

Something mothlike fluttered in his chest. "Maybe it's something you ate. Gas."

"It's not gas." A spasm crossed her face. She pressed her hand against her abdomen. "The pain is really strong, Reuben. Something's very wrong. Maybe it's the water you gave me."

A wave of dread welled inside him. "There was nothing wrong with the water."

"You put something in it—What did you put in it?"

"Just the erasure of the letters, and a little earth from the garden. You saw me. It isn't the water."

"Call the doctor."

His heart turned to stone, and he stared at her, unable to speak.

"*Call* him, Reuben."

"Try to rest, Isabelle," he said, knowing that rest was useless. "Maybe the pains will stop." How long would it take? Minutes? An hour? He had thought that he would feel satisfaction in knowing the truth, but the truth was bitter in his mouth.

She clutched his hand. "I'm going to lose the baby."

"You won't lose the baby," he said, loosening her grip and pulling his hand away.

Jonathan's baby, he thought with a renewed anger that overwhelmed his grief. She had mollified him, had sworn to an oath she hadn't believed was binding, had drunk the water because she had doubted its power.

She hugged her stomach. "Please, Reuben. Call the doctor!" she said, an edge of hysteria in her voice.

"All right. What's his number?" He reached for the phone on his night-stand, punched random digits as she dictated the doctor's number, and spoke to a dial tone. "The answering service said the doctor will phone back shortly," Reuben told her as he replaced the receiver. "In the meantime, try to sleep, Isabelle."

He couldn't bear looking at her lying eyes. He rolled onto his side and pretended not to hear her a while later when she moaned.

Isabelle shook him. "Why isn't he calling back?" she whimpered. "Phone him again, Reuben."

He turned toward her. "He'll call any minute. If it's a miscarriage, Isabelle, there's nothing he can do. He'll tell you to come see him in the morning."

"I'm scared." Her lips trembled, and panic shone in her eyes. "The pain is worse, Reuben. My heart is beating so fast."

Pity stirred within him. He placed his hand on her chest and felt the mad racing. Lifting the comforter, he saw blood on the sheet. He touched her abdomen, hard with guilt. No doctor could save her, he thought, more sad than angry now.

"I have to go to the hospital, Reuben. Something's terribly wrong." She was shivering, but her pale face was shiny with sweat.

"Let's wait for the doctor to phone." At some point he would have to call for an ambulance, just to go through the motions, but there was nothing the paramedics or anyone could do.

"I want to go *now*." Isabelle pulled herself up to a sitting position, then moved off the bed and rose. "I'm so dizzy." She sounded surprised and alarmed. She swayed for a moment, like a palm branch in a gentle breeze, before sinking onto the carpeted floor.

Reuben's heart broke, and his anger dissolved. He hurried off the bed and knelt at her side. "Why did you do it, Isabelle? Why? We had everything."

"The pain," she whispered. She moaned and shut her eyes.

"I love you, Isabelle." Warm tears spilled onto his cheeks. He lifted her hand and pressed it against his lips. "I forgive you," he murmured to her unconscious form, touching the features of her beautiful face so that he could commit them to memory.

The rabbi who married them officiated at the funeral.

"Such a tragedy," he told Reuben. "If only the ultrasound had shown something. If only the ambulance had come in time."

A second ultrasound, the obstetrician had explained to Reuben, would probably have revealed the ectopic pregnancy developing outside Isabelle's uterus. The cause of death, according to the coroner, was acute hemorrhaging resulting from the rupture of the fallopian tube.

Or so they thought. Reuben had listened, nodding at the medical diagnosis, though he knew better. He was awed by the power of the bitter waters, which had caused Isabelle's stomach to become distended and her thigh to collapse, just as the Scriptures had warned. He wished he could share this with someone, but, of course, he couldn't.

They wouldn't understand. And he would have to explain that he'd left Isabelle unconscious and gone to the downtown office, that he'd returned to her side hours later to phone an ambulance, when it was over. He had left her out of love, not anger or revenge. He had left because watching her die, knowing that no one could save her, had been excruciating.

Seeing Jonathan that next day, and again at the funeral, so handsome in his grief, so poignant in his eulogy, had been jarring. Reuben couldn't understand why his brother, Isabelle's partner in adultery, had not yet been partnered in her punishment. Obviously he was guilty. To think otherwise, to contemplate any other possibility . . .

It was only a question of *when,* Reuben consoled himself. God had His own timetable, and Reuben couldn't presume to question Him. Any day now, it would happen.

Reuben could wait.

RONALD LEVITSKY has written four mystery novels featuring the civil liberties lawyer Nate Rosen. When he is not writing mysteries, Ronald Levitsky teaches social studies at a junior high school in Northfield, Illinois. He recently received National Board Certification as a master teacher, and is at work on several short stories not involving Nate Rosen.

Thy Brother's Bloods

▼   ▼   ▼   ▼   ▼   ▼   ▼   ▼   ▼   ▼

RONALD LEVITSKY

THERE ARE ROOMS TOO SORROWFUL even for ghosts. Rooms like caves on some distant frozen mountain where one waits for death a long time. A slow numbing death in which loneliness becomes the only pain, and that too great too bear.

This was such a place. Sweat and cigarette smoke and odors of countless unwashed bodies—and fear that infected even the innocent visitor. A room that once might have been green but in the dim overhead light seemed more a fish-belly white, as if fear had leached even the walls of their color.

Rosen sat on a wooden straight-back chair and stared down at the small square table, chipped and blackened by grease. The chair opposite him was empty. Was the boy coming? He opened the letter that had arrived by courier the same morning. It was unlined, the words written in small, precise letters reminding him of a mathematical equation.

"Four days left. I need to see you immediately. Arrangements made for your visit this afternoon at two. Please." It was signed, "John Kennecott."

Why in the world had the letter been sent? Why was the boy wasting his time on Rosen? Better not to have come. Better—but what choice was there?

Light cut through the shadows to his right, where the door had opened. Blinking hard, Rosen turned his head. When he looked back, John Kennecott sat across from him.

In some ways he hadn't changed at all. The same doughy face that with its blank expression looked as if God hadn't quite finished forming it. Thin lips, a weak chin. Straw-colored hair, now longish and parted in the middle to make his face perfectly symmetrical, as if just one of a million cookie-cut Joes. Only his eyes set him apart. Dark small-caliber eyes, deep set, that betrayed an overriding intelligence. Kennecott seemed more round-shouldered—but perhaps he was just leaning forward. No longer gaunt, he'd finally filled his frame, yet hadn't grown much. Still short—maybe five-six. Nine years had passed. How old must he be—twenty-five, twenty-six?

Leaning against the door, the prison guard, a muscular black man with a shaved head, stifled a yawn, then said to Rosen, "I'll be outside if you need anything."

The door closed, and the darkness scurried back around them. Rosen felt nauseated. He shouldn't have come. What would Kennecott say—this Jew baiter? This neo-Nazi who walked into a store in broad daylight and gunned down an old Jewish shopkeeper. A cold-blooded murder. That's what all the newspapers had said at the time, because that's what Kennecott had boasted at the scene of the crime. That's what he had told the district attorney and the judge. Never a hint of remorse, rather, "I'd wished there had been two kikes to kill." And that's why he was going to die.

The murder had taken place five years before and had been forgotten by the public. Even Rosen had almost forgotten the crime. Yet the past few weeks, with the final appeal running out, had caused the case as well as Kennecott's rhetoric to resurface.

"Of course I expect to die," he had told one newspaper in an exclusive death-row interview. "Everyone knows that the Jews control the legal system, just like they control the media."

Even opponents of the death penalty voiced their opposition in muted tones. So what did this anti-Semite have to say to Rosen?

As if he guessed Rosen's thoughts, Kennecott cracked his lips into what almost was a smile, put his finger tips together, and intoned, "According to Exodus, 'And they went three days in the wilderness and found no water.' Isaiah later says, 'Ho, everyone that thirsts should come for water.' Do you think water symbolizes the Torah?"

Rosen stared uncomprehendingly at the other man. It was as if a dog had spoken.

Kennecott continued matter-of-factly, "You see, I took the phrases literally when I first read them—about the Israelites being thirsty for water. But then I came across a passage in the Talmud that suggested this thirst was really the need to study the Torah. What do you think?"

Rosen struggled to make sense of what he'd heard.

"What's your interpretation?"

"I don't know. I don't. . . . "

"I am disappointed. Unless my memory betrays me, you were once something of a scholar of the Torah. Not quite a rabbi, but certainly not a layman like me. What's the phrase they use—a Talmud Torah man. That's it, isn't it? You were a Talmud Torah man."

Rosen had forgotten how articulate Kennecott was. His voice was well modulated, each word a jewel, yet when spoken together they expressed the haughty self-deprecation of a Boston Brahmin. But these words from his mouth made no sense.

Rosen asked, "What are you doing?"

"Why, I was merely asking a point of clarification."

"What are you doing?"

Kennecott sighed petulantly. "If I'd asked to see a rabbi, my request would have been misconstrued. No doubt the press would've assumed some last-minute change of heart on my part, even a deathbed conversion, so to speak. All ridiculous, yet inevitable given the media is run by the sons of Abraham."

Rosen passed the letter across the table. "Why did you ask me here?"

"It was good of you to come, but, of course, I knew you wouldn't refuse. It's a mitzvah, isn't it? A commandment to help someone in need."

"Stop it."

"Five years in prison can seem like forever. I had to do something to pass the time, so I've spent a good portion of my incarceration studying the great works of your people."

"Why?"

"Why?" He shrugged. "Why are Jews so intrigued with Hitler? A know-thy-enemy sort of thing, I suppose. I'm at a disadvantage not understanding Hebrew—English translations will have to do, but I've become fascinated by the Talmud. Analyzing under a mental microscope every single word uttered in the Old Testament. And each word subject to a myriad of interpretations. No wonder you Jews make such good lawyers. It's really like a book of riddles, isn't it? For example, why does a thief pay as restitution five oxen for stealing an ox but only four sheep for stealing a sheep?"

"John—"

"Is it that, as one scholar contended, an ox is more valuable because it works for its owner, or is it because, as another argued, that the thief must carry the sheep and therefore loses some of his dignity? I think the latter argument is quite clever, don't you?"

"John—"

"Very well, Mr. Rosen." Kennecott tapped one hand nervously on the table. For a moment he seemed to lose focus then, blinking hard, said, "You're here because of what another great thinker, Oscar Wilde, once wrote—that no good deed goes unpunished. Do you remember when we first met?"

Rosen nodded. How could he forget? It was what had brought him here.

"I was sixteen, arrested for distributing what the authorities so arbitrarily called hate literature."

"As I recall, your flyers advocated sending blacks back to Africa and putting Jews into concentration camps."

"But then I had you pro bono—a civil liberties attorney. I expected you to defend me on my constitutional rights. Freedom of speech, after all, that's what you do, isn't it?"

Rosen shifted in his chair. "You were a small-town kid in the big city and in trouble for the first time. I didn't want you to be branded for the rest of your life as a neo-Nazi goon."

"So you betrayed me."

"I had you plead guilty to probation with a few hours of community service. It gave you a second chance. You agreed to the plea."

"As you said, I was a kid. How was I to know what that meant? Picking up kosher trash in front of a synagogue filled with ill-smelling gray beards and tutoring a bunch of ghetto monkeys. Not to mention the respect I lost among my colleagues."

"Those skinheads you ran around with?"

"My friends!" His hands tightened for a moment to control his anger, then he resumed, his voice once again even. "At least they were before you fixed things. I could have been a hero for the cause. I would have gladly gone to jail for my beliefs. They . . . they turned their backs on me. They were my friends, Mr. Rosen. My friends."

Kennecott's face twitched, losing its bland symmetry and, for a moment, betraying his pain.

Feeling his stomach tighten, Rosen said, "I did what I thought was best for you. I thought I saw something in you worth saving."

"Did you really? Well, are you satisfied with the results? Have you followed the progress of my career? Less than a year later I was in jail for hitting a police officer during a demonstration against an affirmative action rally. More arrests followed—for disturbing the peace, harassment, assault—of course when that Spic hit me and I defended myself, I was the one arrested. Then the crown jewel—the murder of the Hebe shopkeeper. That gave me real pleasure. Tell me, do you still think I'm worth saving?"

Rosen couldn't take any more of this. He stood, kicking back his chair. "If this is the reason you wanted me here—"

"No, no. Please sit down. Just a few more minutes of your time. Remember, I don't have very long to live. Less than four days."

For a long time Rosen stared at the prisoner, then reluctantly sat down.

"Thank you," Kennecott said. "It really was good of you to come. Do you remember what Rabbi Yochanan said about his brother-in-law, Resh Lakish? That not having him to discuss Torah was like trying to applaud with one hand. Perhaps that's the way I feel about you."

"So you called me here just to talk?"

"Oh, I've enjoyed our conversation, but as the great Rabbi Heschel reminds us, a Jew must live by actions and not mere words. How did he put it?" Kennecott's head leaned back, his eyes half-closed. "'The deed is the test, the trial, and the risk. What we perform may seem slight, but the aftermath is immense.'"

Rosen fought back his anger. "An anti-Semite quoting Heschel. Surely the Messiah will soon arrive."

For the first time Kennecott smiled, the smile gone as quickly as it came. His eyes widened; they seemed feverish. How could he control himself, knowing he had such a short time to live? Swallowing hard, he said, "I want you to do a deed for me."

"If it's to look into your appeal, I can't do any more than what your attorney has already done."

"Oh, no. You did enough once before as my attorney. Besides, I'm quite ready to die. However, I would like you to review my case. I've made arrangements with Mrs. McNulty, my attorney, to meet with you later this afternoon. I've instructed her to answer all your questions without regard to the usual attorney-client privilege."

"If this has nothing to do with an appeal, why have me look into your case? I don't understand."

"Guard!" Kennecott called, and the door opened.

Rosen persisted, "Why, John?"

The prisoner rose nearer the light; he glistened with sweat. "You ask why, Mr. Rosen? Think of it as another talmudic riddle for you to ponder. I look forward to our next visit. Guard, we're done for now."

The prison, located in a downstate rural area, meant a two-hour trip to Chicago, the criminal court building, and the meeting with Kennecott's lawyer. While driving, Rosen remembered how he'd felt as a boy when his rabbi had given him a difficult passage of the Torah to interpret. Like his meeting with Kennecott, feeling initial bewilderment, attempting desperately to work the problem through like a convoluted maze, reaching a dead end then retracing his steps to try again and again. Sometimes the most difficult ones weren't resolved until, like a Zen koan, a sudden flash of enlightenment revealed the answer. Was that what it would take?

Better to let the scenery drift by. He wasn't used to the country—the green fragrance of corn and the first scent of autumn like a whiff of gunshot. Occasionally he'd pass an isolated farmhouse with its red barn and tall silo. Beautiful, but the isolation reminded him of Grant Wood and Andrew Wyeth paintings with their sad, sometimes sinister moods.

Kennecott was from this kind of farming community further downstate. Rosen thought of Wyeth's *Christina's World,* but instead of the young girl, her back to the viewer, dreaming alone in the fields, he pictured Kennecott. What must the boy's life have been like to fill him with so much hatred?

The boy. Until today he'd thought of Kennecott only as a boy. Even after the murder, Rosen had persisted with that image. Why? Was it guilt for not seeing nine years earlier who Kennecott really was or, worse, for not being able to stop him before he murdered someone?

It was nearly five o'clock by the time Rosen arrived at the criminal court building and hurried up to the second floor.

Sheila McNulty had worked as a public defender for more than two decades. A short, stocky woman whose fiery red hair was threaded with gray, McNulty balanced a passion for the law with a cynicism for the criminal justice system. Rosen had known her for a long time—they'd worked a few cases together. He trusted her judgment and, even more, her instincts.

Rummaging through the folders on her desk, she pulled out a thick file that she handed to Rosen. John Kennecott's.

"Your copy. Keep it," she said. "When we conferenced yesterday, he told me you'd be coming. What's this all about?"

"I was hoping you'd tell me."

"Haven't a clue. I thought maybe you'd found something to help with our final appeal, but I couldn't think what."

"His appeal—any chance of success?"

"No chance in hell. Kennecott doesn't even want the appeal. When I told him state law mandated it, he wanted to challenge the law. You know how many cases I've tried using every trick in the book to keep somebody alive? Along comes this guy who wants the state to kill him."

"Why do you think he wants to die?"

"Beats me. Certainly not remorse. He's been cool as a cucumber from the day he was arrested, and I've never been able to get him to open up. Arrogant little bastard, yet I . . . You'll think I'm going soft, Nate, but I can't help feeling a little sorry for him. Know anything about his background?"

"He's from a small farm town."

"Pine Park, Illinois. Population, seven thousand odd people, and I do mean odd. An only child. Father manages a feed store and mother's a school teacher. Never once visited their son in prison. When I contacted them about the appeal, the father said he was too busy filling a grain order to talk to me. You know what the mother said? 'In His great battle with Satan, the ways of the Lord are strange. John must suffer, as we all must suffer.' What the hell does that mean?"

She continued, "You should see his high school test scores. Brilliant, but growing up in a hayseed town where cows carried on the most intelligent conversation, not much chance to take advantage of his brains. A loner, pushed around because he was different, he turned to the Internet—the world of hate—and finally found a place to call home. To be honest, I wouldn't have been surprised if he'd have put on a trench coat and taken a gun to school."

Rosen said, "Instead, he took a gun into a jewelry store and killed an old man."

"That he did. And in less than four days he'll be paying the piper."

"Sheila, is there any chance that Kennecott's innocent?"

"He confessed, even bragged about the murder." She leaned back in her chair. "You know what happened?"

"Just what I remember from the papers. Can you fill me in?"

"Five years ago, on a hot August afternoon, John Kennecott was a skinhead punk passing out hate literature on Devon Avenue. The only twist was that he passed out the material to Jewish, Korean, and Indian merchants.

Some of the Koreans didn't understand what it was all about—they actually thanked him for the papers. One even posted it in his store window like it was a public service announcement.

"With some others it was a different matter. Kennecott had words with a number of store owners. Got into a fight with a jeweler, Morris Gittelman, age sixty-two, and was arrested for disturbing the peace. Swore to the cops that he wasn't through with 'the Jew squatting on the window sill.'"

"What's that mean?"

"A line from the poet T. S. Eliot, that other erudite anti-Semite. Anyway, the next afternoon Kennecott goes back to the store and puts a bullet into Gittelman. Hangs around for the cops to come, then brags about it."

"'True Christians have a right to defend themselves against vermin,'" Rosen read from the police report. He asked, "Who published the stuff Kennecott was distributing?"

"He did. With a computer, anyone nowadays can be his own William Randolph Hearst. The actual drivel seems to have been culled from several hate groups, much of it from the Internet. Kennecott drifted in and out of a number of local groups."

"Any reason why he never stayed with one of them?"

McNulty shook her head. "Some of these guys are real loners. Who knows? Kennecott's got quite a brain; maybe he could only stand each group of nuts for so long, or maybe he didn't fit in even with them. That would be a laugh, wouldn't it? Too weird even for these weirdos."

"So as far as you know, he was acting alone."

"No organization ever claimed him as a member."

Rosen flipped through the report. "What about the gun?"

"A thirty-eight. No registration. Kennecott admitted it was his. Said he bought it from some street kid a few weeks before and kept it in his car for protection."

"A single bullet killed the old man." Rosen paused to read the report, then added, "Funny angle, isn't it? Upward trajectory, about forty-five degrees."

"Gittelman's blood was on Kennecott's clothes, and powder burns were on both men. The old man must've struggled for the gun before he was shot."

"Any witnesses?"

"Sheila Epstein—a cousin who worked part-time in the jewelry store. She was in back making Gittelman lunch. Came out front just in time to see Kennecott pull the trigger. She screamed her head off and then fainted. Got a concussion and almost became a second victim. So, Nate, what's this all about?"

"You know as much as I do. Kennecott asked me to look into his case."

"To prove his innocence?"

"No. Like you said, he admits his guilt. Even seems proud of it."

"Then why?"

"I have no idea."

McNulty shrugged. "Guess we can file this as a dying man's last request. A sort of charity case. Nice of you to take it on."

Rosen gathered the papers into the folder. "Do you know the Hebrew term *tzedakah*?"

"Something to do with charity, isn't it? When I was a kid, one of my Jewish friends had a *pushke* in her kitchen."

"For Jews, *tzedakah* means more than charity. It's a duty to help those in need. A religious obligation. So you see, I had no choice."

It wasn't his old neighborhood, but it could've been—that is, a generation ago when the store signs were in Yiddish rather than Korean and Hindi, and the women wore babushkas and long dark dresses instead of peacock-colored saris. Old women and young mothers buying food for the evening meal, only this time from grocery stores smelling strongly of curry or kimchi.

Sitting in his car, Rosen closed his eyes against the bright morning sun and imagined the kosher delicatessen that had once stood on the corner of his old neighborhood, the hard salamis hanging in the windows behind a neon Star of David. And the smells—the pungency of smoked fish and richness of simmering matzo ball soup. He kept his eyes closed, even when the image slowly disappeared, to be replaced by that of the papers of Kennecott's file strewn across his bed.

He'd been up late last night, reading the court records in light of what Sheila McNulty had said. Not much more to learn, other than that she was right. It had been a slam dunk for the state's attorney, and the way Kennecott had taken pride in the murder of "the old Jew" made it easy to understand why the death penalty had been sought and granted.

One thing McNulty hadn't mentioned was how Kennecott had gained among a certain community the popularity he'd never had as a kid. No hate group had specifically identified Kennecott as one of its own. However, the police had downloaded newsletters and calls-to-arms from the Foot Soldiers of Odin, Bearers of the True Cross, and other fringe elements that trafficked in hate—mentioning, for example, how "Brother John Kennecott had shown the courage and convictions of a true Christian." Or on another site: "While many of us profess our willingness to die for our cause, only a sacred few, like John Kennecott, are willing to nobly make that sacrifice. Remember, talk is cheap. It's action that counts."

Or another that proclaimed, "Another Christ will soon be nailed to the cross."

When he'd finally fallen asleep, Rosen tossed and turned in a cold sweat the rest of the short night.

The next morning he canceled a nine A.M. appointment and drove to the neighborhood where the murder had taken place. For the past fifteen minutes he'd waited in his car, for what he wasn't quite sure. The jewelry store owned by the victim was no longer there. In its place stood an East Indian video store with colorful posters of Hollywood movies and adventure epics from the subcontinent. Its current owner certainly would have known nothing about the crime.

Scanning the block, Rosen noticed Shapiro and Son Shoes across the street. It wouldn't hurt to give it a try.

The store was another throwback to Rosen's youth. A no-frills poster, dusty overhead lights, paper-bag-colored store. Walls jammed with shoe boxes balanced precariously one atop another like a circus act, and several of the old bear-trap-looking foot measurers scattered along the floor. Displays of cheap sandals and loafers. A young mother and her two children, the only customers, were leaving as Rosen approached the counter. A short, stocky woman in her sixties—hair the color of blue steel, ruby lipstick a little too thick, and glasses held by a heavy silver chain around her neck— looked him up and down.

"What can I do for you?"

"Are you the owner—Mrs. Shapiro?"

"That's right."

"Was your store here five years ago?"

"Five years ago? More like five hundred years ago, it seems. My father-in-law started this store during the Depression. He always said that no matter how poor people were, they still needed to wear shoes. So what's this all about?"

"Did you know Morris Gittelman, the man who owned what used to be the jewelry store across the street?"

Her eyes narrowed. "*Nu?*"

"My name's Rosen. I'm an attorney looking into what happened to Mr. Gittelman."

"Gittelman was murdered by an animal, may he rot in hell. Thank God he's going to be killed in a few days. You know how they do it now? They stick a needle in his arm and put him to sleep like a dog. So nice and kind. Why so nice and kind to somebody like that?"

"Mrs. Shapiro—"

"The old way was much better. Strap him in a chair and turn on the electricity till they fry him good. Monsters like him, I'd like to pull the switch myself."

"Mrs. Shapiro, were you here in the store the afternoon that Mr. Gittelman was killed?"

Just then a heavy man, clutching a sheaf of pink papers, stepped from the back room behind Mrs. Shapiro. He was about the same age as the woman. He had a balding pate fringed with longish gray hair; his thick glasses gave him an owlish appearance. He joined Mrs. Shapiro behind the counter and stuffed the papers into a squeaky file cabinet.

"My husband," she said. "We both were in the store when it happened." To the old man, "This fella's a lawyer asking questions about Gittelman's murder."

"A lawyer, huh? I bet some kind of lawsuit."

"What do you mean?" she asked.

"Whenever somebody dies, even a Gittelman, there's always a lawsuit."

"I bet his wife's behind it, even though he probably left her plenty."

The old man shook his head. "Are you kidding? He dealt in junk. You wore one of his bracelets for five minutes and your wrist turned green."

"Mr. Shapiro," Rosen said, "This isn't about a lawsuit. I'm just trying to clear up a few details about Mr. Gittelman's death. So both of you were here that afternoon?"

"That's right. Such a hot day it was, and when I saw that punk across the street, I knew there'd be trouble."

"You recognized John Kennecott?"

"Sure I recognized him. He was here in my store the day before. Soon as he walked in I knew he was a troublemaker. Something about the way he looked. Just not right."

"What do you mean—'not right'?"

"I'm telling you . . . I'm telling you he wasn't right. Now I told you."

His wife said, "The look of a devil, that's the way he looked. Cold like a killer."

Rosen asked, "What did he want?"

"Trouble," Shapiro said. "He walks up to the counter and hands me a paper like it was an invitation to some block party. At first I didn't understand what it was all about. So he waits while I read it. All about Jews as rats and Spic wetbacks and Indian rag heads. I couldn't believe it. The words, I mean. Why would somebody do that? Here in my own shop. And the kid just stands there all quiet and polite like he just brought me a message from Western Union and was waiting for a tip. I told the son of a bitch to get out of my store and never come back."

Rosen asked, "What did Kennecott do?"

"What did he do? He got the hell out of my store, that's what he did."

"He didn't threaten you in any way?"

"I would've liked to have seen him try. A punch in the face is what I'd have given him. I used to be a boxer in the army."

His wife added, "I was gonna call the police."

"I didn't need no police."

"I was gonna call the police."

"Enough with the police!"

Rosen asked, "Did you see him go into Mr. Gittelman's jewelry store?"

Mrs. Shapiro said, "About fifteen minutes later. I kept looking out the window, because I was afraid he might come back. I saw him crossing the street and walking into Gittelman's store. Right away I knew there was gonna be trouble."

"What do you mean?"

"Well, Gittelman had such a temper. I knew he wouldn't stand for such a thing. Didn't I tell you, Ira?"

"You told me."

"Well, I waited a few minutes, then I was gonna call the police—"

"Again with the police."

"—When all of a sudden Gittelman and this kid come tumbling out of the store, Gittelman on top. Gittelman's yelling and punching the kid. The whole neighborhood came out—oy, such a sight."

Shapiro said, "So then the kid got up, but Gittelman wouldn't let go. They wrestled around a little bit more, then the cops came. They took the kid away, with Gittelman yelling after them. I can still hear it in my ears. Such words."

"From what you're telling me, it seems that Mr. Gittelman started the fight."

"Haven't you been listening? I told you what that animal was doing. What did you expect from Gittelman? Especially Gittelman."

"So he had a violent temper."

"Let's just say he was a man you stayed away from."

Mrs. Shapiro put an index finger to her head. "He was a little meshugga."

"A little? He was a bastard, let's be honest."

"Ira."

"A bastard and maybe a crook to boot. You know the talk about where his jewelry came from." He leaned closer to Rosen. "Wouldn't surprise me if it was from the back of a truck. And there were stories about him being in prison. A knife fight, I heard. Still, he didn't deserve to die like that. Not from that punk."

Rosen said, "The next day, when the murder took place . . . the police report indicates that you phoned the police."

Shapiro said, "Sure. When I saw that punk walk into the jewelry shop, I knew there'd be trouble, so I called the cops."

"Did you see Kennecott with a gun?"

The old man scratched his head. "I don't remember. Maybe. Or maybe it was under his shirt."

"So you didn't actually see the shooting."

"No, but Shirley told us all about it plenty of times afterward."

Rosen remembered the name from the police report. "You mean Gittelman's cousin, Shirley Epstein."

"That's right. She was in back of the jewelry store when she heard the two men arguing. She came out front just in time to see that little bastard gun down Gittelman. Her screams . . . they followed that bastard into the street. And he just stood there, holding the gun in his hand until the cops came. Then he turns the gun over nice as you please. Like he'd been waiting for them. How do you like that? I read in the papers there was Gittelman's blood on his clothes. That's how close he stood. He must've looked him right in the eyes when he shot him. What kind of man does that?"

Rosen said, "I'd like to talk to Mrs. Epstein. Do you know where I might find her?"

Mrs. Shapiro sighed. "In heaven is where you'll find her. The poor woman died two years ago. Heart attack. She was never right after what happened. She'd sit and have tea, and all she'd want to talk about was how her cousin was murdered. 'Like Germany,' she kept saying. 'Just like Germany.' The Nazis couldn't kill her back in Europe, but here in America. *Nu?*"

"What about Mr. Gittelman's wife?"

"That shiksa? She didn't let the grass grow under her feet. His body wasn't even cold when she sold the store. They got a nice condo in Evanston, not far from the lake, or so I'm told. We was never invited over."

"Do you know if Mr. Gittelman owned a gun?"

The old man stroked his chin. "A gun? I don't know. Never saw one. Not that I'd blame him. We was robbed once—a burglary at night. Made me want to get a gun."

"Ira, no," Mrs. Shapiro said.

Shapiro put his arm around his wife. "This was a nice neighborhood in the old days. Everybody knew everybody. You met them at the movie house, in shul, in the *shvitz*. Now, I look around and who do I know? Strangers. Half of them can't even speak English."

Mrs. Shapiro asked, "Could your grandfather when he came over from Poland? Could mine?" To Rosen, "Don't mind Ira. We all get along fine. The people on this block—they're like us. You just want to be left alone to make a little money for your children. That's something all of us understand. It's men like the one who killed Morris Gittelman. Him, I don't understand."

Rosen stared at the store across the street and said, "Neither do I."

After leaving the shoe store, Rosen grabbed a quick lunch and then drove a few miles north to an appointment at a high school. He was defending a group of students who had been suspended for violating the school's dress code. Discussing the case with the principal and the school board's attorney, he kept losing focus, thinking about Kennecott in jail with only three days to live.

An hour later he hurried through the school hallways, watching the kids sprawled against their lockers or jostling one another at the drinking fountain. He concentrated on the loners, like the long-haired boy in black who sat on the bottom step of a stairwell, refusing to move even as some bigger boys in jerseys kneed him as they passed. Could that kid grow up to be another John Kennecott?

He called McNulty, and by the time he'd returned to his office downtown, she'd faxed him the information he'd requested on Morris Gittelman. Mr. Shapiro had been right about the jeweler's having a criminal record. Fifteen years ago he'd been convicted of trying to sell stolen property in a police sting operation. He'd served six months in prison. Two years later he'd been caught again and was also convicted for assaulting a police officer while resisting arrest. He'd gotten two years and served a little more than one. After that his record was clean.

Reviewing the trial transcript, Rosen found no reference to the victim's criminal record. It could have been important to the defendant's case, had Kennecott actually wanted to be defended. However, with a confession from the accused, the victim's past wasn't important. Only that Kennecott was a murderer.

Or so it seemed.

The next morning Rosen drove to the condo of Gittelman's widow. When they'd spoken on the phone the night before, he'd identified himself as an attorney working with John Kennecott's legal team and asked to see her as soon as possible. He'd expected a barrage of questions and ultimately a refusal, but instead she'd invited him over for breakfast.

She lived four blocks from the lake in a red-brick, two-story building with a courtyard shaded by two large oaks on either side of a flagstone path. Some of the leaves had begun to shrivel; a few had fallen before turning colors. Again he inhaled the barest whiff of autumn and trembled a little. A stained-glass dove was encased in the door. He pressed the buzzer, and she rang him upstairs.

"With a name like Rosen, I didn't know if you'd want bacon," Joan Gittelman said, stirring the omelet.

"I'm fine without it," he said, sipping his coffee.

She was probably twenty years younger than her late husband. A brassy redhead, already made up at eight-thirty in the morning, with a cigarette balanced in an ashtray beside the egg carton. She wore a turquoise, high-collared blouse that brought out the green of her eyes, a pair of Polo jeans, and Tevas. Something he wasn't prepared for—he liked her right away.

"My Morrie wasn't much into his religion. Nothing he liked better than my pork tenderloin, but to each his own, I always say. Here you go."

She brought two heaping plates of eggs, potatoes, and toast to the kitchen table and sat across from him. "Dig in."

"This is great," Rosen said. And it was.

"Morrie always liked a big breakfast. You know what they say—it's the most important meal."

While they ate, Rosen said, "Yesterday morning I was in your old neighborhood—where the jewelry store was. Talked to the Shapiros across the street."

"You mean the old guy hasn't coughed out a lung yet? Good for him. That's not the easiest place to run a business."

"I'm sure it can be dangerous. Look what happened to your husband."

She stared at her plate for a few seconds. Someone else watching her might have assumed a widow's grief, but Rosen had seen that look enough on the witness stand. She was thinking hard before saying anything. And, in fact, she waited for him to continue.

He said, "It must've been a terrible shock."

"Think so? You think a cop coming to your door and telling you your husband's been murdered in broad daylight is a terrible shock?" She lit a cigarette, took a long drag, then leaned back in her chair and stared at him, her green eyes glinting cold. "The reason you're here—something about the execution, isn't it?"

"Not necessarily."

"'Not necessarily'—what the hell does that mean?"

He put down his fork and leaned back as well. "It means I don't really know. A long time ago I defended John Kennecott on a minor charge, and two days ago he asked me to look into his case."

"Why?"

Rosen shrugged. "I honestly don't know."

"Is he paying you?"

"No."

"So what has he got over you, some kind of Jewish guilt thing?" She smiled, a big, honest smile, which made Rosen smile too. "Morrie used to tell me all about how his mother used to make him feel guilty about everything—from not eating his vegetables to his choice of girlfriends. I wonder how she would've felt about me."

"How did you two meet?"

"In Vegas. I was a cocktail waitress, and he was in town for some jewelry show. We hit it right off. He had a real good sense of humor."

"I heard he had quite a temper."

She laughed. "That's for damn sure, but that was business. He was all peaches and cream with me."

Rosen looked around the condo. Leather couches, an antique breakfront, a Sub-Zero refrigerator. "Your husband left you well provided."

"Morrie carried a big insurance policy. Said he never wanted me to worry about money after he'd gone. I can guess what the Shapiros told you. That Morrie was a crook. Well, maybe he wasn't the most honest creature on God's earth, but what businessman is?"

Rosen liked the woman even more for the way she defended her husband. He'd better ask now, or he might never. "Mrs. Gittelman, did your husband own a gun?"

Again she took a long time to answer, crushing the half-smoked cigarette into the remains of her eggs. Finally she shook her head.

He said, "I find that hard to believe, considering the neighborhood and your husband's business as a jeweler."

"He couldn't own a gun."

"Because he'd been convicted of a felony and therefore couldn't get a permit."

"You've done your homework. That's right."

"Your husband broke the law before. I think it's quite possible that to protect his business, he might have purchased a gun off the street."

"If he had a gun, and that punk kid walked in, why didn't he—"

"Maybe the gun that killed your husband was his, not John Kennecott's."

"I think maybe Kennecott should be paying you. You sure sound like you're trying to prove something."

"Was the gun your husband's?"

"I told you Morrie didn't own no gun."

"Mrs. Gittelman—"

"It was nice talking to you, Mr. Rosen."

"Why did you agree to see me?"

"What do you mean? Oh, I get it." She allowed herself another generous smile, which froze on her face. "You think I got some kind of guilt trip going on over . . . what's that term you lawyers use . . . over what allegedly happened. No, Mr. Rosen, I was glad to see you. I figured that since you're representing the goddamn little bastard who murdered my husband, you might tell him for me that when they're sticking that needle into his arm, I'll be drinking champagne. You tell him for me. I'll be toasting my Morrie with a glass of the best champagne money can buy."

Maybe it was because he hadn't gotten any sleep the night before. Or maybe it was the way he hadn't gotten any sleep, knowing this was the last day that John Kennecott would be allowed to live. And now, sitting in the prison conference room, Rosen felt the same fear he was sure Kennecott was feeling, a fear that crawled around your belly, not letting you think of anything else.

And when the same guard brought the prisoner in, Rosen knew that Kennecott was scared, and that, at last, there might be hope for something good.

Kennecott sat across the table and didn't look up until the guard left the room. He was even paler, with sunken eyes, and his teeth chewing on his lower lip. Hands gripped tightly as if in prayer. His shirt was stained with sweat, betraying the dank, acrid smell of fear.

Clearing his throat, Kennecott said, "Fourteen hours to midnight. Not much time, not even for a mayfly."

"Time enough for the truth. Will you tell me the truth now?"

"I've already told you the truth. Our little chat three days ago. You know."

"I think I do. There's a story concerning a scholar of the Torah named Rabbenu Tam. He was reputed to be such a genius that later scholars were hesitant to pass judgment on the basis of his opinions. They weren't sure that he truly wanted to interpret a passage a certain way or merely show off his brilliance."

Kennecott's lips twitched into what almost passed for a smile, but he said nothing.

Rosen said, "You went back unarmed to Gittelman's jewelry store. You wanted to make a statement, harass the old man a little more—show your courage, but you didn't intend to hurt him. In all of your run-ins with the law, you never initiated violence."

"Perhaps I changed."

Rosen stood and walked around the table. "Get up." Shrugging, Kennecott did as he was told, staring up like a little boy. It made Rosen feel even sicker, but he continued.

"I'm about the same height as Gittelman. According to the police report, the bullet entered the victim in an upward trajectory, about a forty-five-degree angle."

"Well, I am much shorter than you." There was something in his voice—a suppressed excitement.

"Not that much. You had to be standing close, as close as I am to you right now. You had to struggle for the gun."

"Perhaps we did. Perhaps he grabbed at the gun—"

"No." Rosen made a downward motion with his right hand. "A taller man—the natural motion would've been to knock the gun down and away. But if the taller man held the gun and the shorter man defended himself—" He grabbed Kennecott's wrist and jerked it up. "The gun might be pushed up and back, and if a bullet was discharged against the gun holder's chest . . . that would be about a forty-five-degree angle."

Rosen sat back down and, after Kennecott took his chair, said, "That's what happened. Gittelman pulled the gun. You struggled with him to protect yourself, and the gun went off killing him. It was self-defense. John, if you wanted me to look into the case . . . if you wanted me to help you, why did you wait so long? I'll call your lawyer, but I don't think—"

"You're wrong," Kennecott said, an edge in his voice. "You're wrong. I killed Gittelman just like I said."

Rosen felt like shaking him as if he were a spoiled child. "Then why did you call me? Why the hell did you call me!"

"You seem a bit perplexed, Mr. Rosen. Do you need me to write you a guide?" He was chattering nervously, barely able to suppress his fear. "Remember, I told you it was just to help me pass the time. I needed someone to talk to, and you. . . . I remember how we used to talk when I was younger. You thought you were acting so nobly—a Jew defending an anti-Semite. But even that wasn't enough. You felt sorry for me, so you persuaded the judge to give me probation. I wanted you to see me now. I wanted to give you something in return."

"What?"

"A talmudic riddle to work on. Did you enjoy it these past few days? I'm sure you must've found it interesting, even challenging."

"Do you know what's going to happen to you?"

"Don't I deserve it? After all, I killed a man. What did God say to Cain, 'The voice of thy brother's blood crieth unto Me from the ground.'"

"You said before that you don't know Hebrew. The correct translation is 'brother's bloods.' The word is plural, because when a man is killed, not only does he die, but so do all who would have come after him. Forever. Do you understand?"

Kennecott nodded. "Therefore, whoever saves one life, saves the whole world. And that's why you're trying to save my life, isn't it, Mr. Rosen? Like so many other do-gooders trying to save the whole world. I wonder—would you have done the same for Hitler?"

"Hitler was guilty."

"Hitler never killed anyone with his own hands. I did." When Rosen was about to protest, Kennecott quickly added, tapping his fingers uncontrollably on the table, "Even if we suppose you're correct about what happened between the old man and me, I'm still your enemy and the enemy of your people. Mightn't I one day not kill again—kill many Jews with premeditation? Or grant me that at least I would spew enough venom to encourage others to murder. Then wouldn't I be just as guilty? Shouldn't you want me to die now, rather than take the risk of what I might do for the rest of my life?"

Rosen stared hard at the other man. Kennecott was coming apart in front of him—he was sweating, his hands couldn't stop moving. Yet still he clung to this madness.

Shaking his head, Rosen said, "That's really what this is all about—a martyrdom so that your name can live forever among a few skinheads? You can't mean it."

"'May my death be an atonement for all my sins.'" The statement a Jew in ancient Israel made before his execution. More bravado. Kennecott continued, "Are you so sure now that I'm worth saving?"

Suddenly he relaxed in his chair, his hands growing limp and his head tilting to one side. After glancing around the room, he said, "Perhaps this isn't the best setting for our discussion. I'm from farm country—an outdoors boy. Your Baal Shem Tov used to wander about in the forest, didn't he? A great spiritual leader, but still he enjoyed his games. Yes, the forest. Sometimes when it gets a bit chilly in my cell, I think about my youth and how nice it was to be in front of a fire deep in the woods. You know."

"Know . . . know what?"

Kennecott managed a crooked grin. "Your second talmudic riddle. Or perhaps better to say—my final gift to you. Guard!"

"Wait a minute."

As the door opened, Kennecott struggled to his feet. Again his hands were clenched, the knuckles white. "No more time, Mr. Rosen. Alas, no more time." His voice was trembling. "'Because I could not stop for Death, He kindly stopped for me.' Emily Dickinson. A rather introspective poet, full of angst and self-doubt. She would've made a good Jew, don't you think?"

"John?"

"Goodbye, Mr. Rosen."

Kennecott walked through the door, past the guard who stood silent and immutable as God.

The kettle whistled, rousing Rosen from the table next to his kitchenette. He'd been drifting in and out of sleep most of the evening, and now that it was night, he should have given up and gone to bed. The window was open a crack, enough for the crisp autumn breeze to keep him awake. He made himself another cup of tea, then leaned back in his chair, listening to an old Thelonius Monk album on the turntable. It comforted him, the notes tumbling solemnly like silver dollars from the fingers of that most singular of pianists. Always Monk or Billie Holiday on nights like this—nights hushed as mourners are hushed when sitting shivah. It was the same after Rosen's father had died. Alone at the kitchen table, with the blue jazz cooling his mind.

He thought back to his childhood. He remembered his relatives around the kitchen table, his Great Uncle Zadel putting a sugar cube between his teeth, then drinking hot tea from a glass. Or his mother stroking his hair while, snuggling against her, he ate from a plate of her mandel bread. He always liked the kitchen best, felt safest there. Even now, he smelled the onion and flour of his mother's apron.

All evening he'd been thinking about what had been said to him earlier that afternoon. Those last words about Kennecott being "an outdoors boy" who was used to "a fire deep in the woods." It was, indeed, a talmudic riddle.

He hadn't looked at a clock since arriving home. He didn't have to. It was long after midnight, and Kennecott had been dead for hours. Not the end though—Kennecott had made sure that this was only the beginning. Rosen was tempted to turn on his computer and browse through the hate Web sites, lit up like a firmament of *yahrzeit* candles spread across the blackness of hell. The dead man would be a martyr all right, just as he'd wanted. And maybe, because of it, even more hate and violence. Pogroms with Cossacks on horseback chasing down mothers and babies. Nazis ripping beards from the faces of holy men, their Jewish bodies lining ditches, gold teeth piled high like Pharaoh's pyramids. Leo Frank dangling from a tree.

Maybe Mrs. Shapiro was right; maybe Kennecott was an animal who should rot in hell. Rosen saw the pain in Joan Gittelman's eyes—what the "little bastard" had done to her husband and to her. Maybe . . . maybe.

What Rosen felt for certain was the same dull aching in his heart he'd felt when long ago he'd turned away from his faith. How disappointed his father had been. Nothing Rosen did from that point on ever made a difference. Nor, with his father dead, would it ever make a difference. Why should thinking about a damnable anti-Semite make him feel that same way? It wasn't fair. For God's sake, it wasn't fair.

But, then, the world wasn't fair. It hadn't been fair to Kennecott, a brilliant kid born to parents who didn't give a damn about him—not the way parents should. They'd never visited him in prison during his entire incarceration, not even those last few days. What must it have been like to spend those final hours alone? To know that no one cared about you as a human being—that your only worth lay in your death, and that in the most perverse way?

His head began to ache. He sipped some tea, closed his eyes, and once more tried to make sense of it. Why had Kennecott insisted that Rosen investigate the case? Was it, as Kennecott had claimed all along, an intellectual game—a talmudic riddle—to pass the brief time he'd had left? Was it just one last bit of revenge on Rosen for "betraying" Kennecott years ago by not taking the boy's hatred seriously enough? Trying to convince a judge to deal it away as youthful indiscretion. Was this murder the supreme mockery of Rosen's good deed—of the one ideal he still held sacred?

But Kennecott hadn't committed murder. Of that Rosen was sure. His brow furrowed as the headache worsened. He'd better get to bed. Besides, he was feeling a chill. Closing the window behind him, he finished the tea and leaned back in his chair, remembering the coziness of his mother's kitchen. How he'd liked sitting near the stove when she was baking bread. What's that Kennecott had said about sitting in front of a fire in the forest? Rosen felt himself drifting off, half-dreaming of the warmth of an open fire . . . its crackling, the smell of autumn leaves brought in by the night breeze . . . that single light in a deep dark wilderness.

Suddenly Rosen straightened in his chair. Of course! He waited a few minutes, letting the ideas dance together in his head—dance as the Baal Shem Tov as a youth must have danced in the woods, taking joy in the wonders of God's Creation.

And that famous story about the Baal Shem Tov. Whenever his people were threatened, he would go into the forest, light a fire, say a special prayer, and the threat would end. Years later, his disciple went into the forest, forgot how to light the fire, but said the prayer and still avoided disaster. Later still, another follower could only find the place, yet that had been suffi- cient. And finally, another could do nothing but remember the story and hope that would be enough. Was that what Kennecott had meant about wanting to be near a fire in the forest? His real reason for studying Judaism— not mockery or an attack, but a final plea for forgiveness? Alone, abandoned by his family, he'd lost his way in a thicket of hate and almost lost his soul. But he had remembered the story. And that was enough for Rosen.

He walked to the mantle above the fireplace, where he lit a candle and whispered the first words of the mourner's prayer, *"Baruch Dayan Emet."* Blessed be the True Judge.

LEV RAPHAEL is the book critic for National Public
Radio's "The Todd Mundt Show" and mysteries
columnist for the *Detroit Free Press*. He also reviews
for the *Jerusalem Report*, the *Forward*, the *Washington Post*, the *Boston Review*, and the *Ft. Worth Star-
Telegram*. Among his many books are the Nick
Hoffman series: *Let's Get Criminal*, *The Edith Wharton Murders*, *The Death of a Constant Lover*, *Little
Miss Evil*, and his newest, *Burning Down the House*.

Your Papers, Please

▼   ▼   ▼   ▼   ▼   ▼   ▼   ▼   ▼

LEV RAPHAEL

"HEY—IS YOUR NAME REALLY DARK? I've never met anyone with, like, a soap
opera name! Is that cool or what?"

Dark looked up at Peter Cohen, one of the beginning master's students,
thin, green eyed, flushed with just having harangued their shy hostess to
can Mariah Carey and play some big-beat and techno CDs he'd brought
with him. Peter was so skinny you could draw straight lines down each side
from his shoulders past his hips—it was as if nothing in life had touched
him yet. But his voice was full of phony New York sophistication.

Up until now, the English department party had simply fallen around
Dark like heaps of confetti he was too tired to brush away. Alone in his corner, he had been content to just get drunk and hazily watch people laugh
and dance, watch especially the newer graduate students like Peter—some
right out of college—whose youth whipped the air like crackling, fresh flags.

"It's short for my last name—Darkow. Russian."

"But you look Jewish. Come on, it's a Jewish name, isn't it? Confess!"

Dark nodded very reluctantly.

"I knew it! You look just like my Uncle Morty—but he's eaten way more
corned beef than you ever will. I mean, you must have, what, 10 percent
body fat? 8 percent? No way, Dude! But you're big, too. Maybe we could

work out together some time—I'm really hopeless, no muscles, a super wimp. So, tell me, with this Russian thing you've got going, do you read lots of Dostoevski?"

"Not really."

"I like Dostoevski. The people are so outta control, not like in Henry James."

"I'm doing my dissertation on *The Ambassadors*."

"Oh, that's right, I remember, I heard you'd been working on it for, what, ten years? Seven? Whatever. But James—why bother? Wasn't James senile when he wrote his last coupla books? I mean, nothing ever happens in his books: somebody just moves a piece of furniture and finds a dust ball behind it. Gimme a break. That pathetic crap about 'Live, live all you can!' when he was dead from the waist down. And he was so fucking anti-Semitic. Just like Edith Wharton and Henry Adams. How can you read that clown? Seriously, you should do some therapy and deal with your internalized anti-Semitism, man. Maybe that's why you can't finish your dissertation."

Before Dark could begin an angry lecture or just tell Peter to shut up, Peter bullet-trained ahead: "I'm doing my master's thesis on David Leavitt. Talk about your fucked-up, shame-based Jews! I'm gonna call it 'The Rise and Fall of a Crypto-Jew.' I mean, it's so cool that he ends up getting busted for plagiarizing Stephen Spender's memoir, but doesn't even steal one of the best parts, about Spender being half-Jewish in England and what it felt like. How perfect is that?"

Despite himself, Dark said, "I didn't know David Leavitt was Jewish." He'd read some of Leavitt's pallid stories years ago and had no idea—not that it mattered.

"See what I mean!" Peter whooped. "You can't really tell!"

"But you admire him? You like his writing?"

"Are you kidding? Absolutely not! He's old news, he's the eighties, just like Tama Janowitz. But he's a great case study. And he hasn't published a whole lot and none of it's deep, so it'll be pretty easy to write about. I already have a publisher at Indiana University Press who wants me to turn it into a book."

Dark cringed at the unspoken assertion that Peter would never take years to write anything.

Peter grabbed his arm. "But what's the point of another Henry James dissertation anyway? Wasn't your father a Holocaust survivor? Why not write about something connected to that? Like—" He hesitated. "Oh, how about rhetorical Holocaust pornography—you know, the way everybody and everything gets compared to the Nazis and the Gestapo? It would be awesome."

Before Dark could reply, Peter strutted off to dance as a thumping Fat Boy Slim song came on. Dark hated techno and electronica and big beat and all of that, but he felt obliged to keep up with contemporary music; reading *SPIN* was just as much a vain conjuration against aging for him as vitamin E.

Dark studied Peter, who didn't seem to be with anyone. Though his basketball shirt, baggy jeans, and high-tops were drab, Peter moved with such confidence he was like a lighthouse beacon offering promise in the fog.

And Dark wanted to punch his lights out. He couldn't believe someone just entering the program knew about his father and, worse, knew he was having trouble finishing his dissertation. What the hell had he become, the Ancient Mariner? How humiliating that Peter wasn't just telling him what to write about, but had tossed off a brilliant idea as if it were nothing.

Dark spent a few fierce moments trying to remember who in the department he'd told about his father's past. But the anger faded into despair as he listened to the hateful music and watched people dance. Dark never danced anymore because it made him feel too old. His students, Peter, everyone danced so differently now—like they thought they were gangsta rappers on MTV, moving their arms and hands in ways that seemed as alien as kabuki.

But then everything these days seemed like a performance he didn't understand or care about. Dark was on another College of Arts and Letters fellowship this year, having used up his five years of assistantship support and two extra years the chair had wangled for him because he was a good teacher. And because the department needed cheap labor.

Having long since finished his course work and taken his comprehensives, he was mostly alone writing, or trying to write. Even the people he knew here, people he had gone drinking with, the ex-girlfriends, were no more than carousel horses, passing quickly and smoothly in their private bright circle, eyes dead, manes and legs frozen in painted delight. He was too tired to argue theories, share complaints about illiterate students, or slander professors. He was too tired, and people no longer expected him to show up when he was invited: "If you were an Indian," one of the department secretaries had said, "your name would be Dark Cloud, honey." His work seemed impossible; each new book and article on James filled him with

dread, as if he were watching a horde of lemmings surge to their strange hyp-
notic death.

What had happened to his love of Henry James, the sense of discovery
and escape when he'd read *Washington Square* and *The Portrait of a Lady* in
college, and imagined himself alive in a different era, alive and purged of
the Jewishness he quietly, fervently loathed?

His advisor in college, Mrs. Olson, had warned against James. She urged
him to choose a minor writer no one had handled, as if dissertation topics
were grapefruit at an open-air stand. That seemed like brilliant advice now in
this dreary apartment, which even music, food, and guests couldn't rescue
from mediocrity. The orange seventies-style plaid furniture supplied by the
landlord, the sagging bunchy curtains, the Pullman kitchen, the flimsy un-
painted doors, and the windowless bathroom with its noisy useless fan were
duplicated all over town. Worst were the matted but unframed cheap Renoir
prints, their colors greasy, the smiles and poses somebody's idea of freedom, ease—as pathetic in their own way as the kindergarten wish of a child
to ride frantically speeding fire trucks through traffic frozen by their blare.
If not Renoir, it was generally poster-size nature photos so artificially beautiful they could've been painted on velvet, or cheaply dramatic wall hangings:
geometrics, rainbows, trees.

Dark drank some more Seagram's, mulling over his morning's news. On
a routine physical, his doctor had found what he thought was a heart murmur and had urged Dark to see a cardiologist. He was only thirty-five, but
suddenly those digits were like the room number at the end of the hospital
corridor where he had seen his father seated in a wheelchair a year ago, eyes
crushed shut by pain, thin white hand circling over his stomach. When his father's cancer—sudden, voracious—had struck at their family, Dark had felt
himself stronger than random crazy cells, felt he could counter anything
and not disintegrate.

But this was new. His own body, his lean, diet-purified, marathoning body,
safe passage through the realms of sickness and death, suddenly seemed jeop-
ardized, as if the government extending his permission to travel had collapsed
in revolution and he was unprotected by its mottoes, interests, seals.

"So what's your real first name?" Peter asked, sailing over to sit by him.
Behind Peter the party lurched and weaved like a furious baroque canvas of
historical mayhem.

"Gregory."

"Puh-leeze! What did your parents call you?"

Peter's thin smooth face was as intent as an obnoxious television inter-viewer's, convinced that truth was only a question away.

"None of your business." Wasn't there any way to made this asshole shut up?

"Whatever. You're definitely Dark."

Yes, he was. Because of his black hair and tanned-looking skin, his mother had often called him "Gypsy." Some girlfriends had wanted him to be French or Greek, whatever they thought was sexy and exotic, and made up nicknames to match. And Dark had never said he was Jewish, had kept his background mysterious. So when Sophia in high school had first called him "Dark" it was less a joke or wish than a discovery. Since then, seeing "Gregory Darkow" on paper, even when he'd signed it, had been like dri-ving by a desolate war memorial where each carved name is merely space pushed into stone: form without substance.

Peter leered. "People tell me you've dated a lot of women in the department."

"Most," Dark said flatly, wanting, for effect, to add "All." He thought, dated and negated.

"Really? And?"

Dark flashed to himself at twelve, confidently explaining the garbled world of sex to an open-mouthed nine-year-old cousin whose curiosity was min-gled with disgust and shame.

"And what? You want details?"

Peter looked down and Dark studied the spiky brown hair dyed blond at the tips, the two small gold hoops in each ear, the thin blue-and-red wreath tattooed around his neck. He felt sudden loathing for this . . . kid. Rising to leave, he wished he were really drunk, or that he'd gone into the bedroom where the cocaine was; then he wouldn't care. "Jew boy," he thought, de-spising Peter's big nose, his accent, his arrogance. Peter had suggested work-ing out together; Dark could imagine helping Peter lift a barbell over his chest and then letting it go. How many ribs would it crack? He smiled.

"Hey, I'm sorry," Peter offered.

"I guess you are."

At home he thought of calling Susan, but she would be up from Providence tomorrow and she didn't like him waking her girls. He could hear her saying, "You couldn't wait? What's the problem?" Susan could not even pity herself. A promising pianist, she had fallen from a tree at fourteen and broken both her hands; her father drank himself into kidney failure and death a few years later; her first lover had abandoned her when she was pregnant, revealing he had a wife in Florida; she had lost the child and spent months in a mental hospital. There was more: two miscarriages, a vicious divorce, all of it like the awful printed cards he remembered deaf-mutes thrusting at people in the New York subways, unfairly forcing pity, shame.

But even at forty, Susan did not look battered. She was beautiful, slim and graceful, gray eyed, with dramatic, foaming, black curly hair like a Restoration wig, extravagant hair, sweet smelling, soft. Years ago, he would have admired her past like some historic plundered marble frieze reproduced in a glossy catalogue, found it exciting, the promise of life. How he'd loved sad novels in college, feeling he must surely be spiritually expanded for reading them. But that was distant suffering—pain that was observed, not experienced. Now, since his father's death, it was all too real, and so seeing Susan every other weekend when her ex-husband had the girls was enough for Dark.

On Saturday mornings they usually talked first, casual memoirists of the week, dropping news and information like cards in a leisurely summertime game on some back porch shaded with honeysuckle. But he couldn't this time. When Susan set her weekend bag down in his living room he pulled at her sweater and jeans, wanting to devour her and time. Their sex was ecstatic, quick, surprising him and amusing her. That was a relief because for too long now, he'd been feeling his body reminiscing with Susan, like a cart horse with blinders on, plodding home, the world reduced to always what's ahead.

From the floor she said, "I guess you were glad to see me, huh?" Later, in bed, she asked, "So what's wrong?" She was smoking with cynical grace, ashtray on her Caesarian-scarred belly.

"Me—my heart." He explained what the doctor had told him. He didn't mention his dissertation. He never did.

Susan pressed for facts. "But you're not even sure it's bad? You won't know right away?" Susan shook her head. "Dark, don't be a baby. Plenty of people live with a little heart murmur, swim and climb mountains and live for ever."

"But I feel bad." It sounded illogically petulant, unequal to what was inside. He wanted to shout, "I'll die before I ever accomplish anything," to punish her somehow, but the words made him dizzy. He had never told her about his father, never told her he was Jewish, had kept as much of his past a secret as possible.

As if hearing his inner moans, Susan said, "God, I am so sick of this. Everyone I know is crazy because they're getting old. Women who can't have kids; this writer, he's thirty-seven, never been published; musicians who couldn't make it in Boston, hell they can hardly make it in Rhode Island; real-estate guys want to earn double their age but don't and never will. That's all I hear. Someone told me last week at a party: 'I feel like killing myself.' I said, 'You want a medal? You think it's brave saying that? Try doing it.' I live in a goddamned cancer ward and everyone's terminal."

He winced, thinking of his father's death, his father's ugly deathbed wish: "Make something of yourself! Do something, for God's sake!" It was a bitter assessment of how little he'd achieved so far, especially when measured against the life his father had lost in the camps, never recovered, never discussed. That absence had sucked the life out of his home, driven his mother to alcoholism, himself to—well, to what? Endless delays?

All his life, Dark had listened to his father complain. Why had he come to America? Why hadn't he left the DP camp for Australia, England, wherever his friends had gone? All of them had become rich. Why hadn't he? Wasn't it enough he lost everyone and everything in the camps? Was he cursed here too? Dark's father was so profoundly ashamed that when old friends visited the United States, he was sullen, unwilling to talk about his history of business failures. "A *groyser gornisht*, a big nothing, that's all I am," he would mutter out of their earshot.

And Dark had somehow been supposed to redeem it all, the war and its aftermath, but that was never going to happen at the rate he was progressing.

"A professor you want to be?" his father had sneered, shaking his head. "A *nechtiger tog*—it'll never happen!" As if Dark were doomed to repeat his father's failure.

Showering, Dark felt diminished by a lifetime of scorn, like a tiny tile set into some vast and horrible Bosch-like mosaic, insignificant by itself.

The water drain seemed slow, and he reached down for a small slick ring of hair that for some time now had been growing there every time he showered, like a pearl responding to the irritation of time. His hairline was creeping up, but hair was appearing in strange places, on and in his ears, across his knuckles, like weeds and wild flowers claiming an empty house and yard.

"You're upset," Susan said at lunch in their favorite restaurant. "But that's good. It's better than being miserable. Maybe it'll get you off your butt. You'll end up like some dried-up old man in a Henry James story if you don't do something."

"Is this, what, an intervention?" Did everyone have to hector him?

"Of course not. I'm just tired of people being afraid to get old. It's not death they're afraid of, it's life. My students write about it—freshmen!" She grimaced, and there at the small crowded table in a halo of wine-sipping couples, he wondered why he'd bothered talking to her last year at the Yale conference, or why he'd wanted more than one weekend together.

"You're not listening," she said.

Chianti. Pasta primavera. Peanut butter pie. Espresso.

They could not decide on a movie, endlessly quoting reviews, friends' comments, suspicions. He did not want to go for a drive. She did not want to shop or make love again. Neither wanted to scrounge up someone to visit.

"It's not a good weekend," he managed.

"No." Susan was no longer critical, dismissive, seeming suddenly like a little girl stifled by her expectation of a treat. He did not want her soft or sympathetic, not today.

"I'll go home," she said. "Call me."

Dark slept until 4:00 A.M., woke sweaty, uncertain, pulled himself into the kitchen to brew coffee. He read until dawn—magazines, the *Times Book Review*—and then slept again, went off for a bike ride at noon, tearing past the subdivisions and little farms there at the edge of town, lost in his body, in the pumping of his legs. Then he watched *Abbott and Costello Meet Frankenstein* and *Tora! Tora! Tora!*

In the evening he dragged himself to a local bar hung with a nightmare of Mexican baskets. While he ordered his third Seagram's, he saw Peter walk in, recognize him with a huge smile. Peter headed over, his walk part dancer's glide, part saunter. Tonight Peter was costumed very differently, wearing Gap chinos, Topsiders, and a red-and-blue-striped shirt. Dark thought of Gudrun in *Women in Love* liking those two strong colors together, but she was so complex, and Peter had nothing but his youth.

Peter said, "I'm sorry I was such a creep Friday night. I like to talk, but when I'm happy, and drunk, I can be rude."

"Happy?"

"Yeah—my interview."

Peter ordered Dubonnet on the rocks.

"My Philip Roth interview, coming out in *New York* magazine," Peter went on. And through a sinking deadness, Dark heard Peter talk about the

Zuckerman books and his editor-father's friendship with Roth. "That's how I got into the program here. Roth wrote a letter of recommendation for me, an awesome letter. Not that I deserved it. I mean, my grades weren't really hot, but the letter—"

They drank a lot, Peter raving about New York, his luck, and Roth, while Dark more and more understood the madman in the Poe story, bricking up his wife's corpse in the cellar. Peter was pushy, Peter had connections, Peter would end up on top—without deserving it.

"You're pretty lucky," Dark said.

"I am. I am lucky. I really haven't worked hard at all. I never have. Things always just turn out right for me."

Dark seethed. Peter was young, brash, connected. He had no illusions about his work being a "contribution." It was clearly just a hoop to jump through. He'd find a job without a problem, ending up at some hip, media-savvy English department awash in cultural studies where everything was race, class, and gender, and where texts had no meaning outside their textuality.

Dark thought of all the papers he'd done at conferences, none published, the articles he had sketched and planned and bought file cards for but never finished, and his degree. In college, it had seemed like an elusive, gleaming storybook treasure, but now, within reach, not much more than the campus stickers you bought so that you could park in certain more convenient lots. Yet he still couldn't finish. And if he did? Who would want to hire someone whose specialty was Henry James?

"Is there really a waterfall near here?" Peter was asking. "People tell me it's great."

"It is. Want to see it?"

"Who's driving?"

"I will."

Dark's car was back across the street and they drove twenty minutes along the desolate interstate.

"You know, since we're getting to be friends, Dark, you should know that—"

"You're gay."

"How . . . ?"

"Dubonnet on the rocks."

Peter laughed nervously, and Dark felt as if Susan's contempt had been animating him.

"It doesn't bother you?"

"I don't care," he said, finishing the sentence silently: "about that."

Dark felt the night air had plucked away his haze by the time they stopped at the edge of the state park. As they headed down the unmarked path, he was murderously clear and determined to act. The full moon's silver, on and through the maples, edged everything with a grim brilliance. He walked without speaking, neared the low heedless roar. At a space in the wall of trees, Dark said, "This is it." He plunged down the slope; the waterfall gleamed above them, cruel, private, eating up their silence. Dark was glad to see that the stream was deeper than he remembered, and as Peter moved closer to the water, Dark thought, Now, shove him in now and hold him under.

He grabbed Peter's meager shoulders, but Peter whirled around with a surprised, wild, eager grin on his face and fell to his knees, grabbing at Dark's crotch with eager hands.

When Dark kneed him in the chin, Peter grunted and fell back, his head and shoulders down in the water, and it was very easy then. Dark crouched down and straddled his scrawny waist heavily to hold that clever, empty head under the ice-cold water as Peter kicked and struggled. Eyes closed, Dark squeezed as if he were getting the proverbial blood from a stone, and it wasn't very hard. He was so much stronger than Peter, and had more to lose now.

Shaking the water from his suddenly cramped hands, drying them on his jeans, he wondered how many people had seen them leave the bar together. Could he hide the body?

He was surprised that these thoughts came to him so calmly. He thought of Henry James's cryptic line, "So here it is at last, the distinguished thing." If he could pull this off, he could do anything.

Like steal Peter's topic, change his dissertation committee, and finally get his doctorate.

For years he'd been ABD: all but dissertation. Now it could mean "aided by death."

He laughed.

SHELLEY SINGER has been a reporter and an editor; she presently teaches fiction writing. She has written two PI series, including six books starring Jake Samson and Rosie Vicente. Her most recent, *Royal Flush,* was published in 1999. She is currently at work on a mainstream novel.

Reconciling Howard

▼   ▼   ▼   ▼   ▼   ▼   ▼   ▼   ▼

sHelLey siNGER

HOWARD KAPLAN WAS NOT MY FAVORITE guy in the world.

We had some history. We had grown up in the same Chicago neighborhood, a few years apart. His father and my father had hung out on the same corner when they were young and useless. Our mothers had belonged to the same gin rummy club.

Sometime in the 1990s, my father mentioned to me that Howard was living in the Bay Area and was doing therapy. I didn't bother to ask what kind or whether he was the patient or the doc. I had said something like *"Nyump?"*—and changed the subject.

Why didn't I like him? I don't know. I remembered him as a skinny, tidy kid, with a long, ferretlike face and eyes that always seemed to be looking sideways at me. His pants were too short and so was his hair. He hadn't seemed to like me any more than I'd liked him

So when he called me I couldn't imagine why.

"Yeah, nice to talk to you again after all these years, too, Howard. And now you're right here in Marin County, eh?"

"Yeah. Yeah. Right here. Listen, Jake, my father says you're some kind of private eye?"

Some kind. I've been doing it for quite a few years, but only recently had gone legitimate, working for my pal Rosie Vicente at her new, legally licensed agency. I'd always looked at a PI license as just something else to lose, myself, but there I was.

"You need a PI, Howard?" Probably wanted me to tail his wife or stalk his girlfriend.

"I think so. See—" he took a deep breath "—someone is threatening my life."

Huh. No wonder he sounded so tense. "Call the cops."

"I already told them. They said they couldn't do anything until someone, you know, does something."

"So who's threatening you?"

"I don't know. But a lot of people don't like me. I mean a lot of people do, of course, but the thing is, see, I'm a facilitator." I didn't say anything, so after a pause and a sigh, he continued. "I do groups where people work out their differences. Reconciliation sessions."

"You mean like family counseling?"

"Not exactly. Israelis and Palestinians, whites and blacks, pro-growth and pro-environment groups—people who want to work out their disagreements. Children of survivors and children of Nazis. That kind of thing."

"You've got like, what, a Ph.D. in enemies?"

"They're not enemies. That's the whole point."

"So how's business?"

He hesitated. "It's building." Translation: not so good. "Listen, how about I read you the note?"

"Go ahead."

He cleared his throat. "It's printed, like, off a computer printer. And it says, 'I can't tell you who I am or how I know this, but someone in your next survivor-Nazi workshop is going to kill you.'"

"When's the next workshop?"

"Saturday."

Three days away.

How would a person find out about the workshop and sign up to kill him? I asked him where and how he found the people who came to his groups. "Oh, well, I'm very involved in the community. There's a need out there for this."

"So you what, put up notices?"

"Yes, of course. Community centers and churches. I have some connections in the legal and related professions. Organizations. Private individuals." He advertised to anyone and everyone with enough money to pay for it. That didn't do much to narrow the field. "Do you want my mailing list?"

"Well . . . okay, fax me a copy." I didn't think it would tell me anything and I guess my tone of voice said that.

"Jake, I don't feel that you're taking me seriously."

"I'm taking the death threat seriously."

"That's not what I mean." He sounded hurt and I flashed back to high school. Was I still judging the man by the standards of sneering adolescence? And combining that, now, with adult cynicism? "This is something I really care about. Reconciliation, resolution, forgiveness." No question about it. I was too cynical. Maybe I needed to do a little reconciling with my better self. "And a lot of people," he added, "feel a strong need to participate."

I supposed that was true. There were always some who'd plunk down a few hundred dollars if someone gave them a captive audience and a chance to talk about their own crap. They could fill up a workshop if he didn't get enough people with real problems.

"And now someone feels a strong need to kill you."

"That's what the note says. Will you help me?"

Howard had insisted we all wear name tags, which I found very useful. I kept pretending to scribble in my little notebook; what I was really doing was looking up the participants in my notes, matching faces with names, backgrounds, and lives. Howard had given me copies of their applications, and I'd done some background checks through the agency's online investigative service. They all seemed to be real people with real histories, including a restraining order, some credit problems, one arrest for shoplifting, one civil suit, and a couple of very expensive houses.

We were all sitting on wooden folding chairs in a nervous circle in this meeting room, maybe twenty by twenty, in a church in San Rafael. A room with spotless white walls, a tan-flecked asphalt tile floor, and a row of small windows that allowed us a view of a dusty hedge through half-open venetian blinds. Howard matched the room in a white shirt, brown tie, and tan pants.

There were four offspring of Nazis, six of concentration camp survivors. Including me, Jake Samson, using the name Jake Solomon. Fictional son of a fictional Buchenwald survivor, alleged Realtor, and undercover liar. Before we'd sat down, Howard had let me know he'd never seen any of these people before in his life.

I looked around the circle. What were they all doing here? Lots of shifty eyes and clenched jaws. Unless the note came from someone who just wanted to scare him—always a possibility—one of them was here to kill Howard. But why, I kept wondering as I listened to each, in turn, tell his or her own story, did the rest of them feel the need to be here at all? Especially the Gestapo babies. Why would they come to something like this? Were they so wracked with genetic guilt that they had to pay to get themselves bashed? Or were they going to use this session to tell the world they were innocent victims of unprotected sex? And as for the Jews—did they feel the need to forgive? The urge to punish someone for what happened to their parents? Or did they just want to feel superior?

In any case, I was going to have to figure out who was here for what reason, if I was going to keep Howard from getting murdered.

Howard, whose nametag said Dr. Howard Kaplan, had just asked Steven Grshenko how he really, really felt about his father the Ukrainian collaborator, and the pudgy little guy yanked at his white-blond hair for a moment before he answered that he loved the old man, who had died just a couple of years before.

Barbara Abramovitz, the Berkeley poet—she was the one with the shoplifting record—lit into him.

"He should have been apprehended. He should have been deported. He should have been fucking hanged!" I didn't disagree with her, but screaming at Steven wasn't going to obliterate Hitler. Or change her childhood with a lunatic into a Dick-and-Jane story. She'd already told us at epic length how her mother, a crazy survivor of a Bergen-Belsen adolescence, had driven her American GI daddy out of the house when Barbara was nine and had then proceeded to sink into a pattern of alternating reclusiveness and explosive, violent rage.

"Now, Barbara," Howard said. "Remember: 'From where do we know that it is cruel not to forgive?'" Until that moment, Barbara had deferred to him and, like the rest of the group, called him Doctor. Now she shot him a look of absolute contempt.

"Forgive, Howard?" Her icy glare would have shrunk a normal man to the size of a toadstool, but he didn't even flinch. He was covered with the armor of righteousness. I was impressed. I had a lot to learn in the armor department. The righteousness department, too.

He didn't say anything, so she cranked it up a notch. "Forgive?" she said again. "What are you talking about?" The ice was turning to fire. Barbara was actually shaking with indignation, her frizzy red hair quivering in a weird, electric way. "That Steven is right to forgive his father? Or that I should forgive a murderer? Which is it? And I don't hear Steven talking about forgiveness. Do we even know he thinks there's anything to forgive?" She glared at Steven, who stared back at her in stunned or maybe just blank blondness, scratching the back of his right hand.

Judy Mills, the professor of Holocaust studies, was nodding thoughtfully. "Steven, what about that? I think the group would like to hear how you found out what your father did. And how it made you feel. And—"

"Oh for Christ's sake!" Ralph Witt yelled, jerking forward in his chair like he was going to jump out of it. Ralph had very white skin and very dark hair, and when he flushed with emotion he looked like Snow White with too much makeup. "He's here. He's talking to you. He didn't have to come. How do you think he feels?" Ralph was Gestapo offspring. He was the one with the restraining order, ten years ago. An old girlfriend had claimed he was violent.

Frank Horowitz stood and walked to the window, raising a muscular arm to fiddle with the blinds. Closing them and opening them again before he turned back to us. "Why doesn't he tell us, then?" Frank always sounded neutral, or at least he had during the first hour of the group. He was either the coolest dude in the room or he was hiding his feelings. "And this does bring up a question. Are any of these war criminals still alive? Unprosecuted? Aren't you people afraid we'll send the Nazi hunters after them? We know your names."

Marlene Sharp turned pale and jumped to her feet. "My father was just a boy. A guard. He doesn't live in this area and you're not going to send anyone to get him. Is that all you're after? Revenge?" Her blue eyes looked huge behind the thick lenses of her glasses. Marlene had too much debt on too many credit cards, but if that made her dangerous, we'd need an army on every corner to keep the peace.

Frank shrugged. We already knew Steven's father was dead. Carl Brunner and Ralph both said theirs were, too, but I hadn't been able to find any death record on Carl's dad, an SS guard at Bergen-Belsen.

"And as for that 'cruel not to forgive' stuff, Howard . . . " Oops. Frank had dropped the "Doctor," too. But the look Howard leveled back at him was calm, interested. ". . . it is also written—I can't remember where, but I went to Hebrew school, too—that sins between men—I assume that means people—" he got a small laugh there for the sins between men. Frank was in a twenty-five-year relationship with another man "—are never forgiven until the sinner pays his debt and appeases the one he harmed. And wouldn't there be some question about whether all Jews would have to forgive collectively since the crime was committed against all Jews?" Frank's face was open, playful, like a kid enjoying his first school debate.

"You going to keep throwing Jewish Scripture at us?" Ralph's white face was red again. "How we going to argue against that? Doctor Kaplan?" He tossed a challenging scowl at Howard.

This guy really had me on edge. "Don't worry," I told him. "I don't know any Scripture except 'an eye for an eye and a tooth for a tooth.'" Now it was my turn for Ralph's high-blood-pressure glare. A little late, I realized I should be trying to keep him calm, not pissing him off.

Howard held up his hand, giving me one of his sideways looks. "'It is forbidden to be cruel and difficult to appease.' Maimonides said that." Maimonides. I think my father mentioned that name once. A Jewish philosopher. Middle Ages. That was as far as my knowledge went. My father had strong feelings about forcing religion on people, and religion was one of the few areas where he was willing to give a child the status of person.

"Ya wanna go to Hebrew school?"

"No."

"Okay."

I pulled myself back from the distant past and realized Paul Shapiro was now speaking.

"But the Law says that the iniquity of the fathers will be visited 'upon the children, and upon the children's children, unto the third and unto the fourth generation.' That's in Exodus. And these people are just the children. So they carry their fathers' sins. Don't they?" Wow. Unto the third and fourth. That could take a while. Didn't some of those biblical guys live to be hundreds of years old? Paul was looking around the room, smug and maybe a little vindictive. I glanced at my notes. He owned a pet shop and from his financial picture, it wasn't doing well. Before the pet shop, he'd failed in the restaurant business. But being a schlemiel didn't make him a killer.

"Look," Lael Gold said, "It's not like we're talking about an insult or a stolen goat or something." A stolen goat? "Nobody can forgive someone for something he does to someone else. Only the wronged person can forgive. That pretty much leaves murder out of it. Dead people can't forgive, and we can't forgive for them." She was smiling as she talked. She smiled when other people talked. I could actually picture her writing that note to Howard and smiling the whole time. Creepy. And she had a sweaty look to her, too, or maybe her skin was oily.

A pretty good argument, though. How would Howard answer her? He didn't. He just started asking people about their experiences with forgiving.

No wonder someone said that for every ten Jews there are eleven opinions. Or something like that. How could we help it? There was the Law, and then there were all those old bearded guys interpreting the Law. For a minute there, until Lael had spoken, even I had gotten caught up in the argument about stolen goats and the forgiveness of the dead and stopped thinking about murder. About which angry person in this room had threatened to kill Howard.

It didn't seem to matter that I'd lost my yarmulke years ago and never missed it, that the last time I remembered being in a synagogue was sometime around puberty and John Kennedy had just been assassinated—well, maybe that's an exaggeration. Doesn't matter. You can take the boy out of the yarmulke but you can't . . .

Sherlock Holmes would have stayed focused on the job. He was a Brit. And unlike Sherlock the Cool, I had my own emotions to contend with here. The neighborhood I grew up in, the Holocaust was real. We all knew all about it, if only secondhand. I'd met a couple of actual survivors when I was a kid, people who knew my dad or my mother. I remembered one sweet, pretty woman with a bullet scar on her cheek. And it wasn't helping that I'd refreshed my memory with some online concentration camp sites so I wouldn't make some total schmuck mistake about Buchenwald and blow my cover. Those sites are graphic, to put it mildly.

Over the years, I hadn't thought about the Nazis much more than I thought about the Inquisition. When I'd see a movie, sure. Then there was the time Rosie and I went undercover in a baldness of skinheads. Well, what, then? A herd? A gaggle? But every time I did think about it, I understood one thing clearly: if my parents had been in Europe during that war, I would never have been born.

I had to clear my mind. Which was I, anyway? The coulda-been yeshivah boy? The pissed-off Jew? Sherlock Holmes? No contest today. I was getting paid to be Sherlock.

Marlene Sharp was staring at her red-painted fingernails. Steven, in the chair next to hers, was patting his own knee with a rapid da-da rhythm. He'd been scratching that hand more, I saw. It was almost as red as Marlene's fingernails. Judy was delivering some little treatise on what forgiveness was and was not, complete with historical references. Marlene looked up, her magnified eyes flashing.

"Could we please stop acting like a bunch of hair-splitting rabbis?"

Judy gasped. Lael's dark eyes narrowed dangerously over her white-toothed smile. What kind of weapon would Lael use if she wanted to kill someone? I couldn't picture her with a gun.

Steven rested his raw hand on his thigh and began to scratch it again, staring blankly out the window.

Marlene went on. "Should you forgive us? Does your Law say you should forgive us? Or even that you can?"

My Law. Now there was a concept. I'd always thought my law was American. English common. Not something conceived by a bunch of nomads sitting on a dune or a gang of medieval scholars whose only real country was the Law they argued about.

"What exactly would it take to pay the debt and appease you? Maybe we have to die first? Excuse me, but what a pile of shit! I haven't done anything to be forgiven for. I came here to talk, to—I don't know why I came. Because of my father. Because he was at Maidanek. He was sixteen. You have no idea of what he felt or what he did or what they would have done if he hadn't done his job or how he feels now. But the point is, I'm here because it was all horrible, because I can't even begin to understand how horrible it was or why people did the things they did. And because I wanted to meet you and say that I want you to forgive my father." She started to cry. I crossed Marlene off my list. I couldn't see her threatening Howard. One down, eight to go.

Paul was nodding. "She's right. She's not here to be forgiven, and we're not here to forgive." I looked at him hard. What did he mean by that? Couldn't read him. That alone was enough to worry me.

"So what are we here for, Paul?" I asked

"Jesus!" Ralph exploded. "Another metaphysical discussion?"

"Oh, take it easy, Ralph." Carl Brunner put his thick arm around the other man's shoulder. Carl had been pretty quiet so far. He was a big friendly guy, a contractor, son of a Bergen-Belsen guard. "We're not here to fight."

Ralph grunted and stared at Howard again. "Dr. Kaplan? You tell us. What are we supposed to be doing here?" The others all looked at Howard, too, waiting for whatever he had to offer. I hoped they wouldn't be disappointed. I hoped it would be good. Everyone but the potential killer had come because they thought they needed to do this, for whatever reason. They needed Howard.

Howard sat silent for a moment. Searching Jewish law? Thinking about following orders in the Fatherland? Trying to remember why he was there?

"Reconciliation. Learning to drop the hate and fear and guilt and realize everyone here is just a person who can do better and who can be friends despite history." Carl nodded enthusiastically. He wanted to be friends. "That we are not our history. We are ourselves. We need to recognize one another's humanity. We need to give shape to our grief. Reconciliation comes out of forgiveness. Forgiveness happens inside the person who forgives. Forgiveness of one person by another is complete in and of itself whether or not it leads to reconciliation. But reconciliation takes two. It is the responsibility of both parties." My head was swimming. There were only so many catchphrases I could absorb all at once. I was losing touch with reality. Was he making sense or talking crap? I couldn't get a grip on it. "Now!" he said. "Let's focus our discussion." He tented his fingers and looked at them as if he'd find the focus there. Everyone settled down, seemed to sink into their wooden chairs, waiting.

"When you were growing up, did your family talk about the war? Raise your hands if they did."

None of the Nazi offspring raised a hand. Barbara was the first to react. Then Lael, then Paul.

"Tell us what they said. Barbara?"

"My mother talked about it all the time. Sometimes she'd start talking and couldn't stop until she was crying so hard she couldn't talk at all. Then she'd go into her room for days. Then she'd come out breaking things and screaming." Barbara spoke quietly, looking at the floor. "I wrote a poem about that." She raised her dark eyes and sent a piercing look around the circle, but no one asked her to read it. They were all probably as reluctant as I was to hear her cut loose in verse. Maybe they were just scared she'd cut loose completely.

"Lael?" Howard said.

Barbara jerked her head away from him as though she'd been slapped.

"My mother, too," Lael answered. "She wouldn't talk about it a lot and she never cried." I checked my notes, pretending I was scratching my nose. Lael's mother was an Auschwitz survivor. "But she would tell me how you have to be strong, always aware, always on guard. Her whole life was dedicated to never forgiving, never forgetting. It killed her. I don't want it to kill me." She was positively grinning.

"Paul?"

"They talked about it. They hated Germans, they hated Poles, they hated the English because they tried to keep refugees out of Palestine. But mostly they just talked about how they met in the refugee camp, or about their life in Brazil. But I'm really here about me. Someone needs to make things right for me." Someone? Because he couldn't ever seem to make things right for himself? A whiner, wet with self-pity.

"So, Marlene . . . " Howard shifted his gaze to her. "Your father must have talked about the war a little. You knew he was a guard, that he was sixteen. . . . "

"That's all he said. Not about the war, but about how he was just a boy and didn't know what was going on and had to follow orders. He would never say more than that. He cried, once, talking about that." She shot a vicious look at Barbara, who curled her lip and turned away, opening the purse she'd hung on the back of her chair. She pulled out a long nail file and began to saw at a thumbnail. As she sawed, she stared at Howard, who was sitting right next to her. I thought that was odd, since she was mad at Marlene. I kept my eye on that nail file.

Howard spoke again. "When I first began doing these workshops, a lot of people were angry about them. On both sides. Some said they didn't do anything, that they were born in this country and weren't guilty of anything. And some said there was no forgiveness, not ever, no reason even to talk. Some, like Paul, said we could talk after four generations. Some, like Lael, said the dead can't talk at all and can't forgive. And even if the Law says those things, and people carry guilt that way, more and more people, I think, have come together, or at least talked about coming together. And that's good." He nodded, as if he were agreeing with himself. "How many feel guilty about what happened?"

Three of the four Nazi babies raised their hands. The holdout was Ralph.

"I don't feel guilty," he said, standing and gripping the back of his chair. "I'm sorry it happened. I want to come to terms with it, with what my father did. I want to feel that I've made an effort to reach out. But I don't think I should have to feel guilty—" he punctuated the word by lifting the chair in his hands and banging the legs back down "—and it really pisses me off that anyone thinks I should." He looked puffed up, as if someone had pumped more air into him than his body could hold.

Barbara—she was still holding that nail file—took a breath, but whatever she was going to say didn't have a chance to come out. Howard was right there.

"That's good, Ralph. Very good. You're being honest. You're telling the truth. Is there any more truth you'd like to tell? Anything you might have left out?" Howard's words struck me as silly, but he knew what he was doing. Ralph seemed to have deflated. Now if he'd just sit down . . .

"Yeah. I want these people here to understand, and say they understand, that I'm not guilty of anything."

"Bullshit!" Barbara screamed. That did it. Ralph puffed up again and turned redder than ever.

"It's not bullshit! It's! Not!" He picked up his chair. "Bull! Shit!" He raised the chair over his head and heaved. It sailed over Barbara's head—or really, over both Barbara and Howard—and crashed into the wall behind her, denting and scraping its tidy whiteness. Barbara dropped her nail file and sat, gray faced and frozen in place for a moment. When she leaned over and began to grope on the floor for the nail file, Howard picked it up and handed it to her. Then he stood and turned toward the fallen chair. But Steven was moving faster and got there first. He retrieved the chair and set it down next to Ralph, who glared at Steven, glared at the chair, and sat back down. I noticed that Steven had rolled up his shirtsleeves. His forearms were covered with little scars.

Marlene was crying again. Everyone else was silent.

Howard broke the spell. "Something else I'd like to ask," he said. "How many of you have trouble sleeping?"

Slowly, one at a time, about half the group raised their hands. Pretty soon, they'd be talking about insomnia. Amazing. Was that the way Howard always handled tantrums in his groups? Or was this a special treatment, for prospective killers only? Everyone was still in shock. The wall was scraped and dented. But Howard was acting like it hadn't happened at all. The technique seemed to be working. After all, Ralph was sitting in his chair, not bashing it over Howard's head.

"Anyone want to talk about not sleeping?"

Barbara had come out of her stupor. "Why aren't you throwing this man out of here?" She pointed her nail file at Ralph. "He could have killed someone." Judy and Paul both nodded, Paul scowling, his face dark. His fists were clenched.

"I didn't throw it at anyone," Ralph shot back, jumping to his feet again. "I threw it at the wall!"

Marlene was brushing something imaginary off her blouse. Steven was scratching his hand, watching Howard blankly, his body so tight I could feel it. Lael was smiling. Carl was cracking his knuckles and staring out the window. He stood, suddenly, and reached into his jacket pocket. I tensed, ready to jump him. He pulled out a pack of cigarettes and headed for the door.

I could have sworn the temperature in the room was up by a good ten degrees. If someone started fighting, if the place erupted, that would give the killer a chance to get to Howard and, in the confusion. . . . Was that the whole point of all this? But quietly, firmly, Howard continued.

"We are now talking about not sleeping."

The guy was a real study in contrasts. He sounded and acted silly, sometimes even foolish, stumbling over his own catchphrases. But at the same time he was an in-control iceberg of a man. A rock. Who seemed to know what he was doing. Maybe.

Frank spoke up. "I have trouble sleeping. It's because of the dream, mostly." He hesitated, chewing his lip. Frank's mother had survived Auschwitz and married another survivor. He'd been born the next year.

Paul had settled back down, grudgingly, and so did Ralph. I could still feel Steven's tension, and Barbara couldn't take her eyes off Frank. Carl was walking back and forth outside, smoking.

"I had the dream for the first time when I was little—I must have been about three or four. I was inside a circle of trees and there were Nazis marching around outside the circle and they'd taken my parents and they were looking for me. I waited and waited for them to go away, and then I sneaked out and ran—and then I woke up. I know the dream came from things I'd heard the grownups talking about, it wasn't clairvoyant or anything. But I've had it again, or pieces of it, or dreams like it, all my life. And when I dream it and I wake up I can't go back to sleep. Sometimes I wake up crying." There were tears running down his cheeks now, but he shrugged. "The first few times I did that with Mario, he was really scared." Mario was his boyfriend.

Howard nodded. Judy got up from her chair and went to Frank, putting her arms around him, patting his salt-and-pepper hair. He cried a little more, then smiled and thanked her.

"That's very good," Howard said. "Anyone else?" No one moved or spoke. "Okay, now I want everyone to stand up. I want everyone to just walk around to other people and touch their arms, their shoulders, their hands. I want you to touch everyone in the group, to feel their realness. Their humanity and physical warmth. Do that now."

Oh, great, perfect timing for touchy-feely. They were quiet enough, but no one was relaxed. I was sure someone would touch too hard or say just the wrong thing when they touched. Not to mention what a good chance this would be for someone to jump Howard.

But he was in charge, so we all stood up and wandered around touching one another while I tried to have eyes in the back of my head. Suspects? I had a few favorites. Ralph, because of his temper and his lack of repentance—it might just make him real angry that someone thought he needed reconciling. Barbara, because her mother was crazy and I got the feeling she wanted to punish someone for something. Paul, because he was a failure looking for a scapegoat or someone to beat at something. Steven, because he was like a thick cable full of hot wires. And Lael, because she gave me the creeps.

When Steven got around to touching my arm, lightly and quickly, I took a closer look at that hand he kept scratching. He'd gouged it down to raw flesh. Three bleeding stripes in a field of bright pink. And the scars on his arms could have been from gouges, too. Or knife cuts. Okay, so I'd put Steven at the top of my list.

Ralph tried to touch Barbara, but she wouldn't let him near her and wouldn't touch him. He approached Paul, who jabbed him on the shoulder. I'd been watching and I was there, putting myself between them, bouncing back the heat from Ralph's rage until Paul backed away, sulking. Lael touched no one's actual skin, only clothed shoulders, until she got to Frank. She touched his hand.

After everyone milled around for a while, and the touching seemed to be done, we all stood there with our arms hanging, waiting for the next instruction.

"I think," Howard said, "that it's time for lunch." I heard Lael inviting Barbara to the veggie burger place down the street. I couldn't quite get a fix on Barbara, so I said I'd like to join them. They said that would be okay. Lael smiled. Not her usual generic smile. Something warmer. Oh, good, she liked me.

"I'll catch up with you," I told them. "Just want a word with Dr. Kaplan . . ."

I watched how the lunch groups formed. Carl, Ralph, Marlene, and

Steven clumped together and squeezed out the door. Judy and Frank left chatting with each other. As I watched them, I really studied Judy's face for the first time and saw that she'd had a nose job. A professor of Holocaust history with a cropped nose? What the hell was that about? I'd always thought that a lot of people did it so they wouldn't look Jewish. But maybe she did it when she was sixteen and it was the fashion. Or maybe she'd had a honker that got in the way when she kissed. Then I tried to picture her kissing and just couldn't do it.

Paul wandered off by himself. *Hmm,* I thought. A loner.

When they were all out the door, Howard grabbed my elbow. "What do you think?"

"You've got a few people here who seem pretty unstable. Some who are downright weird and scary. What I'm wondering is how the killer's planning to do it. Only someone entirely nuts would stick a knife between your ribs in front of nine witnesses. And probably would have done it by now."

Howard waved that thought away. "I was thinking poison. When everyone comes back from lunch, why don't I try leaving my coffee cup somewhere in a corner while I have them do an exercise? And you watch. And we'll catch him! Or her."

"We could try that," I said doubtfully. "It might work." I was thinking anyone who wanted to kill him would be smarter to wait until he headed home, follow him, and shoot him.

Lunch at the veggie place was interesting. Barbara was packing poetry, a slim volume of her own stuff, and Lael, being creepy, prevailed on her to read some. It was a lot better than I'd expected it to be. For one thing, most of the poems were short and to the point. Strong rhythms, too. Some of it was almost like rock music, while one or two were more like jazz: wandering, improvisational, moody. But most of what I heard I'd compare to rap. Not particularly foulmouthed, but hostile as hell. Let me tell you, I'd hate to be a bona fide power in the patriarchy and be standing in front of her when she had a gun. But I didn't think Howard qualified as any kind of power.

Lael sat beside me, and from time to time I could feel her thigh pressing on mine. Barbara sat across from me, and if she could have folded her arms across her chest, read her poetry, and eaten her burger at the same time, she would have. After she finished reading a dozen poems, she segued into a lengthy lecture, aimed at me, on the evils of private property, Berkeley style. I couldn't figure out why she was doing it until I remembered I was supposed to be a Realtor. She asked me if I didn't feel guilty selling Bay Area property at its ridiculously inflated price, so inflated that most people couldn't buy their own homes, so inflated that the rich were getting richer.

"Think of it this way," I told her. "Nobody's really getting richer unless they sell out and move to Kansas. Then the average Bay Area homeowner can afford a mansion and enough cash left over to live on for the rest of his life. But if you stay in the Bay Area, there's no profit. You can only go from one inflated house to another. It's like Monopoly money. It isn't doing anyone any good and I agree it's doing a lot of harm. But I can't fix it. And meanwhile, I can help people find what they can afford." I'd had a Realtor girlfriend a couple of years before. We'd talked about that kind of thing.

Barbara snorted at me but didn't really have an answer. Lael reached over and squeezed my thigh. The veggie burger tasted like dust with garlic and tomato.

All I had after lunch was a small bruise on my right leg, the certainty that Barbara had violent tendencies, and gas from the garlic.

Howard was there to greet us all as we filtered back in. He had a paper cup of coffee, and made a big show of taking off the lid and placing the cup on a table in the corner.

"Here's what we're going to do next. We're all going to stand up in a circle and hold hands. Alternating. Carl, take Barbara's hand. Barbara, take Marlene's. And so on."

We did as we were told. Ralph stood safely between Judy and me.

"Now just stand there feeling the other person's hand. Think about how much it feels like yours. Think about forgiveness and love. Think about telling all of the truth and making your apologies to one another. Not a single person in this room was responsible for harming any other person here." We stood there. I was holding Steven's hand on one side and Ralph's on the other. Ralph's hand was hot. Steven's was clammy, but at least I wasn't holding the one that was bleeding. Lael was. I wondered if she'd noticed.

"Now think about being the other person." We thought, or pretended to. "Now you're going to *be* the other person. Frank, you are Ralph. Ralph you are Frank. . . . " He went around the circle and gave us each a role to play. Unfortunately, the numbers were uneven—he had six Jews and four Nazi kids. So after he'd paired off Ralph with Frank, Barbara with Carl, Judy with Marlene, and Lael with Steven, he fudged. "Paul, Jake, you'll be free-circulating and taking on any role you want at any given time." He shot me a quick significant look to let me know he was giving me the opportunity to listen to and watch everybody. "And any of you can switch roles with any-one else anytime you feel it's appropriate." Well, that was loose enough. He made it sound like a plan. I was thinking he didn't have a choice; he just hadn't attracted enough Nazi kids to balance the workshop.

He watched for a while, stepping in once when Barbara dropped out of her role as Carl and threatened to slap Steven for his grinning impersonation of Lael, who seemed finally to have noticed his hand. She was staring at it. He was scratching it again. It was really a mess. There was blood smeared all over it. Pretty soon it would be dripping onto the tan tiles.

Howard said, "Excuse me," and slipped out the door.

Paul went to be Ralph with Barbara. I joined Judy in being Marlene, crying and talking about my teenage dad. The real Carl, playing Barbara, started raving about an eye for an eye and no forgiveness. Then Paul got tired of being Ralph and abruptly announced he was Frank. He started speaking to the room at large, wandering around the edges, saying he was Frank as a little boy, looking for his parents, afraid. And who would take care of him? he asked. Who would make up for his parents' being gone? Then Ralph started crying and asked Paul if he could be Frank, too. It was get-ting pretty chaotic. Paul must have wandered past that coffee three or four times. Everyone was all over the place. I saw Lael bump into the table the coffee was sitting on. Then Howard stuck his head in the door. If he was going to keep popping in and out no one would have a chance to poison his coffee.

"Okay—now, everyone switch roles!" We were way ahead of him. "Take any role you want except yourself. Remember—appease and forgive and rec-oncile! Remember—it is cruel not to forgive! Forgiveness happens inside. It takes two to reconcile!" I was watching Paul. He shook his head. Howard was not convincing him. What was Paul doing there if he was going to be so hard to convince? Then Howard pulled his head back and disappeared again, closing the door. Now we really had chaos because people were being forced to switch from roles they'd chosen on their own. Lael refused to be Ralph when he asked her to switch with him. Marlene started crying again when Frank asked her to be him. It was all I could do to keep an eye on that coffee cup. But I'd been doing some thinking, and I was beginning to get a glimmer of what to look for and who to suspect. I watched.

Howard stayed away for half an hour. By the time he came back, everyone was sitting down, roles dropped, exhausted. I had seen Lael hug Marlene and Carl hug Frank. Ralph clapped me on the back at one point and told me he thought I was a hell of a guy. I sent it right back at him. Steven was clasping his bloody hand, staring at nothing. He looked beat.

Howard went to the table in the corner and picked up his cup. He looked at me. I thought for a minute. Should I make it a definite "no"? I decided against that. I wanted to convey that I could have missed something. So I raised my eyebrows noncommittally and shrugged. He brought the cup to his lips. I saw his nostrils contract as he breathed in the steam. Then he got this funny expression on his face and sniffed harder. He shot me a fierce look, nodded once, and jerked a thumb at the door.

"Lock it, Jake!" I ran to lock it. He whipped out his cell phone and called the police.

The coffee, he told them, had been poisoned. They needed to come and take it and analyze it and find out who in the group had tried to kill him. I swept a look around the room. Everyone looked horrified except for Lael. She wasn't smiling but she looked cheery, like this was the most fun she'd had in years.

The thing was, I'd really had my eye on that coffee all along. I knew damned well no one had put anything in it from the time Howard brought it in and set it down on that table. But I was also sure that they'd find poison in it.

When the police came, Howard demanded that everyone be searched, and I wondered what they'd find. Did he have a fall guy picked out? Had he planted something on someone? Turned out, no. He lacked either the nerve or the meanness to go that far. He was just setting up a puzzle—how did the villain manage to poison the drink and have no trace of packaging or powder on him? Maybe he thought he'd even get on that TV show about unsolved mysteries.

I suggested they search Howard while they were at it. Howard threw me a shocked, questioning look but raised his arms and offered them his body. Everyone else in the room stared at me like I'd lost my mind. Steven brushed the back of his hand across the tears on his cheek, leaving a red smear. Judy demanded to know what I thought I was doing, treating Dr. Kaplan this way.

When they didn't find anything on Howard, I suggested they search his car, and he started dancing around, yelling about search warrants. That of course made the cops suspicious. When they said they'd get one, he fell into his chair all slumped and dismal.

"Oh, go ahead," he told them. Then he raised his watery blue eyes to me. "Don't tell anyone."

I nodded. I knew who he meant. My father. Anyone in Chicago.

"I wanted to put everything I had into this, but I wasn't getting enough people."

"Sorry, Howard," I said.

"I don't think you are. I don't think you ever understood what this meant to me, how important I feel it is, how much I needed to make it work."

"I understand that now." And I could just imagine his fantasy headlines. Brave Workshop Facilitator Foils Mysterious Murder Attempt. Courageous Healer Vows to Continue Reconciliation Work. Who Hated the Hate Fighter?

"And who was I hurting, anyway?" Me, for one. He'd hired me to legitimize his game, hired me to be too dumb to figure it out. But I just shrugged.

I could hear little whimpers and sighs and grunts around me as people began to figure out what was going on, and I should have been keeping an eye on Ralph. Suddenly he was a blur heading for Howard, screaming "You son of a bitch!" I went for him, one of the cops went for him, and together the three of us made a tangled mess on the floor. Ralph had a cut lip, my knee was a throbbing knob of pain, and even the young cop was rubbing his elbow. But Howard never even said thanks.

Whatever he'd used, he'd been dumb enough to leave evidence in his car. Rat poison, I found out later, and the package was in his dash compartment. I also found out later that Howard's workshops had not only not been "building," they'd been getting smaller and smaller. So he came up with a plan to attract attention.

We all had to sit around for a while until the police hauled Howard away. I wasn't sure what they would charge him with. Filing a false police report? I liked reckless endangerment of workshop groupies. After all, I wouldn't have put it past Barbara to shoplift a couple sips of coffee. Or Marlene to weep away all her bodily fluids and reach desperately for the cup. And Steven could have used a transfusion.

I didn't think Howard would have to serve much in the way of time, if anything, but at least the publicity stunt wasn't going to work. He'd be getting headlines, all right. Both Carl and Paul said they'd make sure of that. Carl had a son working for a local TV news show. Paul had a cousin on the *Chronicle*.

"I say we all forgive him," Carl said. Ralph, nursing his lip, shot him an ugly glare.

"If he begs us to," Judy said. She looked pretty angry, too.

"Do we all collectively have to forgive him? Unto the fourth generation?" Marlene said, giggling.

When we were finally allowed to leave that room, Lael, who had stopped smiling when Howard called the police and hadn't smiled since, made a point of saying to Steven, "I'm going to forgive you for making fun of me. I'll have to think about the rest."

We shook hands and said good-bye; there were even a few hugs. But no one looked peaceful or satisfied.

I figured I could probably forgive Howard. All he'd stolen from me, in the end, was time and the money I should have earned. But he'd taken a lot more from the others. He was supposed to be teaching them to forgive and forget, to sleep well without nightmares, to reconcile themselves to their parents' evil. For a while, it almost seemed as if he were doing that. I could feel pity and compassion in the room, as well as the anger and grief. But in the end, it was just a scam. He'd been willing to put us all under suspicion for attempted murder. What kind of message is that when the Law, and the scholars, and eleven out of ten Jews already disagree?

Maybe, after all, I couldn't forgive Howard. And like Lael, I'd be thinking about the rest.

JANICE STEINBERG'S five mystery novels feature Margo Simon, a San Diego public radio reporter. The most recent, *Death in a City of Mystics*, transports Margo to Safed, Israel, for centuries a center for the study of Jewish mysticism. *Death in a City of Mystics* was nominated for a Shamus Award. The author's first midrash, a retelling of the story of Adam and Eve, appeared in the Summer 2000 issue of *Living Text: The Journal of Contemporary Midrash*.

Hospitality in a Dry Country

▼　　▼　　▼　　▼　　▼　　▼　　▼　　▼　　▼　　▼　　▼　　▼

JANICE STEINBERG

LED BY THE PROPHETESS DEBORAH, the Israelites achieved a great victory against their foes, the Canaanites, recounted in the Book of Judges. The defeated enemy general, Sisera, sought refuge with Heber, a man who had separated from his clan (the Kenites) and formed an alliance with the Canaanite oppressors. The bold actions taken by Heber's wife, Jael, were celebrated in Deborah's triumphal song. Deborah not only exalted the victors, however. She also sang of Sisera's mother, who did not yet know that the battle—and her son—were lost.

> Most blessed of women be Jael,
> Wife of Heber the Kenite.
> Most blessed of women in tents.
> He asked for water, she offered milk;
> In a princely bowl she brought him curds.
> Her left hand reached for the tent pin,
> Her right for the workman's hammer.
> She struck Sisera, crushed his head,
> Smashed and pierced his temple.
> At her feet he sank, lay outstretched.

At her feet he sank, lay still;
Where he sank, there he lay—destroyed.

Through the lattice peered Sisera's mother,
Behind the lattice she whined:
"Why is his chariot so long in coming?
Why so late the clatter of his wheels?"
The wisest of her ladies give answer;
She, too, replies to herself:
"They must be dividing the spoils they have found:
A damsel or two for each man,
Spoil of dyed cloths for Sisera,
Spoil of embroidered cloths,
A couple of embroidered cloths
Around every neck as spoil!"

—JUDGES 5:24–30

Two legends exist about Sisera and his mother. According to the Talmud, Rabbi Akiva, one of the greatest figures in Jewish history, was a direct descendent of Sisera. And it is said that the wail of the shofar on Rosh Hashanah is the sound of Sisera's mother's tears.

She Who Slew the General

Jael:

It is said of me that I was so seductive, the mere sound of my voice aroused desire! Seven times that day, it is said, I lay with the enemy general, but not once did I take pleasure in it. It is even said—by the learned men whose brows turn slick with sweat as they imagine themselves within my tent, their holy loins on fire—that I suckled the man I was about to kill with sweet milk from my breasts.

But it is not yet time to tell my story. The other one clamors to be heard, she who sought the truths only I could tell. She who would come to my tent and receive refreshment, as her son had done.

She Who Is Given No Name

Sisera's Mother:

Why did I raise a warrior? Why not an artisan or a merchant? Or one of those small, clever men with oiled hair who stand at King Jabin's side and whisper counsel into his ear?

But this womb of mine was not formed to carry small, meek, oily men! A great general like Sisera can only be born of a woman who is a warrior herself. Erect I stood, wearing the costly blue-dyed robes I had donned to celebrate our victory, as the first ill tidings were related to me: of our nine hundred iron chariots lured into the wadi at the base of Mount Tabor. And of the terrible storm, sent by the Israelites' god, that flooded the wadi and trapped the heavy chariot wheels in mud. My legs lost their strength. Still I remained standing as I heard of the retreat of the army, the men running from their useless chariots. And then the Israelite soldiers—who would have imagined the Israelites, our vassals for twenty years, so bold?—rushed forward and slaughtered them all.

"Surely not all," I said to the sniveling servant who had thrown himself prostrate on the ground in front of me.

"Perhaps not all, mistress," he said, his body shaking. (A man so craven, never could I have given birth to such a one!)

"Do not lie to me!"

"Mistress, I have heard of no survivors. But the word is slow in—"

"Enough!" I kicked his side.

A courageous spirit is no nostrum against grief. Would that it were! I dismissed the messenger and all of my ladies except Nera, who has served me since we were both children. Only then did I allow my boneless limbs to rest, as Nera helped me to a couch and held a cup of wine to my lips.

I thought at that moment I had descended to such suffering I could not endure it. Later I would wish for the suffering of that first day, the sharp, clean loss of believing my son had died a warrior's death.

Only my dear Nera dared tell me the strange story that was next whispered in our defeated city. The Israelites were led by a woman! This woman had not marched into battle at the head of the soldiers. That, at least, was the work of their general, Barak. But he was guided in all he did by a prophetess; he had even refused to march unless she was beside him. There was no honor in this for Barak. And even less for my poor Sisera.

Oh, and if that were all! But the gods had reserved for me even deeper shame.

"What was done to him?" I cried, when our people were allowed to bring my son's body home. "Did they mutilate him thus after his death?"

For his skull was crushed as if some great fist had squeezed the life from him, shattering brain and bone.

Nera and I undressed Sisera. Anyone who believes a woman too delicate to view her child's corpse knows nothing of childbirth! Four babies ripped through my thighs into this world. One of them was pulled from me gray as ash, its umbilicus wrapped around its neck. Two more I buried before they had lived ten years. To handle a dead child does not frighten me.

My son was a massive man, and it took the strength of both of us to turn him. Why did I feel I had to do this? I wondered later. Did I simply want to see and touch every part of my son, as I did after he first fought his way out of my womb? Or had his spirit whispered to me while I slept? Was that why I scrutinized his lifeless body as if I were one of the king's spies?

Like a spy, I discovered a secret. There was no mark of any sword or spear on him. The terrible crushing of his skull was not a blow inflicted after his death. Rather, it was the very cause of it.

"Did he fall beneath a chariot wheel?" I said to Nera, but answered myself: "Surely, if he had fallen among the chariots, he would have suffered injuries over his entire body. And his garments would be torn."

"Perhaps the enemy soldiers seized him and set upon him with their fists and feet. Cowards!" Nera said, tears in her eyes.

"Foolish woman! Would fists and feet have shattered only his head, any more than chariot wheels?"

Nera's eyes are as old as mine but sharp as a maiden's. It was she who discerned something amid the crushed bone and tissue.

"Look!" she said, holding his hair away to expose the side of his skull. "There is a round hole here. Hold the lantern close, Mistress."

I did so as she leaned forward and peered at the wound, which I saw was a circle with cracks radiating out from it.

"The angle of the pierced bone slants inward," she said, "as if some sharp, round weapon penetrated there."

"No spear has such a thick head," I said, putting my finger to the wound; it was as large as two of my fingers.

"Do not block the light!" she commanded me. Only Nera would speak to me thus.

She examined his head for another moment, then went to the door and called for someone to bring us a sewing needle. I asked her why, but she preferred to mystify me.

While we waited for the needle to be fetched, I held Sisera's garments to my face and drank in the smell of him. And if I had felt curious about the wound that felled him, now my mind shrieked questions. For as I smelled my son's garments, I felt as if he spoke to me from the land of the dead!

Surely a place near his collar smelled of milk, as if he had spilled some while drinking. But where does one find milk on the battlefield? The robe also carried, faintly, the fragrance of a woman's perfume. That, however, presented no great mystery. No army is without its trail of whores; Sisera must have invited one to his tent. But then I noticed another sign that seemed strange in a soldier fallen in battle.

"Look at his feet," I said to Nera. "There is dirt under the toenails, but surely someone has bathed his feet."

"One of the Israelites? Some woman who—"

"Then why not wash his entire body? Why bathe only his feet, as one might do for a traveler arrived at one's door?"

A servant came with the needle Nera had requested. I held the lantern again as she probed the hole in my son's skull.

"As I thought," she said. "There are slivers of wood in the wound."

"Wood! Surely the Israelites use metal weapons, just as we do." I summoned back the men—though they were mere lads, all that is left of our army, the pups too young to have ridden to Mount Tabor—who had brought my son to me.

"How did he receive this injury?" I asked them.

They trembled, sick faced, as I forced them to look at Sisera's shattered head. But they claimed not to know.

"Where was he found?"

Again they pleaded ignorance, and although I had two of them beaten, I could not persuade them to tell me. Such is the life of a so-called powerful woman. Lied to and protected, even by pups such as these!

But I do not have to rely on boys to tell me what I want to know. Already, with no help but that of another old woman, I have learned that Sisera was not killed with any weapon commonly used in battle. And I suspect he may have been lured from the battlefield shortly before his death.

I have lived fifty and two years. I have little time left. I vow to accomplish one thing before I die: to learn the truth of my son's death.

How She Gained Proficiency with the Weapon

Jael:

Heber's restlessness! As if the blood of our ancestors ran in my husband so strongly that to remain in one place for too long produced in him a physical sickness.

Or so I believed during the first years of my marriage to Heber, when this man, fifteen years my senior, seemed as much father as husband to me; and I, a mere girl, showed him the same gentle docility I had learned to show my father at home. He had a restless, adventurous spirit, he said, when first he must live near Mount Tabor, then on the plain, and then in the hills again. I blinded myself to the way he always tired of whichever of his Kenite kin we lived among and set to quarrel with them, so that we must once again live elsewhere.

But when I did begin to see how things really were with my husband, what did that matter? Although I attempted both anger and gentle coaxing, never could I influence him to make peace with his family and stay where we were. Not even when he made the final break with the Kenite clan and brought us nearly within Canaanite land.

Each time we moved, it fell to me to gather all of the household goods, take leave of our neighbors (such weeping we women did!), and follow my husband. And each time, I had to raise our tent anew. I learned to grasp the mallet and pound in the wooden tent pins, as if nothing had changed from the days of our wandering ancestors. No other Kenite woman has driven as many tent pins as I!

Those men who imagine me so tempting and voluptuous, would they had seen me after a day of hammering tent pins under the desert sun! Every crevice of my body stank from the effort, and my palms blistered, slivers of wood hidden in the swollen flesh.

A Victory Song Heard by the Vanquished

Sisera's Mother:

I am a woman of considerable stature, and my voice is as deep as that of many men. Can this be a surprise, in the mother of Sisera? I told Nera my plan and asked her to fetch me the garb of a male laborer from the marketplace. "Bring me clothes that have been worn already," I requested, "with the smell of hard work in them."

That evening, I dressed in the garments she had obtained. She insisted on accompanying me, though in form she is my opposite, short and soft limbed, and she had no choice but to appear as a woman. She had purchased simple women's clothing for herself.

Thus disguised, we ventured into the city. This was my first time in the streets of once-mighty Harosheth-goiim since the defeat of our army. The chill night air crackled with fear, like the feel of distant lightning. Fear, and mourning, for was any family spared the loss of a soldier son or husband? At first, I saw few people on the streets. In my wealthy neighborhood, everyone had burrowed inside, as if their lengths of dyed cloth would cushion them. (I, too, will if necessary try to bribe my way out of whatever fate befalls the rest of my people.) Even in the central marketplace, the stalls that only days ago had offered fine embroidery and metalwork from every land were now shuttered as well. But the taverns were busier than ever, and if the merriment seemed forced, the false revelry of people who do not know if they will be slaughtered tomorrow or forced into slavery, it was no less lively for that.

In the first tavern we went to, all talk was of the prophetess who led the Israelites. Such nonsense it was! She was eleven feet tall, one man said. Another claimed she exhaled great gouts of flame from her nostrils. Yes, and arrows shot from her breasts!

We sought another establishment where the patrons had not yet consumed so much beer. In a dark tavern no larger than my closet, a minstrel was playing. Minstrels know more of what is going on than kings. I bought the man a pint of beer and asked what news he had of the battle. He spoke of those things I already knew—the chariots in the mud, the Israelite prophetess, and so on, although he did not allude to her body serving as a weapon.

I let him speak at first, not wishing to arouse suspicion by seeming too eager. But finally I asked, "What of Sisera? How did our brave general die?"

"Ah! Not bravely at all. They say he ran away from the retreating army and took refuge with a woman, who killed him with her own hands."

"Lies put forth by the Israelites to increase our shame!"

"Perhaps their prophetess exaggerates in her victory song. She would not be the first poet to do so."

"What song is this?" I asked him.

He bent close to whisper in my ear. "It is forbidden to sing it."

I placed a gold coin before him. "Who is to mete out punishment for doing what is forbidden?" I said. "The army? None remains. The king's officers? Are they not in hiding with the king? Or are all of them, the officers and the king himself, lying slain?" For these rumors, too, flew from door to door.

"I know only parts of this song," he said.

"Then I will pay for only parts." I reached for my coin, but his nimble fingers had already plucked it from the table.

At first, as he sang, I thought that I would like to meet this prophetess, whose name was Deborah. She was a fine poet who sang praise to their god and to the bravery of their clans who rose up and went to battle. But then the words spoke with joy of my Sisera's death—struck by a woman with a tent pin! She even made sport of my waiting for his return. Had this Deborah ever borne a child? For no mother could so cruelly jest about another's loss.

Nera placed her arm around me to comfort me. I pushed her away. I had no need of comfort. I desired only truth.

"Who was the woman who struck this blow?" I asked. "Was it this prophetess, Deborah, who mocks at a mother's grief?"

The minstrel shrugged. "As I said, I have learned only parts of the song. But what other woman could have brought down Sisera?"

I resolved to see this Deborah. That she breathed fire, I did not countenance. But I knew now the manner of my son's death. I longed to see the maker of it. I was determined to know if it was the prophetess's perfume that clung to my murdered son's clothes.

The Wife of Heber the Kenite

Jael:

Just as, at first, I accepted my husband's explanation of why we must move again and again, so too I admired his efforts to befriend our Canaanite rulers. Did he not tell me many times how admirable and clever this was? Was it not the best course for any man of ambition, to please our superiors rather than resist and antagonize them? he said. How was I, a girl of fifteen years when we wed, to understand such subtle matters as politics and loyalty?

So I smiled and served wine, lamb stew, and the juiciest dates to the Canaanites he invited to our tent. I was flattered when our guests told me I was pretty. Even when they asked to see my hair—I looked to my husband, and he nodded his permission for me to remove my head covering. My hair is long, black, and lustrous; that much of what they say of my beauty is true. And I admit to the pride I felt when these important men admired me. I began to rub oil into my hair daily.

What a silly, vain child I was! The first time Heber asked me to go alone into our tent with a Canaanite official—I will never forget, it was the fat, flatulent tax collector—I was so stupid I didn't comprehend his meaning. I obeyed him, just as I had obeyed my father. I screamed, once, when the tax collector seized me and thrust his hands under my robe. But only once. I quickly realized that this was what my husband wished, yet another way for Heber the Kenite to gain favor at court.

There is no better education for a woman, they say, than to be a courtesan. For how long does an old man perform under the blankets—if he is able, even with great encouragement, to perform at all? (I talk like a whore now. The words come naturally to my mouth.) The wife of Heber the Kenite, lying naked beside Heber the Kenite's guests, offered them wine and sweets, and inquired of them about the ways of the world. From the tax collector, I received an education in finance. The king's counselor tutored me in politics and court intrigue. King Jabin himself taught me never to allow sentiment to affect my judgment. And to trust no one. But perhaps that was a lesson I learned without any assistance.

When Sisera appeared at my tent, fleeing the battle and seeking refuge, I did not turn him away. But I knew well, by this time, the antagonism our own people felt toward my family, their distrust of us who dwelt apart and were seen to benefit from our closeness to the king.

Those with whom Heber had cast his lot were fallen. How would we be seen by our own people now? As misguided prodigals to be welcomed back into the fold? Or as collaborators?

And if anyone came to my tent seeking Sisera, what then? Any other woman found to be sheltering the enemy general could plead that she had no choice but to yield to the wishes of a strong, armed man. But the wife of Heber the Kenite, friend to the Canaanites? Traitor to her own people? No, I knew what I must do.

Our God forbids women to use weapons. But I had no need of any sword or spear. I bathed Sisera's feet and made him comfortable inside my tent. He asked for water. Milk I gave him, to induce sleepiness. When he was deeply asleep, his soul far from his body, I picked up the mallet and a tent pin. My hands were steady as I approached him. He lay on his side. I held the tent pin directly above his temple. Then I struck with all my force. Sisera's body shuddered at the first blow, as if for an instant he would rise. I hammered again. In that, the learned men are correct. I "drove the pin through his temple till it went down to the ground" (Judges 4:21).

Can I be blamed if, with each stroke of the mallet, I imagined that beneath my hands was Heber the Kenite's head?

The Prophetess

Sisera's Mother:

Nera cried and pleaded with me, but I was not to be dissuaded. Nothing would satisfy me but to go into the Israelite lands, into the very midst of our conquerors, and seek this Deborah. Even a thing so small as our venture to the tavern the night before had seemed to Nera an act of great daring. This plan of mine terrified her.

"We will be discovered and killed!" she said.

"You are not going," I told her. "Sisera was my son, and this quest is mine alone."

But Nera is even more stubborn than she is fearful. If I went, she said, she would be at my side. "And do not try to sneak out in the night," she warned me. "Or I will give the alarm and tell our men where to find you."

"We will have to walk," I said to discourage her. I had no wish for a companion on this journey. "I am a strong woman, but not so strong that I can carry you on my back when you tire!"

"And how much have you walked, Mistress?" she challenged me. "Or carried a pack of provisions? Should we not take donkeys?"

"Where will we find donkeys without arousing suspicion?" I asked. Fine horses there were in Sisera's stable, but had I taken one and not returned, a score of men would have begun to search for me.

Nera assured me she could arrange for donkeys, and it occurred to me that I might after all be glad of her sharp mind and eye.

We would dress as we had to visit the taverns, in the clothing of a laborer and his wife. But this time, without the shield of night, I could not simply cover my head and expect to escape detection. I made Nera shear my hair—so thin at my age, it was no loss. She, however, wept as she cut. Never could Nera disguise herself as a man. Even were she as tall and stout as I, she lacks the iron of my heart. I slapped her to stop her crying. "Shed no tears but for Sisera," I said.

The next morning, before dawn, we set out, Nera having given out word that I was sick with grief and did not wish to be disturbed. We carried a few coins in a small purse at my side; other money we hid in clever pockets Nera had sewn into our robes. In a poor quarter at the edge of the city, we met a cousin of Nera's who took one of my gold pieces, held it to his teeth, and bit it; then, satisfied, he led us to a donkey that looked as old as Nera and myself.

"I paid for two donkeys!" I protested. "And I want two live beasts, not one so near to the grave."

But he swore that no more or better animals were to be had. A quarter of the population of Harosheth-goiim was fleeing, fearful of what punishment our new masters might exact for the years we ruled them. But if I wished, he would gladly return the gold of "the mother of Sisera" and find another buyer who appreciated the animal's value. Thus he reminded me that I paid not only for his beast but for his silence.

And so Nera mounted my purchase, and we proceeded—I walking more swiftly than the donkey!—to the gates of the city.

There I saw the truth of what the man had told us. Many people were abandoning the city, though nearly as great a number seemed to be streaming into it, all telling themselves that after losing a war, life must be better anyplace but where they had been. As if, their heads pillowed on new ground, they will no longer dream of their dead! A poor, elderly couple with a faltering donkey aroused no special attention amid the families leading bleating goats and whimpering babes. My Sisera never whimpered! Not because I beat him for crying. But even as a child, he showed a warrior's disdain for tears and complaint.

I thought of his courage when my feet, unused to walking any greater distance than a stroll into the marketplace, began to blister; and I said nothing. But after several hours I began to stumble. Nera made a great fuss then and insisted on stopping by the side of the road, where she inspected my feet and treated them with some ointment. She would not ride on the donkey after that, and why had we bought the beast, she said, except for one of us to ride? Nera is stronger than she appears. She walked the rest of the day, while I rode.

We ate the dried fruit and bread we carried with us, and eased our parched throats with wine. At night, we rested as best we could at an inn so crowded we had barely enough space to lie down. I kept my knife close by my side all night and slept little. I wish I could say that my vow to my son so inflamed me that I leaped up in the morning with the energy of a young girl. Alas, my limbs were no more supple or youthful than my dried-up womb. I awoke feeling pain in every joint. And when I tried to stand on my blistered feet! I did not cry out or complain. But I allowed Nera to persuade me to go astride the donkey again while she walked; for would I not need to be as rested as possible, and thus have my wits about me, when we entered the Israelite land?

This we did at midday. I told a nervous young Israelite soldier who would have blocked our way that we wished only to go to our daughter, who had married an Israelite; she lived near the prophetess, I said. And I slipped into his palm a piece of gold. He told us which way to go and wished us a safe journey.

Here, the roads carried only ordinary commerce rather than refugees, and I hoped to have a more pleasant journey.

As if the Israelite land knew me, however—as if it read my heart—the land itself seemed to turn against me. We had traveled only a short distance when the donkey fell to its knees, pitching me onto the ground. Nera had to stand in front of the animal and pull the lead, while I beat the beast's hindquarters with a stick.

The donkey stumbled again. Again, we goaded him. But, finally, he fell and would not even raise his head. I knelt to listen to his breath; he had none. We pushed the poor animal to the side of the road and covered its body with palm leaves—what else could we do? Then we continued on our bleeding feet, our provisions on our backs. I hoped to purchase another donkey—I would have bought two—from one of the Israelites. But something in our dress or manner marked us as Canaanites, and those Israelites we passed regarded us with distrust.

At night, we found no inn, but instead bedded in a field. Too weary to maintain a watch, I slept deeply. I woke to Nera's cries and the rough hands of men searching my garments. They discovered most of the coins hidden in my robe. That was not all they discovered. "This one is a woman!" one of them cried out. The news frightened them, although not enough that they returned my money.

The robbers gave Nera and me into the hands of another man, I believe the leader of their clan. This one tried to question me. I would speak to no one but their prophetess, I said. The man swore and surely would have beaten me, but respect for my sex and gray head stayed his hand. In the end, he knew not what else to do with us, and so did as I had asked. That night, he bound us and told a man to stand guard over us. Exhausted, I little felt the discomfort of our bindings, and I slept. The next day, leading us by the rope with which he had bound our hands, he brought us to the prophetess.

It was thus—poor, limping, and dragged as if I were a criminal—that I came into the presence of Deborah.

A small, plain-looking woman, Deborah "held court" sitting on a hillside at the foot of a palm tree. Surely this is no great leader who could defeat Sisera! I thought, as I was led toward her. Only the deference on the faces of those gathered around her suggested she was anyone but a peasant woman, resting in the shade of the palm before she returned to herding goats.

But if I doubted her identity, she knew mine.

"Welcome, mother of Sisera," she said, even before my captor had spoken—when, from my shorn head and clothing, she should have thought I was a man. She asked to speak to me privately. Her people withdrew, and I sat beside her under the palm tree. Although she was proud of her people's victory, neither was she insensitive to my grief. She told me, in simple words, of my son's death. And she prophesied. . . . But can I believe what Deborah told me?

The Woman in the Tent

Jael:

They said I lay with Sisera seven times that day, but not once did I take pleasure in it. This is the real matter, is it not, that the learned men wish me to discuss? Enough of Heber's wife's skill with tent pins, I hear them say. What of her skills within the tent?

Patience! I will arrive there, I swear it.

Most of Heber's Canaanite friends were men in positions of power. And is it not a sad truth that a man rarely gains power without also gaining a fat belly, yet at the same time losing teeth and hair? How weary I became of flattering and offering dainty morsels of food to ugly men like the tax collector and the provincial administrator. Like Heber.

Sisera was older than I, but he had not the years of my husband or the other men. And his body was strong from the discipline of war. This I noticed when he first dined with Heber. As a maidservant and I brought out many serving dishes and I answered the men when they spoke to me, I stole glances at our new guest. And I felt him watching me in a way that told me he knew what was said of me among the Canaanites. I grew warm with . . .

But am I to feel shame now? I who have been blessed by Deborah and even called greater than the matriarchs, Sarah, Rebecca, Rachel, and Leah?

And if I say I obeyed more quickly than usual when Heber asked me to go into the tent with Sisera alone; and that after that day, whenever I heard General Sisera was to be my husband's guest, I put on my softest robe and combed oil into my hair until it shone . . .

Before you condemn me, consider: I was nineteen years old, my flesh firm and ripe as a persimmon; my heart bursting as when the fruit is left too long on the tree. And my womb—my husband had taught me how to shield myself against being made pregnant by our guests, and he always checked to make sure I followed his instructions. Yet his weak seed had given me no child!

When Sisera came to me from the battle, I knew what I must do. I wished him to sleep, so I gave him milk. I knew that lovemaking, too, would relax him. So I lay with him.

One time only.

The learned men are disappointed. But they are not finished with me. Still, there is the question of my pleasure.

But now, the words are not ready on my tongue. Those things that I did, I can easily relate. But what I felt? When a man asks if I took pleasure in lovemaking, I have no skill at consulting my own heart for the answer.

Were you to ask the Canaanites who knew me—question them, perhaps at a tavern over a glass of wine—they would tell you the Wife of Heber was a wanton, a voluptuary, capable of deriving pleasure from every imaginable act of love. For was that not what I told my lovers, when they asked if they had pleased me?

"Did your body respond to Sisera?" the learned men demand, impatient.

Ah, if that is their standard of pleasure, I need not have pondered what to tell them.

"Yes," I say. They look at me with scorn. I add, wanting to shock them, "What should any young woman prefer? An old man with a limp member or a strong, handsome general?"

The learned men leave me, shaking their heads.

And yet. . . . After I lay that day with Sisera, I had no hunger or thirst for many days to come. Making love with him the last time, knowing I must slay him, my belly filled and filled with the tears I could not let myself shed.

What Jael Carried

Sisera's Mother:

Nera and I journey astride fine horses, supplied to us by the prophetess. I am dressed as a woman now, in plain but well-spun clothes she gave me. We are even escorted by several of her kinsmen. Deborah is no fool. By thus helping us, she puts us under guard.

We pass settlements of tents clustered together. Within the circles of tents, children play; and at their periphery are gardens, fruit trees, and grazing flocks.

At last, when we have nearly left the Israelite lands, I see ahead of us a tent that stands alone. And there are no children here. One of the men rides ahead to announce our arrival. I see—but only faintly, with my weak, old-woman's eyes—some person come out from the tent and speak to him, and then the person goes back within the tent. Is it she?

I had thought I was prepared for this moment. But as we approach the tent, fury, grief, and excitement beat wildly in my breast. I grip the rein of my horse so tightly that my fingernails nearly pierce my flesh.

As I dismount, a man comes forward. If a man can both rush and hesitate at the same time, Heber the Kenite does so. His arms, flapping up and down, convey effusive welcome as, I have heard, he was wont to welcome Canaanite officials; but his face belongs to another man, a cautious fellow who coughs out a greeting, his eyes fixed on my escorts rather than myself. I have no interest in Heber, however, but in the two women who follow him.

One, a servant, carries a cushion and a bowl of water. Of the other woman, I can discern only a shapely form clothed in rich garments; her head is bent and her face hidden within the folds of her head covering. Who can this be except Jael, wife of Heber the Kenite? My son's murderer. And something else, as well?

I am aware that Deborah's men will seize me if I do her any harm. As if they imagine I have the slightest fear of them. What can they do but take my life? It is not their presence that keeps me from grasping her throat and crushing it as she crushed my son.

Yet, how am I to test the truth of what Deborah told me, a thing that will not come to pass for generations? A descendent of Sisera will be a great Israelite leader, she said. This man's courage will be celebrated for centuries. Was this genuine prophecy or a mere act of cunning, a subterfuge to quell my rage? (And yet, Deborah knew who I was. How am I to explain that?)

"Please allow us, lady," Heber says, as the maid puts down the cushion and the bowl of water, which is scented with sweet herbs.

I sit on the cushion. Jael motions the maid away and kneels at my feet. Then she glances directly at me. I see that despite her meek demeanor, she is a woman of spirit. And I see something else. Does Jael herself even know? For the signs are no more than slight, some quality of her skin and her eyes, perhaps visible only to one who has borne as many children as I.

I allow her to remove my sandals and bathe my feet, this woman who carries Sisera's child.

BATYA SWIFT YASGUR is a freelance writer living in New Jersey. She is the winner of the Mystery Writers of America's Robert L. Fish Award. Her fiction has appeared in many publications, including *Ellery Queen's Mystery Magazine, The Georgia Review,* and *Science Fiction Age*. Her nonfiction has appeared in medical journals and consumer health publications. Ms. Yasgur has a background in social work and is currently working on a book about asylum-seekers in American prisons.

Without a Trace

▼   ▼   ▼   ▼   ▼   ▼   ▼   ▼

BATYA SWIFT YASGUR

As I was going up the stair
I met a man who wasn't there
He wasn't there again today
I wish, I wish he'd stayed away

HUGHES MEARNS

Let's get something straight. I didn't convert because of Rachel. I met Rachel because I wanted to convert. Her father, Rabbi Cohen, was giving me lessons in Judaism, while her mother, the gracious *rebbetzin,* invited me for *Shabbos* and *yom tov* meals. I spent plenty of time with Rachel during those long Friday nights and Sabbath afternoons. We became good friends, or at least as friendly as a very Orthodox young woman could allow herself to be with a single man, and of course I fell in love with her. Who wouldn't adore her lovely dimpled face; her thick, dark hair; her eyes, alternately laughing and serious, the color of the golden *challah* bread? I hadn't known of Rachel's existence when I called her father, a name out of the Yellow Pages, stammering out my interest in Judaism and asking for Hebrew lessons. But once I met her, my religious experience became forever intertwined with her dimples and her eyes, her smiles and her religious guidance.

229

Did I have hopes? I'd be lying if I said I didn't harbor some tiny wisp of prayer, especially once my lessons had run their course, my conversion was complete, and I stepped out of the *mikveh* shining and newborn, my Jewish future unfurled before me like a parchment waiting to be inscribed. When Rabbi Cohen, who served on the rabbinical court that had officiated at the conversion and witnessed my immersion in the watery womb of Jewish commitment, said to me solemnly, "Now you are as Jewish as I am. You can be called to the Torah, and you can marry any Jewess you want," I immediately thought of Rachel: of the hours we spent in easy camaraderie, clearing the table or drying dishes after *Shabbos* had ended; of the worlds of Bible stories she opened up to me, her teeth twinkling as she smiled. Yes, she was younger than me by ten years, but I knew what I saw in her eyes. I hoped. I prayed. I dreamed.

So after the little dinner party the Cohens held in honor of my conversion, as Rachel and I were laboring over the kitchen sink, I broached the subject. And found out that she was dating someone, a rabbinical student. His name was Aaron Minkovich, she told me. She had met him only recently, but it was already clear that he had all the qualifications she was looking for in a mate and they were soon to be engaged.

Quite right. A young man from an Orthodox Jewish background, scholarly and sagelike. Whose shoulders were rounded from bending over holy books, whose soft, white hands were stained only with the ink of the *sofer*, whose eyes beheld the sacred letters of Divine connection. A far more fitting *shiddukh* than a world-toughened policeman, whose shoulders were knotted with the tension of the beat, whose callused hands were stained with the blood of criminals, whose eyes beheld murder, drugs, and the anarchy of gang wars. For whom Judaism, with the minutiae of its orderly laws, the beauty of its Sabbath candles, the haven of its liturgical music, was an escape from the madness and chaos of the non-Jewish world. There was pain, yes, but a sense of rightness as I wished her *mazel tov* on her pending engagement.

I couldn't bring myself to attend her wedding. I told her I had to work overtime on a difficult murder case. But in my heart, I bore her husband no ill will, and I always wished Rachel well. Before falling asleep every night, I closed my eyes and there she was before me, in the richness and splendor of her new life. Rachel, shyly peeping at her groom under the wedding canopy. Rachel, dancing with the traditional handkerchief, beaming at her new husband. Rachel, clearing the table with him after Friday night dinner as we had so often done together, but continuing to the bedroom to do what we had never done. Yes, I know it is a sin to think impure thoughts, certainly to fantasize about someone else's wife. But I couldn't help seeing his sanctified hands moving across her sanctified body, and hearing her soft gasps of wonder and gratitude. And as they became immersed in the blurred *mikveh* of my tears, I silently clothed them in prayer. *May the Lord make His countenance shine upon them and be gracious unto them.*

We sculpt people in memory where they remain, static, while we ourselves grow and age. Rachel and Aaron were still the shy, happy newlyweds of my bedtime imaginings when I received an urgent call from Rabbi Cohen four years after the marriage. Aaron was missing. He had been gone for several weeks. Vanished without a trace. I was a policeman; could I help?

Of course, I came right over to the familiar home, where the kitchen had once rung with Rachel's and my laughter, where the rabbi's study had resonated with the echoes of Sinaitic thunder, where the spirit of God had hovered over the face of the table. Where there had once been light.

I turned down the *rebbetzin*'s offer of tea and cake, my stomach rebelling against what my eyes were seeing. How much weight Rachel had lost, how haggard her face, how filled her eyes with unalloyed torment. Her visage was haunted, a far cry from the dimpled bride of my imaginings.

"Why didn't you call me right away?" I asked.

The rabbi shook his head. "I wanted to call you the very night Aaron didn't return from the *beis midrash,* the study hall at the yeshivah, where he'd been learning Torah with his *chavrusa,* his study partner. But Rachel didn't want me to."

I turned to her. Her lovely face was pale, her eyes cast down.

"Rachel?" I prompted.

"I didn't want to impose." I almost didn't hear her voice, flat and muted.

"Impose? Oh, Rachel!" I couldn't help my reproachful tone.

"Never mind," the *rebbetzin* said, putting a trembling hand on Rachel's arm. "What is important is that you're here now. And maybe you can help."

"The police already tried." Again, Rachel's voice was dull, bereft of its customary richness.

I already knew about the fruitless police investigation. Earlier that day, right after hanging up with Rabbi Cohen, I had spoken to Tony, who was the original officer assigned to the case, and watched him scratch his balding head with an immense paw. "I should've thought of you," he'd said, thrusting a file into my hands. "You're one of them now. You know their lifestyle and all. Maybe you can turn up something I missed, because I got nowhere."

"The police don't know Orthodox ways," I said to Rachel, keeping my voice as gentle as possible. "They might miss important clues. Someone *frum* might have better luck."

The rabbi and *rebbetzin* were nodding vigorously. I had the feeling they'd made the same point to Rachel before. "Where do we begin?" Rabbi Cohen asked.

"Tell me about what Aaron was doing the day he disappeared."

"Aaron was studying to be a rabbi when we got married," Rachel began, in that new, flat voice. "You knew that, right?" I nodded and she continued. "So he spent all his time at the *beis midrash*. Even once he was ordained, he decided he wasn't ready to look for a congregation, and stayed on at the yeshivah for post-ordination classes."

"He was such a learned man." The *rebbetzin*'s voice trembled.

"Don't say *was*," Rabbi Cohen chided his wife. "That makes it sound as if, God forbid—"

"You're right." She glanced nervously at her husband, then at me. "He *is* such a scholar."

"So he generally spent his days at the *beis midrash* studying with Levi Shammus, his *chavrusa*. He got up in the morning as usual, went to prayer at the yeshivah, came home for dinner, and then went back to the yeshivah for evening *chavrusa*. He usually came home around nine o'clock or so."

Rachel began to tear apart a paper napkin.

"On Wednesday—that's three weeks ago tonight—he just didn't come home."

"Did he act any differently than usual in the morning?" She shook her head. "Did he say anything unusual? Do anything strange? Please tell me everything, no matter how trivial it may seem."

"I've thought and thought, but nothing comes to mind."

"Did he have any enemies?"

Another shake of the head, as the hands worked harder shredding tiny pieces of napkin.

"Was he in debt? Any financial trouble?"

She started on a new napkin, the white mound of shredded paper rising, snowlike, on the kitchen table. "Nothing like that. I managed our money, such as it was." She laughed, a thudding, mirthless sound. "Not that we had much on his yeshivah stipend, but we got by."

"How about his family? What do they say?"

Rabbi Cohen answered the question. "Aaron didn't—doesn't—have much family. His parents died when he was quite young, and he's an only child."

I knew that too. Family deceased, the file had indicated with the usual impersonality. But no further information had been supplied. "How did they die?"

Rachel mumbled something that sounded like "accident."

"What kind of accident?"

"He never wanted to talk about it," she said, the bits of paper fluttering from the table onto the floor. "And I didn't want to press. Obviously it was very painful for him."

"No cousins? Aunts or uncles?"

"Some family in Israel," the *rebbetzin* said. "An uncle who isn't Orthodox any more. Aaron has never met the man, and wouldn't even invite him to the wedding."

"Do you know anything about this uncle? Name and address, for instance?"

"Only that he shares the same last name as Aaron and that he lives in Jerusalem."

"What is Aaron like?"

They all began to speak at once. Learned. Scholarly. Intellectual. Holy. But I interrupted.

"What's his personality like? Any hobbies? Interests?"

"He believed that developing any interests outside of Torah was a *bitul zeman*, a waste of time," said Rachel. "Torah was his entire life."

"Is there anything else you can think of?"

All three shook their heads, and Rachel began gathering up the shreds of napkin and crumpling them into a ball. I turned to her.

"I know the police already searched your apartment and didn't find anything significant, but I'd like to have a look around, if you don't mind."

She nodded and rose, glancing at her mother. I understood the glance. A woman may not be alone in a secluded place with a man who's not her husband. Her mother understood too. "I'll come with you," she said.

Rabbi Cohen put his arm around my shoulder as he walked me to the door. "You will find him, won't you?"

Eye met eye in a moment of shared fear, dared hope. "With God's help," I said.

Rachel's apartment was neat. Terrifyingly neat. Not a dish in the sink, not a crumb on the table, not a hair clip on the bathroom vanity. Religious books were stacked on the dining room table, corner to corner, without so much as a paper out of place. Kiddush cups stood like gleaming soldiers in the china closet, while white-bearded sages gazed sternly from picture frames on the walls.

We walked through the apartment quietly. I opened drawers and plowed through closets and pockets, searching for a clue, for even a fragment of a clue. For a scrap of paper with some mysterious jotting, for a matchbook with an incongruous restaurant insignia, for an unfamiliar article of clothing that could bring a gasp of surprise to Rachel's lips.

Nothing.

I thumbed through the ponderous tomes that stood in ancient leather-bound splendor on the living room shelves. Bible and Talmud; Maimonides and Nachmanides; books of prayer, of psalms, of Jewish law. No marginal scribblings, no penciled comments, no papers, greeting cards, receipts, or memorabilia stuck between the pages.

Nothing.

I hesitated outside the bedroom, that sanctum of marital intimacy in which my mind had once tiptoed and peeked during nights of longing and prayer. Some shyness, unbecoming in a hardened cop, kept my hand hovering on the doorknob and prevented me from marching right into the inner sanctum of Rachel's privacy. The *rebbetzin*, sensing my diffidence, pushed the door opened.

More order. Twin beds, with tightly-pulled blankets and hospital corners, separated by a night table. Which bed played host to their gropings and murmurings, their holy dance of whispers and hallelujahs? The question rose unbidden, even as I pushed it from my mind and focused on Aaron's closet with its neatly lined up ties, shirts, pants, and tzitzis. A series of black hats. A drawer with snowy undershirts and crisply folded handkerchiefs. And nothing out of place, nothing mysterious lurking anywhere.

The bathroom looked freshly scrubbed. Had Aaron and Rachel ever showered together, or was that against Jewish law? Rabbi Cohen had always told me he would teach me details of the marriage laws when I was ready to marry, please God, so I knew very little. Toothbrush tube neatly squeezed, towels draped formally over racks, a robe hanging on a hook.

Nothing, nothing, nothing.

"You see?" Rachel turned to me, the flatness in her voice tempered only by tiny sprinkles of defiance, of grim triumph. "The police already did all this."

"I'll do better than the police," I promised, almost taking her hands, then remembering the religious restriction against physical contact with a woman. "I'll find him."

"Please God," said the *rebbetzin* fervently.

"Please God," I echoed.

Rachel was silent.

My visit to the yeshivah was just as frustrating—as barren as the womb of the biblical Hannah. Rabbi after rabbi sang the praises of Aaron in impeccable and ancient phrases. An *ilui*, a prodigy, a sage, a scholar, a tzaddik, a saint. His mind, I was told, was swifter than an eagle, mightier than a lion, more graceful than a deer. I heard of his talmudic prowess and of his insight into the apparent contradiction in Rashi's commentary on Genesis 37:4 and 50:16. No, they didn't have a clue as to his disappearance. He had no enemies. He had no hangouts except the *beis midrash*. He had no vices. They should know, they insisted. The saw him twelve hours a day.

Nor was Levi Shammus, Aaron's *chavrusa* and best friend, any more helpful. Words of praise tumbled out of his mouth in incoherent mutterings. Such an honor to study with him He opened my eyes to deeper understandings. Aaron hadn't seemed unusually troubled or distracted. No, he never had trouble concentrating. He was as brilliant as ever on the day of his disappearance. No, he had never mentioned enemies, financial worries, rediscovered family members. Drugs? Levi laughed as if I had suggested that Aaron had swum the Atlantic or grown wings and flown to the moon. Ridiculous.

Nothing.

I tracked down the uncle in Jerusalem and called him. Between his halting English and my halting Hebrew, we managed some rudimentary communication. The uncle had never met Aaron and certainly didn't know the young man was missing. His father and Aaron's grandfather had been brothers, he said. After World War II, Aaron's grandfather had moved to the

United States, while his own father had made his way to Israel. The two brothers corresponded for a time but lost touch over the years. The last he heard was that his uncle was living in Brooklyn. Sorry, he had no further information. Call again if you need more help, he said before hanging up.

Nothing. The rabbis, the friends, the family, everyone agreed. Aaron had vanished without a trace.

Vanished without a trace. The phrase kept nagging at me. There were none of the usual signals of distress, none of the usual clues, no hook on which to hang an investigational hat. Vanished without a trace, without a trace, without a trace. *Without a trace.* I slept and awoke with the phrase. It snaked its way through breakfast and Morning Prayer, a constant companion, tugging at my sleeve and at the fringes of my tallis. I couldn't seem to rid myself of its haunting melody, like a snatch of *zemiros,* the Sabbath table songs I carried around in my heart all week. *Without a trace, without a trace, without a trace.* And I couldn't find another song to sing.

I tried to push it from my mind and concentrate on the investigation. I reread Tony's files, reviewed my own notes, and went over every interview in my mind. What had I missed? I spent a few days in the yeshivah, sitting in Aaron's customary seat, swaying over talmudic tomes as he had. What did the world look like to Aaron? But I couldn't stand in his shoes while I sat in his seat. *Without a trace, without a trace, without a trace* kept coursing through my mind like blood through my veins.

Another sleepless night, the phrase giving me no reprieve. What did it mean—why did it continue to haunt me? Was I meant to befriend it instead of rejecting it? Was it there to teach me something? *Without a trace.*

And suddenly it became clear. God Himself was speaking to me through this obsessive chant, through its grip and mania, and now I knew why.

Aaron didn't *vanish* without a trace. He *lived* without a trace.

There is no righteous man on earth who does only good and sins not, says the Book of Ecclesiastes. But Aaron seemed to defy the wisdom of Solomon. Torah was his entire life. He was a man without vices.

Torah couldn't be *anyone's* entire life. And no one was without vices.

The phrase was gone. And in its place, a disturbing glance into the dark mirror of truth. I had let my feelings for Rachel shadow my investigative objectivity. I hadn't probed, asked her the questions I would have asked any other woman with a missing husband. My shyness, my fear of prying and violating her modesty, perhaps, or of appearing to have the voyeuristic salaciousness of a spurned would-be lover had sealed my mouth. And my eyes.

Unasked questions jumped and itched like the lice in the Egyptian plague. Why had Rachel been so reluctant to consult me? Was it only the awkwardness of having rejected me and the concern for my feelings, or was there something else? Why did she avert her eyes? Was it only the modesty of a very Orthodox woman, now married to another man? Or was she ashamed of something? Why was the apartment so neat? Sure, Aaron may have been compulsively orderly, but I had known Rachel over many years. She was comfortably easygoing in the kitchen, occasionally giggling over shoving disorderly piles of pots into her mother's overcrowded cabinet and shutting the door, or leaving dishes in the sink and suggesting we go for a walk. There was something uncharacteristic and sinister about the military order of her apartment. And why was she so pessimistic about my chances of finding Aaron? Her parents were calling me every day, often several times a day, to find out if I had any news. Why wasn't she? She seemed devoid of faith and of trust in God and in the future—qualities *she* had once imparted to *me*.

I had to speak to Rachel again.

Alone.

When I rang the bell of her apartment, her face blanched then fell apart, like one of the napkins she had shredded at the table. "What, do you have any news?"

I stood in the hall. She would be uncomfortable if I entered her apartment. "No news. I just wanted to talk to you."

"Why did you come here? Why not see me at my parents' house? You know I've been eating dinner there every night since the disappearance."

"I wanted to speak to you alone."

"We can't be alone together. You know that. Anyway, there's nothing I have to say that can't be said in front of my parents."

I couldn't hold back. I had to say it. "I don't believe you're telling me or them the whole story." The rabbis talk about a leap of faith. This was mine, my plunge into the dark abyss of Rachel's secret soul.

She covered her face with her hands, and suddenly she was crying. Great, racking sobs shook her slender body. She moved aside and motioned for me to enter, leaving the front door open so that we would not be violating the religious restriction against being alone in a secluded place with the door locked. I stood by helplessly, restraining myself from taking her in my arms.

"What do you want to know?"

"The truth," I said.

"What makes you think I haven't told you the truth?" But her faded voice and nervous hands betrayed her.

"I'm sure you haven't told me everything. I want to know what your marriage was really like."

"It was empty. It should have been full, but I felt like I was living with a shell."

"What do you mean?"

She hesitated. "I don't know how to explain it. Aaron wasn't cruel. He never hurt me, he never yelled at me, he never said a harsh word. But he never said anything kind or loving either."

"Never?"

She seemed confused. "I mean, he tried. Sometimes he would recite biblical verses to me. *Eishes chayil,* the woman of valor. Or passages from the Song of Songs. But they were never *his* words."

I felt my cheeks beginning to burn, like Sabbath candles. "I don't want to make you uncomfortable, but I need to ask you this. What was your intimate life like?"

Her voice emerged, muffled, from between the prison bars of fingers that crisscrossed her face.

"I went to the *mikveh* every month, of course. We kept all the marriage laws. But when the time came to be together, he couldn't . . . I mean it wouldn't . . . I mean, we never actually managed to . . . "

Four years and no children. Now I understood.

Four years and no gasps of wonder and gratitude in the silent mystery of the night.

"Did he ever try to get help for his problem?"

She shook her head. "I wanted him to get help. I told him there were doctors who deal with this sort of thing. He wouldn't go. We had the same discussion for years, until I—" She broke off and sat, her hands still covering her face, like the cloth over the holy ark in synagogue.

"Go on," I urged.

"I told him I wanted children. And I wanted a full life. You know what I mean. I threatened to leave him if he didn't get some help." Her voice dropped. "That was the morning of the day he disappeared. He never came home that night."

"When he refused to get help, what did he say? How did he explain?"

"He said God would help. He quoted Rashi's commentary, describing Isaac and Rebecca praying in different corners of the room when Rebecca couldn't conceive. We tried that!" she burst out suddenly. "We *davened* every night together. I stood there." She pointed to the window. "He stood over by the bookcase."

Questions were tumbling out of me like children at recess. "How about this—" I glanced around "—this obsession with neatness and order?"

She shrugged. "He was meshugga about neatness. He never got angry, but he got agitated when anything was out of place. He started to shake. He said, 'Our rabbis say that a Jewish home is a *mikdash me'at,* a Temple in miniature. The Holy Temple had meticulous order. Our house should have order too.' Sometimes I argued. I told him a house should look *heimish,* you know, lived in and homey. But he always looked at me like *I* was the crazy one. I saw how much neatness meant to him, so I did my best."

"Did he ever talk about his family?"

She shook her head. "It's as if he had no childhood at all. And I wanted to respect his privacy, so I never pried after he made it clear he didn't want to talk."

"Do you know where he grew up?"

"In Brooklyn," she told me.

"So he didn't talk about his family. He didn't talk about hobbies. What did he talk about, say, over dinner?"

"He shared the latest insight he had into a biblical verse or a rabbinic concept. Since I've never studied Talmud, he had to fill me in on a lot of background for me to understand what he was saying. Sometimes I told him about my day at school. I'm a teacher. I would tell him the cute things my second graders said. He would smile, but I never felt he was really *there* with me." She paused and suddenly looked at me. A flicker of recognition crossed her eyes. "That's it, you see." She sighed. "This may sound strange, but he was never really *there* at all."

A man who lived without a trace.

Another question pushed its way forward, but I held back. Enough for now. I stood up.

"Rachel, I won't stop looking until I've found him."

"You are a good friend," she said and started to cry again.

I reviewed everything again that night. Aaron's obsession with neatness. His monomaniacal devotion to Torah. His marriage, arid as the parchment on which the Holy Scriptures were inscribed. A man whose distinguishing qualities were his insights into a series of biblical verses. Why those verses, I wondered. I reached for my Pentateuch. I read both verses several times and attempted to penetrate Rashi's commentary, but my Hebrew lessons had never given me smooth mastery over the cryptic and mysterious script with its foreign font and its elusive references. I picked up the phone to dial Rabbi Cohen, then changed my mind. Levi Shammus would be more helpful.

Levi was only too eager to help. "You want to know Aaron's insight into these verses? I'll explain." I heard him take a breath, then assume a professorial tone. "The first verse describes Joseph's relationship with his brothers. You remember how Jacob favored Joseph and gave him a beautiful coat of many colors, right?"

I remembered.

"The brothers were so jealous of him, they couldn't even talk to him politely. Rashi says that this was actually praiseworthy on their part. At least they didn't lie. They weren't phony. What you saw was what you got, and they never pretended to love someone they actually hated."

"What about the next verse?"

"After Jacob's death, the brothers were worried that Joseph would take revenge on them for selling him into slavery. They figured he was just waiting for their father to die. So they told him that Jacob had instructed them to appeal to Joseph after his death and ask him to forgive them."

"Sounds reasonable."

"It was reasonable," Levi said, "but there's one problem, according to Rashi. Jacob had never actually told the brothers anything of the sort. They made the whole thing up. Apparently, it's okay to lie if you're pursuing peaceful ends."

I saw where this was going. "So how could it be okay to lie for peace in one situation but also to tell the truth in another, if telling the truth caused animosity and not peace?"

I could hear Levi smiling. "That was exactly Aaron's question. I must confess, I had never thought of it. Neither had all our teachers. And Aaron explained it by saying that when you are dealing with living people, it's wrong to be duplicitous. People always have to know where they stand. But if you're lying after someone's death to protect the dead or the living from hurt, well, then, it's not only okay, but actually praiseworthy."

Lying to protect the dead. Lying to protect the living after parental death. Was this just another intellectual exercise in the reconciliation of apparently contradictory rabbinic texts? Or was there a more personal meaning for Aaron, something to do with his dead family?

Had Aaron, in an attempt to protect his deceased parents, or perhaps to protect himself from them, buried himself under the weighty tombstone of family secrets, leaving only his ghost to wander through the deserted corridors of his depleted life? Who was his family, and what were their secrets? How did they die? Maybe Aaron's Israeli uncle had some information.

"I don't know anything more than what I told you," he insisted when I called.

"Did your father ever receive mail from Aaron's grandfather?"

"They did wrote to each other, yes."

"Do you have any of the old letters?"

"No, only envelopes. My wife, she collects stamps. So she saved them. But they're more than twenty-five years old. They can't be much use."

"Anything is better than nothing," I told him. "Just read me the return address."

I found myself standing in front of an apartment building in a rent-controlled area of Brooklyn. Small children of various ethnic backgrounds were spraying each other with water from an open fire hydrant, while a few old people sat fanning themselves in folding chairs.

"Excuse me," I said to one ancient-looking lady with stockings rolled around her ankles, a glass of iced tea in one hand and a Yiddish newspaper in the other.

She looked up, spilling her tea.

"I didn't mean to startle you." I found a clean tissue in my pocket and handed it to her. "Have you always lived here?"

"Fifty years, thanks to God." She spoke with a heavy Yiddish accent.

"Did you know a family named Minkovich?"

"Vy you vant to know?"

"Their son is missing. I'm investigating his disappearance."

"Little Aaron?" Her hand shook, and the iced tea spilled again.

"Yes. Did you know them?"

"*Oy,* did I know them." She sighed and I noticed tears in her eyes. "Such sad family, I never saw. But Aaron, he vos grandson, not son."

I waited for her to elaborate, but she fell silent. "Please explain," I finally said.

She looked at me for a long time. "If you are trying to help poor Aaron, I help you." She held out her hand and I took it. "I am Sadie Miller. I tell you stories."

I perched myself on the front steps next to her chair. And a good thing too, because her stories took several hours, between her labored English, her labored breathing, and her own life story of European persecution and American struggle. I left as it was already getting dark, with the greater darkness of my newfound knowledge weighing on me like a stone.

My good informant had managed to flee Poland together with her husband and children, her hopes and dreams smashed and burning along with the windows and walls of her Polish home. "Ve vere de lucky vuns," she told me. And indeed they were. Despite the hardship and privation of immigrant life, they had escaped from the jaws of the Nazi beast; its hot, flaming breath rained ashes on the land they left behind.

The Minkoviches hadn't been so lucky. They had gone through the concentration camps and arrived, bleeding, in America, the poisoned darkness of the Old World still injecting its venom into the day-to-day life of the New World. They had always been a little peculiar, even before the War, Sadie told me. She had known them all her life because they had lived in her shtetl; in fact, it was she who had found them the apartment in her building when they came to the United States. "It was a strange, crazy family," she said. "They were meshugga."

They'd apparently had a child during the war, a little girl that Mrs. Minkovich had thrown from the death train into the waiting hands of a peasant. "I never find out how the child come to America, how she find parents, but she come and she find her *mamma* and *tatte,*" Sadie said. "She come with no man and with little baby." Her voice sank. "She leave baby with his *bubbe* and *zayde* and she kills herself."

Sadie gathered that Aaron's mother had wanted him to be raised by a stable, loving family, but because she had not had contact with her parents for years, she had no idea that they were anything but stable. In fact,

Aaron's grandparents spent a good deal of their time in and out of mental institutions.

"Aaron, he used to come to mine apartment after school. He never knew if his grandparents was home or at hospital. There was terrible screams at night. The *bubbe,* she hit him with frying pan. The *zayde,* he just sat and cried. Only *Shabbos,* it *vos* a *bissel* quiet. Aaron, he run away to shul. There he find safe."

The kind rabbi of the shul had taken Aaron under his wing. Discovering the boy's brilliance, the rabbi turned Aaron into his protégé, spending long hours studying Talmud with him. "When Aaron came home from a study session with the rabbi, his eyes were shining," Sadie remembered, "and he looked happy and peaceful. *Oy,* the rabbi, he's dead now," Sadie said. "And the shul, it built up bigger. It is school now. Public school. But he was an angel of *Gott* for the poor little boy. Like a father to him."

One day, when Aaron was nine years old, he returned from the rabbi's study to find police barricading the door to his apartment. A tearful and shaken Sadie had told him what had happened. His grandparents had gassed themselves. She had offered to take him in, but the rabbi arranged for Aaron to board at a yeshivah. Boarders were generally high school or college age, but Aaron's precociousness and brilliance allowed him to be admitted to the dormitory and to the highest classes. Aaron continued to live at the yeshivah until he grew up and married Rachel. No, Sadie had not seen him in years. Not since the day he told her he was moving to the yeshivah.

"I cry hard," she recalled, wiping her eyes as she told me the story. "I beg him, he should write. But already he vas different. Not the little Aaron drinking milk in mine apartment. Like his *bubbe* and *zayde* stole his *neshamah,* his soul, and took it to heaven with them."

A boy without a soul. A man without a trace. A man who wasn't there.

But where was he now? He hadn't returned to the warm milk of Sadie's apartment. He hadn't called his uncle. He hadn't given his friends, rabbis, or devoted wife a hint as to where he was going or what he was planning.

Maybe he wasn't planning. Maybe he had just run away. As he had run away into the world of Bible and Talmud so many years ago, leaving the frightened, lonely little boy behind in the gas chamber of his apartment.

Where would he run? There was only one place I could think of. It was a public school now, where children laughed about sports and clothes, chewed gum, played basketball, and learned math and social studies. But once it had been an Eden of safety for a little Jewish boy, fleeing the roaring, flaming breath of the dragons of his grandparents' memory.

I found him in the dusty storage room of the school, a room that had, according to the janitor, once been the rabbi's study before the building was taken over by the local board of education. A few boxes of crackers were strewn around the room, together with moldy *challah* rolls and fermenting grape juice. Their sour odor mixed with the overwhelming scent of leather-bound books, the brand-new religious tomes stacked on an old teacher's desk flanked by unused math and science textbooks, a few deflated basketballs, and some broken children's desks.

Aaron was emaciated, like a concentration camp survivor.

When I softly pushed the door open, he did not look up or acknowledge me. He was sitting on a kindergarten-size chair, clutching a volume of the Talmud and swaying over it, intoning the Aramaic words in ancient singsong.

"Aaron?" I touched him gently on the shoulder.

He swayed at a faster pace.

"Aaron, do you know who I am?"

His chanting grew louder.

I squatted in front of him. "You can't stay here. This is a school, not a shul."

His swaying became frenetic, frenzied.

I slipped out of the room and reached for my radio. An ambulance was soon on its way. Then I went to call Rachel.

One hospital after another, one medication after another. Specialists from near and far, with impressive credentials appearing in sonorous alphabetic progressions after their names. Needles gleaming with crystal drops of sanity, a rainbow of pills and potions meted out daily. Some made him sleep, others made him wake. Some made him sit, others made him walk. Some made him sway furiously, others made him mumble and stare.

None made him talk. No, I take that back. None stopped him from talking. Talking to God in prayer. Talking to imaginary teachers and friends, explicating intricate talmudic passages and obscure biblical commentaries. But nothing in the psychiatric arsenal made Aaron *speak*. Communicate. Open the locked door of his imprisoned heart and allow it to fly free.

Nor did he seem to recognize anyone—his rabbis, his yeshivah buddies, Levi, Rabbi and *Rebbitzin* Cohen, Sadie.

Rachel.

I watched Rachel, my sweet, sweet Rachel, fade into emaciation worse than her husband's. Day after day, she sat at his side, talking to him. Sometimes she asked him to study Talmud with her. Sometimes she told him about her children in school. Sometimes she just sat quietly, watching him, her honey-colored eyes dry until after she reached the street, where they became the waters of the Shiloach.

"I thought he noticed me a little bit more today," she sometimes said. Or, "He stopped his learning and actually looked at me."

This was progress, I thought bitterly. To have your husband notice you.

"The new psychiatrist says they're going to try electric shock therapy. They've tried everything else—private sessions and groups, medicines and shots. Maybe, maybe."

I didn't need their fancy polysyllabic labels, their learned mutterings, as esoteric as the talmudic *pilpul* of the man they were diagnosing. It was abundantly clear to me what had happened to Aaron. If you became a pillar of salt by looking back at ruin and damnation, you became a pillar of ice by refusing to look back. You became the tombstone of those undead ghosts who prowled through the netherworld of your denied heart and your depleted soul.

Hopeless, the psychiatrists said after the last electric shock treatment had been tried and failed. And told Rachel that she'd better move on with her life.

"What are you going to do?" I asked Rachel that night. We were taking a walk outside her parents' house, the sobbing of her mother following us like a cloud.

"What can I possibly do?"

"You heard what the psychiatrist said. Move on with your life."

She stopped and turned abruptly to face me. "You don't understand, do you?"

"Understand what? The great love you have for him? Your dreams of having him back so you can return to your life together? Admit it, Rachel. You can't possibly love him anymore."

"Anymore? I never did love him." Her voice was so low, I could barely hear her.

"You, what?"

"I said, 'I never loved him.'" She spit the words out like unclean insects.

"So why did you marry him in the first place?" It was the question I had always wanted to ask her, the question that had fluttered inside me that day in her apartment, a question that had given me no peace since the innocent, blissful couple of my imaginings were scrubbed and flushed away by the disinfected order of Rachel's apartment.

"I had to marry someone quickly," she said, her voice muffled.

"Why?"

"Never mind. I can't talk about it."

"Rachel." I touched her arm and drew my hand back, as if from fire. "Whatever it is, I can take it. I deserve to know the truth."

"You want to know? You really want to know?" The words were stampeding out of her mouth, like Noah's animals released from the ark. "All right, then I'll tell you. I'll tell you. I felt the same way about you as you felt about me. I loved you too."

"But you said—"

"I know what I told you." Her voice rose in anguish. "I couldn't tell you the truth. That my father forbade me from marrying you because you are a convert."

And the earth opened its jaws to swallow my frail hopes, my dreams, my innocence, my God. I tried to reach for her with my hands but they closed on nothing. I tried to say her name, but no sound came out.

"My father said he would never dance at my wedding. That marrying you would damage the *yichus* of our family, our pedigree. He urged me to marry Aaron. A fine young man with a glowing rabbinic future. 'But I don't love him!' I kept saying. He laughed at my idea of love. An American Hollywood invention, he called it. He quoted the Torah to me. How Isaac brought his bride, Rebecca, into the tent of his mother, and then he loved her. This is the correct sequence of events, he told me. You don't fall in love, and then marry. First you marry someone who is appropriate for you, and then the love starts to grow."

Rabbi Cohen. Who had said, Now you are as Jewish as I. Who had said, Now you can marry any Jewess you like. Rabbi Cohen, who had sold his daughter into the slavery of her arid marriage to save her from my tainted genes.

"Do you regret it?" I asked Rachel now, my voice as ragged as the shredded napkins of another, more innocent time.

"Yes. Oh, yes." She began to cry, leaning against a tree for support.

Against all odds, against all reason, I heard tiny whispers of hope, felt them wriggling around my insides, tingling, alive. She regretted her marriage. She had once loved me. I thought, I was sure, that she loved me still. I watched her clutch the tree, sobbing against its solidity, and I knew that I could be that tree for her. The tree of real knowledge of the difference between good and evil, truth and falsehood. The tree of a life whole and splendid beyond her imagining. The psalmist's tree planted by the river, giving fruit in its season, never wilting, but yielding success in all its endeavors.

"It isn't too late for us." My voice had stopped wavering and had become calm, confident.

"But it is too late. You don't understand."

"It's not too late for me. I still love you. I will always love you."

"It's too late for me." Her voice rose in anguish and she began to pound on the trunk of the tree.

I watched her fists flail, watched the droplets of blood congealing on her lovely skin, and took her hands. She wrenched them away and used them to cover her face. "I can never marry now. I'm an *agunah*."

"What's that?" Somehow Rabbi Cohen had not covered this in his Hebrew lessons.

"A woman who's stuck with a man who can never be a husband to her, but whom she can't divorce."

"Why would that happen?"

Her voice had taken on the teacher's tone, and I felt like one of her second graders. "By Jewish law, if a husband is missing and there are no witnesses to say he's dead, or if he's mentally incompetent to make legal decisions, or if he's mean and possessive and just doesn't want his wife to be free to marry someone else, then the woman is stuck."

"Stuck?"

She nodded, clutching the tree again. "A man in that situation wouldn't be stuck. If his wife is missing or nasty or insane at least he has some recourse. That's because the strictest Torah law allows men to have more than one wife. So if he's in a mess, he can collect the signatures of a hundred rabbis who give him permission to basically take a second wife." Her voice sank and shook. "But a woman can't do that because she's not allowed to have more than one husband. So if her husband can't or won't divorce her, she remains married to him forever."

"Surely there's some sort of legal dispensation, a loophole, a rabbinic decree that would allow . . . "

Rachel shook her head.

"No, no, it's impossible," I protested. The Torah of the Lord is pure, it restoreth the soul. The Torah is just.

The Torah is pure and just. That doesn't mean it's easy.

Or fair.

She shook her head again, her jaw set. I was struck by the difference in her demeanor. No longer appearing gaunt and ravaged, she looked detached, almost scornful. "Fairness is a modern American concept. Only God decides what's fair."

Those must be Rabbi Cohen's words. Or maybe the chilly voice of Aaron speaking from within the burning bush of Rachel's heart. Not her voice, not the voice of a lovely young woman, condemned to a life of celibacy and separation from the man she loves.

"Rachel, you can't possibly believe that. It goes against everything, *everything* I thought Judaism is. Everything *you taught me* about the love of God, and the beauty of His laws."

"Do you think Orthodox Judaism is all sweetness and light? Kugels and *Shabbos* candles? Children laughing in their costumes on Purim or giggling over the hidden *afikomen* matzo on Passover? Pretty melodies in shul? Did you think you could pick and choose, keep only the laws you find palatable and ignore the rest? Didn't you know what you were getting into when you converted?"

"But this is wrong!" I burst out.

"Only God decides what's right and what's wrong," she repeated. "He dictated the Torah to Moses. The written and the oral laws. They have been passed down from generation to generation in their original and pristine form and they can't be changed. Do you understand?" And in the new hardness of her voice, I heard the frozen echoes of Aaron's ice world, devoid of the heat of passion, the warmth of love, the scorch of pain, the light of truth.

She began to walk toward her house. She turned around once, and in the moonlight I thought I saw tears covering her face as the knowledge of the Lord covers the earth. As I watched her retreating back, I wanted to shout, to scream, to run, to hurl myself at her and sweep her into my arms. But I stood and watched her. I was silent and immobile.

I had become a pillar of salt.

So what was I to do? I chose the quintessential Jewish response Aaron himself would have been proud of: study. Study, study, study. I left the police force, enrolled in rabbinical school, and became a rabbi. But not Orthodox. Reform.

I still love the spicy sweetness of the kugels, the celestial melodies of the liturgy, the beauty of the *Shabbos* candles. I can allow their light to shine through the benighted corridors of memory, dispelling the darkness of rigidity, of historical shackles, of the fanatical enforcement of primitive origins. For the Torah is not in heaven, says the Book of Deuteronomy, but in our human hands to enact. From my pulpit, I preach the wedding of ancient rituals to modern ethical sensitivities. I speak of our right, our obligation, our behest, our heritage to choose. To pick and choose. My congregation listens, their faces rapt.

My new wife listens, her face rapt as well. She is not only my *rebbetzin* but also a rabbi-to-be in her own right. In fact, we met at rabbinical school. And after Friday night services, the candles dancing in slow and sibilant undulation before us, we sing *zemiros* of purest joy and celestial harmony. We study biblical and talmudic texts together, understanding that God speaks through them, but even more important, through us. That Revelation is both historical and ongoing.

And later, when the books have been reshelved, when the table has been cleared, when the dishes have been washed and dried, when the candles have taken their leave, we go upstairs. There, in the recesses of my bedroom, I hear God's truest voice as my wife and I climb our own mountain of Revelation to its peak of jubilant and thundering hosanna.

But afterward, as we lie intertwined and trembling, I close my eyes and there is Rachel before me. Rachel in her twin bed, modestly covered and devoutly alone. I hear the singsong chant of the absent Aaron's talmudic *pilpul,* the haunting strains of the Book of Lamentations, the Sabbath *zemiros* swirling in slow parody around the shadowed room. And as she becomes immersed in the blurred *mikveh* of my tears, I silently clothe her in prayer.

   May the Lord make His countenance shine upon her and be gracious unto her.

Continuation of Copyright Page

Spirituality/Jewish Meditation

God Whispers: *Stories of the Soul, Lessons of the Heart*
by *Karyn D. Kedar*

Eloquent stories from the lives of ordinary people teach readers that the joy and pain in our lives have meaning and purpose, and that by fully embracing life's highs and lows, we can enrich our spiritual well-being. Helps us cope with difficulties such as divorce and reconciliation, illness, loss, conflict and forgiveness, loneliness and isolation.
6 x 9, 176 pp, Quality PB, ISBN 1-58023-088-1 **$15.95**

God & the Big Bang
Discovering Harmony Between Science & Spirituality AWARD WINNER!
by *Daniel C. Matt*

Mysticism and science: What do they have in common? How can one enlighten the other? By drawing on modern cosmology and ancient Kabbalah, Matt shows how science and religion can together enrich our spiritual awareness and help us recover a sense of wonder and find our place in the universe. 6 x 9, 224 pp, Quality PB, ISBN 1-879045-89-3 **$16.95**

Six Jewish Spiritual Paths: *A Rationalist Looks at Spirituality*
by *Rabbi Rifat Sonsino*

The quest for spirituality is universal, but which path to spirituality is right *for you*? A straightforward, objective discussion of the many ways—each valid and authentic—for seekers to gain a richer spiritual life within Judaism. 6 x 9, 208 pp, HC, ISBN 1-58023-095-4 **$21.95**

   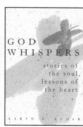 

Discovering Jewish Meditation
Instruction & Guidance for Learning an Ancient Spiritual Practice
by Nan Fink Gefen
6 x 9, 208 pp, Quality PB, ISBN 1-58023-067-9 **$16.95**

Meditation from the Heart of Judaism
Today's Teachers Share Their Practices, Techniques, and Faith
Ed. by Avram Davis 6 x 9, 256 pp, Quality PB, ISBN 1-58023-049-0 **$16.95**;
HC, ISBN 1-879045-77-X **$21.95**

The Way of Flame: *A Guide to the Forgotten Mystical Tradition of Jewish Meditation*
by Avram Davis 4½ x 8, 176 pp, Quality PB, ISBN 1-58023-060-1 **$15.95**

Stepping Stones to Jewish Spiritual Living: *Walking the Path Morning, Noon and Night*
by James L. Mirel and Karen Bonnell Werth
6 x 9, 240 pp, Quality PB, ISBN 1-58023-074-1 **$16.95**; HC, ISBN 1-58023-003-2 **$21.95**

Minding the Temple of the Soul: *Balancing Body, Mind, and Spirit*
through Traditional Jewish Prayer, Movement, and Meditation
by Tamar Frankiel and Judy Greenfeld 7 x 10, 184 pp, Quality PB, Illus.,
ISBN 1-879045-64-8 **$16.95**; Audiotape of the Blessings and Meditations (60-min. cassette),
JN01 **$9.95**; Videotape of the Movements and Meditations (46-min.), S507 **$20.00**

Spirituality—The Kushner Series
Books by Lawrence Kushner

The Way Into Jewish Mystical Tradition
Explains the principles of Jewish mystical thinking, their religious and spiritual significance, and how they relate to our lives. A book that allows us to experience and understand the Jewish mystical approach to our place in the world. 6 x 9, 224 pp, HC, ISBN 1-58023-029-6 **$21.95**

Eyes Remade for Wonder
The Way of Jewish Mysticism and Sacred Living
A Lawrence Kushner Reader Intro. by *Thomas Moore*
Whether you are new to Kushner or a devoted fan, you'll find inspiration here. With samplings from each of Kushner's works, and a generous amount of new material, this book is to be read and reread, each time discovering deeper layers of meaning in our lives.
6 x 9, 240 pp, Quality PB, ISBN 1-58023-042-3 **$16.95**; HC, ISBN 1-58023-014-8 **$23.95**

Invisible Lines of Connection
Sacred Stories of the Ordinary AWARD WINNER!
Through his everyday encounters with family, friends, colleagues and strangers, Kushner takes us deeply into our lives, finding flashes of spiritual insight in the process.
5½ x 8½, 160 pp, Quality PB, ISBN 1-879045-98-2 **$15.95**; HC, ISBN -52-4 **$21.95**

Honey from the Rock SPECIAL ANNIVERSARY EDITION
An Introduction to Jewish Mysticism 6 x 9, 176 pp, Quality PB, ISBN 1-58023-073-3 **$15.95**

The Book of Letters: *A Mystical Hebrew Alphabet* AWARD WINNER!
Popular HC Edition, 6 x 9, 80 pp, 2-color text, ISBN 1-879045-00-1 **$24.95**; *Deluxe Gift Edition*, 9 x 12, 80 pp, HC, 2-color text, ornamentation, slipcase, ISBN 1-879045-01-X **$79.95**; *Collector's Limited Edition*, 9 x 12, 80 pp, HC, gold-embossed pages, hand-assembled slipcase. With silkscreened print. Limited to 500 signed and numbered copies, ISBN 1-879045-04-4 **$349.00**

The Book of Words: *Talking Spiritual Life, Living Spiritual Talk* AWARD WINNER!
6 x 9, 160 pp, Quality PB, 2-color text, ISBN 1-58023-020-2 **$16.95**;
152 pp, HC, ISBN 1-879045-35-4 **$21.95**

God Was in This Place & I, i Did Not Know
Finding Self, Spirituality and Ultimate Meaning
6 x 9, 192 pp, Quality PB, ISBN 1-879045-33-8 **$16.95**

The River of Light: *Jewish Mystical Awareness* SPECIAL ANNIVERSARY EDITION
6 x 9, 192 pp, Quality PB, ISBN 1-58023-096-2 **$16.95**